Kerry Ann
May all your
adventures
magical
David E Daigle

RISE OF THE DARK QUEEN

The Frontmire Histories - Book II

By David E. Daigle

ISBN: 1-4392-3913-4
ISBN-13: 9781439239131

Visit www.booksurge.com to order additional copies.

Dedicated To:

My lovely, loving wife, Eileen who supports all my dreams, endeavors, and who continues to endure countless hours of reading and editing.

Peggy Watson who inspired me to write.

In memory of
Dr. Gilman Moreau, teacher, mentor, friend.

Many thanks to all who read Book I and insisted that this sequel be released, especially to those who assisted in the funding of the publishing costs for Book II.

Cover art by Jerry Halkyard. Known as Dragonfrog in his gallery at renderosity.com

Other Works by This Author

Novels:

The Frontmire Histories:

Prince of the Elves: princeoftheelves.synthasite.com
The Rise of the Dark Queen: darkqueen.synthasite.com
Kravorctiva: kravorctiva.synthasite.com *
Vanished!: vansished .synthasite.com *
blog: davethedc.wordpress.com

Magic Kingdom: Foreclosed *
A spoof based on Terry Brook's Magic Kingdom: Sold

Short Stories:

A Loon Called From the Opposite Shore *
A Prayer for the Barley *
Lily *

Plays:

It's a fetish, Jerry! *

* Yet to be Published

FOREWORD

Dear Reader.

Firstly, I would beg thine indulgence that thou might not be overly distraught. Many of those who participated in bringing this work to its ends have struggled to endure this problem (or so, perceived problem). And thou, noble reader, art above thus.

It happens to have happened, in this time, in this era, in this place, that the language of the Elves does not contain capitol letters (Alas!): therefore, a sentence, by need, does not begin with a capitol letter. I pray thee: Do not despair, for greater minds than of thine have fallen prey to this folly.

Except. Except that, as in any renown language, for the exception of Bahal, which means *to scorch*. Over the cycles of the sun, *bahal* (in the Elven language) became Bahal in the hands of the Humans, and it became known as Mount Bahal.

Otherwise, I welcome you to the sequel to Prince of the Elves: The Frontmire Histories – Book I. Those whom I know and have read Book I have clamored for Book II's release.

So without further ado, here it is.

Tables Measure

Time

- Course of the sun: the time from sunrising to sunsetting. In Frontmire, this is approximately a 12 hour period depending on the season.
- Quarter course of the sun: the course of the sun is divided into four quarters of about 3 hours each.
- Quarter of the moons course: the moon's course is also separated into four roughly three-hour quarters depending on the season: one week.
- Moon's course: the time from sunsetting to sun rising.
- Moon's cycle: time from full-moon to the next full moon
- Spans: roughly one hour whether of the moon of sun.
- Cycle of the sun is roughly equivalent to one year.

Distance

- Span: a rough measurement approximately the width of a hand, generally accepted to be about five inches. It is from this measure that the measure for time is derived – one holds his hand to the sky and measures the time involved for the sun or moon to travel that distance.
- Pace: approximately three feet.
- League: approximately seven miles.

Weight

- Stone: approximately two pounds.

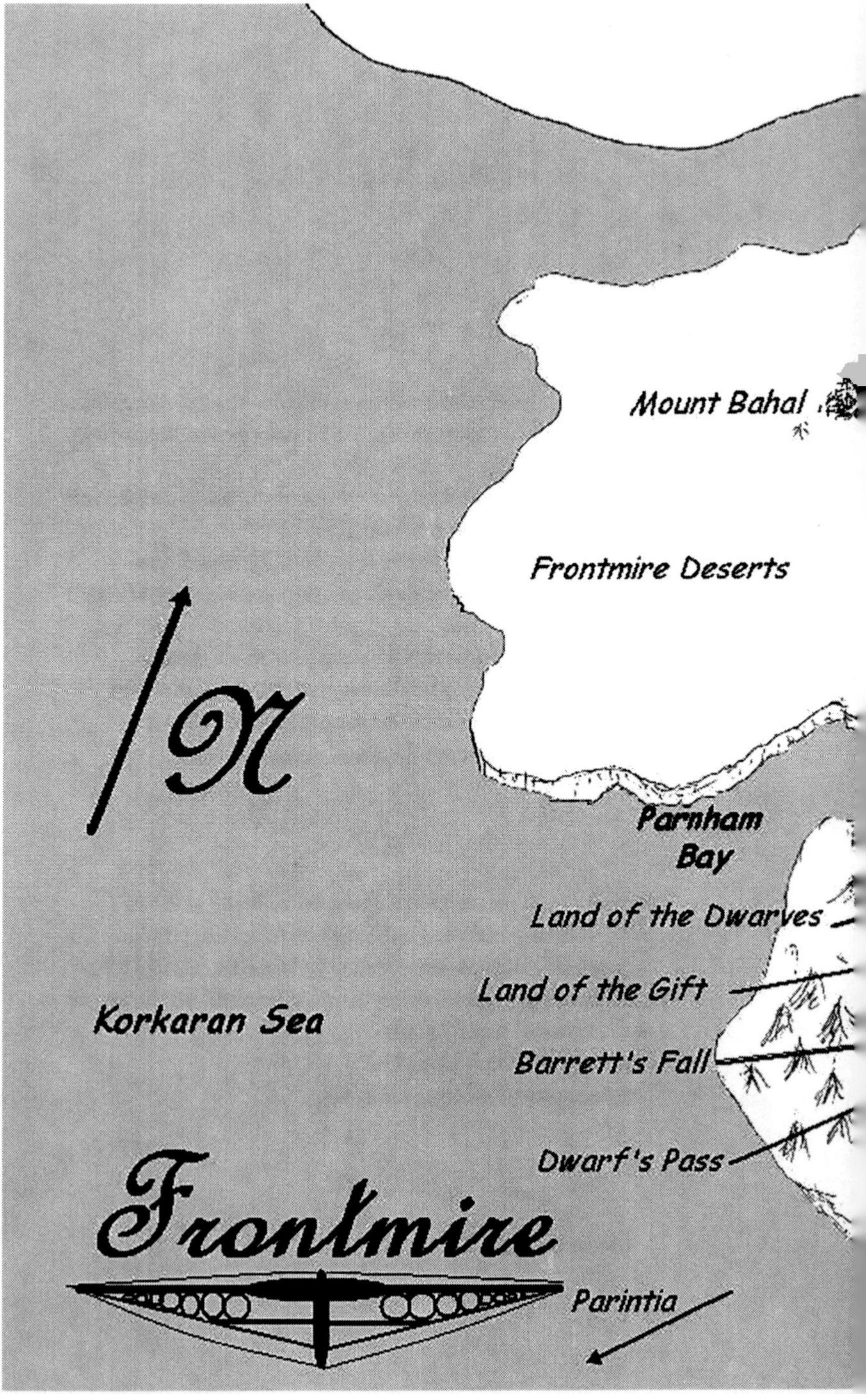

Mount Bahal

Frontmire Deserts

N

Parnham Bay

Land of the Dwarves

Land of the Gift

Korkaran Sea

Barrett's Fall

Dwarf's Pass

Frontmire

Parintia

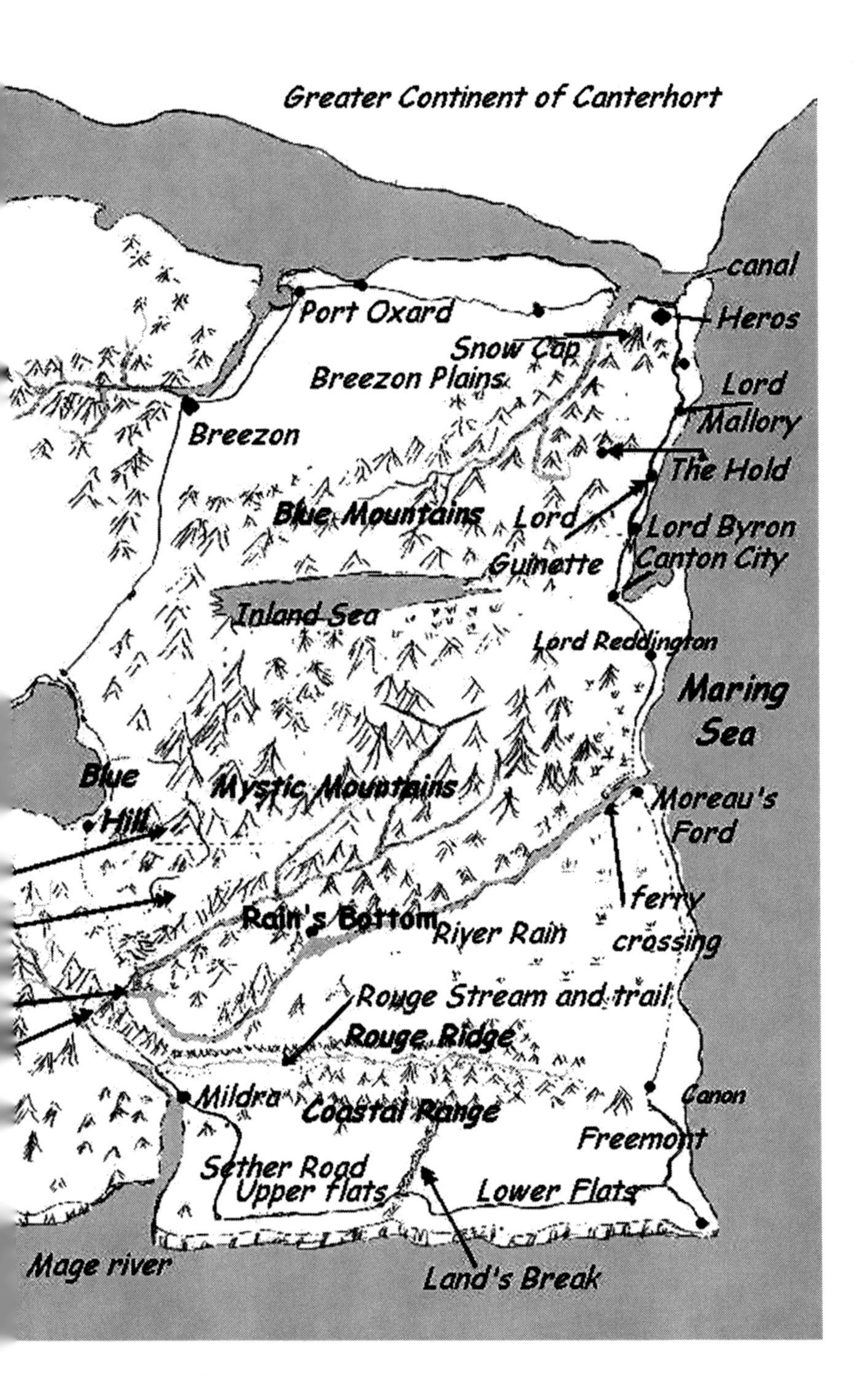
Greater Continent of Canterhort
canal
Port Oxard
Heros
Snow Cap
Breezon Plains
Lord
Mallory
Breezon
The Hold
Blue Mountains
Lord
Lord Byron
Canton City
Guinette
Inland Sea
Lord Reddington
Maring
Sea
Blue
Hill
Mystic Mountains
Moreau's
Ford
ferry
crossing
Rain's Bottom
River Rain
Rouge Stream and trail
Rouge Ridge
Mildra
Coastal Range
Canon
Freemont
Sether Road
Upper flats
Lower Flats
Mage river
Land's Break

Frontmire Histories – Book II
The Rise of the Dark Queen
Glossary

Note to those who read in the Common Tongue: There are **NEVER** any capitol letters in the Elvish language of Frontmire. Please do not be dismayed by this.

acdec: ăk' děk: Blue Elfstone pertaining to the magic of escape or safety. Also, see Elfstone. Note: there are no capital letters in Elven writings.

acrch: ăkrk: Elven rune of *life and health*. Also Elfstone and Faerie creature by same name. Also, see Elfstone.

Ahliene: Elf maiden who falls in love with Commander Stanton. A true Healer of the magic of *acrch*.

AlhadStone: Dwarf king present at the forging of the Elven knife (*Gildar* in the Dwarf tongue).

Andreanna: Human girl from BlueHill who becomes traveling companion of Jerhad and Stanton. Also descendent of the ancient Elven king's lineage. Jerhad's 'girl'.

Argentus: Name given by the Druids to the Faerie Elven element of magic: source to the Faerie magic, which is an ancient and powerful earthen magic.

Arts: The group of the three magics, which were that of potions, spells and incantations. They are the White, Gray and Black disciplines.

Atkans: Master Filinhoff's Druid grandson.

Avenar: A wizard of the Grey Arts of magic, who dwells in *The Hold.*

Bahal: bā' hăl: Live, but not very active, volcano in the northwest of Frontmire. From the ancient Elven tongue meaning *to scorch*. Note: Though the elven language contains no capitol letters under any circumstance Bahal has been capitalized because of its prolonged use by the land's Humans.

balak: bā' lăk: Elven rune of death and sickness. It also exists as an Elfstone. Also, see Elfstone.

balan: bā' lôn: Elfstone of purification. Black in color. Also, see Elfstone.

balat: bā' lăt: Elfstone of destruction. The Elfstone is unique to Andreanna as it was formed of a blending of White, Gray, Black and Faerie magic, blending with her innate magic and personality.

Banta: A Mountain Gnome that becomes one of Andreanna's "body guards".

Bantin heifer: Giant heifer from the Homeland of the Giants. Evidently known for its noisy mating.

Barrett's Fall: Large waterfall on the River Rain where an earthquake rerouted the river. The falls is allegedly named after one Barrett who discovered it too late and went over to his death.

Baros: Jerhad's grandfather, Lewin's father.

Baby: A she-wolf that becomes one of Andreanna's traveling companions.

Black creatures: Daektoch's servants, which are referred to as black creatures or dark creatures. They were formerly wizards of the Black Arts that Daektoch has altered magically. They are known for having sharp poisonous claws that are lethal, invulnerability to conventional weapons and the ability to turn to mist and travel at great speeds in this form as they come and go.

blending: the effect of combining contrary magics. The common effect was neutralization of the wizard's magic – rendering him powerless. In Morlah's case, the blending was considered pure and united the magics to their full potency.

BlueHill: A village of mostly human inhabitation on the central west coast of Frontmire. Andreanna's hometown.

Blue Mountains: Mountain range in the northern parts of Frontmire running from the East to West coast of Frontmire.

Blushing Maiden: Inn belonging to Master Kline and Miss Molly, located on the River Rain in the town of Rain's Bottom.

BondBreaker: Giant, son of Jorolant, who is the replacement *Nourisher and Keeper of the land of the Gift of the Elves*. He replaces Mordock as Keeper.

Bonawock: The collective of the damned. "Ghost" of the collection of souls of the ancient city of Pernham, city of the Mountain. They were condemned by the Faerie creatures for the offering of their children in blood sacrifices to he necromancer or *Kataruk*.

Bornodald: A horse-like race of great intelligence, speed, strength and endurance. Capable of communing with each other (and others who are capable of it) by mindspeech. Their land of origin is that of Karob.

Breezon: One of the major cities of Frontmire located on the Breezon River, on the north coast. A walled and prosperous city.

Boy: A he-wolf that becomes one of Andreanna's traveling companions.

Bull: One of the male giants.

Canon: A small city on the Southeast coast of Frontmire. Though of human inhabitants, it does its commerce with the Elves of the south coast due to geographic isolation.

Canterhort: Larger continent of which Frontmire is a southern peninsula.

Canton City: Human city on the central eastern coast of Frontmire.

The Castle: Giant schooner of which Master Forbonder is skipper.

Catrina: Jerhad's mother. Elf with a question of Dwarf mixture in her lineage.

Cave Gnomes: A variety of gnome found in Frontmire which are of a thin frame and are shorter than a Dwarf by one head. They live primarily in the eastern Mystic Mountains, but they do come out and have interactions with the other races. Their intelligence is equal to that of the other main races. The Cave Gnomes spent many years in subservience to the wizard, Avenar.

Cave Troll: A variety of troll found in the Blue Mountains of Frontmire. Considered dull witted, they are powerful individuals that are tribal and factitious. They are approximately two heads taller than the average human and weight about half the weight of a cow.

Coastal Ridge: Mountain range running east to west in southern Frontmire, south of the Rogue Stream.

Course: See appendix of time, weights and measurements.

Cycle: See appendix of time, weights and measurements.

Daektoch: The Black Mage, practitioner of the Black Arts of magic. Known for his greediness and lust to possess of destroy all other forms of magic.

Derrin son of Kalborn: Dwarf smith who forged *Gildar* (*Ember*).

DiamondHeart: One of the giants who will remain on Frontmire when the Giant schooners leave for the Homeland.

Doeg: dō' ĕg: Replacement leader for the gnomes after Thogg.

Dolan: dō' lə: Word from the dwarf language meaning rock or fortress. Also the name of the mountain or home of the Dwarves in the Western Mystic Mountains.

Dort: A Dwarf who goes by the nickname of Nose. He has the ability to detect the scent of different ores while they are still in the ground.

Druids: Originally known as Ryer's Clan. A studious clan living on Parintia who after there near annihilation became reclusive and were given the name *Druids*, which they later adopted.

The Druid Histories: Chronicles kept by the Druids of their own history.

Druid Queen: Formerly named *Ryer's Maiden*. Ship belonging to the early Druids and whose crew was murdered by Daektoch's servants. She becomes a ghost ship after she is burnt and sinks out in Nickolii Bay north of Heros, and she is said to haunt the waters off of Heros with her crew.

Druid Sleep: A state of unconsciousness induced by herbs and Gray magic that deters the effects of time and disease or injury to allow healing and restoration. The use thereof prolongs life by reversing its deleterious effects.

The Dwarf Histories: Chronicles (kept by the Druids) of the Dwarves' history.

Dwarf's Pass: A road constructed by the Dwarves after the elves migrated to southern Frontmire in the days of the ancient king of the elves, Windermere. It followed a gulch in the western mystics and was the only connection from the south to the north that was passable on the West coast, and it connected the two in the vicinity of the Mage River just north of the Rogue Stream and led to Barrett's Fall on the River Rain. The eastern end of the mountains was passable.

Elfstones: Stones that are a manifestation of the earthen magic of the element Argentus. Each manifestation contains a particular characteristic of the magic and its power. They frequently have a humanoid or Faerie manifestation associated to then, also. Mentioned in the story are *acrch, acdec, balak, balan, esord, igini, licri, urcha.* They are usually plain, colored, but not precious or semi-precious stones. The names are derived from the ancient Elven language and are never capitalized, as capitol letters do not exist in the language. Seven of these stones are contained in the handle of the Elven blade *Gildar* (or *Ember)*.

<u>The Elven Histories</u>: Chronicles (kept by the Druids) of the Elves' history.

Elise: Morlah's Druid niece.

Ember: Name of Jerhad's knife of Elven magic also known as *Gildar* in the Dwarf tongue.

esord: ĕ' sōrd: Green Elfstone meaning foe finder, with ability to detect the presence of enemies. Also, see Elfstone.

The Fair Lady: Hawkins' ship on which Jerhad, Andreanna and Stanton go to Breezon and Heros from Parnham Bay.

Filinhoff: Druid. Master of the Black Arts.

Fonta: The manifestation of the Faerie isini as a Cave Gnome child. She accompanies Andreanna in her search to find the Faeries.

Forbonder: A Giant. Skipper of the schooner *The Castle.* Leader of the giant's expedition to Frontmire.

Fortis Root: Also known as "root": used as a stimulant and similar to caffeine.

Frontmire: Peninsula on the south of the greater continent of Canterhort. Homeland of Dwarves, Elves, a population of Humans and Cave Trolls.

The Gift*:* Short for *The Land of the Gift of the Elves to the Giants.* A central western Frontmire parcel of land given to the Giants by the Elven king of old, in gratitude for stopping the war with the trolls.

GladdenStone: Son of StoneBreaker, father of HeartStone and King of the Dwarves.

Gnomes: There are two varieties of gnomes in Frontmire – the more common and well known are the Cave Gnomes, and the reclusive gnomes, which are the Mountain Gnomes. See each respectively.

Gnonanock: Term used of the leader of the Rock Troll tribes.

Gildar: gĭl' där Dwarf name of Jerhad's knife of Elven magic. Known as Ember in the common tongue. The blade contains argentus in the steel and Elfstones in the handle. Also, see Elfstone.

Gram: Dwarf matriarch, mate of the late Swarf King RavenStone, mother to the late GladdenStone and grandmother of King HeartStone and SixFists and "seer". She assists Andreanna in controlling her magic.

GreatHand: Giant who delivers the news of BondBreaker's death.

Grotton Brewen etch Kepchenlcher: Giant language for 'The Keeper and Nourisher'. This is the Giant who is appointed to care for the *Gift* on Frontmire, also known as the *Gift of the Elves.* Every one hundred years the Keeper would be replaced with another. The position was determined by and given to the winner of the Contest held in the Homeland of the Giants.

The Hammerstar: Giant schooner.

Hawkins: former Breezon army sergeant but now captain of *The Fair Lady.*

HeartStone: Son of GladdenStone king of the Dwarves. He becomes king after his father's death.

Heros: hĕr' ŏs: Capitol of Frontmire on the northeast coast. A city of human inhabitation and location of Daektoch's secondary dwelling.

The Hold: Avenar, the wizard's dwelling. Formerly a military hold belonging to Heros until after the *Ten Year Troll War* when it was abandoned.

igini: ĭ' gĭ nē: Purple Elfstone of the magic of 'harmony'. Also, see Elfstone.

isini: Name of the Faerie who accompanies Andreanna in her search of the Faeries. She is manifested as a Cave Gnome child. Her name means mischief.

Inland Sea: Large landlocked sea north of the Mystic Mountains and south of the Blue Mountains.

IronLeggs: Dwarf commander over the ten thousand Dwarf troops sent by King HeartStone to Mildra.

IronLeggs: Dwarf commander over the ten thousand Dwarf troops sent by King HeartStone to Mildra.

Jerhad: jâr ĕd: Main character. Elf, son of Lewin, son of Baros, descendant of the Elven king's lineage and inheritor of the magic Elven blade, Ember.

Kassandra: Female Giant who has an eye on Mordock as a possible mate. Also, one of the giants who will remain on Frontmire when the Giant schooners leave for the Homeland.

Kataruk: Necromancer that beguiled the population of Pernham, City of the mountain, into offering their children to himself in blood sacrifices.

Keeper: Same as *Grotton Brewen etch Kepchenlcher.*

Karob: kä rôb: land to the southeast, across the Marring Sea; land of origin of the Bornodalds.

Korkaran Sea: Sea to the south and west of Frontmire and Canterhort.

Kline: Known as Mater Kline. Owner of the *Blushing Maiden Inn* in Rain's Bottom.

Lend: Lendon's nickname.

Lendon: The Prophet of the Long Awaited for Queen. Citizen of the Mystic Mountain city of Pernham, city of the Mountain.

Lewin: Jerhad's father and mayor of Mildra.

licri: lĭ' krē: Yellow Elfstone. *licri* meaning strength or mighty. Also, see Elfstone.

The Lord's Inns: Inns formerly owned by the lords of Heros which were built a day's journey apart along the eastern coast of Frontmire. From north to south, those that remain are: The Lord Mallory, The Lord Guinnette, The Lord Byron and The Lord Reddington.

Mage River: River of western Frontmire emptying into the Korkaran Sea and forming the Port of Mildra at its mouth.

Marcus: Member of Stanton's former squad in the Breezon army.

Marietta: Female Druid gardener.

Marring Sea. Sea to the east of Frontmire and Canterhort.

Master Kline: Owner of the *Blushing Maiden Inn* in Rain's bottom.

Mermaid: Name of Parintian ship.

Mildra: Port town of Elven inhabitation on the southwest coast of Frontmire. Located near the mouth of the Mage River. Jerhad's hometown.

Mingus: Dwarf who accompanies Jerhad in Andreanna's rescue in Book I and now builds bread ovens for Andreanna in Book II.

Miss Molly: Master Kline's wife of the *Blushing Maiden Inn.*

moor cat: large powerful gray predator with light brown stripes that lives in the moors of eastern Frontmire.

Moreau's Ford: Village at the ford at the mouth of the River Rain on the east coast of Frontmire.

Mordock: mōr' dŏk: Giant who was the *Grotton Brewen etch Kepchenlcher* and befriended Jerhad and Stanton. Also, one of the giants who will remain on Frontmire when the Giant schooners leave for the Homeland, as are Kassandra, DiamondHeart and Tahmat.

Morlah: mōr' lä: Druid who possess a *blending of magics* of White, Black and Faerie Elven Magic. Lives in the *seilstri* on the Isle of Parintia.

Mountain Gnome: A very tiny (two heads shorter than a Cave Gnome or three to four heads shorter than a Dwarf), more primitive gnome of leathery wrinkled skin. They are tenacious, bold and wiry and live reclusive lives, mostly living in the southern and central Mystic Mountains. Their intelligence is equal to that of the other main races.

Mountain Trolls: A variety of troll which lives in the Mystic Mountains: of great size -equal to that of a Giant, immense in strength, solitary in habit, except for mating season and of terribly low intelligence, though more intelligence than most animals.

Mystic Mountains: Immense complex of mountains in central Frontmire.

Nan: Name of a former and now dead Druid healer. The Faerie *acrch* uses the name in her interactions with non-Faeries.

Nickolii Bay: Large bay to the North of Frontmire, opening west to the Korkaran Sea and connected to the Marring Sea by a man-made canal.

Nimbus: Dwarf scout.

Nose: Nickname to Dort the Dwarf, who has the ability to detect the scent of different ores while they are still in the ground.

Nourisher and Keeper: Same as *Grotton Brewen etch Kepchenlcher.*

Orenald: dwarf that accompanies Jerhad to raise the alarm about the impending Troll invasion.

Pace: See tables of time, weights and measurements.

Parintia: Island to the southwest of Frontmire. Homeland of the Druids. Formerly known as Ryer's Island.

Parnham Bay: Bay on the central, west coast of Frontmire. Located near Blue Hill and the land of the Gift of the Elves.

Pernham, City of the Mountain: City in the Mystic Mountain, which lies in ruin. Home to the ancient race now become a 'ghost' known as the *Bonawock*.

Port Oxzard: Port city of human inhabitation on the north coast of Frontmire. The port is a center of commerce serving Breezon.

Rain's Bottom: Human village on the River Rain in central Frontmire. Hometown of Master Kline and Miss Molly.

Raven: A Bornodald given to the Druid's as a gift by the Prince of Karob. Later joined up with Morlah and was transformed by magic to that of a Pegasus.

River Rain: Large river with its origin in the south central Mystic Mountains. The River, formerly emptying into the Korkaran Sea via the Mage River, was diverted by a shift in the continent during an earthquake and now flows east to the Maring Sea. It has its origin in the far western Mystic Mountains and flows southwest over Barrett's Fall and then turns east to the Marring Sea. Above Barrett's Fall, it is named *the eastern turn* of the river. Below the falls, it is named *the eastern turn*.

Rogue Stream: Stream running, between the Rogue Ridge and Coastal Range, East to West in southern Frontmire. The Rogue empties into the Mage River, just north of Mildra.

Rock Troll: A variety of troll that lives on a distant island to the northwest of Frontmire and Canterhort. They are taller than a human by four or five heads and a bit shorter than a Giant. They are loyal to each other and to those they hire out to as mercenaries. And they are of intelligence equal to that of humans, Elves and Dwarves. They are renown as fierce warriors.

Rogue Ridge: Impassable ridge running north of the rogue Stream in southern Frontmire.

Ryer: Founder of Ryer's Clan on Parintia.

Ryer's Clan: First term applied to the segment of the Human population on Parintia, who later become known as the Druids.

Ryer's Maiden: Name of a ship owned by Ryer's Clan. It was later renamed *The Druid Queen.*

seilstri: sēl' strē: Castle keep on Parintia, which the Druids inherited. It became the center of their community life. It is named from the ancient Elven word meaning learning or knowledge.

Sether Road: Road that follows the south coast of Frontmire.

ShortBeard: Dwarf military messenger.

SixFists: Loner Dwarf who becomes traveling companion to Andreanna. Grandson of King GladdenStone. Cousin of King HeartStone.

SnowCap: Mountain on the Northeast end of the Blue Mountains, just south of Heros.

Span: See appendix of time, weights and measurements.

Stanton: Human, former Breezon army squad leader and traveling companion of Jerhad. Now, he becomes the Commander of the Elf Army and the object of Ahliene's affections.

SteelHand: Dwarf in charge of the mining of gold and construction of Mildra's fortifications.

Stewart: Breezon army captain. Friend of Stanton.

Stone: See appendix of time, weights and measurements.

StoneBreaker: Father of GladdenStone king of the Dwarves.

StoneSon: Dwarf soldier that has a bit of a drinking problem. Stanton uses him as a source for obtaining a stiff drink on a few occasions.

StoneWorth: Leader of the crew of Dwarves who maintained the aqueducts in Heros – now assisting in the mining stone and gold in Mildra.

Tanodo: A Mountain Gnome that becomes one of Andreanna's "body guards".

Tahmat: tă' măt: One of the giants who will remain on Frontmire when the Giant schooners leave for the Homeland.

terensil: As named by the Faeries, Elvish meaning The Watcher's Eye, the name given to Morlah's argentus staff, as within it, he is able to see untold distances.

terenden: As named by the Faeries, Elvish meaning The Watcher's Flame, the name given to Morlah's argentus knife.

Thogg: thŏg: First gnome leader.

Tobac: Nickname of Tomstock, the Dwarf tobac merchant.

Tom: Master Kline's son.

Tomstock: Dwarf tobac merchant, also nicknamed Tobac.

Troll: There are three varieties of these humanoid creatures, which live in Frontmire (except for the Rock Troll). They are the Cave Troll, the Rock Troll and the Mountain Troll. They are all tall, large and powerful and varying in levels of intelligence. See each one respectively.

urcha: ûr' kă: White Elfstone. *urcha* meaning shield or defender. Also, see Elfstone.

urcha-ac: ûr' kă – ăk: The name the Faerie *acrch* christens Stanton's sword at Moreau's Ford. Elvish meaning Defender of Life - Ursha in the common Tongue.

Werme: A leviathan/serpent of the Inland Sea that feeds on magic.

Windemere: Last of the ancient Kings of the Elves when they lived in northern Frontmire in the area of what is now the Breezon Plains.

Witch's Dew: Herb known to be extremely poisonous unless used within one course of its being picked, which then can be used to induce a hypnotic or trance-like state.

Woody Betany: Wild herb with tranquilizing, sedation, and pain killing properties.

Lineage of Jerhad: Jerhad, son of Lewin, son of Baros, descendent of Koro, son of Dandle, son of Minneras, descendent of Baros, son of Habald, son of Pands, descendent of Windermere, descendent of Pavillione.

Lineage of the Dwarf Kings: HeartStone, ur (son of) GladdenStone, ur StoneBreaker, ur RavenStone, ur ElkHunter-Stone, ur WhiteStone, ur AlhadStone, ur ThunderStone, first King under *Dolan.*

Chapter 1

The Black Mage sprinkled a pinch of powdered leaf of Witch's Dew into the simmering cauldron. He sighed. It did not satisfy him as he had expected, as he had hoped; nothing did. His centuries of existence were lost in bitterness and hatred. What was it? Six, seven hundred cycles? No, it was longer than that. It was six hundred cycles since he had come to dwell among the inhabitants of northern Frontmire. There had been a time when he had dwelt among others, but he did not remember that anymore. Why did they hate him so? Why could he not find rest for himself? It did not matter, for soon they would all pay and pay dearly at that. A little longer, and then, he would have the satisfaction of being the only one in the land able to wield magic. *Then*, he would savor the fruit of his labors.

Adding the last ingredients, the mage motioned with his hands, and the large wooden ladle began stirring the potion. He stepped back as a large noxious bubble burst on the potion's surface. It released a venomous green vapor, which he sent away with a wave of his hand before adding a handful of gold ore; he had been laboring at the concoction for one cycle of the moon. Tonight, the moon was full, and its stimulus would bring the brew to its full potency, activating the malignant mixture. Daektoch's plan was to, once and for all, put an end to all opposition, to at long last bring to fruition his struggles for supremacy. With this, he would overcome the Faeries who continually had involved themselves in the thwarting of his endeavors; he would cut them off from the very source of their power. The Faeries dealt with, the Elves would follow.

Daektoch the Black Mage vaguely remembered a time when he had been happy, when he had not lived in isolation, when he had not found it necessary to hide like some leprous outcast, but that was a faint and distant reminiscence, like that of the aged stains on his robes. There had been another life. He did remember the *Kataruk*, the evil necromancer who had stirred Daektoch's longing for power, the beginning of the change that had led to his quest for might in the forces of magic. It had been a long path, and now his ends were at hand.

The mage turned his eyes to one of the shadows that stood along the cavern's wall; the shade understood. With a resonating but hollow harmonizing, it began to chant, power throbbing throughout the chamber as its twelve fellows along the walls joined in, the final element of the curse. Within the labyrinth of Mount Bahal, within the Black Mage's lair, the incantation grew in strength. The volcanic mountain seemed to sway to the voices of the subverted wizards who were no longer Men, and the solidified magma throbbed to the Black magic's momentum. Down in the depths of the mountain's crater, the molten lava that normally bubbled began to spit and boil; outside under the moonlight, the mountain grew ominously dark, shrouded from all sight as lightning pierced the obsidian murk that hung over the pinnacle, yet without illuminating its slopes.

From the mountain emerged a venomous, long, fluorescing green tendril. It seemingly meandered aimlessly southward, as a great serpent seeking prey. Only, it knew where to find its quarry; it went south, deep within the Mystic Mountains where the Faeries dwelt. There, it would begin its work, an endeavor that would be slow and insidious but nevertheless effectual...*and lethal.*

Daektoch laughed mirthlessly, seeking within himself to find the joy of his labors; the dark creatures continued the incantation. A few more heartbeats and the trap would be set. The Faeries' demise would begin!

The mage left the chamber, leaving his servants to finish the work, for he had other enterprises at hand. The Cave Trolls needed to be brought into subjugation again. Being dim-witted made them easily turned into a swarming horde, and their tremendous strength and size made them formidable opponents. The mage emerged from a tunnel that appeared as a skeletal eye socket on the mountain's eastern face, and he stood on the narrow ledge that ended in a steep plummet. He looked out to the northern Blue Mountains inhabited by the Trolls, gazing through the night, sending out his awareness as a creeper, searching for his minions' minds.

He enveloped them with his will. His thoughts would be their thoughts. His desires would be their desires. His purpose would become their purpose: *the Elves' destruction!*

The Trolls would be well equipped, for Heros, the capitol, was also his, and he had seen to it that they had built many garrisons with armories stocked full. The Trolls would plunder them and be armed for the deed. A hint of satisfaction wisped through him at the thought. Puny Humans! They had been so easy to sway and bend to his will. They never questioned why the Trolls did not attack Heros as others Humans were. Yet, Heros had stockpiled lances, maces and broadswords as if war were at their very gate.

The Trolls were now in motion, but it would still be awhile before they amassed in numbers. The most difficult part of controlling the Trolls was to suppress the constant fighting among themselves and their tremendous appetites.

Without constant control, they would endlessly feed and fight amongst themselves and be useless. The effort of controlling them would cost Daektoch a continual exertion, but he could manage.

Within Bahal, the chanting ceased; the spell was finished. Daektoch turned and entered the mountain, returning to where his servants waited. Arriving within the cavern, he randomly chose four and cast a spell on them, mutating, mutilating the demon-like wraiths into bat-like creatures the size of horses. Four of the other shades mounted these and left, two flying south to the land of the Elves and two to *Dolan*, the mountain in the western Mystics where the Dwarves dwelt. The Dwarves! Oh, yes! They too would feel his wrath. Too often, they had meddled and assisted in thwarting his plans, but that would end soon. They thought themselves secure in their mountain habitat. Daektoch almost laughed. *Dolan*, the Dwarf word for rock or fortress. He would show them how worthless that fortress could become.

There were but two other obstacles. The Human city of Breezon and Morlah the Druid. He had plans for them too. But for tonight, he had expended enough energy. The mage needed to regenerate his powers. A short season with his spirit in the Netherworld was needed, and then he would set his plans into full motion.

Déjà Vu?

Jerhad lay half asleep under an ancient Silver Willow common to the southwest of Frontmire. He watched as an old man cloaked in a gray mantle made his way up the road past the house, where he lived with his parents. The Elf laughed to himself, feeling as if he were viewing a scene from his past when Morlah the Druid had come up that very road, seven cycles of the sun before, looking much like this dream apparition did now. The subsequent events had turned Jerhad's life upside down.

He remembered watching Morlah, passing himself off as an old man, approaching him and saying:

"Hot! Is it not?"

Jerhad bolted to a seated position, "Morlah! I thought I was dreaming."

"Thou mayest well wish thou wast, mine Elven friend." The Druids, to this time, still spoke in the ancient version of the Common Tongue.

"Not another delivery!" Jerhad pretended to chide, putting his hands up as if to push Morlah away or ward himself from evil.

"No...not a package but an errand, mayhapst."

"You'd have to pay me a lot more than six golds to send me off on another Druid errand, Morlah. I don't think you could afford it," laughed Jerhad.

"Wouldst a gold mine be enough for thee?" the Druid inquired with a conspiratorial grin breaking across his face.

Jerhad laughed even more, "You're on. You give me a gold mine, and I'll run your errand."

"Done then," smiled Morlah, mischief beaming in his eyes.

Then, Jerhad came forward and embraced the Druid. "Well-met, Morlah. Well-met! Where have you been? We haven't seen you in some seven cycles of the sun."

"Sleeping...the Druid Sleep, but now is the time to awake. Trouble doest begin again in the land. But enough of that for now. How is Andreanna?"

"Great! She's put her weight back on, fiery as ever. Looks great as ever too though she still gets dark circles under her eyes when she's tired. You missed it. We were wed about one cycle after she came to Mildra. We have a daughter now, Kendra...four cycles old. Andreanna's...you know...woman things...took a while to catch up before she was able to bear," the Elf finished a little awkwardly.

Andreanna, though Human in appearance, had a good part Elven blood in her ancestry and, as was Jerhad, was a descendant of the royal lineage of the Elves; there had not been a recognized King or Queen for hundreds upon hundreds of cycles. She had long auburn hair, almond-shaped, chestnut-colored eyes and was extremely beautiful, even if she did not have Elfish-pointed ears. Andreanna was now in her twenty-seventh cycle, and she had become a vibrant addition to the Elven community of Mildra.

"It doest mine heart good to hear this, Jerhad. I wish thee both well...and many children, though they willst challenge thine heart in ways that Gnomes, Trolls and wizards have not."

"What in the gods' names is that supposed to mean?"

"Time willst reveal this mystery to thee if thou doest not know," Morlah chuckled.

"Druids! ...You staying or you gotta run, like you usually do?"

"If there is room at the local inn, I wast think...."

"Oh, cut that out!" interrupted Jerhad. "You'll stay with us. Andreanna would kick me if I let you stay elsewhere. She still speaks of you often...quite fond of you actually, for some unknown reason," Jerhad teased. "We're living with my mother and father. Father's home from the sea for a spell. You'll get to meet him.

"Better get ready. My mother still tells the story of the ten Trolls she killed with her longbow...only now, it's grown to thirty or forty and at one thousand paces. Like cheese, good wine or any story worth telling...gets better with age."

"Is thine family at home now?"

"No, they're all down in the market. The tarpon run was early this cycle. Andreanna helps Mother down there, and they take Kendra with them. They're up to their elbows in fish. Father's helping out, too."

"And thee, why doest thou not help?"

"I just got here about one-half span before you arrived. Just finished planting the summer wheat, then took the midcourse ferry back. I ate some and thought I'd get me a nap in the shade before I go down to help. Was up one span before the sunrising to get to the fields every course of the sun for the past quarter-moon's cycle."

"How is thine grandfather?"

"Oh, ...He died...just last cycle, in the late summer. We had expected it to be a long time before. He had fallen off the roof of his cabin while fixing a leak...just before we were wed. He wouldn't hear of being moved into town, so I went up and stayed with him. But then, he mended and perked right up and did rather well until he died.

"It was really strange, Morlah, but it seemed in those times, when I took care of him, that I was sharing something with him that helped him get better...but that's just crazy... isn't it?"

"Is it? Doest thou not bear the *acrch,* Elfstone of Life and Health? I wouldst like to see where he didst live. Is the cabin still there?"

"Left it just like it had been.... You know...he just died in his sleep one night. The course before, he was in good spirits, and he even gave me his books. One of them is a copy of the *Druid Histories*. The one dating to two hundred cycles of the sun ago, and there are older copies of the *Elf* and *Dwarf Histories*, too. I keep them up at the cabin."

"They art very valuable sources of knowledge. Thou shouldst keep them where they wouldst be safer. Hast thou read them?"

"I do. I read them quite often in fact. I was familiar with some of what I read, from Grandfather's stories that he used to tell me when I was a boy. But now, it's all so much more real since I've seen Dwarves, Gnomes and Trolls...and Daektoch...."

"Ah, yes...Daektoch...but come. Let us walk as we speak," he said as they turned and headed south along the way. "Jerhad, I fear that Daektoch is about again."

"Fire and demons! I thought we'd seen the last of that miserable wretch. I'd hoped I'd never see that soulless wizard again!"

"I fear that thou willst, Jerhad. Thou doest know of his lust to possess all magic and to destroy that which he canst not possess. Thine Elven blade, *Gildar* or Ember, is magic. Thou hast innate magic. That, he canst not possess, so he willst seek to subvert thee or destroy thee. The Elves have dormant magic. In his mind, he doest perceive this to be a threat to himself; they must be destroyed also. He doest fear all who wield magic as potential enemies, so he seeks to annihilate them. Thou willst not escape his attention; neither willst I. We two art the most powerful forces of magic, for the cause of good, that I am aware of...next to the Faeries of course, but they do not intervene much into the affairs of mortals. Daektoch willst not tolerate our presence."

"Always there with an encouraging word, Morlah; aren't you? But...about me and my magic.... I'm confused. We never did have time to talk about it before. Sometimes I feel the magic is in the knife.... Then, it's like the knife is in me, or I'm in it or...I don't know. How was I able to use the magic, if it's in the knife, when the Gnomes had possession of it? And then, when I fought with Daektoch, I never even touched it. It was like the magic came out...from inside me. Good thing Kassandra showed up when she did." He smiled at the memory of the female Giant who had saved his life in his fight against Daektoch, and he became lost in thought for a span of heartbeats.

"This is the nature of the magic that thou doest posses. Thou doest remember I spoke to thee of it several cycles past; I didst tell thee that magic is the Elves' destiny and that the knife wast not all."

"Yeah...so?"

"Magic is inherent and innate to the Elves. Over the cycles, after the Elves moved to southern Frontmire it didst become dormant from lack of use. The knife is Dwarf steel with the element argentus mixed in at the forging, as thou doest know. Argentus is an Earthen power, the very source of Faerie magic and therefore of Elven magic. The Faeries art the embodiment of the magic, which is said to possess an intelligence of its own. Some of the magic is expressed in a humanoid form that we doest know as the Faeries, while other portions of the magic (or intelligence) prefer different forms."

They made their way down the lane, two figures walking under the oppressive midcourse sun.

"One such form is that of the Elfstone. Some go further and will express themselves as both, or in ethereal entities. For example, the *acrch*, the stone of Life and Health, is expressed in the Elfstone which thou doest bear in the handle of thine Elven blade. Though she doest remain in completeness in the stone, at times she hast chosen to appear in Faerie or another humanoid form, such as an old woman, a dream creature.... This power is also within thee, Jerhad, innate as a descendant of these distant relatives, if thou wouldst. It is a part of thee, equal to thine own life force, and canst not be separated from thee."

Suddenly, the Druid stopped and looked behind, gazing over his shoulder toward the unseen Mount Bahal, which lay many leagues away, listening, his eyes searching the skies and frowning as if in deep concentration. Morlah shook his head, concern clearly visible on his face, sighed and turned south again. Dislodging Jerhad from his northerly gaze, the Druid propelled the Elf forward with his hand on Jerhad's elbow.

"The magic hast its source within the argentus, the same power that is within thee and the Elfstones. It hast been dormant in the Elves, so a catalyst wast needed to awaken and guide in its use; this wast the purpose of the knife, Ember. At first, when thou didst use its power, it wast that of the knife only, but then, the magic didst awaken within thee at the stirrings caused by the blade's power. Then, the ability in thee wast able to become its own independent force with a life of its own and intelligence of its own, yet not separate from thee or the argentus." He glanced over his shoulder towards the unseen Bahal again.

"When Daektoch didst take Andreanna at Moreau's Ford, and thou didst fight with the dark shade, his servant, the ability didst awaken completely within thee. Thou wast able to wield the magic without using the power of thine Elven blade. Later, thou didst handle the magic without the knife's presence, in its full force. It didst come to its fullness, perhaps prematurely. Stanton didst finally speak to me of what had happened. *Thou wast almost lost.* The memory of it shouldst not be stirred within thee.... No, do not ask," he said raising his hand, warding off the question as it began forming itself on Jerhad's lips.

"Suffice it to know that thou didst destroy the creature with force from within thee alone. After thou wast healed of thine wound, the magic of the stones and that within thee didst work as if answering face-to-face in a looking glass. That which thou doest perceive within the knife is perceived within thee by the stones in the knife's handle.

"In this way, the stones didst quicken thine innate ability and teach thee its use. The knife willst always be a source of power to thee to strengthen and focus that which is already within thee; but in contrast to myself, who once am separated from the argentus, am powerless, except for that which I have of the Arts, thou art a source of power that hast not been known since the end of the Kingdom of the Elves in the north, both in the manifestation of magic and in the strength thereof. Doest thou understand this?"

"I hear you, old man, but I don't know if I understand."

The blade they spoke of was one given to Jerhad by his grandfather upon his rite into adulthood seventeen cycles of the sun in the past at the age of fifteen cycles. It was, by any standard, an odd appearing knife. The double-edged blade was about three spans long and two fingers wide and was made of (his grandfather had claimed) steel forged with Elven magic, sharp enough to shave with if the Elves had such need. The handle was of a golden-colored metal (but not gold) of a wrought braid-like work, into which, someone had interlaced oiled leather strands. Peculiar to the handle was the row of dull-colored, acorn-sized stones mounted within, not gems or precious jewels but perfectly round stones numbering seven. These were set completely within the handle so that they showed on both sides; they were ordered (from blade to pommel) white, yellow, blue, green, purple, black and silver-white: Elfstones of Earthen magic.

Within the bowels of Mount Bahal, Daektoch festered in his hatred of the Elves and Morlah the Druid. Actually, he hated all life that he did not control. At least Daektoch had the compensation of knowing that GladdenStone, the Dwarf King, had died in battle though it was only a bitter satisfaction now. How had they gotten forty Giants involved? Where had they come from? That, he did not know. He knew of the one who guarded the land that was gifted of the Elves to the Giants. He had taken care of that one. But forty! How would one even find so many Giants in Frontmire?

A large portion of the Trolls that Daektoch had brought against Breezon had been slaughtered in the fighting seven cycles past, just courses of the sun before they would have achieved the breeching of the walls; it would have been easy plunder from there. Frontmire's second largest army would have been destroyed. He had wanted to destroy the Breezon army to eliminate any possible interference from them. As it stood, the surviving Trolls had been routed back into the Blue Mountains with two thirds of their ranks left dead, lying on the Breezon Plains or drowned in the Maring Sea. Those wretched Giants and Dwarves had shown up and flanked the Trolls, killing thousands and assisting in what had led to the final rout of the entire horde.

Then, there had been the unrest that had risen in the east, which had led to the final dread, panic and stampeding of Trolls into the river and sea and the following rout of the remaining Trolls back into the mountains. What had escaped his notice was the two dinghies containing the ghosts of the dead Druids that he had slain some six hundred cycles before. By means of Morlah's magic they had crossed from the mist where they existed, waiting, longing for vengeance against Daektoch. Their very presence cast fear and terror into the hearts of mortals. They had caused no small unrest on the Trolls' eastern flank and had proved to be the undoing of Daektoch's minions. To add insult to injury, Daektoch had been desperately wounded, first by Morlah in battle, and then by the Elf, Jerhad, whom he had seriously underestimated. The Elf's magic was powerful! More powerful than his own. Only, the Elf was inexperienced in its use and without malice in his heart, which had almost proven to be Jerhad's undoing. Daektoch's injuries from fighting the Elf had been too great for him to confront either Druid or Elf again, and so he had slithered back into the labyrinth of lava-wrought mazes within Bahal.

Morlah and Jerhad walked on into the heat of the afternoon, up to Jerhad's grandfather's cabin. It was a small log structure tucked away in the foothills of a solitary mountain (the first of the Coastal Range) to the south of Mildra. The sea could be seen in the distance to the southwest, large cumulus clouds being blown briskly far out over the water and spanning out to the horizon. The area before the cabin bore a level field with great Canterhort Firs growing sparsely about the front of the cabin and turning into a dense stand of towering spires around the back and up onto the great stone of which the mountain was comprised.

Spring wild flowers grew in abundance in the field; their sweet fragrance hung heavily on the air in the afternoon's heat as they displayed bright rainbow shades of colors. A cooling breeze from the Korkaran Sea faintly stirred the grasses, swaying, giving a feel of life and motion to the otherwise still setting.

The cabin itself stood in stark contrast; it was old, having been built by Jerhad's father's grandfather nearly one hundred cycles past. The dampness of the winter sea air produced a thick moss cover that clung throughout the cycle to the hand-hewn-cedar shakes on the roof, still solid and weatherproof. The cedar logs, streaked with cracks of age and drying, were an ancient home to the spiders and insects, which lived in their darkened recesses. On the front, a narrow porch of thick fir planks was enclosed with pole rails that guarded a lone rocking chair. Two flat stones, a smaller set on a larger, made the stair leading up into the cabin. From the roof on one side, rose the stone-masonry chimney Jerhad had helped his grandfather replace some cycles past. This setting, serene and peaceful, was one that Jerhad often used as a refuge for thinking or reading the *Histories*.

The two companions went to the rear of the cabin, shaded by the huge firs, and drank cold water, using the ladle that hung from the side of the cedar-slat barrel, which housed the spring.

"Now, I willst show to thee the payment for thine next errand. Am I correct in assuming your grandfather didst leave his land to thee?"

"Payment? ...What errand?"

"The land, is it thine?"

"Yes, yes.... How did you know? What errand?"

"It wouldst follow logic that he wouldst leave it and his books to the one who didst attend to his stories and needs. I knew thine grandfather many cycles back, as I didst tell thee. Every generation, I didst visit thine family and didst send the eldest male on the same quest I didst send thee upon; I have met thine father and grandfather, though, I didst arrange it that they didst not remember.

"Your grandfather wast the first in many cycles to have believed in magic. I thought it wouldst have been him in whom it wouldst first awaken. But it wast not to be. Thine father didst not believe." The Druid droned on in his discourse of logic. "So I wouldst expect thine grandfather to hold thee dearer for thine attention to his stories, which thine own father didst have no time for, even from an early age. Then, when thou didst return into the north of Mildra wielding magic.... It wast a logical conclusion."

"What's this payment and errand you're taking about?"

"The one we didst agree to earlier. Thou didst say that if I didst pay thee a gold mine, then thou wouldst undertake mine errand."

"Oh, no, you don't. No more errands for me, Druid. I had half of Frontmire trying to tan my hide last time. No more! No thanks!"

"Come. We willst speak of that later. Come see." They climbed the hill behind the cabin until they reached a small plateau, the last after the rise that ended the foothills and gave birth to the mountain. They crossed about one-eighth league to where the mountain rose again. Coming to a boulder, which was easily double the size of the cabin they had just left behind, they stopped.

"When I wast with the Faeries in the Mystic Mountains, they didst instruct me in many things: of argentus, of magic... of your magic, of their purpose in bringing the magic back to the Elves, that is, to balance the power between the forces of good and evil that hold might in the land. For evil is destined to rise again and again. It is appointed to the Elves, for now to thee, to keep and maintain the equilibrium.

"The Faeries didst tell me of the coming need for a different power to achieve these ends, monetary power, the power needed to establish a kingdom. It willst be needed to see the Faeries' purposes come to their fullness. Let me show thee what they didst speak of to me."

He lifted his staff into the air. It was a polished, Black Oak staff with a silver-white orb fixed to the top. The fist-sized argentus orb lent its power to the wood and through it, to Morlah. While in contact with the argentus through the staff, the Druid could wield the mighty power of the Faerie magic. The Faeries had named it the Watcher's Eye or *tenensil* in the ancient Faerie and Elven tongue.

Tenensil came to life, magic visible in the silver-white light that it radiated, and then, the power shot out and wrapped itself about the boulder. Without breaking a sweat, Morlah lifted the boulder into the air, steady and sure at the end of the shaft of light, and placed it to one side.

"Here is what the Faeries didst tell me of."

Jerhad was not listening. He was still pondering the moved boulder. Morlah walked to the stone face of the mountainside where the boulder had lain, pulling his solid argentus knife and working the stone for a heartbeat or two before turning to hand Jerhad a piece of what he had dug out. The knife was also given a name by the Faeries: *tenenden* – The Watcher's Flame, for it contained an ominous power.

"Gold!" exclaimed Jerhad. He went over and studied the rock wall where he saw a vein of pure gold, not a mixed ore, the width of his hand and twice his height. "O, ye gods, will you look at that! How did you know this was here?"

"Thou art not listening to me...again," Morlah continued in his deliberate fashion. "The Faeries didst tell me. Now step back."

With the same ease, he returned the boulder to its original position, hiding the enormous vein of wealth that was now Jerhad's.

"Here, take this," he said removing a leather purse drawn closed with a rawhide strand. "There art one hundred large golds within this pouch. Thou willst use them to hire Elves to mine this gold. There is the wealth of a kingdom, a rich kingdom, hidden in the mountain. The Dwarves art coming. Two hundred of them; they willst act as thine security and mining consultants, and they willst provide some labor to mine the gold. It willst probably not be possible for long, but it willst be best to leave the knowledge of this to the Dwarves and Elves for as long as thou canst. The Dwarves willst be at thine service. The gold willst be melted into bars by the Dwarves while another group of them willst transport it to *seilstri.* We doest have the means to keep it safe there until it is needed here. Thou willst pay the Dwarves twelve bars of gold per moon's cycle; they have agreed to this already. When thou doest return from thine errand, thou willst begin to mine the gold. Very few thieves or robbers willst have the resources to deal with the Dwarves. As thou doest remember, they art rather fierce fighters, almost like Giants packed into smaller bodies."

"I'm not going on any Druid errand!" Jerhad protested vehemently.

"Let it suffice. Hast thou food and a bed for an old man?"

"Yeah, sure. But I ain't going on no errand. Do I need to help you to walk, too, 'old man'? Come on."

"More elderberry pie and sweet cream, Morlah?" asked Andreanna.

"No, I thank thee, mine dear; I have eaten enough for a troop of Dwarves. Methinks I willst rupture."

Andreanna laughed. They had just finished evening meat at Jerhad's home and sat in the living area of the charming cottage.

"Oh, Morlah, it's so good to see you again. What brings you to Mildra anyway?"

"Well, thou...."

"Tobac, Morlah? How about a pipe of tobac?" interrupted Jerhad, rising to his feet and pushing his tobac pouch into the Druid's hands. "The Dwarves have reopened the pass to the north, and now trading between the Dwarves and Elves is commonplace." He continued to stand directly before Morlah. "We now smoke some of the best and freshest Dwarf tobac available. You really have to try a pipeful. Have you seen the pass?" Morlah took the tobac pouch that Jerhad held before the Druid's face.

"I didst come down that way after I didst visit the Dwarves," nodded Morlah as he pressed a large pinch of tobac into the bowl of his long-stemmed, White Ash pipe. "As I recall, an earthquake is reported to have closed it to traffic some four hundred eighty-six cycles past. It hadst been known as Dwarf's Pass, carved out through the mountains by the Dwarves soon after the Elves had migrated here from the north."

He reached up with his staff and prodded Jerhad, moving him so that the Druid might view the others in the room. "The earthquake didst loose one side of the gorge used as the general route of the pass and didst fill it some two hundred paces deep with stone rubble." He leaned close to a candle on a nearby table and lit his pipe, great white puffs of the sweet aromatic smoke rising toward the ceiling. "*The gods* know how they manage such things - the Dwarves, their fathers bless their beards, have bored through the rubble and made an arched tunnel of stonework beneath it," the Druid spoke from around a billow of tobac smoke. "The work is as tight as a Gnome's mouth when caught in a lie. Ah, yes. This *is* good tobac."

"What was that you said, last time you were here, about Andreanna having Elf blood. Here have some more java..." said Jerhad, still attempting to run a diversion from the "errand" topic.

"Yes, it doest seem that three hundred four cycles ago Brandier, son of Habald, son of Pands the miller, didst leave Mildra and went north," said Morlah, ever the scholar, allowing himself to be diverted from his topic while showing no notice of Jerhad's tactics. "He didst visit the Dwarves and the Giant at the *Gift of the Elves to the Giants*. Then, he went to Breezon for a season and there didst wed a Human before returning south. They settled in BlueHill to the end of their cycles." Morlah sat forward, to the edge of his cushioned chair, his finger poking at the air as he spoke. "Then, some one hundred eighty cycles ago, Koro son of Dandle, son of Minneras the fisher, didst leave Mildra and made it as far as BlueHill. There he didst meet and marry a descendant of Brandier, Melissa by name. Well, thou doest know how likes in appearance attract, she and he both with the Elven eyes and ears.... They married and had children. Then, one hundred and twenty-five cycles ago, Jerhad, thine own great-great uncle went to BlueHill also and didst marry one Marion descendant of Dandle, descendant of Brandier. Now, if that is not a strange enough play of fate, one hundred fourteen cycles later, thou, Jerhad, hast wed Andreanna, descendant of Dandle, descendant of Brandier. More so, each of these males is in the direct lineage of the Elven King Windemere as art thou, Jerhad. Fate has her hand upon this lineage!" Morlah blew a great ring of smoke up toward the ceiling.

Jerhad was out of diversions, the wind having been knocked out of him with that last comment. He fell back into his chair defeated.

"But now to mine purpose. Seven cycles ago, I didst return from Frontmire to *seilstri*, the keep, home of the Druids. I didst enter into the chambers that we doest use for time spent in the Druid Sleep. After I didst seal the chamber from within, and the guard wast posted without, I went into the Druid Sleep. Perhaps having a guard is a little overly zealous of us; but after Daektoch's attempt on us, *seilstri's* Guard doest leave nothing to chance.

"So I went into the Druid Sleep in order to preserve myself as I have done for many cycles. I didst wake from seven cycles of the sun of sleep, mine body healed and restored as if I wast four cycles younger. I had set a spell to awaken me if Daektoch's presence wast out in the land again.

"*Daektoch hast come out of hiding*! He bothers not to conceal himself any longer," said Morlah finally getting to the crux of the matter. "*He willst come for the destruction of the Elves!*"

Jerhad threw his hands up, jumping to his feet. "No! I don't want to do this again!"

"Ye gods in the heavens, he's coming here?" asked Catrina, Jerhad's mother. "Ah, and me out of practice with my longbow. Why I'd just like the chance to let two arrows fly into that foul beast's heart...."

"Mother!" blurted Jerhad.

Andreanna reeled about and stood before Jerhad, "Listen, Elf Boy!" Jerhad knew that he was in for it now. For Jerhad, Andreanna's use of "'Elf Boy", was equivalent of a Human mother using a child's full name.

"You going to hide your head under the pillow and hope that the things under the bed don't bite your toes? What's the matter with you?" She missed her attempted swat at his head as he pulled back. "If Daektoch comes looking for us, we'd better be ready. Hiding isn't going to keep him or a band of Trolls from slaughtering us."

"Ain't no Trolls going to get us while I have my longbow," continued Catrina.

Lewin, Jerhad's father, rolled his eyes. "I think you'd better stick to filleting tarpon, Cat."

"Why I'll have you know, the last time those Trolls...."

"We know! We know," sighed Lewin. "We've heard about it already, and thank the gods that Jerhad was able to do that... whatever he did and stop the whole thing before you all were killed." Lewin always hated to admit that Jerhad possessed of magic. He did not believe in magic, nor did he want to believe in it. But the whole village had seen it happen, so he could not deny it had...at least not openly.

"Andreanna, I don't want to get involved in this. I don't want to go wandering all over Frontmire again," protested Jerhad. "We were just lucky last time that we just didn't end up dead. And now, there's you and Kendra and the tarpon need to be smoked and pickled before they spoil...."

She successfully smacked him upside the head and put her hands on her hips, legs spread apart, reminding him of the first time he had seen her in her chain mail and with a shortsword on her hip.

"That's exactly why you'll do as Morlah tells you. You need to protect your family here," she said, continually poking him in the chest as she scolded. "You're the only one with magic among our people. If you hide and we all die...of course you wouldn't...*your magic would protect you.* Then where would you be? I'm going to bed. Why don't you sleep at Grandfather's cabin tonight to think this over!" She turned and went to her room.

Morlah's face went through a series of contortions, most of them tending toward a grin or a smirk. "Well, thou art correct about one thing, Jerhad," he finally smiled, "she hast lost none of her fire.... Now, if someone wouldst be so kind as to show me to mine room; even though I have slept seven cycles, I still need to rest from course to course.... The effect is not to the same end." He exchanged good nights with them and was shown to his bed by Catrina.

"...Did I ever tell you about the time I killed forty-six Trolls..." Catrina said as she escorted him to the rear of the house.

"Seven cycles she's told that story...I thought she would wear it out, but instead it grows. Perhaps she does have Dwarf blood, which would explain the exaggerated tales," said Lewin to Jerhad, "But she's as good a mate as any male could want. If you want a female, there's just certain things you have to endure... Son, I don't need to tell you what I feel about this magic thing, but I know there was the Troll war up in Breezon, and it made its way down here. Our ship barely made it through the booms on the river as we left Breezon. I saw what was happening there. I saw the pile of ash and Troll bones on the field to the north of town where the Giants and Dwarves burnt the dead Trolls. If trouble is about to come upon us and Morlah thinks there's something we can do to stop it...then let's do it."

Jerhad flipped the gold nugget to his father.

"This is pure. Where did you get it? Enough for two small golds in this."

"Up the hill behind Grandfather's cabin. You're all fired up to help Morlah? You just bought yourself a job as foreman of the mining crew. Dwarves are coming to do security and melt what we mine to gold bars for shipping to *seilstri* for safekeeping. Morlah wants us to hire Elven labor and pay them with this." He threw the pouch of golds over to his father who went wide-eyed staring into the purse.

"Looks like I'm going on another Druid errand. Don't know where or what yet. Meanwhile, that nugget will probably get you enough supplies for a start at opening the mine. Keep it quiet for now. We start when I get back, I guess. If I get back. Daektoch almost killed me last time we met. If Kassandra hadn't walloped him upside the head...I would have been a goner." Jerhad had to laugh; he could still vividly see the surprise on the mage's face as the wizard had hurtled into the brush.

"Now I'm going to see if I can sleep in my bed tonight. Between you and Mother and Andreanna, I doubt I'll get any peace around here until I play go-fer for the Druid again. Night, Father." Then, he went off to see if he could reclaim his space in his own bed. The only thing he loved more than Andreanna was simply to sleep next to her at night.

Chapter 2

The chilly, hazy ochre morning sky found Jerhad at the woodpile splitting cedar and pine logs for the hearth, to get the chill out of the house before break fast cooking started. Jerhad, now in his thirty-second cycle was a tall slender Elf of golden hair with brilliant-blue, almond-shaped eyes. He had the typical pointed and nearly lobeless Elven ears. He was a handsome male who had lived with his parents his entire life, a common occurrence among the Elves whose children took care of their elders as age claimed them. Jerhad had been snatched from his secure life in Mildra by the Druid's previous errand and had been sent throughout Frontmire in dangers, perils and adventures, only to discover that he possessed magic. He had courageously faced magical, black creatures, Gnomes and even the Black Mage himself.

Morlah came strolling around the corner. "The Trolls willst come; it is just a matter of time," said the Druid in his direct and long-winded manner. "The Elves throughout the land have heard of thee and thine deeds. Take a few Elf hunters, males, who art reliable, males who art good with bow and knife, and cross from here to Canon and call the Elves to arms. Tell them to ready themselves for battle. Each village is to prepare defenses and send a small force to Mildra to form a larger fighting force, an army, one might say, a force to use to meet the enemy head on, and not wait for each village and town to be assaulted individually. Tell them to wall their communities to the best of their abilities. I have set thine father to the task here in Mildra, seeing that he *is* the mayor. The Dwarves willst be here soon, and thine father willst set them to work under the guise of building a defensive position while waiting for thee to return and open the mine. He willst also use the coin I have given thee to begin the task until the mine is opened and canst pay for laborers. Look for help when and where least expected. Be of good courage, Elven Prince. Ja speed." With which, he turned and left.

"Good morning to you, too, Morlah...hey wait...how...? Damned Druid!"

"Who are you talking to?" asked Andreanna, coming around from the other side of the house. Morlah, as if by magic, was already out of sight. "Talking to yourself? Stanton warned me that you did a lot of that. I hadn't believed it till now. What's holding up the wood? It's cold in there."

"Yes, dear," mumbled Jerhad beneath his breath; it was a sure way to get the last word in.

So arrangements were made for Jerhad's departure, and a few courses before he left, the Dwarves arrived. The whole village was astir with excitement at their presence. Whether a work crew or military detachment, Dwarves dressed and looked the same: chain mail and steel helm, mace or axe at their side, stout and determined, like a cross between a miniature Giant and a bull, carrying themselves with an aura of strength and confidence and all with long beards, which were held in high esteem among them.

Jerhad had approached four of the town's most reputable hunters, the *Elves' best* and also friends of his. He paid them each one large gold now, and another to be paid when they returned. The first was Darcus, a loner, a tall slender, platinum-haired male of few words who lived in a cabin a couple of leagues north of Mildra. He had been involved in the fighting against the Trolls seven cycles back, so he did not need convincing. He listened to what Jerhad had to say, bit the coin to see if it were pure and nodded. "Let me know when we leave." He had turned and gone back into his cabin.

Jasson, Lehland, and Hash were the other hunters. Jerhad had forgotten Hash's real name; everybody just called him that because that was all he ate when out on the trail. These three always hunted together, working as a team. Each cycle they supplied their friends and relatives with fresh meat – elk, turkey, geese, venison and bear in abundance. They were both quiet and quick in the forest. They were loyal to each other and the town. Moreover, Jerhad would trust them with his life.

Jerhad had found them at Jake's Tavern the night he had gone looking for them. The inn was frequented mostly by unwed males and travelers. It was a large rammed-earth structure, painted a bright red and roofed with gray slate. A large hearth burned with a hot fire at one end.

"Jerhad, sit with us," called Jasson through a mouthful of mutton pie, as Jerhad had entered Jake's. "What brings you out this late in the course? If the men of the village weren't so scared of your mate, I'd say you'd be in danger of having her stolen with you leaving her home alone."

Everyone within earshot laughed. Jerhad flushed a little and sighed, knowing there was more truth than not in what Jasson had said, more than most males would want to admit to. They never did tire of rubbing it in that Andreanna could wallop the pants off every male in the town, including Jerhad.

"The Trolls are being moved against us again," said Jerhad. These three had been involved in the defenses of Mildra in the last Troll raid also. They had just come in from the forest and had missed the recent news and happenings.

"How'd you know that?" mumbled Hash.

"The Druid was here.... Wants us to mobilize the Elves along the coast to prepare for the defense of the villages. You see the Dwarves that are afoot?"

They nodded.

"They're going to help build a defensive wall. The Druid wants me and four others to go raise the standard, or something like that. Darcus has agreed to come. Pay you each one gold, a large one, before we go and another when we get back."

"Excellent!" said Lehland. "We expect to see any fighting?"

"The Druid didn't say. He just told me what he wanted me to do."

"Andreanna coming?" grinned Jasson.

Jerhad gawked at him in disbelief, "We have a child! Ye gods, what are you thinking; she's a mother!"

"Too bad, we could have used her if we ran into trouble. I'd feel a whole lot safer," Jasson finished, setting everybody, except Jerhad, to a howling laughter.

"Yeah, we'll be coming, Jerhad, lad. We've seen these Trolls before. If we can do anything to help defend our people...we'll be there. Count on us," mumbled Hash.

"Thanks. This was easier than I expected. I guess I'm the only one offering resistance to all of this, except, between Andreanna, my parents and the Druid, that's all been kicked out of me."

"You'll be better off with us and the Trolls," they called to him as he left, setting the house off into a roar of laughter. So just like that, it was settled.

The rising before Jerhad left on his errand, the Dwarves surveyed the terrain, searching for the best advantage for a location for a defensive wall. The grassy meadow that lay some one thousand paces north of the town was solid ledge about one to two paces below the rich topsoil. They would dig down and lay footings there to build the wall, which would be of stonework, built of interlaced blocks fashioned with overlying steel keys set into carved locks in the stone; keys would be left open on the inside to interlace any future widening and heightening.

The Dwarf leader, SteelHand by name, spoke to Jerhad. "Morlah instructed me on this matter when he was in *Dolan*. He told me of the gold. This is what I propose to do.... Hey Nose," he called to a short fat Dwarf sitting with others who were engaged in exchanging lies and tales, seeing who could outdo the other yet still be somewhat credible.

"Jerhad this is Dort, son of RockBreaker. We call him Nose. Nose, what is it I have in my left hand?" Nose was shorter and much stockier than most Dwarves. He had a ragged-briar-patch of a beard with his two glistening, dark-brown eyes and bulbous nose, the only other facial features to be seen between bush and brow. Uncommon to the Dwarves was the unstrung longbow that Dort carried slung over his shoulder.

Nose's nose wiggled a bit, "Coppers.... Coined in the early cycles of GladdenStone, is it?"

SteelHand shook his head in exasperation. "I hate it when he's exact like that. What's in my right hand?"

Again, Nose's large proboscis moved about as if sniffing the air, "Silver. Mined in the..."

"That will be enough." interrupted SteelHand in feigned disgust. He opened his hands showing the copper and silver coins respectively. "Nose has a unique gift of being able to smell metal. Do not ask me to explain it. His father did it as well as his grandfather unto five generations. We think, maybe, that one of his female ancestors went over to visit with the Faeries.... Who knows? But what we do know is that he can smell metals, including gold.

"What we do is open the mountain to quarry stone for the wall. This is *easy* work for us." This was a bit of necessary Dwarf bragging.

"Morlah has already described the layout to me." SteelHand went down on one knee and scratched a diagram of what he spoke of in the dirt. "So we follow the vein from one pace away for now; Nose will keep us at the right distance so we do not run into the gold. Later, when we want to move the gold, we just peel that last layer of stone like peeling the skin off of a boiled tomato. Meanwhile, we can put the troops to work. It will give us our stone for the wall and make the mining a breeze. 'Two Trolls with one stroke!' At the word Troll, the Dwarf's hand instinctively moved to his mace and rested there.

"We will begin cutting tomorrow and also set a crew to excavating the soil so we can set the footings for the battlement. What we need from you is a supply of food.... Fresh tarpon would be nice; we have not had that in a long time. We will do our own cooking... brought our own cooks. Then, I need eight yolk of oxen on plows to break the soil, eight more to put on scoops to pick up the loosened earth. We brought some scoops with us that we have had good success with in *Dolan*. You will need to supply the plows. Then, we will need another eight teams with sleds for hauling stone down from the quarry.

"We will be cutting the stone with diamond-studded cables...a gift to you, Elven Prince, from King Hearthstone, son of GladdenStone, in *Dolan*. This is going to be more fun than we have had in a long time. Cannot wait to get going...and we get paid, too!" he said rising to his feet, his face beaming with delight.

Next sunrising, before the town began stirring for the new course, Jerhad and his four companions quietly left the town, unnoticed. The yellow rising sun was magnified by the haze, a remnant of the light, night fog that was quickly burning off. Leaving the last of the houses behind, they passed by a dozen or so Dwarves finishing break fast under a tree.

"Thought you Elves were going to sleep all course," they called. "Half the sun's course is already past. Where have you been?"

"I am Orenald," spoke one Dwarf as he approached the Elves. Orenald was a lean and muscular Dwarf. His long braided hair was a lighter brown than most Dwarves. His eyes were intense, revealing a unique intelligence. From his belt hung a two-edged war axe on one side and a steel-headed mace on the other. His chain mail shone brightly. "SteelHand said we should go with you and have one of us stay behind at every third or fourth village to help direct the building of fortifications. We will have the entire south coast at work in no time. The good part of this is that many villages lie along the cliffs off the coast; half of the defense is already there."

"The more the merrier," surrendered Jerhad. He introduced the Elves and was given the Dwarves' names. He did not remember one name by the time they had been through them all.

"Jerhad, Dwarf-Friend," said Orenald to Jerhad, pulling him aside as in conspiracy, as the Elves and Dwarves spoke to each other, "King HeartStone, son of GladdenStone, conveys his greetings to you specifically. He charges me to tell you that he has not forgotten that you bear his father's token of favor, which is now his token of favor. He has sent one hundred large golds to help pay for his own people's wages here, from his own monies. He has also sent the cutting cables at his own expense, a great expense they are, *I might add*."

King GladdenStone, father of the present King, HeartStone, had given Jerhad and his traveling companion, Stanton, each a copper coin that were the token of his favor, seven cycles past. The bearer of the token was promised aid from any Dwarf it was presented to, by word of the King. GladdenStone believed that Jerhad was the fulfillment of the prophecy spoken by Morlah in *Dolan* at *Gildar's* forging: *Gildar* in dwarfish, Ember in the Common Tongue. "*In that time, Gildar, the Elven blade, shall return to this mountain. The bearer shall be he who willst restore the magic to the Elven Kingdom. The Black Arts shall begin to crumble at his coming. The dark and wicked ones shall learn to fear. Through him, the Dwarf Nation shall reunite with the Elves and the path to peace be embarked upon.*" The son had promised to honor his father's word. Now, the King held to his promise even though Jerhad had not asked for help: such was the Dwarves' goodwill.

"King HeartStone also will be sending ten thousand warriors at his expense. They will rotate with the miners. This work will keep them limber for the times of fighting; they will set up a defensive perimeter beyond the building of the wall during its construction." The Dwarf paused, sheepishly.

"Begging your pardon, Elven Prince...but would I be permitted to see it?" Orenald asked in a hushed tone.

"It?"

"You know...," he said, his eyes indicating Jerhad's knife. "...*Gilda*r...it is just...well, I have heard so much about it. How it was forged in *Dolan*..."

"Sure," said Jerhad slipping the longknife from its sheath, offering it to Orenald, handle first.

"Oh, no. I could not take it. I just wanted to see it, if you please, especially...since it is...doing something," said the Dwarf, gawking at the Elven blade.

Jerhad looked down at the knife, wondering what the Dwarf was talking about. In the past, the green stone, *esord* (foe-finder from the ancient Elven tongue), had glowed to warn of danger. The other stones also had glowed for their own reasons; but the purple stone, *igini*, harmony or unity, until now, had not shown any signs of life or magic.

The stone shone brilliantly!

"What does it mean, Elf Prince?"

"Jerhad, call me Jerhad...and as to what it's doing...I haven't any idea."

Jerhad felt as if he were in a dream with everything that was happening about him. He had watched as if from a distance while the whole of the past few courses, since Morlah's appearance, had played themselves out around him. Fate had set her hand in motion again, and he was going along for another 'ride'. He did not look forward to it either. He worried about leaving Andreanna and Kendra, not having been separated from his mate for more than a couple courses since Morlah had brought her back from Parintia. He worried about the Trolls and *Daektoch*. And the village...what if the Trolls did come in force as they had in the past? The Dwarves and Elves could not stand up to such an offensive. *Damned wizards*! If he ever got the chance, he would invite the mage to a pig roast...and Daektoch would be the pig.

The Dwarves got their heavy, buckskin packs on, fell in behind the Elves and took up a marching song:

"Pace by pace, along the road
    pace by pace, we bear our load.
Pace by pace, we march when told
    pace by pace, our song unfolds.

We sing our song as we march along
    Beat our feet to dusk or dawn.
We sing our song as we march along.

League by league, hot or cold
    league by league, our pace we hold.
League by league, the course ain't old.
    league-by-league, our tale's untold.

We sing our song as we march along
    Beat our feet to dusk or dawn.
We sing our song as we march along

Step by step, though legs are short
    step-by-step our song exhorts.
Step by step to any port.
    step-by-step we're a dusty sort.

We sing our song as we march along
    Beat our feet to dusk or dawn.
We sing our song as we march along.

Hotter and hotter, the sun may glow.
    hotter and hotter, but our legs won't grow,
Hotter and hotter, but we don't slow.
    hotter and hotter, we're the Dwarves you know!

We sing our song as we march along
    Beat our feet to dusk or dawn.
We sing our song as we march along...."

They went on for two spans of the sun without pause in their song, which was quite catching. The Elves were soon found moving to the Dwarves' pace.

Chapter 3

Daektoch was one of the very few wizards left over from the era of the original studies of the Arts of Magic. Those who had studied the Black Arts had become greedy and covetous of their power and ultimately had caused the demise of the Schools of the Arts. Then, Daektoch had set about to destroy those who were a potential threat to himself. The Druids who also studied the Arts had fallen prey to him, as they were apparently considered able to cause him harm. Though the Druids were a gentle people without interest in the mage, he had set about to eliminate them, as he had the wizards. Daektoch had come short of total annihilation of the Druid clan and had in his arrogance and pride thought them not worthy of a second effort. He now had Morlah as his chief adversary as a result of that mistake. Daektoch hated mistakes.

Back in the present, Daektoch, with the assistance of two hundred hired Rock Trolls, was organizing the Cave Trolls again. He had had to pay the Rock Trolls dearly, for they were not like their feeble minded cousins, the Cave Trolls, whom they despised. But gold coin, highly esteemed by the Rock Trolls, was easy to obtain considering Daektoch had the Heros Council in his hand. Tax monies were easily diverted from the city coffers from the eight hundred thousand population of Heros.

The Rock Trolls were bigger and stronger than their smaller counterparts. They were fierce fighters and had never known defeat in battle. They were only slightly smaller than Giants. The two had yet to meet in battle.

In their secluded home in the Mystic Mountains, something was terribly wrong. The Faeries were ill (if that was what one could call this effect on magical creatures)! A Faerie being sick or dying was unknown of (unless one was destroyed by powerful magical forces). The condition was mostly ambiguous; the Faeries were becoming listless. They felt that ever so slowly their power and very life force was weakening.

Daektoch observed with deep pleasure as this progressed. This was his greatest and best work ever!

It was the first course out on Sether Road, pursuing their mission of rousing the Elven nation to arms. As Jerhad and his companions came to the first village, Klisterie, half a league from Mildra, Jerhad suddenly wondered how he was going to go about doing what was needed. *Would anyone even believe him? Would anyone even listen? How had he gotten into this mess? Was he about to become the laughing stock of southern Frontmire? Imagine, calling the Elves to arms when they had never even seen a Troll*! Much of Frontmire's reality had become legend and myth to the Elves in their geographical isolation. *Morlah! He should have made the Druid run his own damned errand*!

"Hey," someone shouted. "Isn't that Jerhad, son of Lewin, who slew the Trolls up in Mildra?" The town's population, wondering at the sight they beheld, stared and then fell in behind the troop of Dwarves and Elves who walked past, heading to the town square, a picturesque area encompassed by colorful, pictorial storefronts. The bordering edges of the market area were lined with beautiful flowerbeds and stone-paved walks. The buildings, most clapped with cedar-shakes, were painted in bright reds, blues, yellows, lavenders and oranges.

Few had ever seen more than one or two Dwarves at a time; but now there was a dozen of them led by five Elves, one of which was famous among them; that was Jerhad. *licri*, Elfstone of strength, luminesced on Jerhad's Elven blade's handle. He had not called upon it, but it had become lively, strengthening him of its own will. The purple stone, *Harmony* or *igini*, also was brilliant. It was just as Morlah had said, 'magic speaking to magic', Elven-blade magic speaking to the heart of the Elven Prince, teaching, instructing, leading him and now about to speak to the dormant magic within the Elves.

"Friends," Jerhad called. The crowd that had been gathered by the power of *Harmony* quieted. "You recall seven cycles past, how the Trolls attacked Mildra. The Dwarves cornered them and held them until they were finally defeated." Jerhad did not mention that he, single-handedly, had annihilated the Trolls. "The Elves of Mildra also fought, raining arrows upon them with their longbows. Even my mother was out with her bow and shot ten Trolls."

The friendly crowd laughed and then quieted again.

"The Black Mage, Daektoch, was the one behind the Trolls' movements. He controlled them and sent them against us because he is afraid of us. Magic...," *Where were these words coming from*? Jerhad would have never dared speak to more than four or six people at a time in the past. "...is the heritage and destiny of the Elves. For both the good and the protection of our people, it belongs to us to bring back what was lost. Daektoch doesn't want any to possess magic but himself. He is active again and is gathering the Trolls against us. They will destroy us unless we arm and defend ourselves.

"The Elves must rise to the occasion! We will not be defeated! Magic must become part of our lives again. Friends, prepare to defend yourselves, your families and your homes. HeartStone, King of the Dwarves has sent help. One of these Dwarves will remain behind and assist in erecting the best possible defenses."

He stepped down from the well-crafted, wooden bench that he had somehow climbed onto, as a platform, as he had spoken; the crowd cheered. The mayor, Allaire, stepped out from the crowd, hand extended to greet Jerhad. The mayor was an elderly, widowed Elf. He had the typical long hair worn by both male and female Elves though his was white with maturity, one of the few signs of becoming old normally revealed in aging Elves. His smile was warm and disarming.

"Well done, son. I thank you for the warning to our people. I was in Mildra when we attacked the Trolls. I would not want such to happen here and to be caught unprepared. What can I do for you, to help you?"

"You saw the Trolls? Well, sir, you could be a tremendous help. You are a man known among the Elves. If you would come with me to even just a few villages to help encourage the Elves to organize, we may be able to save lives."

"Consider it done, my boy; but I doubt you need my help for that. Look how you've stirred these people on your own!

"I will travel with you two courses eastward to the villages of Starborne, Mindar, Kotton, and Bannon. Then, I will break off and take the route to the north and back westward to warn the people of the hamlets and cottages that lie off the main road. Then, I will return here to help coordinate our defenses. Also, I should be able to help convince some of the leaders in other villages to take up your cause and go with you, if you desire.

"Ah…is it true what I hear?"

"What?"

"That you are descendant of King Windemere?"

Jerhad blushed. *The Druid has been here*, he thought. "So I'm told," he answered the mayor.

"Imagine, a descendant of the ancient King here in our midst…and with magic! I saw you destroy the Trolls that course of the sun. Very well done!" he said with a shudder.

"Scared the pants off of me, you did…but well done. With you on our side, we can't lose."

"I am but one. I can only be in one place at one time. A village can be ravaged while I'm but a league away."

"Point taken, my boy.

"You'll all stay the night at my home. We'll leave for the village of Starborne at first light."

"Any place a poor Dwarf can get a meal around here?" butted in Orenald with a grin, his dwarfish appetite complaining with a loud rumble of his stomach.

Jerhad felt *licri* go silent (*igini* continued her glow). *Had he used the magic to influence them? Had the magic used him to influence them? Had it* ***used*** *him? Magic! Maybe Stanton was right. It was far too complex for him whatever anyone said.* He wished that he could just go home and help smoke the tarpon and then sleep with Andreanna tonight.

The Elfstone, *igini,* had glowed – first in *Gildar's* handle, brighter and brighter, and then, in him until he had felt as if he held their hearts collectively as one in the palm of his hands, molding them to his will. No, not his will…but to *igini's.*

Well, actually, they had not done poorly. Things had gone far better than he could have hoped for. His fear had been that they would not respond, that his warning would fall on deaf ears, or worse, that they would simply laugh at him, mock him, and then, they would be destroyed by the Trolls.

And so, village by village they went with *igini* growing stronger and stronger within him, the people responding with increased fervor and determination, until eighteen courses of the sun later, they stood on the outskirts of the city of Canon.

Walking into the Canon, the largest community in all the south (actually the only city in the south), they made their way to the city hall. Canon was almost exclusively Human in its population although it was now separated from other communities of Men due to the disrepair of the only road connecting it to the north. Many cycles past, Heros, the capitol, had given up financing the maintenance of the road, and now it was almost all but impassable, allowing for difficult foot travel only. The city, therefore, relied on the Elven population to the south of the mountains for all trade, including the use of the Port of Mildra for shipping, the reefs making safe landings near Canon impossible.

No one paid attention to the travelers as they walked through the streets, for it was common for both Elves and Dwarves, or Gnomes, to be seen about. The group had slowly dwindled to the five Elves, one Dwarf, Orenald, and Weill, the mayor of the last Elven community that they had passed through, Fraise.

"We'll go to *The Brent House* and get rooms at the inn. From there, we can wait on the council's response. Then, I'll see if we can be granted a hearing by the council tonight," said Weill. "I'll take care of all the arrangements."

Not long past, Jerhad would have been uncomfortable being among so many Humans; but now, after his travels and adventures of his last "errand," he felt quite at ease among them. The five Elves and Orenald gathered in the dining hall of *The Brent House* and had evening meat while waiting for Weill to return.

This was by far the largest inn that Jerhad had ever seen though not by any means the most elegant. But its solid maple planked floors were clean, worn dark with age and wear, as were the long wooden tables that could seat a score at each. The place was airy, well lit and was heated by two great fieldstone hearths, one at each end. The beds in their rooms, Jerhad had noticed, were free of vermin, and the linen changed between guests. The mattresses were feather, not straw. Weill had picked up the tab for food and lodging. Returning from the city hall, Weill explained, "I was able to convince them to meet with us tonight, one span after sunsetting." He sat and joined them for evening meat and shared in a pitcher of warm ale.

Later that evening, Weill led the group into a small building two blocks up the street from *The Brent House*. It was a very plain wood structure on the outside, but the inside was finished in expensive wooden panels, well polished and stained a rich natural-oak color. The furniture was fine, solid oak crafted and polished to a shine that allowed one to see his own reflection. Around the matching conference table in the middle of the only room, sat six Humans all looking grim and, maybe, impatient. *igini* and *licri* were silent, for the Humans were without magic to respond with. Jerhad became nervous, unlike as in his encounters with his own people.

"Friends," Jerhad spoke to the Humans. "I am Jerhad, son of Lewin, descendant of King Windemere, of the town of Mildra. We have come on our journey to warn the entire south coast of the impending invasion by the Trolls. Morlah the Druid says that the Black Mage, Daektoch, is about again and that he plans to attack the Elves. Though he has no intention towards the Humans at this time, we thought it worth warning you since it is likely that any large movement of Trolls might come around the east side of the mountains. That would put Canon directly in their path and, knowing how Trolls behave, it is unlikely they would simply pass you by. King HeartStone has already sent aid and will be sending ten thousand Dwarf warriors to assist us."

"Who says the Trolls are coming this way?" asked one who apparently was leader of the council, in a gruff voice.

"Morlah, the Druid. Though he did not say they would come this way, he did say they would come to southern Frontmire, and he asked us to warn everyone."

"How does he know this?" continued the spokesman. His eyes were narrowed, his brow furrowed and his jaw set.

"His magic has allowed him to detect Daektoch's activities. Seven cycles past, the Trolls made their way to the fields just north of Mildra before the Elves and Dwarves stopped them. Daektoch himself was injured in some of the battles he involved himself in and subsequently went into hiding again, until now."

"Morlah hasn't seen him then?"

"No, but he doesn't need to because he can sense him with the use of magic."

The meeting was apparently off to a bad start. The council members had not introduced themselves nor asked for introductions nor did they give any evidence of having any interest in the message. They seemed to be as mules with their minds set against whatever was to be presented.

"I was told you have magic," continued the councilman. Jerhad pulled his Elven blade, Ember, from its sheathe and laid it on the table before him, not offering it to them, keeping it within his reach.

"Looks like a child's toy," muttered a pale-skinned, dark-bearded man opposite Jerhad. "What does it do?"

"Magic." Jerhad's companions became restless. It was becoming more and more obvious that they were not welcome and that their message was even less.

"Magic. Like what?" persisted the bearded Human.

Jerhad breathed deeply. *If they did not want to hear him out, they just had to say so. He could have been on his way home.* He reached deep within himself, combining precise portions of *licri, balan*, and *esord.* He pointed his finger at the bearded man across from him, lifting him from his chair and up into the air, as Morlah had the boulder; with a thud, Jerhad pinned the man against the wall up near the ceiling. The man flailed his arms and legs, terror inscribed upon his face and bulging eyes.

"It does a lot of things," he shrugged, "but it won't save you from the Trolls if you don't defend yourselves and your city. I came here to warn you. I have done so. You will live or die by your decision. The blood of your families and people will rest upon your decision. The Elves and Dwarves will help you as they can if you so desire." Then, he set the man back into his seat. The man, once free of the magic's hold, jumped from his chair, toppling it over, and hurriedly backed to the wall and away from Jerhad. The council stared at him as if he were a Troll babbling in its native tongue.

"I see by your faces what your choice will be. Magic is not only in my blade, but also in the Elves themselves. We might be able to help." He turned and left. For a heartbeat, everyone sat in stunned silence. Then quickly, his companions rose and followed after him.

Mayor Weill caught up with him. "You should have been more patient with them. They would have come around...."

"I saw it in their eyes. They didn't believe a word I said. No.... I saw it in their hearts. They think we are fools, superstitious fools. They have no use for or belief in the magic even now after I showed them a token of its power. I will help them if they ask. It's time to go home. I have decided." Jerhad recomposed himself and remembered his manners. He took Weill's hand and shook it.

"Thank you for your help, Mayor Weill. We'll leave at sunrise, go straight west to the Rogue Valley, and follow the stream to Mildra. We'll save a few risings of travel that way. Unless you prefer we escort you back to Fraise? I miss my mate and daughter and would like to get back home soon."

"No. I will stay behind and speak to the council members individually to see if they can be persuaded. Perhaps I can reason with them."

Jerhad gave him five large golds that he had obtained from Morlah's pouch. "These will pay for your time and assistance and help to buy arms and materials for the defense of Fraise. Be alert, and don't forget to send some males to Mildra to form a main force."

And so, they all went to their respective rooms.

Chapter 4

Jerhad lay awake in his bed at *The Brent House* that night. It was quiet except for a solitary cricket that chirped from somewhere in the darkness. Jerhad was in a turmoil about what he had done. Never in his life had he been so assertive, so forward, so decisive or sure of himself. But he *had* seen. The magic had shown him that he was wasting his time with the council.

How could he have promised them help to begin with? Who did he think he was? He was no leader or ambassador. Mildra did not answer to him. Neither did the Elves. He had no approval or authority to make decisions or promises that would bind others. Yet, he had been so sure of himself at the time. He had felt it in the magic.

He lay awake into the night, and it was not until three-quarters of the moon's course that he finally slept. Then, he alternated from dreams of a Magic Kingdom of Elves to dreams of Daektoch and his dark servants hunting him.

One span after sunrising, the five Elves and one Dwarf left Canon. They would circle the foot of Freemount, the last mountain peak on the Coastal Range, and cross along the trail leading to and then following the Rogue Stream, which flowed almost straight in its containment between the two ridges, all the way to Mildra.

Jerhad and his friends were camping their last night on the trail. By midcourse tomorrow, they expected to be back in Mildra. The night air was cool and without a breeze, and the fire was comforting to body and soul. As they sat by the fire talking and resting from their passage along the tortuous Rogue Trail, the Dwarf passed a pouch of tobac for everyone to dip their pipes into. The aroma of the tobac was sweet whether in cut leaf or smoke.

Jasson was in the process of spinning one of his famous fish stories. "...and so, with a hook as long as my hand, made of cast iron and tied to a rope, I slipped a whole chicken on it and threw it in...."

The starless, overcast night echoed with the sounds of an abundance of crickets, toads, frogs and spring peepers, harmonizing in the nocturnal forest. It was just like the old times with his buddies when all they had to do was fish and hunt; that was when they were not occupied getting the winter's firewood stocked up or smoking and pickling tarpon.... Jerhad found that he missed this type of life. No responsibilities, no cares, no worries.

How had life become so complicated?

Not that he would be without his mate and daughter, but still, he felt a longing for the good old times...no Druids, wizards or Trolls. No obstinate councilmen to sit there staring at him with a look of adamant antagonism and defiance! All he had ever wanted was a quiet simple life with no one butting in to complain or complicate things. Just to be left alone.

Why couldn't he have that? The Druid, that was why. Damned Druids! Daektoch too.... Damned wizards! From the time Morlah had sent him out on that first 'errand', things had never been the same. Of course, he had met Andreanna as a result of it. *O ye gods, he loved her.* He could not imagine life without her now. *Still, the good old times....*

"...and now the fish is pulling so hard that it was dragging the mule towards the water...." The Dwarf's eyes sparkled at the spinning of the yarn.

There were sounds in the brush about them. They all heard them. They all knew that it was not an animal, for whatever it was came straight in toward their camp from all directions.

Jerhad felt the fool! Jasson stopped his story in mid sentence and looked up. They had been out on the trail for courses, knowing Daektoch was about again, and had not set sentries or night watches while in camp. Andreanna would skin him alive if she ever heard of this. This was a mistake she would not have made.

Slowly, cautiously, as not to appear as if alerted, they reached for their weapons - the Elves their bows, the Dwarf his axe, Jason's storytelling dwindled to a stammer. They were at a definite disadvantage having been idly chatting about the fire and gazing into the flames; their eyes were now blinded to all but the immediate circle of firelight. They had neither water nor sand at the ready to dowse the flames. Though excellent in their forest skills, it was not natural for the Elves to think defensively, having had no enemies in their homeland for hundreds of cycles, except for the one Troll raid of seven cycles past.

The circle of intruders closed in tighter about them. Arrows were notched, and bowstrings pulled back at three-quarter draw. No one spoke as they stood staring out into the now foreboding night, backs to the fire. They waited. The night sounds about them went quiet. Time slowed, and breathing quickened. A Night Hawk called, three screeches in three sets. In astonishment, Jerhad wondered if it were possible! He chirped three sets of three of his cricket imitation, stirring the nearby crickets into a determined chorus. The Night Hawk repeated its call.

"It's alright. Put your weapons down; they're friends," spoke Jerhad to his companions. "Come on in," he called out into the threatening darkness.

Stanton, a Human, slipped into the light before Jerhad. "Elf Boy, we had you *dead*!" he laughed as he pretended to run a blade across the Elf's throat. They hugged each other. "Good to see you, Elf Boy. You're looking great. Can't say much for your camp watch.... Married life seems to agree with you," he said, one arm still around the Elf's neck and patting Jerhad's very slightly rounded belly.

"Ye gods, Stanton, you scared us!"

"Better me than Trolls," the Human grinned, and then, he roughed up Jerhad's hair and playfully pushed him away. The four other Elves and the Dwarf relaxed and lowered their weapons.

"Don't tell Andreanna about us not having a watch... she'll kill me. I'll hear about it for weeks and probably get my head smacked more than a couple of times. She seems to think she can make me smarter by doing that."

"And what if I *doo* tell her," teased Stanton.

"Then, I'll just have to let her have you for weapons practice," Jerhad smiled wickedly.

"My lips are sealed. My word on it! I vow it." Stanton and Andreanna had had weapons practice together in the past as they had traveled together. Though Stanton was a warrior, ten cycles a soldier in the Breezon army, she had given him his money's worth. Not to mention that he had not been able to beat a 'girl' with a three quarter staff and he with a sword.

"I have some friends with me. Can I bring them in?" asked Stanton.

Jerhad nodded.

Stanton, ever the soldier, looked over at the Elves and Dwarf to see if they were in accord.

They all nodded.

"Come on in.... The Dwarf's tobac pouch looks full enough for us all," he called into the night. Out of the brush, from around them arose four large figures. At first, Jerhad thought that they were Trolls. He gasped. The Elves and Dwarf brought their weapons up at the ready again.

"Giants!" whispered Jerhad, his mouth fallen open. "Giants, you're still with the Giants!"

Out of the darkness boomed a voice, "Well-met, Jerhad, Giant-Friend." It was Mordock! The Giants stepped into the firelight. "Greetings, little friends," Mordock laughed. The Giants loomed up to a height that of double the Elves'.

The Giants were infectiously friendly and soon had the Elves and Dwarf at ease. Orenald offered up his pouch of tobac but then looked doubtful when he saw the size of the Giants' pipes.

"Do not worry your beard, Master Dwarf," chuckled Kassandra, the female Giant, "Stanton was only poking fun. He had planned to say that from the heartbeat he saw there was a Dwarf in camp." She pulled a pouch of her own tobac from her pack, which the Dwarf thought he might have fit into himself.

The Giants were immense, towering above all other races. Like the male Dwarves did, both sexes of Giants normally wore battle gear, chain-mail coats, meshed steel pants, steel-reinforced boots and light helmets. The males did not produce facial hair as the Humans and Dwarves did. The male Giants wore their dark hair to the shoulder while the females wore long braids that fell to their sword belts.

Then the Giants were introduced. The first was Kassandra. She came and knelt down before the Elves and Dwarf to get closer to their own height. She was quite attractive to look upon, even for Human, Elf or Dwarf.

"Well-met, little Elf-friends. Jerhad, I have made a song of our battle against the Black Mage, Daektoch. It is two settings and one rising in the singing. It gives me great joy to have battled at your side, Prince of the Elves, against such a foe." Reaching down she embraced Jerhad as if he had been a little child.

"Here," she said, rising again, "this is Mordock the former Keeper and Nourisher of the Land of the Gift of the Elves to the Giants. And this is DiamondHeart, a mighty warrior and worthy seaman. He is the son of Jorolant and BondBreaker's brother." BondBreaker was the Giant who had been Mordock's replacement as Nourisher and Keeper. He had been slain by the Trolls while defending the Land of the Gift of the Elves to the Giants.

"We have almost finished BondBreaker's song. It is ten settings in length. It speaks of his great deed in the slaying of hundreds of Trolls in the defense of the Gift, of his strength, of his worth, of his deeds in winning of the contest to become the Keeper," continued Kassandra, swelling with pride for BondBreaker. "We have also made a song of the Battle at Breezon: Dwarves, Giants, Humans, the spirits of the dead Druids, and Morlah on the flying Bornodald in battle against hundreds of thousands of Trolls. We would sing it for you, but it is not brief. It will be for the Giants of the Homeland who can endure such a Giant song.

"This Giant is Tahmat. He fought at Breezon also and slew over eight hundred Trolls and stood over the fallen Dwarf King, GladdenStone, and defended him until the Dwarves could pull him from the battle. He also was first mate on the ship *The Hammerstar*, the Giant six-masted schooner. We will sing of his deeds also.

These Giants were from a land many leagues from Frontmire in the western Korkaran Sea. It was their love of the sea that had brought them to Frontmire in the times of the Elf, Dwarf, Gnome and Troll Wars. The Giants, as a race, were a warm, kind and gentle people but also great warriors and very capable of defending themselves. They were a long-lived race, their life spans reaching seven or eight hundred cycles, and the populace was steeped in culture and tradition. They were extremely fond of story telling, songs of heroic events and general conversation. In their native speech, stories and songs were told over one to several courses of the sun, either about fires, during feasts or as they worked.

"Weapons practice has never been the same," Stanton, former Breezon Army Squad Leader, said to Jerhad as the Human sat at the fire, playing with a long branch, poking at the coals. "Fighting a Giant is no small task; but I've learned a lot. The Giants have taught me much of fighting a larger opponent. *Trolls should be easy now.*"

"Well, Commander...you might just get your chance," said Jerhad.

"Don't call me that. I'm not in the Breezon Army any more and not interested." Stanton had briefly acted as Breezon's Commander in the last Troll war.

"I wasn't talking about the Breezon Army. I was thinking we could use you as Commander of the Elven Army."

"What?"

"Don't you know? Daektoch and the Trolls are about again."

"Trolls? Daektoch? How do you know all this?" asked the soldier with concern.

"Morlah's back, and he says that he senses Daektoch. He expects an assault on the Elves. We've just come back from warning the Elves along the coast and asking them to prepare to defend themselves."

"The Trolls have so soon forgotten," said Kassandra. "They are of brief memory. It has been but seven cycles that we drove them back into the Blue Mountains."

"It's not their fault, Kassandra," said Jerhad. "Daektoch darkens their minds." He turned back to Stanton. "Will you do it? Will you lead the Elves' army? ...What there is of one."

"I don't know.... I was just fun'in when I spoke of fighting Trolls. I *really* didn't want to do that again."

"You think I want to?" offered Jerhad.

Mordock reached out and toppled Stanton over like a toy. "Stand up and be accounted for, soldier! **The Prince has given you command!"**

"Why you big.... I should box your ears...."

"You may attempt to do so in weapons practice, master Stanton," answered Mordock with a bellowing laugh. "Meanwhile, you have been recruited. Give account of yourself."

Then, it came back to Stanton, the vision he had had of Jerhad in his true essence back at Moreau's Ford, the revelation of Jerhad as King of the Elves in a radiance of majesty that Stanton had witnessed while traveling in the dream world with Nan, the Faerie creature. What he had seen had changed Stanton and his relationship to Jerhad permanently. He rose and stood at attention. "Commander Stanton ready for duty, my Prince. I am yours to command."

"Oh, cut it out, Stanton. Just a yes or no would do," moaned Jerhad.

They spent a span of the moon's course catching up on recent events, how the Dwarves were sending aid, how they had begun to help the Elves prepare to defend themselves....

"You're a long way from having an army that can stand against the Trolls. You don't have defendable positions. You don't have a trained army. No cavalry! This could be ugly, Elf Boy," said Stanton with a shake of his head. "But you're not given much choice are you?"

Kassandra reached over and smacked Stanton behind the head, almost toppling him. "You address the Prince as 'Elf Boy'?"

"It's alright, Kassandra. Really," said Jerhad. "I'm not a prince."

"I would not say such!" objected Kassandra.

"Silence, my dove," said Mordock. "He does not see what is to be."

"My dove?" laughed Jerhad. "Last time I saw you two, Mordock was running for his very life every time Kassandra came around."

"The ways of a female are not to be understood by the males of a race. Once they set about to capture your heart, there is little that a male can do. Would you not say so, my Prince?" taunted Mordock.

"I couldn't agree with you more," laughed Jerhad, remembering his own 'capture'. "You will all come to Mildra then," said Jerhad. "We could use a few Giant hands. The Dwarves have begun building a stone wall. I will see you are paid whatever you request."

"Yes, done then," said Mordock. "I will come and help. It has been long since I have labored with my hands. It will do me good. You, my dove and brothers, will you come?" All were agreed. They had toured the land for seven cycles, and were becoming restless for something constructive to do.

"I believe the tarpon have just run the Mage River. This could be a feast fit for a Giant," said Kassandra.

"There's plenty of tarpon, *more* than we can handle. Enough for a Giant's feast. I think we should turn in and get some sleep so we can be off early in the morning."

"Jerhad," said Kassandra, "spend the first watch with me. I have missed you. We will catch up in brief on the events of the past seven cycles."

At midcourse after the next rising, the party arrived in Mildra. As they came over the last hill overlooking the work, the Dwarves saw them and sent up a cheer. The Giants answered back with a bellowed greeting. The wall was going better than Jerhad had expected. Already, twenty paces of two layers of stone were laid on the northern wall, and the trench for the footing of the remainder of the wall was under way. The fortification was being built six thousand paces away from the town to allow inside maneuvering of the army and future growth.

Lewin came out to meet them. "I see you have brought more help, Jerhad. Well-met, son."

Jerhad introduced Stanton, the Giants and the Dwarf to his father.

"Yes," said Mordock. "We have come to work, but I will talk to the cutters of stone. They can stop cutting these tiny blocks and get some real stone down here." He left and headed toward the quarry. Jerhad followed Mordock as the rest of the party disbanded in different directions.

Once at the quarry, Jerhad was impressed with what he beheld of the Dwarves' work. They had set up a series of block-and-tackles with the diamond-studded cables in them. Both on top of the hill and at the bottom were crews of Dwarves and Elves, each taking turns pulling the cable across the stone. The pulley system increased the distance the cable drew by tenfold. It resembled two men on a saw; one crew lugged, then the other, only using their arms' length as they sawed.

They sang:

> "Rock to dust," sang the top crew as the others pulled.
> "Stone we'll bust," sang the crew on the bottom, as the top crews heaved on the cables.
> "Dawn till dusk.
> We're mighty and strong.
> So, it won't be long
> 'afore we drink our ale.
> It won't get stale.
> To quarry stone.
> The mountain's bone.
> Rock to dust.
> Stone we'll bust..."

There were five of these crews, each with a cutting cable. Others poured water to keep the cables cool and help form grit, which aided in sawing the stone while other crews loaded the finished blocks on sleds.

"Well-met, friends. I didn't know you were about, Mordock Dwarf-Friend," said SteelHand.

"Yes, I am, and three more Giants. We stayed behind to visit the great land. And now, I am even more glad of heart that we did. We will join the Dwarves in their stonework. Now you will see what both can do together. It will be an awe-inspiring undertaking. But now, we will ask you to cut your blocks to twice their size. We will put two Giants here to assist in loading the stone and two to place the stone on the wall. The Dwarves will direct us, for the craft is yours. We will be your beasts of burden. If you have the peg and feathering* crews cut all of the stone to the size of those about to be cut over there." He indicated a block that was the size of a four-wheeled wagon. "That should suffice."

"If we do that," said SteelHand with a tear of joy in his eye, "the work will prosper many fold! Ah, it is good to have Giants in the land."

"We will now go greet some old friends and then begin with you at the rising," said Mordock. Jerhad and Mordock returned to the town where they found Stanton speaking with Lewin near the wall.

"Jerhad, if you continue here...," explained the army veteran, "expanding the trench another ten paces away from the outside of the wall, you would gain three paces of height and make a trench which can be shored up and paved with stonework. The drop would break the momentum of any charge, even that of Trolls, and at the same time give you extra height. At this point, where the stonework is up to now, would be a good position to place a bastion. That way, archers can rake the walls with arrows without putting themselves at risk. Raise the height of the wall on the bastion so that it is a less likely place for an assault and put a ledge with a parapet on the top. Place one every three hundred paces; they will greatly add to the defensibility of your barricade. Then talk to the Dwarves to see if they can build spouts to allow for boiling oil to be poured through, rather than over the top... and extend the platform on the inside behind the bastions where a setup for boiling the fuel can be placed. This exposes your men to less danger if you intend on scorching Troll."

Jerhad laughed. "That's what I pay you all that gold for, Commander. Anything else?"

"Yes, I'd like to see the army."

---

* A process that cuts large blocks into smaller ones.

"Ah! That's going to be a little more difficult. They haven't been gathered yet."

"Well, then, Elf Boy," he said turning his eyes to Mordock to see if he was about to be swatted again. "You have them out on the field one span after sunrising tomorrow for review."

"I'll get the word out," agreed Jerhad.

"Until then, how about me seeing if I can box your ears, Mordock?" said Stanton. He walked over to the Giant and, with his chest pushed forward against the Giant's thigh, pressed against Mordock as if to provoke him to fight.

The Giant laughed, "It would be a great pleasure, Commander. Swords, maces, or three-quarter staff?"

"You with mace, me with full-staff. We haven't tried that combination in a while."

DiamondHeart and Tahmat were already at work unloading blocks from sleds. The Dwarves had been using an elaborate system of levers and rollers to unload the stone and move it into position. Now, the Giants simply picked up the stones and set them in place. Some nearby Dwarves grumbled, "Sort of takes the fun out of it."

"I will go tell the diggers to expand the trench. What about the dirt Stanton?" asked Jerhad.

"Use it to make ramps on the inside to allow easy access to the top of the wall. Where can I get a full-staff?"

"Where else? Probably the only one in the village. Andreanna! I'll go with you to fetch it."

"Be right back, Mordock," said Stanton.

Later, DiamondHeart retrieved a dead tree from the forest and soon had it chopped into a pile of firewood. In no time, he had a great fire burning. "Tarpon over hot coals will be a fabulous feast. Too bad there's no ale."

"Says who?" a Dwarf piped up. "What do you think that stack of kegs over on that wagon is? Though with Giants' thirst, we'll have to send for more."

Chapter 5

Stanton and Jerhad arrived at his home where Kassandra sat outside with Andreanna, Catrina and Kendra. Kassandra held Kendra in the palm of her hand. Kendra squealed with delight as she played around on the female Giant's palm.

"You have made a beautiful child, Jerhad. It makes me long to have my own," said the Giantess.

"Stanton!" cried Andreanna as he entered the yard. "This is too much!" She rushed him. Stanton braced himself, expecting to be decked or tripped. Instead, she jumped up, wrapped her arms around his neck and kissed him on the cheek. "Well-met, Squad Leader! Six cycles. You *really* should come around more often."

"That's Commander, now," said Jerhad. "Stanton agreed to take charge of the army."

"Great! When's weapons practice?" she asked brightly, releasing Stanton. "Want a go at it now? Afraid I might be a bit rusty though." She was not.

"Well actually, I was hoping to borrow your full-staff. Mordock and I are going a round. I got some great moves I could show you that he taught me on taking on a larger opponent."

"I'll join you," she said with excitement.

"Don't I get a 'hello' first?" inquired Jerhad.

"Ah, yes, my dear. A peck on the cheek for now, and we'll deal with the *rest* tonight," she said giving him a meaningful batting of eyelashes. She kissed him and then ran off to get her gear, leaving him well flushed and thoroughly embarrassed.

That night the whole village turned out with wagons of food. They set up large stakes and spits and roasted whole tarpon, wrapped in fresh seaweed, over the coals of DiamondHeart's fire. The Dwarves sang songs and Tahmat the Giant told a brief story. It was a time of great joy and festivity in the shadow of the darkness that waited to envelope them all.

By the first span of the sun's course, about one thousand Elf males had gathered on the field near where the wall was being built. Stanton had them line up into formation and looked them over. He turned to Jerhad. "No weapons?"

"Well, not exactly. Every male and almost every female owns a longbow and a longknife. There may be one or two swords in the whole village."

"Ye gods, Elf Boy! This is a far cry from an army. But I guess we'll have to do with what we've got then," he sighed, shaking his head. Then he perked up. "We'll have a fine group of archers...."

"We'll have ten thousand more Dwarves. HeartStone is sending them," added Jerhad.

"Excellent!" exclaimed Stanton, his mind obviously already working at his strategy. Just then, a large, mule-drawn wagon pulled up behind them. They turned to see Morlah sitting at the reins.

"Morlah! Well-met, *old man*," Jerhad teased. "What have you got in the wagon?"

Morlah stood and pulled the tarp back from his load. "Pikes anyone? Eight hundred."

"Morlah, how on earth do you do it? Right place, right time, every time," said Stanton. "Now, this is something we can use. It'll be easier to teach the Elves the use of these against the Trolls rather than attempting any swordplay."

"Six more wagons hired and on the way with more weapons," said Morlah.

"Where'd you get it all?" asked Jerhad.

"Avenar's hold. It is still stocked to the hilt with weapons left by Heros when they abandoned it. Just a matter of recruiting a few Gnomes and wagons."

"Gnomes!"

"Yes. Let us say that they doest owe me a favor," said Morlah with a grin. With the Druid's killing of Avenar, the Gnomes had finally become free of their enslavement to the wizard tyrant. The Gnomes had vowed an eternal indebtedness to Morlah.

"Ye gods, look at that!" exclaimed Stanton as an Elven caravan of ox-drawn wagons came up the road toward Mildra. There were thousands of Elves. An Elf on an ass came to meet them. It was the Mayor from Klisterie, Allaire.

"Jerhad, Lewin, friends! Well-met. After beginning an unpromising attempt at making a defendable position of our village, we decided not to. We determined that, if you will have us, that our sweat would be better spent here as one force rather than many small forces."

"Now you're talking," said Stanton. "Get your men up here in formation. Weapons training begins. What else you got coming, Morlah?"

"Shortswords, more pikes, lances, one catapult, shields and some light armor and mail."

"Jerhad, what'd you think if we suggest that the other villages join us here. Easier to defend one large position rather than several smaller ones. They probably would be overrun within a course of an assault," said Stanton.

"No one told you? Starborne, Mindar, Kotton and Bannon are on the way," said Allaire.

"Where'll we put them all?" asked Jerhad.

"If you do not mind my saying, Masters, you have a sawmill on the river down here. It could be a matter of a couple courses to raise barracks to house the males if we had the lumber. The females and children could be taken into the homes," offered Orenald.

"Great idea! Father, go talk to Minus, the sawyer. I'll get Mother to take charge of the females and children. She can tell them her Troll slaying story. Imagine all those ears!"

"What about food?" asked Stanton.

"We've got smoked tarpon, fresh tarpon, pickled tarpon. Fried tarpon, baked tarpon, tarpon casserole.... Shall I go on?" said Lewin. "The village has fishing vessels that can keep us supplied."

"Didst I not inform thee that thou hast paid eight bars of gold for six ships of grain from Parintia?" asked Morlah. "They shouldst be here by the quarter-moon cycle's end. Better build a greater granary by the mill while thou art at building."

"Well, folks, we have a lot of work to do; let's get to it," said Jerhad.

By midcourse of the next sunrising, the frames of two large barracks stood ready to be boarded up. The stone wall was going up in leaps and bounds with the Giants' help. The trench work was done now, with the help of all the extra males. Jerhad's father had charge of assisting the Dwarves and Elves, organizing the work and furnishing a constant supply of materials for them to use. They had more hands than they knew what to do with.

The sounds of grunts and the clashing of weapons from the training Elves intermingled with loud calls of Stanton's admonishments were heard throughout the entire course of the sun. The gold mine was opened causing an infectious sense of excitement about Mildra. Jerhad felt the glow of the purple stone, *igini,* within him at all times. People from other villages arrived by the wagonload, and it began to look like the whole south coast was moving to Mildra. This could soon be a bit much to handle.

Three courses after the opening of the gold mine, SteelHand came to Jerhad with four large burlap sacks. "Here you go. Morlah asked me to deliver this to you," said the Dwarf as he heaved the bags from his shoulder and onto the ground with a solid, dull thud.

"What's in them?"

"Take a look," said the Dwarf.

Jerhad opened one. It was full of gold coin! He pulled one out and looked at it. It was the size of the large gold minted in Heros, and his profile was imprinted on one side with the inscription on the top *The Kingdom of Mildra.* On the bottom beneath Jerhad's profile was *Jerhad Prince of the Elves*. On the opposite side was the ancient Elven rune *acrch* with an inscription below it, *In the First Cycle of the Kingdom of Mildra.*

"Who did this?" asked Jerhad, a bit put out.

"Morlah. He brought the molds when we began mining the gold. He had us start making coin and said you should have these. Good likeness of you, Prince Jerhad," smiled SteelHand. "There are three thousand of them in those bags."

"Mine?"

"Yes, yours."

"I'm sort of rich then?"

"Yes. I suppose you are. You probably could buy the whole village."

"Buy the whole village? Now that's an idea," said Jerhad talking to himself. "Thanks, SteelHand." Jerhad counted out three hundred coins. "Take the rest of these to my house. Tell Andreanna to take care of them, or my mother, or whoever is there...." Then he ran off.

Later that course, Jerhad called together the mayors from the Elven villages. "I have a proposal for you. I'd like to trade the land from your villages for land here outside of Mildra on the south side of the town. I will give to every family, who is willing, a lot of one hundred by six hundred paces. My grandfather left me a large parcel of land leading to the mountain. I also have purchased all the fields on the south side of the town this very course. If your people agree, we will trade parcel for parcel. I will pay the difference for parcels that are larger, and I will buy all fields that are farmable and hire the sellers to farm them for me at fifty percent of the crop they produce and eight large golds per cycle for pay.

"I have the Dwarves surveying the plots as we speak. I also have several crews of Elves digging to prepare the base for roads from the town to the mountain. We will use the debris from the quarry to make the roads solid and mudless. There will be twelve roads; I figure about three hundred sixty lots per road. That's about four thousand families.

"The Giants have gone up into the mountain behind the mine and will bring down enough logs to the mill to get the basic structures erected as soon as possible. The Giants estimate that this should only delay their work on the wall for two courses. There should be enough wood to keep the mill busy for quite a while. We have enough extra hands around now, so we can get the houses up in no time. If I had to guess... ten per course once we get the wood cut. That means that three hundred sixty houses would be built in ten courses. It would take a lot of pressure off of the village for space. Later, those who want to hire on to farm the land that I buy will be able to live in their former farmhouses without charge. Speak to your people and let me know." Though a very generous offer, the Elf's proposal would leave Jerhad owning most of the southern coast of Frontmire.

Jerhad left them to discuss his proposal. They would also need more barracks soon for more people kept moving into Mildra. He should also send the farmers back to their fields to ensure a fall harvest; but they should have protection of some kind in case of Troll attacks. He would speak to the Dwarves about it.

Morlah sat on a small rise watching the quarrying of stone when Jerhad joined him. The Dwarves had mined a width of three hundred paces and a distance of approximately one hundred paces back into the mountain. The wall about the village kept growing. It already had gone far beyond the short wall they had originally planned, and now they were going to extend it all the way south to the east side of the mountain, enclosing the land Jerhad proposed to sell to the Elves. The cutting of stone had stopped its northern progress into the mount and had taken off perpendicularly, east and west in opposite directions, excavating a trench of fifty-paces width through the mountain.

"Why are they doing that?" asked Jerhad, mostly to himself.

"Must be the quality of the stone," Morlah lied, but not convincingly.

Jerhad let it pass.

"The *MayBest* hast unloaded her cargo of grain. There art four hundred bars of gold ready to be sent to Parintia. We willst send these to *seilstri* aboard her. I willst accompany the gold, with two score Dwarves, then return and go north to see what doest transpire there. Keep thineself informed through the Dwarves of what is happening in the land about thee. They doest have much information of the goings and comings in the land. I willst purchase more grain, also. There art large fields in Parintia."

seilstri was the name of the fortified castle, home of the Druids in the Island of Parintia, which lay several leagues to the southwest of Frontmire. The name was the ancient Elvish word meaning knowledge, for the keep had been a center of learning in former times.

"Parintia use to sell her grain to Heros, but seeing that thou canst pay more, it willst easily be diverted here. I willst also see what other stores and weapons may be purchased and sent here. The town willst have to learn to sustain its growth. With time, because there is coin, what is needed willst find its way here from throughout the inhabited world. Thine thoughts of sending the farmers back to work the land art good. It is to be hoped that the Trolls doest not come through and lay all to waste. I willst go now and supervise the loading of the gold. Hast thou enough coin?"

"Enough? It will take me cycles to use this all up."

"I doest doubt it. The expense of running a city is tremendous, especially when it doest grow this fast. Thou willst also need to attend to securing a reliable supply of fresh drinking water against the chance of the Trolls fouling the present supply. Stoneworth and the Dwarves who worked Heros' aqueducts are about. They willst know what to do." Having said all this, he left.

A few risings later, Jerhad talked with some Dwarves. He had asked them how the farmers could be protected when out away from the walls and into the villages beyond. IronLeggs, a stout, bow-legged Dwarf, captain over the Dwarf force of ten thousand now in Mildra had an answer. IronLeggs looked powerful and plainly dangerous. His shoulders were broad, his arms and legs bulging with muscle and his voice like a growl. He had a short broadsword, a longknife, a war-axe and a mace hung on his belt. Over his shoulder was slung a brass buckler. His hands were like steel as were his eyes. The way he carried himself revealed the underlying warrior, waiting to unleash his strength if the need should arise. Otherwise, he was quite a likeable fellow.

"In times past when the Trolls would run raids down from the Blue Mountains, we would house scouts and sentries in small holds so that they could be safe," said IronLeggs. "The garrisons were built of interlocked stone, top, side and bottom, and could not be dismantled except from within. The stone door was interlocked within the walls and held closed with iron pins." IronLeggs went down on one knee and began tracing his design in the dirt.

"Air shafts came underground from a distance and were hidden so that fresh air was available against any attempts to smoke them out. Slits in the upper walls allowed archers to shoot out. It would take a miracle to get an arrow into them from the outside. The hold was two floors tall, the lower for bunks and food, water, and stores, and the upper for defense. Often there would be a well dug within for fresh water.

"Not one was ever overthrown, and they could be held by a handful of troops. Well, I say held; that was only for effect. Actually, the defenders could just sit about and let the Trolls beat the stone walls, if they chose to. But you cannot get a Dwarf to just sit idly by while there are Trolls about that *neeeed* killin'," the Dwarf stated through gritted teeth, slamming his iron fist into his open palm a few times. He relaxed.

"A smaller version of these holds could be built at each village, preferably on top of an existing well or spring. We have much stone at the quarry that will not be of any use to us in the city's fortification. I can get a crew to work a model for your purpose. Just give me the word."

"Great. Let's do it. I own more than half the land out there now. I've traded it with the Elves for properties between the quarry and town. We'll use wells that are on my lands to do it. I'll get you a crew of one hundred Elves to work with you. By the way, why has the mining of stone turned rather than gone straight into the mountain?"

"Oh, I thought Morlah would have told you. It is to be a dry moat about the castle."

"What castle?"

"Why, yours, Elf Prince. You cannot have a kingdom without a castle. You may not know this, but even HeartStone has a castle within *Dolan*, though it is carved on the inside of the mountain. The east wall is open to the valley so it is open to air and light."

"Kingdom?"

"Look about you. Are you asleep? Have you not seen what is happening here?"

Jerhad went home that course very much overwhelmed with this revelation. While he sat staring at nothing and lost in thought, Andreanna was in the process of counting out gold coins for Mingus, one of the Dwarves who had assisted in her rescue from Daektoch. Finally coming to his senses, Jerhad asked, "What's going on?"

Mingus, a relatively short Dwarf, was a male of few words but of great prowess.

"Bread! Mingus is making me a bread oven down at the market square. I bought the empty store and the lot behind it; the one next to Mother's. Mingus is building me an oven of stone that will bake two hundred loaves at a time. Liele, the potter, has agreed to fire brick to line it."

Mingus flashed a broad smile at Jerhad.

Jerhad laughed, "I should have guessed you'd be up to something like that."

"Someone has to make bread for all those workers and soldiers. It might as well be me. Think of the all the help I'll have. And besides, think of the coin I will earn!"

It was about half of the moon's course into the night when Jerhad was awakened by the calling of rams' horns, blaring away, over and over. He sat up in bed. The stomping of feet running in step could be heard in the distance...and then, as one who had heard it many times over would recognize, the sound of clashing steel and the awful, sickening sound of battle.

"O ye gods, it must be the Trolls," groaned Jerhad. "Andreanna, please stay here with Kendra and my parents. I know you would like to get out there, but please...."

"Yes, my Prince. I will do as you request."

Jerhad raised an eyebrow and looked at her. *Who was this female in his bed? That was not the Andreanna he knew*. In the past, she would have run him over to be the first in battle.

He threw on some clothes and with *Gildar* in hand ran off toward the northern wall where the fighting was engaged. Torches had been lit up along the top of the partially finished battlement. As he gained the wall's top, the Elven archers were gathering, but they could only stand and look out into the darkness where the sounds of combat were heard. Steel rang against steel in the darkness. Cries of pain echoed and the grunts of laboring combatants resounded in the night.

Stanton stood nearby. "Don't know," he said before Jerhad could ask. "The Dwarves sounded their battle horns, formed ranks and moved out into the field. Must be Trolls, but no one really knows what's going on, except those who are out there."

Jerhad jumped up onto the unfinished parapet and raised his knife, mingling some of the white and yellow Elfstones' forces. Light sprang from *Gildar*, the Dwarfish name for Ember, forming a pillar extending to the clouds and lighting the whole of the Mildra area all the way to the mountains as if it were midcourse of the sun.

There were some four thousand Trolls out on the field. About half of them had been engaged by a detachment of Dwarves, while the others meandered about not sure where to inflict damage. With the presence of the light, they saw the bulwark lined with Elven archers and attacked. But now the Elves saw them too. At Stanton's command, six hundred archers released their arrows into the oncoming rush of Trolls. The charge halted, Trolls looking down at themselves, confused about the arrow shafts sticking out from them. Some fell, but most renewed their surge. Another volley of arrows left the wall; more Trolls dropped, but not enough, and the others kept coming. Five, six, seven volleys of arrows followed. About half of the charging Trolls had fallen now.

"Move aside, friends," said Mordock as the Giants came up onto the wall and dropped down to the ground below. They bore small round shields and carried war-maces, which were tried to their wrists with chain. The Giants spun their hammers like windmills in a gale, making a sound similar to that of swarming bees. Trolls fell into broken masses on the field as they encountered the Giants.

The Dwarf detachment that had initially engaged the Trolls were pushed back eastwardly.

"Sir?" said one Elf to Stanton.

"Yes, what is it?"

"Elf infantry waiting your orders, sir!"

Stanton turned and looked behind him where twelve hundred Elves, were ordered in ranks, armed with pikes and lances. He looked over to Jerhad. "Do we let them?"

"Your call, Commander. Are they ready?"

Stanton paused. He nodded. "Infantry! Through the gates! Form ranks before the wall. **Double step!**"

The infantry jogged out in formation.

"Squad Leaders, look to your men. **March!**" Stanton's orders were passed down from squad to squad across the field, using the style of battle communication common to the Dwarves.

The Elves went down the field at double-step and then slowed to battle-step as they reached the Trolls. The Giants had shown the Elves how to modify the pikes that Morlah had brought to give the smaller Elf an advantage against the heavier Troll. They had sharpened the back end and lashed a cross piece as the Dwarves had used in Breezon in the past. As a Troll would attack, the soldier would dig his pike end into the ground allowing the Troll to use its own weight to become impaled upon the pike. The Troll would be stopped dead (literally) in his tracks. Oftentimes, a Troll would be left suspended leaning into the pike. The soldier would then fall back to be rearmed with a new pike at the rear of the ranks. The impaled Trolls would form their own wall that would slow their fellows. The battle lasted but a few dozen spans of heartbeats before these Trolls were all down. Injured Elves groaned and wounded Trolls howled.

Stanton started shouting new orders, "Infantry squads! Formations to the east!" Ranks reformed. "Double-step."

The Dwarves who had initially gone out on the field were still locked in fierce battle. They had been caught by surprise by the Trolls and had swiftly sent out a token force into the field to delay them but were quickly losing ground. The Elves swooped down on the rear flank of the Trolls as the main force of Dwarves came in from the south where their camp was laid out. The rear line of Trolls went down with pikes through their backs, cries of rage and pain rose over the battle's din. Many of the Trolls, still unaware of the rear attack, were brought down by the second line of pikes. Now, Trolls turned to defend themselves and were skewered on the third line of pikes, as Elf infantry surged forward, but now the impaled Trolls blocked the infantry's progress.

"Demons and fire," cursed Stanton. "This isn't working out. This maneuver was designed for a constant oncoming charge."

"Can you get them flat on the ground?" asked Jerhad.

"Flat on the ground? ...I don't know. ...on the ground? How about on their knees?"

"If that's the best you can do, do it quickly."

"Infantry! Make way for archers," he bellowed. The infantry dropped to one knee, a maneuver to allow archers to fire low over their heads. "Archers, hold!"

Jerhad lifted his hand and pointed Ember at the line of impaled Trolls. Magic erupted from *Gildar,* and its fierce flame swept through the impaled Trolls. They fell to the ground in heaps of smoldering ashes.

"Not bad, Elf Prince," said Stanton. "Infantry, forward!"

Once more, they repeated this, and then the Dwarf main force struck and swept the remaining Trolls away.

Jerhad let his light continue glowing while the wounded were taken from the field. Several scores of Elves had fallen, one hundred seventy-six dead, two hundred eighty-some wounded. There were three hundred sixty dead Dwarves and some two hundred wounded.

"I've been stupid, thinking we wouldn't be attacked from the north without warning from *Dolan*," lamented Stanton.

IronLeggs, the Dwarf leader, was with them now. "So were we, Commander. We had thought that our brethren would alert us of any Troll movement to the north. We were caught off guard. Obviously, something has happened at *Dolan* to prevent them from warning us, or the Trolls found another way down here. We were not battle ready, as we should have been. It grieves me to have to report this to King HeartStone," he sighed in dismay. He slipped his longknife from its sheath and began working the handle with his deadly grip. "But, it *will not* happen again."

"Will you bear your dead to *Dolan*?" asked Jerhad.

"No. The King has requested that if any of the Dwarves fall here, they should be buried here, by your leave of course," answered IronLeggs, his thumb testing his longknife's edge. "He has ordered this to show the sincerity of his service to you, and as a sign that our people should be one again, as when Elf and Dwarf fought side-by-side in the great wars of the past."

"So it will be done. I will purchase the field that was fought upon. On the north side by the forest, and below the hills, we will bury our dead together," responded Jerhad, grasping IronLeggs' mace-wielding-hardened hand in a show of friendship and union.

Everyone was off the battlefield now; Jerhad turned *Gildar's* flame toward the field and, with magic, burned all the dead Trolls to ash. He did not want the females and children to see them in the morning. Having finished, he let his light go out.

Chapter 6

The next course, Lewin, Stanton, Jerhad, the Giants and the Dwarf leaders met together.

"We took our enemy too lightly," said IronLeggs. "From now on, we will stand watch at battle readiness."

"We will have the Dwarves stand watch about the wall and the northern and eastern perimeters throughout the night. Sentries will also be posted a quarter league out," added Stanton.

"Stanton, the Elves proved themselves last night in battle. I want to use them with the Dwarves for sentries," said Jerhad.

"Done," said Stanton.

"We will add to the watch," said Mordock. One Giant will roam between sentries during the night. We will establish a call system that will not easily be found out. This will establish that the sentries are about and alive. One Giant should be enough."

"Good," said Jerhad. "IronLeggs, could you send out scouts to see where the Trolls came from?"

"That won't be necessary," replied Stanton. "I sent out one-half squad of Elf hunters this rising to do the task. The Elves are excellent trackers; they are up to it. So far, it looks like they came down straight through Dwarf's Pass. I've sent the scouts three courses north. That will take them to *Dolan*. IronLeggs also dispatched Dwarf messengers to go with them.

"Also, we will maintain eight scouting parties. Four to the north and four to the east. Two will be coming and two will be going at all times. They will weave a repeating pattern so that they cross each other's paths at each rising and at each setting."

"Any more business?" asked Jerhad looking around. Everyone shook their heads. "That's it then, let's get back to work."

The construction of the wall was making headway. One layer of stone had progressed beyond the eastern end of the town and had taken its turn southward. "What about gates?" Jerhad had asked Orenald.

"They are on the way. King HeartStone is having them forged in *Dolan*. They will be brought down in parts. They will be for outer gates. Bars as thick as your arm. We will construct inner gates made of wood and plate them with iron here in Mildra. We will need a hard wood, but not one that splinters easily. One with a bit of resilience and fire resistant if possible."

Jerhad laughed, "You don't ask for much, do you? I'll ask the sawyer; he'll know what to use. Just let me know the size of timbers you need. I'll cover the cost."

Jerhad returned home where he found Andreanna with Kendra. She looked worried. "What ails thee, my beauty?" he asked.

"I'm not sure. Last night, when the Trolls attacked, I was restless, so I went up on the roof to see if I could make out anything. I saw you standing on the wall. I saw the magic light up the sky and land. Then my hands grew warm, and light glowed about them. Oh ye gods, Jerhad, it scared me so bad. What's happening to me? Could it be something to do with Daektoch's spell?"

"I don't know. I don't think so. Morlah said you are of Elven descent. It could be Elf magic. We'll speak to Morlah about it the next time we see him. Maybe this is the right time to give it to you."

"Give me what?"

He pulled a stone fixed to a cord from his belt pouch. "It's the black stone that was found when Morlah removed Daektoch's spell from you: a result of the blending of magics. Master Filinhoff had said you should have it. He said it was *balat*, but I don't know what that means. Morlah said you should wear it." He handed her the stone.

Andreanna took it but held it by the cord from which it was suspended, at arm's length, and stared at it with her brow furrowed. "Does it **do** anything?" she asked with distrust.

Later that course, while Jerhad was at the mill inquiring about timbers for the gates, an Elf ran up to Jerhad. "Andreanna wants you home. Now!"

"What's wrong?"

"She didn't say. She just said for you to get your pointy ears up there, *fast*."

Jerhad reached down into the magic and ran. Those who saw him were not sure that they had; he passed them in a blur. It seemed to Jerhad that he had just started running when he arrived, an eighth league's sprint. He burst into the house.

"Andreanna? Where are you?"

"In here, Jerhad."

He rushed to her. Andreanna sat on a stool, looking grim; on the floor before her was Kendra, sitting, playing. About the child glowed a rainbow of colors as she juggled an array of toys in the air above her. They danced about, twisting and twirling in the air.

"Want to play, Daddy?" Kendra asked.

He dropped to his knees in disbelief. He reached into the colors...magic! *Pure Elven magic.* Strong Elven magic! Each color was a perfect blend of power harmonizing with the others.

"I see the Faeries in you too, Daddy."

"Not Faeries, sweet pea. Just magic."

"No, real Faeries, Daddy."

"I'm not ready for this," said Andreanna, glaring at Jerhad as if in accusation.

"Neither am I. Don't tell anyone. Kendra would you promise me something?"

"Alright, Daddy."

"Don't play with the magic outside. Only when you're alone with your mother in the house. It will make me happy if you do this for me." The last thing Jerhad wanted was for word to get out that his child possessed magic. That would probably buy her Daektoch's personal attention.

As Kendra played, Jerhad investigated the colors, the combinations of power, that she produced, his own magic responding. A whole new world of power opened to his understanding. His comprehension expanded, and new possibilities became evident. She was dealing with the purest and most complete magic he had yet seen.

"My sweet child, where in the gods' names did you ever learn this?"

"Not me, Daddy. You. At night, you sleep. Your Faeries come out and play with me."

"My Faeries?"

"Yes. The blue, the yellow...the green...white one too... and purple and Nan. But not the black. She said she doesn't know how to play, so she stays with you."

Andreanna scowled at Jerhad. She resembled an angry Moor Cat.

"Hey, I didn't do nothing. Don't look at *me* that way!"

"Mommy play too last night. Mommy's Faerie camed and played with us."

"What Faerie?" insisted Andreanna, losing her glare.

"Your Faerie, Mommy. She was yellow like Daddy's coins you hide under the bed. Your black one not like Daddy's. She scared me."

How many of these did Morlah wish upon us? thought Jerhad.

Four courses of the sun later, a Dwarf patrol came south to Mildra. They went directly to IronLeggs with their report. Then, IronLeggs called for the Giants, Stanton, and Jerhad. "ShortBeard has just come out of *Dolan*," he said to them. "ShortBeard, give your report again."

ShortBeard stepped forward. He was as his name, with a beard only to his mid chest. "Six courses past, the Trolls came out of the north along the west end of the Blue Mountains. They have laid siege around the western side of *Dolan*. There were a few skirmishes but no outright battles. King HeartStone had the tunnels collapsed once the Trolls discovered them. Hundreds of Trolls died in them. Now they seem content to sit about and wait. The western mountains are covered with tens of thousands of Trolls, led and kept in line by Rock Trolls. They have not gone deeper into the mountains toward the valley yet. We do not know if they are aware of it.

"We had to use the long tunnels to come out; they come out almost a league away from *Dolan*. King HeartStone has given specific command that the Dwarves who are in Mildra should remain here. He prefers to have a distant force kept in reserve. He is filtering another ten thousand troops through the long tunnels to the north, to have a force there also. The

King would also prefer to honor his father's token and leave a large detachment here in Mildra.

"There will be messengers regularly sent for communications. You are to do the same. They must be Dwarves. We will not reveal the location of the long tunnels to any; few of our own people know them."

"Well, that explains why we weren't alerted of the Trolls who came here," said Stanton. "We need to intensify our watches. We need to increase the number of our own scouts going and coming to and from the north."

"What of the Gift of the Elves to the Giants?" asked Kassandra.

"When was the last time you were there?" asked ShortBeard.

"About five cycles back. We have toured the country extensively since then. We were on our way back to see the Giants there when all this began."

"Three cycles past, the four Giants, who hold the Land while waiting for the next Keeper and Nourisher to arrive, decided to take measures to see that the same problem that happened with BondBreaker did not repeat itself. They went through the forest and cut into logs all trees that were blown down by the wind. These they have planted into the ground to form a great wall from the cliffs of *Dolan,* along the western border of the Gift, onto the peaks of the southwest Mystics above the River Rain. It was a labor of five cycles. The Giants also dug a dry moat before the wall. They had just completed it when the Trolls came.

"When the Trolls came upon them, the Giants threw out great logs over the wall. One log would take down fifty to one hundred Trolls at a time. The Trolls quickly lost interest and moved back to *Dolan.* A few Trolls are still there camped at a distance and watch the Giant's wall. When the Giants go out to confront them, they run like wild dogs, but return when the Giants return within their fortification. This goes on course by course. HeartStone has sent two thousand Dwarves to reinforce the Giants."

Mordock rose. "We must speak of this at length, my little friends. We will tell you what is to be done by the Giants after we have spoken." When Giants spoke at length it meant they could be at it for courses or quarter-moon's cycles.

The two Giant schooners had returned to the Homeland seven cycles ago, and the Giants there were probably still discussing how to handle the matter of the fall of the Keeper and Nourisher, not to mention telling the tale of the battles fought and making songs of all that had transpired in Frontmire. Four Giants could not hope to stand against that many Trolls alone. Though, they might hold on indefinitely from behind the wall, within the fortifications, with the assistance of the Dwarves, as long as the Trolls did not come over the mountain behind them.

IronLeggs rose from his seat, "Come," he said to the Dwarves, "we will discuss our watches and defenses in case of attack." They also left. Jerhad sat alone with Stanton, who was irate that the groups did not yet function as one army, but instead, the groups tended to govern themselves individually. Jerhad sniffed at the air, and his eyes lit up.

"Well, how about some hot bread and stew?" said the Elf with a push at the Human's shoulder, rousing the man from his thoughts. "Andreanna has fired up the ovens that Mingus made, and if my nose doesn't deceive me, I think there is bread that is just about ready for testing. Let's go see how they work."

Morlah stood at the base of Mount Bahal, the last place where Daektoch, the Black Mage, had been seen. The ghost ship, the *Druid Queen* and her crew were anchored off the north coast of Frontmire, keeping an eye on the mage to make sure he did not leave. They had trailed him there seven cycles past after his battle with Jerhad, and he had not left since then. Morlah had spoken to the *Druid Queen's* captain a few courses earlier; the captain had wanted to go with Morlah.

"What canst thou do against him if thou doest come?" inquired Morlah.

"It is not known what the dead canst do against the Black Mage. We doest not know if the terror our presence brings over the hearts of men willst affect him. Thine magic is different than his. It doest protect thee enough, but we also bear no malevolence toward thee. I doest believe that is a factor. Also, I doest not believe his magic can harm us, but there is no way to know."

Morlah had not agreed to allow the captain to accompany him and had finally persuaded the him to hold off. It might be better to have the crew of the *Druid Queen* remain in reserve until Daektoch was at some disadvantage. Then, the crew might be of greater use or effectiveness. There were just too many unknowns.

Morlah's plan was to go in after the mage; he would make this an encounter unto death. Only one of them would survive. Daektoch's attempts to destroy all magic he could not possess would end; his pushing of the Trolls to the destruction of the land's races would end. The Trolls were only half bad if left to themselves in their home in the Blue Mountains. It was Daektoch's doing that they were such a pestilence.

Along the base of the mountain, Morlah ascended the passage that led to an entrance. Daektoch would be waiting for him. He was sure of it.

"Druid, you are a fool," mindspoke The Raven to him from the plains of Breezon where he was grazing. "You walk into an ambush. You have no knowledge of what awaits you. You are blind, outnumbered and in ignorance. Even a mere horse would not undertake such a mission." Since their first contact using mindspeech, the Bornodald had had an uncanny ability to know what the Druid was thinking.

"Silence, Bornodald. What wouldst thou have me do? This mage is a thorn in Frontmire's side, and I doest mean to extract it."

"Now is not the time, Druid. You have no advantage. How do you hope to succeed? I hear the mage laugh at your presence. You're a fool. There are none who possess the power you do to do good with, except the Elf. If you die within the mount, who will champion the cause of the Elves? Jerhad is too inexperienced."

Morlah stopped. The Bornodald raised a good argument; the Druid hated that. Against his basic desire, but brought to his senses by the Bornodald, he turned and left. He would leave and return when he had a real plan or wait until he could catch Daektoch unprepared.

The Raven was a Bornodald, a horse-like species in appearance only, of superior intellect, and with the capacity for mindspeech with any who were of great magic or intellect. The Humans of the land of Karob, who had managed to capture and raise them in captivity, had bred Raven. Raven had been a gift to the Druids and had eventually become teamed up with Morlah. Together they had become an essential element in the events of the last Troll war. Also, Morlah had enchanted The Raven and turned him into a winged Bornodald. Together they had flown into battle against Daektoch and then against the Trolls that besieged Breezon.

Deep within the Mystic Mountains in a location that could not be found unless allowed, the Faeries had their domain. These were the embodiment of different fragments of the Earthen power. Specifically, the magic found in the element argentus. The element was pure, raw power. It contained an intelligence. The magic was older than the Faeries, for it had been since the planet's beginning. It manifested itself in the Faeries, in Elfstones and other forms. These were living beings, essences of magic, manifestations thereof. Still, they were individuals. Not all expressions of this power were embodied in humanoid form. Some preferred to be as trees, others as stones; those who were in inanimate expressions were still able to show themselves, when they chose, as life forms, without leaving their preferred manifestations.

The magic's ultimate goal was harmony, the harmony of life, of health and of all things that pertained to nature and magic: the Life and Health of the land. This is why *acrch* was of the most powerful among its manifestations.

The Faeries had at one time roamed freely throughout Canterhort; but with the rise of the population of Humans, other races and the rise of Black magic, they retreated to the Mystics and lived over Frontmire's largest vein of argentus. Argentus was their source of life, their source of power. They were the essence and the life of the magic made manifest. The rise of Humans, Elves, Trolls and Gnomes kept the Faeries deep within the mountains, though these races all had their origins in the Earthen power in the beginning. The Faeries were shy creatures in many ways, in spite of their tremendous power. They did not fear the Black Mage but rather were revulsed by his sorceries, and so they withdrew, living in harmony in their habitation. They were strong and vibrant. In their seclusion, they still affected the life, health and harmony of the land. In times past, it was true that they had allowed themselves to mix with the first mortals of the planet though nature, law and essence prohibited it; the cross had produced the Elves.

The Elves, therefore, had innate magic. Early on, they had been strong in power, but somewhere along the way, complacency gave way to disuse, and the magic became dormant. Thus, the Elves became just another race. The balance of power of those who sought good and those who sought evil was disrupted. Now, the Faeries sought to restore the balance by awakening the Elves' innate abilities.

But all was not well in the Faeries' habitat; lethargy continued creeping in upon them. At first, it had not been noticed, but now they knew something was wrong. Their balance was disrupted as if one string on a twelve-stringed lute were out of tune by only a little; a trained ear heard it unmistakably. This had never been; none knew what it was or what to do.

It was one-half moon's course into the night when Andreanna woke. She did not know why she had awakened, but *something had* roused her. She lay in the bed and listened, hearing nothing except Jerhad's soft breathing beside her. Rising, she went to Kendra's room where the child lay quietly sleeping, so Andreanna returned to bed. Then, there was a tinkling sound, which somehow seemed familiar, like a voice she had heard long ago. Maybe in a dream. Maybe in a nightmare.

"Andreanna," sounded the chiming; the voice carried a scent like that of sweet Jasmine. The Human was not startled or afraid, for the voice precluded that. Rather, it was a comforting and somewhat pleasing call.

"Andreanna."

She sat up to find Nan standing at the foot of the bed. The Faerie's eyes were a bright whitish-blue, her hair long and flowing, a lively silver colored silken flow; she had an aura of...Life and Health, emitting that sweet fragrance around her, and sounds like that of tinkling bells accompanying her movements. She was the height of a Dwarf, though without the stockiness, and her face was radiant with the beauty of the manifestation of all that is good. As Nan stood gazing into the Human female's eyes, Andreanna noticed that the Faerie's feet did not touch the floor.

"I remember you. You were in the void," said the mortal woman. The memories of that period were still vivid nightmares for Andreanna.

"Peace, Andreanna. Come touch my hand."

Andreanna did so, immediately being soothed, the pain of the memories beginning to heal.

"Yes, I am the one," spoke Nan. "I was there in your darkness. Now, I need you in mine. The Faeries are sick. We do not know the cause, hence, we know not what it is we truly seek, but there is an insidious festering that grows by the heartbeat, one that we do not know or see.

"Once upon a time, you were of no consequence to the grand scheme of fate, no more, no less than most. That is not to devalue you and your worth as a life. But then it happened, as if by your own choice, that you were thrust into Jerhad's destiny and thereby into the Elves' destiny and the fate of all of Canterhort, if not that of the entire world. Now, it appears that Frontmire and even Canterhort will live or die by your hand. This we know. How, we do not understand.

"We do recognize that the magic that you have within you from your Elven ancestors must be awakened soon. To do so, you must travel to the Mystic Mountains and seek the Faerie creatures that abide there. They will attempt to awaken the magic in you. It may be premature, but it must be attempted soon. Go to them as quickly as possible, for time is precious." And she was gone.

Andreanna lay back down. *What a crazy dream.* Only problem...she was awake. *Was it a dream*? She had recognized Nan from somewhere, *or is that part of a dream*? *This is too confusing. Go searching for Faeries! As if!*

She returned to sleep.

Twelve courses of the sun had gone by since Nan's visit. Every course, every span of the sun's course, every span of the moon's course, Andreanna thought of Nan. A dream that had told her to search for the Faeries in the Mystic Mountains. She became obsessed with the thought, and it ate at her and pressed her to the point that she could not sleep and did not eat.

Damned Faeries, what do they want with me anyway? She remembered word for word what Nan had said; she knew what they wanted, *to wake the magic within me. But why?*

"You're not looking well lately," said Jerhad across from her at the break fast table. They were alone for the heartbeat. "Are you feeling alright?"

"No, I don't! You and your damned Faeries are going to drive me to an early grave," she spat. "I'm sick of it. I don't want to hear about it. ...So just leave me alone or I'll take your head off!" She slammed her fist on the table, got up and stormed out of the room, her chair falling over with a clatter.

"Good morning to you too," he said to the empty table across from him, cowering a bit. He quickly proceeded to sneak out the back door fearing that she might indeed take his head off. *Better to let this cool a bit.* Though he would probably be in trouble for not pursuing it. *Too early for a pitcher of ale,* he thought. *Time to go find Kassandra.*

A span later, Jerhad found Kassandra helping Mordock lift a large hewn stone block onto the bulwarks. The digging of the trench left an odor of freshly turned earth under the hot sun, its scent heavy on the air. The ringing of maces on stone-cutting chisels echoed continuously.

"Jerhad, well-met, friend. We took a bit of time from our much speaking of what to do about the Trolls and the Gift. A bit of stonework will help get fresh blood into the head. Maybe we will have better thoughts," said the male Giant, turning to greet the Elf.

"Maybe," said Jerhad. "Mordock, do you mind if I borrow Kassandra for a bit? I need to talk to her."

"For you, anything. Only do not steal her heart, for that is mine."

Kassandra smiled and winked at Jerhad. "Males! They are so easy to tame."

"True, my dove, but not as easy to domesticate," laughed Mordock.

"Come, let us walk and see how the stonecutters in the mountain fare. We will speak on the way." They walked south toward the quarry. "What troubles you, my little friend," asked Kassandra after they had walked a ways, "for worry is inscribed upon your brow."

"It's Andreanna," said Jerhad. "Something is eating at her. She's distracted. She doesn't talk, doesn't eat. I tried to talk to her about it this rising, but she almost bit my head off; actually, she threatened to. Then she stormed out. I'm worried about her. I don't know what the problem is. I'm scared it might have to do with the sickness she had when she almost died after her ordeal with Daektoch."

"Fear not, Giant-Friend. If that is all that worries you, I will seek her out. There are places that females can go where males should not tread. I will find her after the sun's setting and know what the problem is. Only, I say not that I will tell you the problem. This only I promise to tell you, I will say 'yea' if you have a great worry, and I will say 'nay' if you do not. Beyond that, it may be up to Andreanna to tell you of the matter."

"That's good enough for me. It's good to have friends nearby to help with problems."

Kassandra laughed. "The problem is only so great when it is the only one you see, little friend." They continued on to the quarry to see the stonecutters' progress.

The Dwarves had a unique method of communication. Word would spread throughout the entire camp within half a span if a message needed to be passed on; yet, it was an unobserved phenomenon. As Jerhad and Kassandra walked into the quarry, a Dwarf backed away from his work and with all casualness said, "Messengers for you at the north wall, Prince Jerhad."

Jerhad turned to Kassandra, "How do they do that? We just left there. I don't remember seeing anyone go by in this direction."

"They are like bees in a hive. When one speaks, all know," she laughed. "Come now, my Prince. If you will allow it, I will place you on my shoulder and will have you back to the wall in a few heartbeats."

"Well, it's a bit embarrassing if you want to know, but I guess we should go see what's up."

She picked him up, setting him on her left shoulder, and set off toward the wall at a Giant's pace. Arriving at the wall, Jerhad now on his own feet, they met the Dwarf's scout party.

"Are you Prince Jerhad?" asked the lead Dwarf, Celeront.

"No. I mean, yes...just Jerhad, please. Skip the prince stuff."

"Yes, my Prince... ah, Jerhad."

"Just go on."

"Trolls coming south, about two leagues north of here. About six thousand of them. Came out along the north side of the River Rain early just before sunrising and crossed over the mountain at the Pass. Do not know how or where they came from, but it is clear that they are coming here. They should be here by midcourse of the sun."

"Fire and demons! It's going to happen again. I can't believe it! Somehow I hoped it would just go away." Just then, Stanton showed up. "Dwarf-Friend, this is Stanton, Commander of the Elven Army. Please repeat your message to him and then to the Dwarf commander."

"I already have reported to IronLeggs, my Prince." He went on and repeated the message word for word to Stanton.

"Well, the numbers are in our favor. Though, I don't know how ready we are for this." Looking up to an Elf on watch, on the wall, Stanton said, "Soldier, sound the general alarm!"

The Elf turned and called down the wall, "Sound general alarm." The call was repeated along the wall. Then, rams' horns called out a long eerie and woeful call, causing goose bumps to rise on Jerhad's arms. The call was answered on the south end and the southwest side of the town and finally by the river on the northwest side of Mildra.

Dwarves and Elves swarmed like ants on an overturned mound. Archers lined the parapets. Infantry ranks formed before the defenses, ten thousand Elves along the north wall and five thousand Dwarves protecting the unfinished eastern wall. Five thousand Dwarves lined up in ranks east of the north passage. Both Elf and Dwarf infantry bore the long, modified pikes that the Elves had used in the previous encounter; only the Elves supplemented much of their ranks' needs with fire-harden-wood lances. The Elves wore shortswords on their belts, and the Dwarves long-handled battle-axes.

A valuable lesson had been learned in the last attack. That was, that arrows did not affect the Trolls enough; it could take up to half a dozen of well-placed arrows to bring down a Troll. Morlah, having foreseen this problem, had sent one of the Druid alchemists to help. Using an extract from a well-known jellyfish, the GreenStar, that often infested the mouth of the Mage River, he showed the Elves how to make a quick-acting toxin to coat their arrow tips. Then, they sent some lads out in boats to net the slimy creatures, filling bucket upon bucket with the jellyfish. Finally, they had gone through the messy process of boiling them down, straining the end concoction, boiling it again and finally adding sulfur to the resulting broth. In the end, they had two barrels of an acrid, blue-green syrupy venom.

They had no means of testing it, but the Druid alchemist asked that all of the army's arrows and pike tips be painted, dried and painted again with the substance and warned that everyone be aware that the toxin should not be touched. They were also instructed that the arrows be used sparingly, one or two per Troll until they knew how well they would work. The results should be known quickly. Stanton had agreed to the whole scheme; they had little to lose, and he had also seen such tactics successfully used by the Breezon Army.

It was just before midcourse when a ram's horn rang in alarm out of the forest on the north side of the field. Shortly, two Elves, one with horn in hand, raced toward the fortification. A half span later, the Trolls emerged from the forest, milling around, surveying the field and wall. Several Rock Trolls were among them; the Giants sat on the wall and watched.

The battle plan was simple: allow the archers to inflict as much damage as possible, and then let Elf and Dwarf infantry attack from the east and south. When, not if, driven back, the Elves would retreat, funneling through the doorless gate while the Dwarves retreated to the east perimeter, where they would be joined by the five thousand who would be waiting there defending the partially walled area. The Giants would keep the gate while the infantry withdrew from the field and then retreat within the bulwarks with the Elves.

Half of the Trolls came forward; Jerhad stood on the wall with Stanton and watched. Then, at three hundred paces distance between the defenses and Trolls, Stanton ordered the longbows to release one volley. What resembled and sounded like a swarm of bees rushed to meet the oncoming Trolls. As always, when hit with a volley of arrows, the Trolls stopped and looked down, puzzled by the shafts protruding from them. The Troll horde resumed its charge, but now several of them stopped again and stood swaying, staring, drooling. Longbows sang as another volley of arrows went out to encounter the Trolls.

The second half of the Trolls, which had remained behind, charged. Several Trolls from the forward line dropped headlong to the ground with dull thuds while more came to a standstill, stupefied; it looked like the toxin was working. Horns blared and the infantry moved forward, pikes pointing to the clear blue sky, as the Elves marched in unison and the archers released several more volleys.

"Well, at least they look good," said Jerhad of the infantry.

Stanton answered him with a scowl.

A solitary horn blared, and the pikes leveled to meet the Trolls. The horn blared again, and the infantry surged forward. The sound produced by the two forces clashing was sickening. The nauseating sound of spears penetrating flesh and maces crushing bodies rose. Trolls screamed in rage. Elves and Dwarves cried in pain. Metal clashed as sword, mail, shield and helmet met. Impaled Trolls flailed, hung up on pikes and lances. Their fellows pushed past faster than the first line of infantry moved back, and many Elves fell under crushing blows from stone maces. Defenders were crushed and ripped apart. Assailants fell by the score. A gasp rose from the battle, as if the sigh of death. A cool breeze swept down from the mountains carrying the smell of Troll, blood and death back to the wall. The Dwarves charged into the Trolls flank while the archers let their arrows fly over the infantry into the second line of the Trolls' attack. The defender's arrows sounded like a peppering hailstorm.

Then, the whole field turned into a melee, the entire Elf-infantry line breaking up while a wedge of Trolls drove deep into the Dwarf formation. Retreat was sounded and the Elves, in broken ranks, poured through the opening in the wall. Trolls overtook them and mauled the Elves. The Dwarves were routed toward the southeast, and the Giants took up positions at each side of the gates where they met six Rock Trolls, while the infantry poured in through the opening, funneling in behind the Giants. The archers rained death on the Trolls from close range now; hundreds of Trolls dropped.

The Rock Trolls engaged the Giants as Jerhad and Stanton ran toward the gate, the Commander shouting orders to reform ranks to defend the opening. Dwarves fell by the score to the southeast. Cries of agony and anguish echoed. The eastern defense of Dwarves would hold no more, seeing what was about to turn to massacre of their brethren out on the field. With a rush of booted feet, they charged the rear of the Troll assault, leaving their positions of guarding the site of the future eastern wall.

Stanton cursed. He ordered twelve Elf squads to take up the vacant position along the eastern defense and the others to stand ready to defend the gate. Weapons and armor clanked as the soldiers settled into position.

Back at the gate, swords clashed violently, as the Giants were hard pressed by the Rock Trolls. Both Giant and Troll wore heavy mail. Then in a flash, Mordock took a sword point to the throat and went down. Rage thundered from Kassandra as she stepped forward, straddling Mordock's body. She decapitated two Rock Trolls in one stroke as DiamondHeart and Tahmat rallied to her side and fended off the others.

To the east, the tide turned, and Trolls fell to being slaughtered between the two lines of Dwarf infantry, the rearward Dwarf offensive having put the Trolls in turmoil. The surviving Trolls broke and ran toward the mountain, quickly leaving the pursuing Dwarves behind.

Along the walls, Cave Trolls finally succumbed to the poisoned arrows, moaning in anguish as the toxin coursed through them, sending them into fits of seizures and frothing at the mouth. A large mace was swung and released by one of the Rock Trolls, catching Kassandra square in the forehead. The splintering of bone sounded loudly. She crumpled. DiamondHeart and Tahmat took up positions in front of their fallen.

Jerhad cried out for the Giants to fall back, but they did not move. Again, he called out and ordered them back; they hesitated and then retreated through the gate, fending blows from the Rock Trolls. As the black glow of magic enveloped Jerhad's hands, he reached out with his magic and took hold of the four remaining Rock Trolls, lifting them into the air as a mass, with the Elven power of *balan* and *licri* pulsing about him. He was about to crush the life from them when he was suddenly surprised by the intelligence that he perceived within them; they were not like the mindless Cave Trolls who were more like stupid beasts.

"This is not necessary," he spoke to them. Jerhad found no hatred or anger within himself. *balan* had cleansed him. Actually, he felt something that resembled a love for the creature, a love for the life within, a bond.

One turned his head and made eye contact with him. "We have pledged our services to the Black Mage."

"This is not necessary, friend," Jerhad repeated.

"I die at the hands of an honorable warrior. Do what you must, for if you let me down, I will slay you and yours."

Tears poured down Jerhad's face as he extinguished the Rock Trolls' life force and turned them to dust. The battle was over. Dwarf, Elf, and Troll littered the field. Mordock lay with blood spurting from his neck wound, Kassandra with blood oozing from her ears, eyes and nose. She barely breathed. Jerhad left the wall and went home, head bent low and badly shaken. As he came to the house, his mother met him at the door.

"Andreanna is gone, Jerhad. She's gone!"

"What do you mean 'gone'?"

"That's what I said. Ye gods in the heavens, she's gone! I came home when the alarm sounded...to get my bow.... There she was, all dressed up like a soldier, with a mail coat and a sword and boots.... She said to tell you she had something to do and not to worry. She asked me to take care of Kendra while she was away. Then she ran out of the house and down the street toward the river. She's gone, Jerhad, she's gone!" Catrina paced about, frantic. "Ah ye gods, what are things coming to. Who's going to take care of the bread?"

Jerhad ran out the door and looked down the street. Andreanna could be anywhere; he did not know where to begin looking. He sat on the step and wept.

Chapter 7

Andreanna had heard the horns sounding the general alarm. She was consumed not only with the thought of seeking out the Faeries but also with the *need* to. Jerhad would never have let her go; she could not tell him about it. So now, she had her chance. With everyone distracted by the Trolls coming out of the north, she slipped back into the house and dressed in her battle attire, knee-length chain-mail coat, metal mesh pants, steel-reinforced leather boots and belt that carried a shortsword and a longknife. She packed food, a water skin, an oiled-canvas-outer garment that she wrapped around her bedroll, a bit of extra clothing for warmth and her three-quarter staff. Then, she waited, knowing Catrina would be up from the market with Kendra shortly; it was not long before Catrina entered the house with Kendra in tow.

"I've come for my bow. The Trolls are...." Catrina paused and gawked at Andreanna. "Child! *What are you doing*?"

"I have to leave for a while. I have something that needs doing. Please take care of Kendra for me. Tell Jerhad not to worry." Not giving Catrina time to respond, she kissed them both and then ran down the street toward the river. There would be no one down there with the Trolls about to invade.

Once at the riverbanks, she turned north and followed along the shore, following the docks. When she came to the point where she was in sight of the north battlements, where arms clashed with ferocity, she gathered a few logs, lashed them together and placed her pack and supplies on it. Then with her longknife, she cut some leafy branches and set them on her float for camouflage, wading into the cold water almost to her neck, covering her head with the branches too. She paused to smell the sap of the branches she had cut, Sweet Rosemary.

Slowly, she moved up the river. No one looked in her direction. It took her a full span of traveling before she felt it was safe enough to come out of the water, and then moving quickly along the trail that followed the banks, made her way to the Rogue Stream, crossed it at its ford and continued along the Mage. She figured she would be unlikely to run into Trolls now.

It was dark before she was dried out from her 'swim.' She climbed up into a Great Live Oak to spend the night in its natural cradle-like arms, settled down and ate. Then with blanket and oiled coat covering her, she slept.

She woke with the dawn, stiff and sore. It had been a long time since she had slept in a tree; she was getting soft with all this wedded life stuff. Still it felt good to be out in the wild again. Birds chirped in the early morning. Nearby, a crow cawed. A light breeze carried the scent of water up from the nearby river. It had been *too* long.

"Wat'cha doing?" came a tiny voice from above her in the tree. Andreanna looked up to see a small face peering down at her.

"Ah, well.... I was sleeping. Who are you?"

"Fonta."

"What are you doing up the tree, Fonta?"

"Watchin' you sleep. You pretty when you sleep. My Ma pretty when she sleep. Pa snore an' mouth opens. Drools sometime."

"Thank you.... Where do you come from?"

"Home."

"Where's home?"

"There," she said pointing in some vague direction.

"Are you alone?"

"My Ma an' Pa with me; don't know where they are. We walk and walk an' walk an' then we eated an' sleeped in a cave."

"I'm going down to the ground, now. Do you want to come down with me?"

Fonta nodded vigorously.

Andreanna climbed down. O ye gods, she was stiffer than she had expected! Fonta came down and stood before her. She was a young Gnome girl, no bigger than a varmint.

"You're awful far from home aren't you?"

Fonta shrugged.

"When did you see your parents last?"

"I sleeped in the tree three times since the big ones came an' took them. Ma said I should stay in the tree. I sing a lot a wait an' wait an' wait, but Ma an' Pa not come back. I tell myself stories too. Want to hear a story?"

Ye gods, now what was she to do with this child? It looked like the Trolls might have killed her parents. She could not leave her here, and she could not return to Mildra.... "No thanks. I'll do without the story for now."

"I hungry."

"I suppose you would be. Let's eat."

So, they sat and ate and talked about girl things like dolls and playing house. Finally, it was time to go. This would slow her down, but the only thing she could do was take Fonta with her. "How old are you?"

"Seven cycles."

"I'm going for a long walk. Do you want to come?"

"I supposed to wait for Ma an' Pa in the tree."

"I don't think they'll be back this way. I can take you home. I'm going that direction."

"I come."

"How is it you speak the Common Tongue?"

"Pa go see Humans for milk an' stuff. He bring me an' I play with 'il ones."

"Let's get going then."

The Forest Gnomes were a short thin wiry people who inhabited the eastern Mystic Mountains, a tribal folk who mostly lived in isolation; they had been subject to Avenar the Gray-wizard but had been freed when Morlah had dealt with him. Previously, Andreanna's only exposure to the Gnomes had been when they had pursued her, Jerhad and Stanton, having been sent by Avenar with orders to retrieve the Elfstone Jerhad carried in a pouch.

It was dark now; Jerhad lay alone in bed. Andreanna was not back. Her scent lingered on the soft, goose-down quilt. *What was with her anyway? It wasn't like her.* He also was worried about Mordock and Kassandra; both were near death. Jerhad had gone to see the Giants several times. One of the barracks was cleared and the injured were laid in them. The Dwarves prepared graves for their fallen as well as for the fallen of the Elves. There were many graves. The Dwarves and Elves were still gathering the Troll bodies and burning them. It could be a long time before they were done.

Jerhad thought the whole thing to be a disaster. Stanton had disagreed with him. Counting the strength, size and number of their opponents, he thought that the new Elven Army had performed well. They *had* been lucky for the help of the poison arrows! It would become a standard feature for the archers. The troops were pulled from weapons practice and put to work on the wall with the Dwarves. A wall was easier to defend than an open field, and they needed *at least* a rudimentary defensive barrier in all haste. Besides, they could get in shape moving stone. The wooden gates would be assembled tomorrow and set up within a couple of courses.

Jerhad felt helpless. He also could have kicked himself for having intervened so late in the last battle; he had magic that could annihilate the whole Troll horde. Yet, he had only given help at the very last heartbeat.

What's wrong with me? he thought.

"There's nothing wrong with you," came a chiming voice from somewhere. He bolted up in the bed. The fragrance of Life and Health filled the air. "Follow me, Jerhad."

"Who...where are you?"

Nan appeared in the doorway of his room. "Come with me."

He rose and followed her. He had never met her before, but instinctively he knew who she was, as if she were an old friend. She led him down the street, up to the wall, down past the sentry who saluted him. No one else saw Nan. They came to a space where he could speak without being heard. The night air was still and the town was quiet, as if in mourning and somber reflection of the course's battle.

"You have a lot to learn, Elf Prince. Sit here and let me speak with you. It is not given to one individual being to hold the lives of all within his hand. Daektoch takes such action; he decides who lives and who dies. Look at the monster he is. It should not be so with you. It is not yours to play out the whole of life and death and the struggle thereof. This course's battle was fought as it should have been. The magic within you has an intelligence of its own. It acted as it should have; hence, you acted as you should have. Will the armies stand by and watch you destroy all enemies and not taste of battle and death? Death is as much a part of life as is birth. You must allow fate to play her hand. Trust your instincts. The magic will lead you."

"But I could have saved all those soldiers if I had but acted. I could have saved Kassandra and Mordock."

"Have you not heard me?" she said, reprimanding him. "Are you a god to take these matters completely into your own hands? You must allow the Elven nation to come into its own. You cannot be in all places at all times. They need to learn to fend for themselves. Do you know who I am?" she continued.

"Yes, you're Nan."

"What else?" she chimed.

"Well... you're a Faerie creature."

"Is that all you have understood?"

He thought. "...*acrch*, you're the *acrch*. The stone in my knife or, the magic within the stone.... I think."

"What is the *acrch*?"

"...the Elven symbol of Life and Health."

"The symbol is but a symbol. I *am* Life and Health, Jerhad. It was I who rescued you from the harm that you sustained at Moreau's Ford. It was I who kept Andreanna alive until Morlah could get her to the Healers...."

"Why didn't *you* heal her?" interrupted Jerhad

"Think. I was contained in the pouch. I was not in my rightful place on *Gildar*. Both of these limited me and what I could do. I also was limited in that there was none to wield my power; that is there were none who knew how. Now is the time that you must learn this. The magic is not in the knife only, but within you, as much a part of you as is your heart and mind. You alone among the Elves have the full magnitude of the power of *acrch* within.

"Now listen! As I have said, it is not yours to have power over the lives of all your people. Will the Prince spend his courses at bedsides, healing the sick and dying? Will you raise the dead on battle fields where you were not present to prevent death?"

"But if I have the power, shouldn't I use it. Look at all the wounded!" the Elf insistently persisted.

"Listen!" she demanded. The sound of her voice changed from a tinkling to that of a bell containing a tone of irritation. "It does not belong to you! Let the magic guide you. It will lead you and let you know when it is time to use it and how to use it. In *your* mind and from your perspective, *you* would never allow one single person to ever die. That is not natural. Death must exist as well as birth."

"But if it is so, the Elves will hate me if I let their fathers and sons die out there. If I could have saved them or healed them and I don't, I'll be some kind of monster to them, like Daektoch."

"No! It is not so. The Elves have magic, though dormant. They understand what is right and what is wrong. They understand life and death. The magic will guide them. Look how they've rallied to you and your call to arms; it is the magic. Everything else will work itself out if you only let it and not force your hand. I know that this is difficult for you. Trust me. Trust the magic. All will be well.

"But now, there is a different matter at hand. This land is not that of Giants; BondBreaker died in this land and it has been a great battle for him to complete the Final Journey, being so far from his Homeland. The land and forces of their Homeland are suited for them, and Giants send their dead off with great zeal, which also helps them in the Final Journey. If not for the presence of his brothers and sisters here, he would have only made it as far as the Netherworld. That would have been a tragedy and an evil end for such a noble spirit. BondBreaker's death has upset the balance of much in this land in relationship to such things. It wasn't meant that Giants should die here.

"Therefore, tonight you must use me, *acrch*, to give the two wounded Giants their lives back, for they're about to die. This must not happen! That two more Giants should die in this land *must not* come to pass! Go to them. Trust your instincts. I will not speak to you more of this matter, but I'll be with you. You must seek the path on your own. As it is not yours to hold all power over the Elves, so it is not mine to control matters that are yours. Go!" She vanished.

Fire and demons! Only a moon's cycle ago, life had been so simple. Now, it seemed to spiral down into the depths of complexity; his whole world was turned upside down. Silently, he rose and went to where the wounded were laid.

DiamondHeart and Tahmat sat with the two wounded Giants. A large tent had been erected because they could not get the two into the barracks; a fire burned nearby to help keep them warm. The thick, heavy smell of blood and sweat mingled with the odor of cedar smoke from the fire. Jerhad spoke to the watching Giants in a soft voice for a while, and then turned to look at Mordock. A large blood-soaked bandage was wrapped about his neck, his color pasty white, and his skin cold and moist. He did not respond to voice or touch. Mordock's breathing was labored, and occasionally, a grunt broke from his throat, as if his dreams were troubled. Kassandra had dried blood around her nose and ears; she did not look any better. Her breaths were shallow and few. Her face was bluish and her skin mottled.

Jerhad almost broke down and cried. Then suddenly he knew, he understood. "You must trust me. You know that

I honor and love these two great hearts. You must trust me if I am to help them," he spoke to DiamondHeart and Tahmat.

They both nodded. "Yes, Prince of the Elves. We trust you. Do what you must if you are to help them, if you can help them."

"Remove the dressing from Mordock's neck."

They did as was requested as he drew his Elven blade, Ember in the Common Tongue, for as Morlah had prophesied, *it was to kindle the fire that would restore the Elves to their heritage*; he knelt next to Mordock's head. He glanced at the two Giants watching him, afraid of what they might do. They nodded as to encourage him to continue. Using Ember, he reopened the still-oozing wound in Mordock's neck. Dark stagnant blood gushed forth, spattering Jerhad's clothes.

DiamondHeart gasped and started to rise, but Tahmat put his hand on the other's shoulder and, with a resounding thump, sat him back down. The purplish blood poured freely from the wound as Jerhad slipped Ember's full-blade's length into it. Again, DiamondHeart gasped, his hands involuntarily moving forward, but with a great effort, restrained himself as enormous tears flowed down his face, distress etched upon it.

Jerhad reached within himself and touched the magic of *acrch*; it felt as a warm magic. He felt it, Life and Health, and it filled him with a sense of well-being. He breathed *Life*! It coursed through him in might! He wanted to shout and let the world know that he was *ALIVE*!, but he contained himself. The scent of sweet Jasmine replaced the smell of death within the tent. The Giants saw the change in him, for he glowed with the silver-white light of the Elfstone. Ember glowed with Faerie magic. The silver-white stone in *Gildar's* handle was ablaze. "I am with you, Jerhad," he thought he heard Nan's voice speaking within him. A cloud of quiet peace filled the tent.

Gildar continued to glow until, soon, Mordock himself was aglow. Then, the Giant sighed and shifted in his sleep. Color returned to his face, his skin warmed and his breathing became normal. Jerhad slowly withdrew *Gildar* over the period of a quarter span. The wound sealed itself with healing tissue as the blade crept back. Then, Jerhad fell back. Tahmat caught him.

"I must rest. I need food and water." He lay next to Mordock and went to sleep. It was one span of the moon's course before the sunrising when he awoke. He ate and drank, and then, he checked on Mordock. "He sleeps. Let him do so until he wakes on his own. He will live."

With great weariness, Jerhad turned his attention to Kassandra, but her heart beat too slowly. She was nearly dead. Jerhad hoped that he was not too late. Placing the butt of the knife handle where the *acrch* Elfstone was located, on her forehead, where she had taken the blow, he felt the bones in her massive skull move under the weight of his hand. The bone shards of her skull grated together, and blood from her ears, eyes and nose began oozing again. *Ye gods, she's hurt bad.* Her skull was shattered.

Jerhad wept. His heart ached with pain that would have broken a Giant's heart. DiamondHeart and Tahmat watched as the glow of *acrch* spread from the Elf to Kassandra, the glow of the magic becoming intense. The two Giants were driven to turn their heads to shield their eyes. Kassandra breathed what appeared to be her last breaths.

The sun rose as Dwarves and Elves gathered outside, around the tent, in silence. The tent glowed with *Life and Health*. They basked in the radiance, feeling alive and feeling respectful for what was happening within. Then, some began carrying the injured and placed them about the exterior of the tent. The glow continued one span…two…three…. Groans of pain diminished with the passing of time. Many who had been carried there by this time walked off on their own power. Finally, Jerhad collapsed next to Kassandra and slept. Outside, many who had been dying now slept peacefully. One could not be in the presence of such strength of magic and remain unaffected. Among the uninjured who stood there that course, many would go on and live to twice the normal life span for their race. A few among the more seriously wounded died peaceful, pain-free deaths.

Kassandra sighed in her sleep and rested, healed.

Morlah leaned against the rails of the *Druid Queen's* decks, staring out at Mount Bahal. His mood was sullen, even bitter. He desisted from all talk and refused to listen to all reason. Despondency seemed to lap at him like the waves at the ship's hull. He wondered what it was with him; he felt old and useless. Over six hundred cycles old, nearly two hundred of those spent in the Druid Sleep. He had been alive too long; now he longed for death.

He had not understood when Nan, the Druid Healer (the one the *acrch* named herself after) had refused to take part in the Druid Sleep any longer. Now he understood! Too many deaths had taken place over the cycles. Too many changes. Too much of everything. The land was not of a temperament for its creatures to endure such a long life. Yet, the Black Mage lived on, and while he lived, the land was in peril. Who was he, Morlah, to have appointed himself as protector of the land against the mage? Yet, nobody else had taken the job.

Then, in all stupidity and recklessness he had almost entered Bahal to challenge Daektoch. What? Was he stupid? The move had gone against all reason and sanity. If not for the Bornodald, he would have gone in to Daektoch's lair and most likely to his death. His cycles of labor would have ended in vain.

The Raven had flown in to take him away and had flown Morlah to the *Druid Queen* where he sat and brooded; thirty risings, as the Queen reckoned her own time, had gone by since then. As time did not exist in the land between that of the living and of the dead, he experienced no hunger, thirst or fatigue. He brooded the courses away.

"How long will you sulk, Druid?" mindspoke The Raven.

"As long as it damned well doest please me. Leave me alone."

The Bornodald responded with silence.

Chapter 8

Andreanna and Fonta crossed through Dwarf's Pass and up the River Rain as Jerhad slept next to the recovering female Giant. They crossed the tortuous trail that trekked behind Barrett's Fall's cascading waters and up the eastern portage; the roar of the falls and the crashing of its waters at its base were intimidating to experience from that trail. A heavy mist clung to Andreanna and Fonta as they crossed the moss-encrusted path that meandered behind the cascading waters.

Andreanna could not believe the energy Fonta had. She skipped and jumped and climbed over out-of-the-way objects. She ran ahead and then ran back.

"Don't you ever stop or get tired?" asked Andreanna.

Fonta giggled. "Ma say I got fire in m' pants. Do you got fire in your pants, Miss 'dreanna?"

"I used to, but it might have gone out," replied Andreanna with a weary sigh.

"I set fire to Ma's hat. It made smoke an' Ma was mad at me an' say if I play with fire she toast my little buns an' then me an'...."

Late during the course, with the sunsetting, they turned off the path a ways and found a large Live Oak to bed in. The pale-yellow sun peaked below the overcast, lavender cloud cover before it slipped behind the darkening horizon. Fonta scurried up the tree like a squirrel; Andreanna felt like an old woman in comparison to Fonta's endless motion and energy.

She followed up the tree. They ate and drank and found large limbs to settle down on for the night.

Andreanna woke; it was dark. Fonta was next to her.

"Shhh," said Fonta. " 'rolls."

" 'rolls?"

" 'rolls...like ones that took Ma an' Pa."

"Ah, *'rolls*," responded Andreanna with understanding. Then she heard them moving down on the trail, the sound of hundreds of feet plodding along the path. The tramping of Troll feet continued for nearly a quarter span, until finally, there was silence.

"I guess they're gone now. Why don't you go to sleep, Fonta?"

"I like sleep with you?"

"Why not?" She let Fonta climb onto her; the Gnome could not weigh more than a couple of stones. She was so tiny and fragile looking. They settled in and went back to sleep as the silver moon, from between passing clouds, stole a glance upon them from between limb and leaf.

Andreanna awoke about a half span later. Fonta was somewhere high up in the tree humming to herself. Something did not quite add up about that Gnome, but Andreanna could not put her finger on it. She was not familiar with Gnomes in this way, until now, having only known Gnomes as those who had pursued her and Jerhad to try to steal the pouch he had carried and kill them. She had never thought of them as being parents or as having children, nor had she considered them as having homes or a domestic side. She listened to Fonta's humming.

Still, she thought, *something is not quite right. Even her humming...there was something about it,* but she could not put her finger on it. She liked Fonta...a lot. *Maybe it was because she missed Kendra. Maybe she was just feeling a bit guilty. After all, she had just up and left her daughter and her mate. No warning, no explanation, just up and gone. That wasn't like her. If something was strange, it was with her.* Andreanna shifted on her branch-bed.

"You wake?" Fonta asked, her silhouette appearing on a limb above Andreanna. "Heard you being 'wake."

"Why aren't you sleeping?"

She sighed. "Ma say that t'me, *Why don't you sleep!* She say, *You never sleep!*" Then she shrugged. "Not tired."

"Well, I am – I'm going back to sleep."

Sunrising found Fonta sleeping at Andreanna's side. The verdant canopy filtered the sunlight into a soft, warm, green glow. They climbed down to the ground and ate. Soon, they were on the trail again, Fonta talking incessantly, running, skipping and climbing. They followed the River Rain on the south bank of its *northern turn*, as it was called; the south bank became the north bank of the *eastern turn* after its bend below Barrett's Fall. Andreanna had decided that this would be the easiest way to get into the Mystics and not be forever running into Trolls.

Andreanna and Fonta walked throughout the sun's course along the river, Fonta never letting up in her chatter and activity. It seemed as if the Gnome were in a competition with the water's murmurings and churnings.

"No wonder you're so small," Andreanna chided her. "You burn all your energy up talking and moving. There's nothing left to grow on."

The direction they took was usually only followed in the autumn and winter by trappers; it was a wild unsettled land. The north bank of the river here was off-limits to all. A great portion of it was that of the Land of the Gift of the

Elves to the Giants, followed by a large portion that was the east end of the Dwarves' domain. There was no trail on the south side of the river, travel normally being made by canoe, so Andreanna and Fonta walked through the deeper woods where the undercover and brush was lightest. Underfoot, conifer needles muffled the sound of their passing.

They stopped later, the sun well into the end of its pilgrimage, that course and fished the mouth of a small stream, catching several Green-gilled Trout, which they cooked and ate, wrapping what was left in leaves that would help to preserve the fish. Andreanna also dug up some roots and boiled them for future use. She had had enough provisions for a few courses, but now that she was also feeding Fonta, she would need to begin restocking earlier.

They enjoyed the quiet of the sunsetting from beneath the great oak, which they had chosen to spend the night in. Weariness slowly stole over Andreanna in the same way that the night did the sunlight.

Andreanna, trained to a Sixth Level Proficiency in Weapons by the Druids, had also studied Survival with them. One of the habits that she had acquired was that when there was no one to keep watch at night, one slept where it was more difficult to be gotten at. The Great Live Oak served well. These trees were tall and not readily climbed, and the great limbs were often sunk in on the top side, as they left the tree, making a natural hollow to sleep in. The boughs were so large that the danger of falling were next to none.

"Let's go up the tree," said Fonta, who suddenly seemed quite agitated.

"It's a bit early," said Andreanna.

"No. We go up now. Time to sleep." She pulled and tugged at Andreanna and ran back-and-forth to the tree like a dog trying to lure its master to something. Andreanna, becoming tired of the Gnome's whining, gave in.

No sooner were they in the tree, than a pack of large wolves materialized from the forest about them. Most wolves had a healthy fear of Humans and Elves, or at least a fear of longbows. Here in the wild, this pack did not seem to have such apprehensions, and apparently, all was prey to them though they were unsure of Andreanna's scent. However, Gnomes were definitely good eating! The wolves circled the tree, keeping their distance as they investigated the scents.

"Did you know those wolves were out there?" asked Andreanna, puzzled, wondering if there was a link between Fonta's agitation and the wolves' appearance.

"Time to sleep," she said. "Sleepy time. Tell me story."

Andreanna was not convinced. Still, she felt that something was not quite right about the Gnome child.

Suddenly, one wolf came in running and managed to scramble half way up to their limb, fangs bared and sharply snapping at the air between hunter and prey. Its claws scratched at the smooth bark, attempting to gain a foothold before it fell back to the ground. The wolf circled the tree at its trunk, staring up at them, its narrow, slanted eyes giving it an evil appearance.

Andreanna was shaken; she felt rusty. Back when she had been fresh in her training, this would not have bothered her. Tonight, she felt afraid! *Were her skills up to the challenge*? She felt unsure of herself, not a good sign, for self-doubt could become a debilitating weakness.

Andreanna and Fonta climbed up to a higher limb just for the psychological comfort, even if it were unlikely that the wolves could reach them. Soon, the whole pack roamed at the tree's base, sniffing where Andreanna and Fonta had sat and eaten, consuming the discards of cooked fish that they could find and eyeing their treed prey. About a half span later, it became obvious to the wolves that there was no more to be had. A large male gazed back at Andreanna and Fonta from over his shoulder. He growled a sound that invoked a paralyzing terror into Andreanna. The wolf barked once, and the pack went down to the riverbank, heading south.

Jerhad woke in his bed. What a dream! He sat up and looked out the window where he saw that it was at least one half course of the sun. He looked down and saw that he was still dressed; there was dried blood all over him. It had not been a dream.... Somehow, he had been carried to his bed without being awakened.

"Daddy, Daddy, Grammy say I can play with Kassandra tomorrow. She not sick anymore. Mordock too. Why they sleepy all the time?"

"...They're probably just tired."

"You tired? You sleepy all the time, too. Where's Mommy?"

"I.... I don't know. She said she had to go do something... somewhere."

"Did the Trolls eated her, Daddy? Jenny say the Trolls eated her."

"No, I don't think so. She just had to go somewhere."

"Ah, ye gods in the heavens, you're awake. I am so proud of you and what you've done," said Catrina, entering the room in a bustle. "Healing the Giants and all those Elves... and Dwarves too. Where did you learn all that? This magic thing must be catching, look at this. These flowers were about dead. I was talking to them and telling them why I had forgotten to water them, and then, they were all fresh, full of green leaves and flowers in bloom. Ye gods, Jerhad, what's going on? Have you ever heard of such a thing? I haven't. It's like living in a Faerie tale."

"That just might be the answer, Mother. I'm starving. Is there anything to eat?" They were interrupted at that point by a knock at the front door. It was StoneWorth. Catrina let him in, and Jerhad met him in the kitchen.

"Scout reports just in from the east, my Prince."

"Just Jerhad is fine, StoneWorth."

"Yes, my Prince Jerhad. Trolls have razed Canon, Fraise and Steill's Knoll and still are coming west. About forty thousand of them. Not moving fast, but coming steady. Their numbers grow by the span."

Jerhad dropped into a chair. More Trolls! They probably would see quite a few more before this was over. If only he could bring Daektoch to an end, then the rest would also stop. "Do Stanton and IronLeggs know?"

"Messengers have been sent to find them, Prince Jerhad."

"Alright, find them and tell them I'll meet them at the north wall gate in about one span. I'm going to eat and get washed up. I'll meet them there. Want some pie?" The smell of the, freshly-cooked, honey-sweetened berries filled the room.

"No thanks...just finished *one* myself. These wild berries that grow in the south make the best pies I ever did eat, a second great use for Mingus' ovens. Got to get going. Oh, the first row of stone on the east wall was just finished, all the way to the quarry. We will be using the wall to move the stone out of the quarry now, like using a paved road. Work is going real good."

"Thanks, StoneWorth. Are you enjoying the work?"

"Ah, it is fine stone, my Prince. Wonderful work. I have to go."

Stanton and IronLeggs were already at the north wall when Jerhad got there. DiamondHeart and Tahmat were there also, and they smiled broadly and gave Jerhad a deep bow as he approached. Chain mail squeaked on leather as the two Giants stooped.

"There you are, Elf Boy," said Stanton. "This is the plan I'm hoping you'll approve. I want to take half of the Dwarves and half of the Elven forces that are here to go meet the Trolls. The east wall isn't defendable against them, being that its still far from finished. There's no point in waiting here for them. If they overrun us in the field, they'll do it here, too. Actually, if we can get to the Break before they do, we might have a chance using it as a defensive position. That way the battle would take place away from Mildra. We could gather more troops from the villages as we go. Meanwhile, those left behind will put all their efforts into finishing the wall. What do you think?"

"You're the boss when it comes to the army. I don't have a clue. I guess it would make sense that we meet them there."

"We? You weren't coming! I was leaving you behind to help defend the town. If they get through us, the town will need you."

"No, I'm going with you. If the army marches, I'll be with it and that's that."

"So, when do we leave?" said Stanton. Jerhad was surprised that Stanton did not argue the matter any further.

"That's your decision," Jerhad said.

"First light tomorrow, then. Be there or be left behind. East side of the town, beyond the wall, that is, the wall to be."

IronLeggs and Stanton left to organize their departure. DiamondHeart and Tahmat stayed behind.

"Mordock and Kassandra are recovering well, thanks to you, little master. They have taken some broth and are speaking when awake, though they still sleep much. We have no time to make all the songs that need to be sung of the things that have happened here. But this we have time to do," Tahmat said, both Giants dropping to one knee with clenched right fists to their chests, heads bowed.

Together they said, "We pledge ourselves to your service, Jerhad Prince of the Elves. We are yours to direct in coming and going, until death take one, the other, or all. We are yours to command. This we do in payment of our debt and the debt of the Giants to you for saving the lives of Mordock and Kassandra."

"....Nooo! Don't. You can't do this. I don't want you to do this."

"It is done," stated Tahmat. "It will not be undone."

Jerhad thought for a heartbeat and sighed. "Well, if it is going to be, then, this is what you will do. You will remain behind and protect Kassandra and Mordock onto your deaths from any who would harm them while they recover. And having done that, if it is in your ability, you will help in the defense of the town. But Mordock and Kassandra first."

"It will be as you have commanded, Elven Prince."

"This 'prince' stuff is getting to be a bit much if you ask me," said Jerhad as he left and returned home to prepare for the next rising's departure.

Andreanna and Fonta had been walking throughout the course of the sun's travel.

"... an' my sister Moanat is ten cycles, an' my cousin Baratih is nine cycles, an' we play house with dolls, an' they eated honey cakes, mint tea, an' we play hide-an'-seek, an' Moanat cheats an' look when we hide. An' then she finded us but it not fair..."

Andreanna was beginning to think that the Gnome girl's parents had maybe had abandoned her out here rather than having been captured by the Trolls. Fonta had been at it for two spans without taking a breath. Just as Andreanna came up from crossing under a fallen tree, she found herself face-to-face with a pure-black wolf. Its lips curled back, and it showed her its teeth.

"...an' Ma say that if she look when we play hide-an'-seek that..." Andreanna dug her fingers into Fonta's shoulder, who was about to walk straight into the wolf. She pushed Fonta to the side bringing up her three-quarter staff whirling, cracking the wolf on the head. The wolf whined, turned and ran. The other wolves circled about. Andreanna backed herself and Fonta against a group of small alders that grew too thickly together for the wolves to come through; it provided a good back guard.

The wolves took to their hunting tactics, one trying to draw Andreanna off as another came in from another direction. Andreanna was scared, but soon found that the situation was manageable, since the wolves had no weapons but their teeth. Frightening rumbles erupted from the wolves' throats. Fangs lashed out threateningly. She would pretend to be drawn in one direction and usually got a good solid blow to the one attacking in from the opposite side. She tried not to hurt them seriously, only enough to discourage them.

Only problem was that they were not discouraging and soon doubled their effort.

Becoming a bit more desperate and deciding it was time to put a stop to this situation, Andreanna grew more intent. She was beginning to tire, her stamina not what it had once been, even though it had been seven cycles since her experience with Daektoch. It was time to end this.

A brindled male feigned an attack and got thumped in the ribs, which cracked loudly. The wolf cried a high-pitched whine and desperately stumbled away. The one coming up behind received the staff butt to its forehead with a loud crack and crumpled to the ground. The remainder of the pack gathered together, their demeanor changing from that of hunters to that of pure aggressors. This was their territory, and they were not about to be manhandled by any trespasser. They closed in as a group, the hair on their backs standing, lips snarling, fangs flashing. The sound was terrifying.

"No! No! No hunting! Hold on. Stop!" carried a man's voice from the distance. The wolves looked up in the direction that the voice had come from, holding their ground. A young, bearded man with jet-black hair frantically came tumbling through the woods. His clothes were all of buckskin, and his hat was a fur pelt with mummified eyes, ears and nose on the front, appearing like some kind of mounted badge. He was a handsome man who obviously lived without female influence. The odor about him was of acrid animal fat and of clothes too long worn.

"Hold on, don't hurt them, please. They don't know any better. Alright, guys, back down. Down! Back!" he commanded. "Fland, my name is Fland." The wolves took on a submissive posture, tucking their ears and tails down, as he walked among them. A couple of what appeared to be younger wolves danced about him looking for approval, yipping their greetings. "I'm so sorry," he said to Andreanna. "Are you hurt?"

"No.... Just a bit frightened by the whole experience. Who are you?"

"I'm Fland, son of Nathaniel, son of Joyboch. I live out here. My cabin is up the ridge, to the left, there," he said, pointing into the forest and going down on both knees to check the unconscious wolf that seemed to be waking. "I didn't know you were about. It's all my fault; I sent them out to hunt. They really don't know the difference."

"You sent them out to hunt?"

"Yes, they live with me. I raised the black female and the gray male from pups. Bear killed the mother and the rest of the litter. These others are their pups. They usually wait until I give them the 'hunt' command before they go out. I had to teach them how to hunt; it wasn't easy. Who's your friend?" he said as Fonta finally peaked out from behind Andreanna.

"This is Fonta. I found her in the forest. I think the Trolls got her parents. I'm Andreanna."

"What are you doing in this forest? It can be dangerous out here."

"No more dangerous than the trails where the Trolls are moving. The Trolls are all over the place in these times. They're a lot of trouble too. Me...well I was just taking Fonta, here, back to the Gnomes," she half lied.

"Would you to like to come up to my cabin and have evening meat with me? You could stay the night if you like...," he said as the wolf that had been unconscious tried its legs.

"...ah.... I don't know. We have a long way to go."

"Oh, come on. It will be dark soon."

"We'll come for a while," she said, somehow afraid to go and afraid not to. Something ate at her, not to mention hearing Stanton reproving her somewhere in the recesses of her mind. Come or go, she was not feeling quite safe. Even less safe now that there was a *Human* involved. Fonta was silent and stayed behind her. They followed Fland up to his cabin, the wolves now behaving like pups around him, running and playing, while the one she had cracked in the head seemed none the worse for wear.

They arrived at the cabin a while later, a small log structure, well constructed with a hand-hewn-shake roof. There was no glass in the windows, only reed weavings to cover them over. A small stone hearth stood in the center of the rear wall. A couple of logs were set about, used as seats and a crude table made of lashed poles was set in the middle of the room. In one corner, on the floor, was a palette covered with reeds and some animal skins. The odor of the wolves and the unkempt Human male mingled in with the lingering wood smoke that clung to the structure's interior. Fland was quite talkative, though he was rambling, saying nothing. He also appeared to be growing increasingly nervous.

Not having been there but a quarter span, Andreanna suddenly stood. "We really should be going. We have a lot of travel to do and...I wouldn't want to have to...hurt you."

Fland stopped his chatter and looked up at her. She realized that she had not noticed how wolf-like his eyes were; they grew narrower. He lunged for the door, and having slammed it shut, he bolted it. All pretenses fell away. He removed his outer layer of clothes and stepped toward her, as the wolves outside suddenly became restless, whining and scratching at the door. How many had there been? Six? Eight?

"Get behind me Fonta," Andreanna whispered, her mouth and throat suddenly dry. She did not know if she was safer in here or outside. Outside it was just the wolves. Inside, there was Fland! She had her three-quarter staff whirling in front of her now; Fland grew cautious. He was easily twice her size.

"Please don't, Fland. I don't want to hurt you, but I will if I have to." *Ye gods, even his grin looks wolfish. Am I dreaming all this*? She hoped she was but knew it was not so.

Fland tested her with a few feigned attacks, but Andreanna did not respond, remaining on her guard. They circled each other, going around the table. Fland was being quite cautious, not knowing if she could or would use the staff or how he could get around it. As he came back around by the door, he picked up his own staff, which leaned in the corner. She observed that he held it like a novice. Twice he lunged at her without eliciting a response; she never broke eye contact, her staff whirring.

Suddenly he made his move. Thwack! Thwack! The blows to the sides of his head resounded. He fell back with a clatter, wide-eyed.

"That was your first and last warning, Fland. Stop this, or I'll have to hurt you."

He was coming to the door again, as they continued circling the table. He unbolted it and opened it wide. The wolves stood looking in; they were in an excited state. Fland pointed to her. "Hunt!" he commanded them. The wolves were frantic and confused, pacing about and going in and out of the doorway, whining continuously. "Hunt!" Fland repeated with increased authority in his voice. The two wolves, she had hurt earlier, hung back while a couple of others bared their teeth, a deep, frightening rumble erupting from their throats.

Then, everything about Andreanna's training finally came back to her. The whole scene slowed. Her adrenaline kicked in. In one quick move, she spun around, setting Fonta onto the windowsill, and instantly faced her attackers again. One wolf had thought to take advantage of her offering her back; he ran straight into the three-quarter staff, meeting with it square between his eyes and crumpling to the floor, blood flowing through his nose. The sound of the cracking bones made Andreanna's skin crawl. The wolf lay still as its tongue slowly sagged to the floor.

And then, somewhere deep within her, the Elven magic of *licri* awakened. Everything slowed down about her even more, to the point that her adversaries appeared almost motionless. Stepping forward so easily and what seemed ever so slowly, she brought the three-quarter staff about to meet two more wolves' skulls, collapsing them like eggshells with a crunch. She stepped back and saw the anger in the Fland's eyes. His eyes showed that he would not be reasoned with. He breathed with a grunting, growling sound.

"Please stop this," she begged.

"Oh, I'll stop it all right," he snarled. "Hunt!" He lunged at her, leaving his staff behind. The move that ended his life was quick, as the staff met him as it had the wolves. A dull crack resounded as his skull broke. She stepped to the side and let his dead body tumble to the floor and up against the wall with a muffled thud. Three more wolves met the same fate. The two she had hurt earlier stood in the doorway with ears down and tales between their legs. They whined with a piercing intensity and postured submissively.

"Bad man! Bad doggies," whispered Fonta.

The female skulked over to Andreanna, squatted and peed; then, she rolled over and exposed her throat and belly. "Alright, baby. I won't hurt you." But then in wolfish fashion, she reached down and took the female at the throat, clamping down, pinning her to the floor. The she-wolf did not flinch. Andreanna went down nose to nose with her and gave the most convincing growl she could muster. The she-wolf licked at her face, trying to appease her. Andreanna let up and stood. The she-wolf got up and danced around her legs. The other wolf cowered in the doorway. Andreanna dropped to her knees and wept. She mourned having had to kill the wolves. Fland had made his own bed. He could lie in it. Yet, it made her close to being sick at the thought of having killed a Human, and guilt consumed her. She suspected the whole thing had been a set up from the very start. It had been a long time since she had been so scared, since she had... killed...a man.... The she-wolf continued her dance of submission, licking at her. Andreanna was quite shaken now that it was all over.

"It's alright, baby," said Andreanna, petting her. "Easy." The young male cowered and then crept up to her, peeing himself and whining. She petted him also. "You're okay, boy. You're alright," she repeated.

Fonta sat on the windowsill. "Nice doggies. 'dreanna didn't have hurt you. Other doggies bad. Man bad. Ma tell me stay away from bad man. She say, *bad man hurt Fonta*. 'dreanna hurt bad man an' doggies. Fonta had a doggy, but Moor Cat eated him. Moor Cats bad. 'dreanna ever see Moor Cat? They big cat. Not nice."

"Come, Fonta. Let's get out of here."

She lit some branches, with her flint and stone, on the first step of the cabin and then added dried wood until she had a blaze going. The fire crackled and spat as it began licking up the walls and around the doorframe. It was some kind of burial she was performing, but she did not really know for what, who or why. They turned and left as the cabin became engulfed in flames. The smoke seemed to follow the group, carrying the stench of burning hair and flesh. "Baby" and "Boy" followed.

Chapter 9

Morlah sat on a coil of rope by the rail on the deck of the *Druid Queen,* where he had been sulking for twenty courses of the sun.

"Haven't you brooded long enough, Human?" mindspoke The Raven to him. "You've been at this for three spans of time as counted by your kind in the land of the living."

"What?"

"You heard. Three spans is long enough a sulk." Time on the *Druid Queen* was whatever the captain wanted it to be in relation to time in the land of the living. The dead knew no time. One could be on board (if he could protect himself from the terror that the presence of the dead brought to the living) one course and come back to the land of the living to find that one thousand cycles had passed or vice versa, whatever the captain chose.

This time the captain thought it best to let Morlah enjoy a good long bout of self-pity and moodiness without having him waste time in the land where he belonged. Finally, the captain approached Morlah.

"Get off my ship, thou lazy landlubber," spat the captain with the eerie hollow voice he spoke with, as if speaking from a distance, from the land of the dead. Thou doest sit about thinking thou willst get free grub and not work? Thou willst walk the plank first!"

"Captain," said Morlah, not playing to the "nasty captain" routine, perhaps not even noting it. "I have felt like an old man lately and perhaps a bit useless. For all mine efforts, Daektoch is still at-large."

"What, art thou a god, landlubber brother of mine? That thou shouldst have the upper hand in all matters among the living and the dead?"

Morlah stopped and thought; then he said, "Thou art a wise man, Captain. Yes, there art things that art outside of my control.... I never thought I wouldst say this, but I mayst withhold from the Druid Sleep in the future and make the Final Journey. Methinks that six or seven hundred cycles is long enough a lifetime for one who doest not bear a Giant's heart."

The Elves and Dwarves moved eastward out of Mildra; one half of their force would stay behind for defense. They marched out in ordered columns just after the sunrising. The sound of armed males treading together in step echoed in the short village street. Stanton, Jerhad and IronLeggs rode three of the few available horses.

Stanton longed to have cavalry. Infantry was just too vulnerable to face a full force frontal attack by the Trolls. The archers were actually more valuable than the infantry armed with the modified pikes and lances. Their fighting would be mostly defensive, allowing the Trolls to impale themselves as they charged. *Ah, but for five hundred horses and experienced riders!*

Jerhad rode a small red mare. He was not a very good rider, so he chose a smaller, less spirited horse for himself, traveling alongside of Stanton, behind the first company of Dwarf infantry that led the march. The gray overcast skies reflected the mood of the army and community. Trolls were a formidable foe; many of the troops would not be returning home. The remainder of the Elves were out to see the two armies depart. Watching in sober silence as the ranks marched eastwardly, many wept without sound, mouths open, sorrow upon their faces. Jerhad saw Catrina with Kendra and waved good-bye. Catrina's face was pale and her countenance disheartened. Kendra cried.

Stanton pushed the march at a steady and swift pace; he wanted to quickly cover the distance to Land's Break. They would push the march until two spans after the sunsetting, only stopping long enough for the men to drink and eat a few morsels before going to sleep. Two spans before sunrising, they broke camp and moved on.

The goal was Land's Break, a geological rupture in the plain that went from within the Coastal Range of mountains to the cliffs overlooking the sea. The land appeared to have been heaved up, forming a sheer and jagged cliff in what once had been an uninterrupted, flat prairie. The eastern flats were the low side, and the west stood some ten paces above the lower grasslands. It was as good a natural defensive position as could be hoped for. The militia hoped to get there ahead of the Trolls and wait them out. Onward they marched.

Travel was becoming more and more difficult as Andreanna and Fonta went along the River Rain. The mountains were rising steeper along the river, turning what had been a valley into a gorge; they would soon have to leave the turbulent, rushing river. They had long ago gone past the Gift and the Dwarves' lands and were now moving into the southern Mystics, not encountering anyone since Fland. The forest was dense with Red Cedars dotting the riverside.

But as the gorge narrowed, the trees became fewer and smaller. The waters churned more violently. The two wolves, which ended up keeping the names *Baby* and *Boy,* followed. It appeared that Andreanna had replaced Fland as their alpha. Fonta continued talking, running and jumping; Andreanna wearied.

It was midcourse of the sun when the time came that Andreanna and Fonta could go no further along the foaming river, for the walls of the gorge ahead of them now rose straight up from the dark water, swift, cold, and deep. Going up the side to the top of the mountain was a deep fissure in the stone wall. Andreanna was about to have Fonta climb onto her back to be carried when the Gnome girl scurried into the crack and ran up the mountainside. Andreanna and the wolves followed. It was almost sunsetting by the time they emerged onto the plateau, which ran a few leagues along the river. The sun's sinking orb resembled the orange citrus fruit from Northern Canterhort. They stopped for the night, finding a White Pine to climb and sleep in.

Andreanna cut some branches and wove them together, making a platform they could sleep on. After almost a quarter span of whining, the wolves gave up trying to convince Andreanna to come back down and left to go hunt for themselves.

Andreanna was sore when she woke the next rising; the climb up the mountain had proven a lot more trying than she had anticipated. She went back to sleep. Fonta, further up the tree, was talking to herself. It was two spans past the rising when Andreanna woke again. She had not slept that late in ages. Fonta was still up above, presumably asleep..

Suddenly, the tree began shaking as if it would be uprooted. Dry pine needles fell in a shower. The great tree rocked perilously, and its branches swayed forcefully. At first, Andreanna thought it was an earthquake, but she quickly noticed that other nearby trees were not moving. The platform she was on fell apart. She dropped into some large bushes, which cushioned her fall.

There at the base of the tree was a Troll. Not a Cave Troll. That much she knew. He was immense and naked. Taller than a Cave Troll by three or four heads, almost as big as a Giant, with large round eyes spaced too far apart on his square, flat face, he had large nostrils gaping from a flat nose that snuffed at the air.

The Troll shook the tree as if he would tear it down, roots and all. His skin was a stone-gray color; his arms would have hung down to his knees if he had stopped shaking the tree for a few heartbeats. His posture, when he paused, was stooped, like one of the great apes from a far away land she had once seen in a drawing. His body was covered with a coarse gray hair that did not grow nearly thick enough to cover his hide. He reeked of musk like a Billy Goat in rut.

The Troll's large head turned in her direction as Andreanna fell into the bushes. Cavernous nostrils sniffed for her scent. He turned and came after her, surprisingly fast for his size. Andreanna managed to roll across the branches of her dismantled platform and onto her feet. She found her three-quarter staff and moved away. Was it possible to even hurt something this big and ugly? Somehow, she had always thought that the uglier an opponent was, the less pain it would feel.

This one definitely would feel no pain!

His long hairy limbs reached for her. Ducking, she rolled away coming up alongside of him and gave him a solid jab to the ribs with her staff. The strike thudded dully. The large head turned and looked at her. His long hairy arm came about in a back swing. It would have crushed her if she had not tumbled away. Up in the tree, Fonta continued talking and singing. Andreanna rolled away again. Quickly, she climbed a large boulder and jabbed the Troll at the base of the skull from behind. It twisted, shuffling its weight back and forth, foot-to-foot, turning toward her. As it found her, she jumped straight into its face, smacking it right between the eyes with her staff. She pushed off with her feet and somersaulted back behind the rock, which shook as a massive fist slammed down onto where she had just stood. The Troll, a Mountain Troll, moved the boulder out of the way with a sweep of his hand, apparently uninjured by her effort. The ground trembled as the boulder rolled away.

What the heck does this creature want with me?

Mountain Trolls were a rare breed of Troll that lived in the mountains throughout Frontmire. They were, fortunately, rarely encountered by anyone. Having a strong territorial instinct, they viewed all visitors in their terrain as a threat to their domain. They simply killed and ate them. They were only seen in groups during mating which took place every ten cycles. The males fought for the females. It was said that the mountains shook during this season. Otherwise, they were solitary creatures.

Andreanna was at a loss. She could have easily outrun the Troll, but Fonta was still in the tree. Unable to hurt it with her staff and loathe to attack it with her shortsword or to try to kill it, her mind raced, trying to figure out what to do. Deciding to lead it away, circle back and retrieve Fonta, she called out to Fonta and told her to stay put, that she would be back for her. Andreanna led the Troll along the ridge for a span. The Troll was eager to pursue her, and he followed with a chatter of excited grunts, throaty murmurs and eager croaks. Having left him behind, she made a run for it and quickly outdistanced him. She went south a few hundred paces and then turned east and made here way back through the brambles. The travel here became slower. Finally, she arrived where she had left Fonta.

The Troll was there, shaking the tree!

Andreanna hollered at it to get its attention, also venting frustration. The Troll stopped shaking the pine. It turned toward her with a lumbering gait. Within her, the magic of *licri* began to glow. Not really thinking of what she was doing, she ran to the Troll, slipped beneath its grasp and placed one shoulder against its leg. She pushed. Nothing happened. She reached deeper within herself and into the magic and pushed again. This time the Troll toppled over, crying out in surprise as it fell to the ground, with a loud snapping of a cluster of alders. Before it could recover itself, she pulled her shortsword and, with the flat of the blade, thwacked him on the shin and stepped back. The Troll screamed with rage, flailing his arms and legs. Then, just as he began to rise, she rushed in and repeated the blow. Again, the Troll raged, blade-sized welts appearing on its leg. Over and over, the process went on until finally she allowed the Troll to get up. He looked down at what was now one large welt over the entire front of his shin. He took a step toward her and limped; he stepped another step and stopped. The Troll whimpered like a small dog.

"Well, big boy, had enough?" she called. The Troll looked somewhat subdued. She raised her sword into the air and waved it about. The Troll raised his arms in a defensive posture. He whined.

"Go on, get moving," she called out to him as she began walking toward him. The Troll turned and limped away, mournful cries of pain and defeat erupting from his throat.

Poor boy, she thought, *he is sort of cute.*

Andreanna was exuberant; she had managed to get rid of the Troll without killing it. Then, she realized what had happened, how the magic within her had taken over allowing her to perform an unbelievable feat, startling her. She had overnight gone from being a mere Human with an Elven ancestry to being more like an Elf with a Human ancestry. She had Elven magic! She had Earthen power that responded to her need and will! Only a short quarter-moon's cycle past, she would not have believed it.

"Fonta, are you up there?" she called up into the pine tree.

There was a rustling of branches above. Bits and fragments of bark fell, and then, a tiny face peered out from the branches. "Bad 'roll gone?"

"He's gone. I don't think he'll bother us anymore. Let's get going." Just then, Baby and Boy returned from their hunt. They must have been successful, for their bellies were bulging and firm.

Suddenly, they were surrounded by a band of very small, leathery looking Gnomes; they were as small as Fonta. One heartbeat the clearing had been empty. The next heartbeat, it was as if the brush had spit a horde of Gnomes into the opening. They all wore loin clothes and carried short spears. Though tiny in stature, they appeared quite fearsome.

"Now what!" sighed Andreanna.

One Gnome came forward, speaking in its native tongue, of which Andreanna understood nothing.

She shrugged.

The Gnomes went back-and-forth, urging her to follow them.

"Fonta, do you understand them?" Fonta remained silent, hiding behind Andreanna's legs.

The wolves bared their teeth and growled, so Andreanna took hold of them by the scruff of the neck, forcing them to quiet down. The Gnome became frantic in whatever he wanted to communicate and finally gave orders to the others who then, with their spears, prodded Andreanna to move and follow them. The wolves stayed close to her, growling.

These were Mountain Gnomes; they were smaller than the Forest Gnomes of the eastern Mystic Mountains, about half the size of an adult Forest Gnome, not much bigger than Fonta. Living deep in the mountains, these were rarely encountered. Though related, the two had no dealings with each other. Their leathery, tallow skin was wrapped tightly about their deceptively-frail-appearing frames, yet it was deeply wrinkled and creviced. Unlike Mountain Trolls, they were hairless. They led her on through the dense forest.

Andreanna did not know what to do. She did not want to hurt them, for that would have been like fighting children. She would go along for now, since their direction took her deeper north into the Mystics, and would await her chance to get away. The march went on for spans without a break.

Finally, just before sunsetting, they arrived at the Gnomes' village, one hundred to one hundred fifty in population. The village was a series of tunnels and caves perched high in the face of the cliffs. The leader blew a high-pitched whistling from a reed pipe when they arrived at the base of the cliffs, and a rope ladder made of braided vines with rungs fabricated of branches was dropped down to them. A large basket woven of small branches was lowered also. The leader motioned to Andreanna to put the wolves in the basket.

This took a fair amount of persuasion. After a few sessions of having the wolves pee, indicating their submission but not necessarily willingness or obedience, they were finally were all on their way up to the main camp. Up the steep cliffs they went, with the creaking of straining hemp rope, the wolves in the basket and Andreanna and the Gnomes on the rope ladder.

Once at the top of the cliff, they went along a large tunnel, though Andreanna did have to crouch to get through. The tunnel ended in a huge space, open to the dark starry sky, which seemed to be the center of community activity. A Gnome dressed in a multicolored garment made of brightly-dyed reeds met them. The leader of Andreanna's captors went forward and spoke, hands and arms flailing about, voice squeaking, and gesturing toward Andreanna.

The red-blue-yellow-and-green-garmented Gnome grunted orders, and the others ran about excitedly. Before long, a group came out with a large lashed-pole palanquin, ornamented with similar-colored-reed weavings and flowers. Andreanna was convinced, at spear point, to sit in it. Fonta clung to her tightly. The wolves sat one on each hand, looking about nervously. Food and drink were brought out and laid on a long table.. Drums beat with a deep resounding, and a rhythmic, mesmerizing dance began.

It was obviously a feast of some kind, although Andreanna could not imagine of what, knowing nothing about these Gnomes. The females served roasted meats and herbal mixes with rooty-tasting sauces to her. She was offered a clay bowl of honeyed, mashed fruit to drink. Fonta ate and drank of Andreanna's provisions. The wolves devoured some kind of raw meat on bones, which they guarded greedily. The feast continued into the night, and then just at the rising, Andreanna was led to a small cavern chamber containing a reed hammock. Lying with Fonta on her and the wolves beneath the hammock, she went to sleep.

It was half course of the sun when she woke, a large group of Gnomes stood outside of the cave staring in.

Her head ached and the sunlight hurt her eyes. She let her head fall back onto her bed, her thoughts swimming with a short-lived confusion. The Gnomes fell back when they saw she was awake, and then, a lone female bearing food and drink entered. The Gnome resembled a somewhat poorly crafted doll made of burlap and straw. She was knee-high to Andreanna, and her eyes were dark, revealing an intelligence above that of animals.

"... you... wake, O Great Queen... brought food... for you eat."

"Oh good, someone who speaks the Common Tongue. What's going on? Why was I brought here? What's your name?" The Gnome backed away, overwhelmed with Andreanna's verbal onslaught.

"No.... No speak good," she said with dismay.

Andreanna slowed herself. "Alright...name. What's your name?" she spoke, loudly and slowly.

"...yes...name.... Name Pentka, Great Queen."

Great Queen? Andreanna could make out the beginning of a problem. "Pentka, why was I brought here?"

"Here? Gnome home..., Great Queen. Like prophesy. Great Queen with Wolves. Slayer of Mountain Troll."

"Ah, I see. Now what are we going to do?"

"...do? ... Great Queen no know?" Pentka asked, now puzzled. "Great Queen live with Gnomes.... Defender.... Ruler.... Queen. Queen who rule with wolf. Protect from wolves that eat Gnomes."

Fire and demons, what was she going to do now? "How is it you know the Common Tongue?"

"Pentka...catched by man. Keep as toy for children." At which she spat to the ground in hatred. "Pentka undo chain...run home."

Queen? How had she got herself into this mess? They must have seen her deal with the Troll. She had to find a way out. "Pentka, listen, I'm not a queen. Not queen for the Gnomes. Not queen of any kind. I did not slay the Troll. I just ran him off.... And the wolves well, how the heck do I explain the wolves?" she acquiesced.

Pentka gasped! "Not queen? ...No say that.... Great Queen scare Pentka. Gnomes killed Pentka if say not Queen."

"Horse poop!"

"Horse...poop?"

"Nothing. Forget it. I guess I can be queen for a while. What a mess!"

Andreanna remained under guard in the cave throughout the course of the sun. It did not seem to be a problem for the Gnomes to have a queen and to keep her prisoner at the same time. The wolves were restless. Fonta had gone out to play with the Gnome children. When evening came, the Gnomes brought Andreanna out to the 'throne' again, and they prepared to feast and dance throughout the night. Come dawn, she was returned to her cave.

Course after course, the scenario replayed itself, the Gnomes celebrating the capture of their queen, Andreanna not daring an escape lest she end up killing some of them. But she could not stay here forever, playing token monarch. She rarely saw Fonta anymore, who spent her time playing. It was during the night of the tenth course of the sun that she had been there, that she dreamed of Gnomes and Faeries.

During the dream, one Faerie approached and spoke with her. It was *too much* like the dream she had had when she had lain dying from Daektoch's abuse, and the Faerie *acrch* had come to her. This Faerie appeared as if she were lit by a crimson sunset within her though her skin was a vibrant purple color. She was as small as Fonta. Her hair was pitch-black. Unlike *acrch, igini's* voice harmoniously resonated as with the sound of strumming lute chords.

"Andreanna, I am ***igini****, for your purposes, in your tongue you may call me Manna," spoke the Faerie. "I am also known as* ***Harmony****, at least that is the effect of my presence and power. The Gnomes here are a very religious people. Throughout their history, they have had their mystics and prophets. Do not allow their size to deceive you. They are intelligent, and they are strong.*

"In their prophecies, it was spoken many hundreds of cycles past, that a Queen would arise from among the Elves to rule the Gnomes. Though not appearing as an Elf, she would be known by the Gnome child and two wolves that she traveled with. Through her, the Gnomes would find safety and peace to live in the mountains and bring to an end the predation of wolves upon them."

"I'm not a queen, I don't belong to the Gnomes, and I need to get to the Faeries in the Mystics so I can go home and get on with my life. I have a daughter and a mate who doesn't know where I am, and I'm being held prisoner here! So butt out, Faerie Manna."

"This I understand, Andreanna, but please be patient. Tomorrow, the chief of the Gnomes will present you with a stone, a brown stone. Accept it graciously and keep it with you always. It is an Elfstone of magic. He will also give you a metal pin; it is a key. Guard it safely."

From there, her dreaming deteriorated into a nonsense of dancing Faeries, Gnomes, and Elves. Trolls leered from the forests about them, licking their lips, drooling in hunger, and her wolves, now the size of oxen, sat at her side. Daektoch's laughter could be heard echoing in the distance.

Soaked in sweat Andreanna sat up, awakened from her dream. The Gnome guards, ever vigilant, stood in the mid morning light, stationed at the cave's entrance. The early course was cool and silent. Baby and Boy slept beneath the hammock. Baby woke from sleep and looked up at the Human.

"It's alright, Baby, go back to sleep." She petted the wolf's head and scratched its uplifted chin. *What a person in distress will dream! But, that had been way too much like the Nan dream. Way too real*!

The dream brought back memories of the ordeal she had undergone as Daektoch's captive back in the castle in Heros, which had almost resulted in her death. Jerhad, Stanton, Morlah, and Raven the Bornodald with his new set of wings and some Dwarves had rescued her. She still felt the taint of the Black Mage's touch. Though Morlah with the help of the Druid, Master Filinhoff, had removed the death-spell from her, she still felt tainted, though she never mentioned it to anyone. Jerhad had worried himself into Troll blains over her, and she just could not bring herself to tell him about this lest he fret more.

After her rescue, subsequent events had turned things into one of the best times of her life. She had gone to Mildra and lived with Jerhad's family; his mother, true to her word, had kicked Jerhad out of his room and sent him to live with his cousins, and Andreanna had moved in. Catrina had nurtured Andreanna with love, care and wholesome food and had brought her back to health. Jerhad's love and devotion had helped heal her spirit. Within that sun's cycle, they had wed.

Andreanna had feared that the Elves of the community would frown upon bringing a Human in; but her fears were pointless and unfounded. The Elves were only too eager to embrace her as part of their population. It was an added benefit to find out that she was part Elf, descendant of King

Windemere, though it did not show in her features, except perhaps a little in her almond-shaped eyes. She lay down and returned to sleep.

Andreanna slept again and later awoke to the sound of drums, the hot sun barely breaking the midcourse mark. The group of female Gnomes that attended to her came to retrieve her from the cave. Usually, the Gnomes did not do this until evening. Baby and Boy followed. Andreanna was dressed in a long robe of dyed-woven reeds. Upon her head was placed a large majestic headdress that was adorned with long blue feathers and a variety of wild flowers. She was set up on her throne; it always exasperated her. It was going to be a long course of the sun!

The feasting and dancing went on throughout the sun's course. She was fed and given fermented red berry juice to drink; it was wonderfully sweet with a sharp bite of alcohol in the aftertaste. The wolves were given several rabbit carcasses, which they devoured. Fonta was nowhere to be seen. At sunsetting, the drums and dancing suddenly stopped. A procession of Gnomes dressed in dyed-woven reeds came out of a cave in all the formality and elegance that they could muster. Everyone stood silent as the procession approached Andreanna. Andreanna was convinced to a stand by the butt of a spear poking through the back of her throne. The chief came forward and spoke....

...*Gibberish*. He went on long and waxed eloquently, speaking to her and the tribe in his thin squeaky voice.

Andreanna fidgeted.

Then, from a pouch, he pulled out a string of woven Troll hair that bore a brown stone, the stone from her dream.

Oh, this was way too much!

The chief, holding the stone up for all to see, continued his discourse for nearly another span and then, *at long last*, stopped. Stepping forward, standing on a lashed-pole platform to get him up to her height, he presented the stone to Andreanna. He placed it about her neck.

"*...toba ominaltta cantonick balasta* to take, to keep, to guard to the end of your courses. I present to you the Stone of Magic, my Queen." Then he placed about her neck another string, holding a metal pin. "... the Key of the Power of Knowledge."

"What did you say?"

The chief looked at her and cocked his head, somewhat puzzled. "From the beginning or just the last phrase?"

"Never mind. How is it you suddenly speak the Common Tongue?"

"But surely, my Queen, you know I have never known or spoken any language but that of the Gnomes. Do you jest with me, my Queen?"

It couldn't be! Had the dream been real? She removed the necklace to look at the stone. The chief's words turned to an outcry of gibberish. She quickly returned the stone to her neck.

"...and must never be removed in the presence of your people, my Queen. It is sacrilegious!"

The stone must be magic, an Elfstone! How was it that just when she finally thought she had most things in life figured out, that her world had to be turned upside down? She now possessed, of all things, an Elfstone. She had magic. *And* the magic worked for her!

Jerhad's experiences of coming into his power, the struggles, the difficulties in believing in it came rushing to her mind. She suddenly longed to see him again. But she knew she needed to finish her quest. She had magic, a power that allowed her to understand the Gnomes, and more importantly, to make the Gnomes understand her. Deciding to play a hunch, she spoke loudly.

"I am on a journey by command of the Faeries."

The Gnomes fell back and gaped as one at her words, and a hush fell over the festival.

Did they understand her?

"I must depart at sunrising. This is the command of the Faeries. This is my command."

The Gnomes fell to their knees, foreheads to the ground. In unison they answered, "We hear and obey, Great Gnome Queen." Their chant sounded as the calling of a flock of Purple Wrens.

"We will come with you, Alpha Female," spoke Baby to her.

"You too? Have I gone mad?"

"I don't understand what you ask, but I am glad that at least you hear me now. It is not right that the Alpha should not heed the words of her pack."

"Blazes, fire and demons," whispered Andreanna.

"Come, you will return to your cave that you may rest before your journey," said the Gnome chief.

"Can we do without the guards?"

"My Queen, would you shame your servants by refusing to allow them to protect their Queen?"

"Oh.... I guess it's alright then. Bring them along," she sighed. Talk about a turn of events. A bit of magic and everything became different; all it had taken was this brown stone and she was free to leave. *And,* she was Queen of the Mountain Gnomes too. She wondered if there were any benefits that went with the job.

"And talking wolves too," she said aloud.

"We have always spoken, Alfa-female, it was you who was silent," spoke Baby.

Chapter 10

Waking with the sunrising, Andreanna opened her eyes to see Fonta sitting at the cave's opening. Outside, large billowing clouds swept by high in the atmosphere, driven by winds from off the Korkaran Sea.

"Goin' for walked 'gain 'dreanna? I go with you too. Me, Baby, Boy, Tanodo an' Banta."

"Tanodo and Banta?" inquired Andreanna. Fonta pointed to the two guards positioned outside the cave's entrance. "A whole troop! I guess they'll be insulted if I say no."

"They be very sad. Fonta sad once. Ma spanked me on bottom for eating all her cakes. Then, when she not looking', I eated all the pie, then I was sick. You ever be sick Miss 'dreanna...?" The run on conversation started up again.

"And you Boy, are you coming too?" asked Andreanna. Boy cowered but did not answer.

Andreanna emerged from the cave to find the Gnomes lining the way to the cliffs. She walked along the gathering in her departure, and the Gnomes sprinkled flower petals along the path, before her feet. Some waved smoldering bundles of wild sage, leaving, as if, a mystical cloud along the path. They cried out cheers and bowed deeply as she went by. At the lifts, she put Baby and Boy into the basket that would lower them to the ground below. The chief returned Andreanna's travel pack, restocked with provisions. As she was lowered to the ground, her subjects broke into a song of praise to their

Queen. The singing continued long after her departure, and she heard it for nearly half a span of travel.

The Human female had inquired of the Gnome chieftain pertaining to the whereabouts of the Faeries. Andreanna still was not sure as where to find them. The chief had simply pointed north into the Mystics. He also pointed northwest and then northeast. Andreanna went north, the two wolves leading, Fonta talking and two Gnome guards following.

Andreanna wondered about the magic and why she had any ability at all. Sure, she was part Elf, but she was mostly Human. Perhaps it had to do with the little magic that she might innately possess. Or, was it an effect of what Morlah had done with her in freeing her from Daektoch's spell? And, maybe, it was something Jerhad had done when he lay the Elfstone *acrch* on her chest as they had escaped from Daektoch, or a combination of all these things. Andreanna decided not to think about it, being sure a wonderful headache would develop before long if she did.

The Mystic Mountains were of a high elevation here, leaving the air cool and dry and the sun seemingly more intense. There still was some snow on the taller peaks, though she would not be climbing that high. Bleak-gray stone comprised most of what they saw. Travel became difficult as they scaled a ridge only to have to descend down as far to get to the foot of the next. Trees that grew here were noticeably stunted and more spindly, an effect of a harsher climate. The mountains consisted of an igneous rock formation; huge cracks split their sides, boulders strewn about at their bases. Occasionally, large clouds would suddenly pass, enveloping all in a heavy fog and moisture, only to disappear as quickly, allowing the sun to warm and dry them again.

A lonesome feeling shrouded the whole of the mountains. The mountains had an otherworldly appearance and feel to them. The bleak series of ranges were unwelcoming and desolate. Though there were forests in the deeper valleys, the way the group went showed little signs of life whether plant or animal. In spite of the company Andreanna traveled with, a dreariness and a sense of isolation crept into her. Cold gusts of wind suddenly blew upon them and then disappeared, whispering within hidden crevices and hollows.

Toward sunsetting, Andreanna sent Baby and Boy out to scout for a cave or shelter to spend the night in. They returned shortly, having found a small cavern a short distance off, and led the travelers to it. Arriving there, the two Gnomes quickly had a fire going in the area before the cave and soon had evening meat cooking. Andreanna thought she could get used to that aspect of having them around. Fonta talked on, though, no one really heard her anymore. As the bipeds ate, the wolves went out to hunt. The course grew dark and the evening sun seemed to simply fall from the sky as it rapidly set, leaving the night air bitterly cold.

Andreanna was not sure what to do about setting a watch. If she volunteered to take part, the Gnomes would surely be offended. She decided to ask them what they planned. Baby and Boy returned, looking quite satisfied, and set themselves to licking and washing themselves. They had found something to eat, something that, apparently (one could tell by the odor they brought with them), was well aged.

"Banta," she inquired, "will you be setting a watch during the night?"

"Yes, my Queen. Tanodo and I will watch and keep you from harm," he responded in his mousy accent.

The "Gnome Queen" almost laughed. The two of them were so small that she doubted they could take on a badger together. "Would it not be better if the watch was split into three? Then you would both be better rested to travel."

"Yes, my Queen, but we are only two." He was not going to catch on to her hint.

"But I am here too."

"Yes, my Queen. That is why we are here, and therefore, we will watch in the night." He sounded *far too* patient! But she had not expected much better.

"Alpha-female, Boy and I will watch. There are no two-legs that can watch as a wolf. We can watch better than the Gnomes, even in our sleep. Tell the little two-legs to sleep. We will see to it," Baby spoke with a guttural intonation.

"I doubt that they will want to do that."

"Try it. They are very impressed that you speak with us, though they don't understand your speech when you do."

"They don't?"

"You are not aware? How is it you demonstrate such weakness, yet you are alpha?"

"I guess I just hadn't thought of it."

"They will take to the suggestion if it comes from you and you have a plan that is acceptable to them."

"Baby, is it seen as weakness if an alpha is willing to learn what was not known?"

"I am not sure," she replied. "I had not thought of it in that manner."

"An alpha should have known," grumbled Boy. That was the first that Andreanna had heard him communicate.

"Ignore him," said Baby. "He thinks he is alpha, yet he still needs me to help catch his food. Males are foolish that way, but I guess they can't help it. I think that it has to do with the odor they give off."

Andreanna laughed. "Baby, you may have a point. Banta, would it be acceptable to you to have the wolves keep watch? They say they can do better than any two-legs can, even while they sleep."

The Gnome's eyes opened wide, with one eyebrow rising up a bit more than the other. "If the servants of my Queen say so, then it will be so."

Well! That was easy. So, the Gnomes, Fonta and Andreanna settled down for the night within the cave, Boy and Baby taking up positions at the entrance. All were soon asleep.

Andreanna suddenly sat up in a cold sweat, fear gripping her heart. Everything about her was dark and silent. She could not tell how long she had slept. Apprehension shrouding her heart as a veil. The foreboding night wrapped itself about her like a tight garment.

"Why are you in fear, alpha-female?" asked Baby.

"She is not alpha; smell the fear on her," spat Boy.

"I don't know, Baby. It must have been a dream," she answered. "Boy, you don't need to follow me; you can go off on your own if you have trouble being with me.

"I never asked you to come."

He answered her with silence.

"I begin to understand, that though you are alpha, there are many things that you don't know about wolves. It often was so with Fland. I suppose patience is needed even with an alpha when that alpha is not a wolf."

"Thank you, Baby," said Andreanna. "I am willing to learn if you are willing to teach. I have no desire to be alpha over either of you, but you may come along."

"Why do you reject us so?" lamented Baby with an outcry that sounded as if she had been stung.

"Reject you?"

"You proved yourself to be alpha-wolf when you killed Fland and the others. We have submitted to you, and yet you refuse to acknowledge that we are pack. You confuse us and take our worth from us. How long will you punish us this way?"

"Punish?" Andreanna realized that she needed to start paying attention to the wolves and their needs. It seemed crazy to her, but Andreanna made up her mind to be alpha to the wolves. "Come to me, both of you," she said sternly. Baby came quickly with her tail tucked and licking up at Andreanna's face. Boy came along slower, cowering submissively but also obviously quite unhappy.

Suddenly, Andreanna had them both at the throat and on their backs. "I am alpha-female," she growled at them. Boy struggled but Baby lay still. Andreanna unknowingly reached down into *licri's* power, doubled her grip on Boy's throat until he made raspy, gasping sounds. "I am alpha," she growled again. "We will be pack. There are many things I do not know and cannot do. I am not a wolf but a two-leg, but I am still alpha."

Boy stopped squirming, his breath almost completely cut off. Andreanna let up a bit. "You are alpha," he squeaked out, but it was evident that he was not pleased with the situation. He would eventually be trouble if he ever got up the nerve to challenge her. She would have to keep a close eye on him.

She had killed Fland, the leader of their pack; it had never occurred to her that they would have replaced him with her in needing a new leader. Boy was obviously feeling his hormones and felt he should be in charge. Andreanna gave him another good shaking before releasing him. Both wolves got to their feet and licked at her face, displaying their submissiveness.

Again, fear gripped at her heart! "What's out there?" she asked them.

"Nothing but the wind," replied Boy in disgust. Boy was unhappy that the alpha smelled of fear.

"No, there's more than just the wind. I feel it." She took the opportunity. "You think you should be top dog and yet do not sense the danger that is out there? There are things that are dangerous that you know nothing of, Boy. You still are a pup!" She could feel the rise of his anger.

Then, the wind clearly turned into a distinct low wailing and moaning of voices. Boy snapped at the sound with his bared teeth, cowering. Baby and Fonta took up a position behind Andreanna who still rested on one knee, looking out over her shoulder as they all stared out of the cave. Tanodo and Banta were suddenly at the cave's entrance with their weapons, but it did not look like they were about to go further.

Fonta pulled at Andreanna's arm. "Miss 'dreanna, Fonta scared. That the *Bonawock*. Ma say it steal babies in night. Don't let *Bonawock* steal me."

"What's the *Bonawock*?"

"Don't know. Don't let steal me."

The moaning grew louder, and now the wind seemed to be directed straight into their shelter. The hair on Andreanna's neck stood. Boy whined. Fonta and Baby pressed against her back. The moaning increasingly took on the sound of a voice.

"*...Who dares enter the domain of the* ***Bonawock****? Who trespasses...?*"

The wind swirled at the cave's entrance. It took on, as it were, a Human form, made of a white mist that could be seen by all in spite of the darkness. Andreanna was frozen with fear. The Gnomes fell to the ground, quaking in terror.

Then, *licri* began glowing within Andreanna's bosom, calming and quieting her. She relaxed; the smell of fear from the others in the cave was strong, but it did not register with the Human that she actually could smell their fear, nor did she notice that Fonta did not smell of fear. Or that Boy's was the worst. Suddenly, the wind and howling stopped, the white form at the cave's mouth backed away.

"Who are you?" commanded Andreanna.

The form stopped, "*We are the **Bonawock.** Do not harm us. We did not know...did not recognize you, **licri.** Please do not torment us for our error. We thought you to be trespassers. You had said we could protect our land. Have you changed your mind?*"

Andreanna felt she was caught in some dream or game. First, she had become guardian to Fonta, and then, Queen to the Gnomes and alpha to the wolves. Now, the *Bonawock* was giving her the role of a Faerie creature. It was doubtful that things could become more confusing.

"Who are you?" she repeated. "Who or what are the *Bonawock*?"

Now voices stirred within the figure. "*She torments us... she is displeased. Asking what she already knows.... She will punish. Not fair! Not fair!*" The voices within the *Bonawock* united into a cry, "*Not fair, do not punish, not fair....*" Without the magic of the *licri*, Andreanna would have died of fright at the sounds of lamentation that rose from the mist. Though not aggressive, their whining was even more terrifying than their initial threat.

"Speak!" Andreanna commanded. "Who are you, and what are the *Bonawock*? ...And stop your damnedable whining!"

All sound stopped. The shape moved forward a pace. "*We are the **Bonawock.***" The voice sounded definite, as if the term explained the matter.

"Who are the *Bonawock*?" repeated Andreanna.

"*Tell her.... No, she mocks us...she will punish....*"

"Who or what are the *Bonawock*?"

The voices quieted down to one voice but still containing the resonance of thousands of simultaneous utterings within it. "*We will answer you. Only, do not punish.... The* ***Bonawock*** *is the soul, or the collection of souls, of the dead of Pernham, City of the Mountain. Six thousand and forty-eight cycles past, Pernham, City of the Mountain was sentenced by the noble Faeries because of the great transgression. Please do not punish us. Pernham, City of the Mountain was a city of eight hundred thousand souls, rich and prosperous, a metropolis of the purer race of Humans, ancient ancestors to many of the humanoids of this age. Isolated in the mountains, the city grew for and onto itself. The food we grew was rich and strong. Our people were strong and healthy. The mountain, in that era, was warmer and the soil of the valleys fertile. The people multiplied and grew in knowledge and number.*

"For many cycles, joy and happiness reigned among the people. Then, the time came when the ***Kataruk*** *arrived out of the east with the sunrising. The* ***Kataruk*** *was evil and full of malice, powerful in magic. He seduced us and deceived us into thinking that he was a god. We served him with all vigor. Soon the* ***Kataruk*** *led us into the offering of our children to himself in blood sacrifices. This was practiced with much zeal. When the Faeries heard of it, they were wroth with us...as is just.*

"In all fury and power, they came upon us and destroyed the ***Kataruk****. For thirty courses of the sun, the* ***Kataruk's*** *dark form hung on the gallows in the city center for all to observe as the crows ate his flesh, the gallows that remain to this age. Then, the Faeries cast their sentence upon us: as each one would die, we would be added to the collection that is the* ***Bonawock****. We were allowed to die natural deaths. We also would bear no more children.*" A lamentation arose in the voices at the last statement.

"Silence or she will be wroth!" hissed some of the voices. *"Over the next seventy cycles, the population passed on, their essences and life forces added to the whole of the* ***Bonawock.*** *Now, in your wisdom, O Faerie Princess, and that of your sisters and brothers, we have been condemned to wander the mountain where we lived. The blood of our children, which we so foolishly offered to the* ***Kataruk,*** *cries in our ears by night and by course of the sun. We sinned against our flesh and blood. We lament, we grieve, we repent in dust and ashes for our dark and evil crime. We confess freely and with deep shame that we are guilty! Do not punish us further, for our crime has haunted us as we have haunted these mountains since we became the* ***Bonawock.*** *Be merciful and torment us no more*!"

The tears flowed down Andreanna's face, as she was moved with pity for the *Bonawock* who were tormented by their guilt and their sin.

"And you have been tormented for over six thousand cycles?"

"*Yes*."

"And when will your torments cease?"

"*When the sun forgets to rise*!" the weeping voices cried with an anguish that made the hair on her arms and neck stand again in spite of *licri's* influence.

Early dawn was in the sky, displaying a splay of golden rays that cut into the dark specter of night. The form continued its presence before Andreanna.

"You will not harm my companions. Come. Show me your city that I may see where you dwelt." The form moved, keeping close to the ground, going west. Andreanna turned to her traveling companions. "You must all stay here until I return."

"No, I come with you," wailed Fonta, clinging to Andreanna's leg.

"Alright, the rest of you stay here."

As she left the cave, she heard Baby reproving Boy, "I do not remember having heard of an alpha whine as you did, pup." He did not respond.

Following the shimmering, ghostly form of the *Bonawock*, which silently swept along the ground, Andreanna walked for nearly two spans until it stopped. Still as death, it hovered at a cliff's edge. Andreanna came to where the *Bonawock* stood and looked out into the vast valley below where she beheld the distant ruins of an ancient city built of stone. The roofs on the buildings were mostly collapsed and some walls toppled in places. Not a plant or weed grew from its ground. In some places, streaks of whitewash still clung to the stone, but for the most part, it was all a bleak gray. The fountains in their gardens were dry. Large specter-like remains of great barkless Elm trees lined the lanes. Many were fallen over. Barely visible from where she stood, in the city center, towered the scaffold where the *Kataruk* had been hung by the Faeries.

"I want to go into the city; show me how to get down."

The *Bonawock* hissed! "*No, it has not been done. We have not entered...the blood of our children cries against us from the gardens of sacrifice. We would not enter again. Please.... No....*"

"Alright then, just show me the way in and wait."

Nearly one span later, she walked down a large boulevard leading to the city's center. It had been a vast and magnificent city, planned with a precision of symmetry and architecture. Large stone pillars lined the front of buildings, engraved with flowers, leaves, and other figures. The streets, a grid of lanes and boulevards, were all paved with large quarried slabs of pink granite. Ornate walls enclosed what had once been gardens complete with fountains, stone planters, winding paths and arbors.

Andreanna made her way down toward the city center. She passed by several white, marble altars, which were still darkly stained with the blood of the sacrifices offered upon them. Completely repulsed by thoughts of what had happened here, the Human could not help thinking of her own child; Fonta clung to her. At the city center, she saw the remnants of the gallows where the *Kataruk* had been executed by the Faeries. Small bone fragments still lay on the ground where they had fallen, his remains never having been touched. Andreanna was turning to walk away when a voice, which came from the gallows, reached her.

"*Come back to see your work...after all this time.*" Andreanna jumped! It was then she saw the barely perceptible shade in the air, swinging as if on the end of a rope.

"You're the *Kataruk*!" Andreanna gasped. "How is it you survive to this time?"

"*Ha! You mean you don't know?*"

The Human girl was being cast into yet another role that she knew nothing of.

"*Your magic was strong enough to destroy but my body and hold my life force here as an eternal curse.*"

"What are you?"

"*I don't know what game you engage in, Faerie creature, but I'll play...not having much else to do but hate you through the past millennia. I am the* ***Kataruk****, a sorcerer - by some, a necromancer. I gained great power here through the thousands of children the city offered up in my name. I still to this time smell the sweet fragrance of the blood of their offerings. There isn't a chance that you are here to offer...that little one up to me...is there?*"

Andreanna shuddered! She gathered herself up and spat on the ground between them. This evil creature must have been mistaking the Elven magic in her and carried in the Elfstones for the creatures themselves.

"...Ah, I thought not. A shame, for I believe such a sacrifice even now would give me the strength to escape my bond. Nevertheless, the Pernhamites freely offered them and those that they kidnapped from the country about when they had no children of their own left to offer. If not for your meddling, I would have become the greatest force of magic this world has ever known. My power was not great enough, when you ruined my plans, to deal with you Faeries collectively.... So what do you want with me now?"

Andreanna was overwhelmed, repulsed, by the glory the creature had in his evil and in his crimes. She became calmer as *licri* began glowing powerfully within her. Her hand reached up and grasped *balat,* the Elfstone Jerhad had given her, the one Morlah found in the ashes of the burnt tree when he had freed her from Daektoch's spell. *balat* was hot in her hand. It was not of the same magic as *balan,* purification, as Jerhad possessed. It was not *balak,* sickness and death, but *balat* — **Destruction!**

Now, the intelligence of the Elven magic infused into her mind. Andreanna knew and understood the magic, at least a portion of it. She also understood what she would do.

"*Why do you torment me with the presence of the child. I hunger and you flaunt this morsel before me,*" complained the *Kataruk*.

"You bastard!" Andreanna breathed out with vehemence and might.

The *Kataruk* was taken back by the sudden strength of her fury, the sudden rise of the magic of *balat* and the intensity that rose up within her. "*What do you think you're doing? You've done your deed, thousands of cycles back! Leave me alone!*"

Andreanna smelled the fear coming from it, something she gained from the brown stone and her link to the wolves. *balat* grew hot, hot enough to burn; but it would not harm her. It was her stone. It was almost *her*.

Seeing her intent, the *Kataruk* cried out, "*No! You must not.... There was hope while I was here...all this time I waited.... You can't!*" His voice turned to despair.

She raised the hand that held *balat*, its power striking out with ferocity to destroy the depraved creature that hung in its magical gallows. Her role was now that of executioner. She would finish what the Faeries had not, lest this vile beast ever manage to gain its freedom. As she wrapped her magic about him, she took of his substance, drawing it into the stone but burning the evil from the power he contained, cleansing the power for her Elfstone and herself.

As the last traces of the *Kataruk* disappeared, she thought that she heard Fonta laughing, but looking down, she only saw a terrified Gnome child. *Something is not quite right with this child*. She let it pass.

As they left, Andreanna and Fonta made their way toward the city's boundary, investigating buildings, gardens and stonework of unbelievable craftsmanship and beauty. Andreanna carried Fonta.

"There," said Fonta pointing to a large building that resembled a temple.

"What's there?"

"Want to go there."

"No, I really think we should be getting back to the others."

Upon which, Fonta began to scream and cry, going into hysterics. "Want to go there." She squirmed down from Andreanna's arms, catching Andreanna by surprise. Fonta raced toward the edifice.

Andreanna, a little less energetic, still a little overwhelmed with what had happened at the city center, followed behind at a walk. "Alright," she shouted to Fonta in exasperation. "Wait up; I'm coming."

Fonta disappeared into the building through the large, weathered, wooden doors, which hung askew on rusted hinges. Andreanna entered the building. The first thing she noticed was how lit up it was, having expected the inside to be dark. She looked up and saw that the domed ceiling had been a stained glass structure; broken pieces of red, rose, green, blue, violet and white glass lay scattered across the floor below the open roof. Then, she saw that the stone part of the ceilings and the walls were painted in magnificent and still brilliant colors, apparently undimmed by the ages. The painted murals and frescoes were of gardens, trees, Faeries, gods, animals, Humans, Elves, Dwarves, Trolls, Gnomes, Giants, Bornodalds and other creatures that she did not recognize. The images looked too alive. Coming to herself, she looked about. No Fonta.

"Fonta, where are you?" There was no reply, which caused Andreanna's impatience to burn within her; she was in no mood for hide-and-seek. A small partially closed door in the far end of the main room creaked. "Fonta, get out of there. Let's go!"

Still no reply.

"I'm coming to get you. If you don't come out by the time I get there, I'm going to toast your two little buns for you!"

Still no reply.

As Andreanna pushed the door wider, the pungent sweet odor of Jasmine incense and burning candles told her she was not dealing with Fonta. She slowed, looking around the door into the tiny chamber, a prayer closet. It took a few heartbeats for her eyes to grow accustomed to the candlelight. The walls of the chamber were draped with wool tapestries.

The one opposite her had a Faerie, wearing a crown, and in her hand was a black stone with a ray emitting from it, wrapping itself about the form of a man hanging from a rope on a ghostly gray gibbet. To her right, the tapestry showed a female Gnome wearing a crown, seated on a throne and with a large group of Gnomes bowed to the ground before her. The Gnome Queen wore a black and a brown stone hanging from golden chains around her neck. An ox-sized wolf sat at each hand.

To the left, the tapestry portrayed a solid-black she-wolf on a snowy mountaintop, also wearing a crown. Andreanna slowly entered the room and looked to the wall next to the door where the tapestry showed an Elven King and Queen sitting on a mountain, the sea behind them. The two on the thrones looked uncomfortably like Jerhad and she. All the tapestries looked *too* alive!

A whisper caught her attention. On the floor, on hands and knees and with face bowed to the ground, was a small figure in a robe, the coarse cloth the same color as the stone, which explained how she had so easily missed him. He was a withered, bald Human with a long, white beard, which was stretched out on the floor to a length that equaled his height.

"I am not worthy, O great, Long-Awaited Queen, of your presence. I am but a worm in your presence. At long last, you have come."

Chapter 11

"Who are you?"

"I am the prophet and priest to the Awaited for Queen."

"Did you see a Gnome girl go by here?"

"No, my Queen. Long have I waited to fulfill my destiny and give to you the *Book of Secrets* that has been in my keeping since the condemnation of the city by the Faeries. Now, I will be allowed to pass on. Although the cycles have been long and many, I have not fainted in my duty. I am fulfilled."

"No Gnome girl? ...Since this city was condemned?"

"Yes, my Queen. The prophecy spoke so: that the one who would remain true would live to see the Queen. Now, I can lay my bones down and make the Final Journey, for I have seen the Queen!"

"So you're going to kneel there with your face to the floor and tell me you've been here waiting for me for over six thousand cycles!"

"Yes, my Queen."

"What makes you think I am the queen you wait for?"

"I know it in my heart. I saw you sit on the throne of the Gnomes. I saw your beginnings of taking the throne of the wolves. I saw you destroy the *Kataruk*. I see the time coming when you will sit with the King in the mountain."

Andreanna felt her skin crawl on her scalp and arms. *This was way too weird.*

"As I have said, I am the prophet."

"Get up. Why are you talking to me with your face to the floor?"

"As you wish, my Queen. Though it is not fit for one such as I to speak to you, face speaking to face." The little man arose. He was no taller than a short Dwarf, scrawny, withered and his eyes frosted with age. His skin was a mass of wrinkles and crevices and of a tawny hew.

"It is my regret that the eyes of my flesh cannot see you, my Queen; but what is that to one who serves *you*!"

"You're...blind?"

"Yes, my Queen. Does it displease you that such a blemish be found in your Prophet?"

"...Ah...no." *Oh, this was all too confusing. Yet another role to play. Was there no end to it? Should she play along? The coincidences were all too uncanny to ignore.* She decided to play along.

"Alright, so now that I've come, what do we do?"

"It is mine to deliver *The Book of Secrets of the Queen* to you, my Sovereign, to answer to the best of my abilities all questions you may ask and then to make the Final Journey."

"Can I sit? I've been walking a long time. Are you sure you didn't see a little Gnome girl?"

"I have not seen her, though I sense her presence in a nearby chamber. She is safe. She sleeps." The Prophet pulled a large pillow out of a pile of furs and offered it to Andreanna. "A seat for you, my Queen." Andreanna took the pillow and sat down on it, and then, the Prophet sat on the floor before her.

"What's your name?" she asked, preoccupied and discomfited by the tapestries.

"My name?"

"Yes, your name?"

"I'm not sure I remember. I had not thought of it for many cycles...." He reflected for a score of heartbeats. "Lendon. Yes, that was it. My friends just called me Lend."

"Lend, ...if what you tell me is so, you are over six thousand cycles old. How can this be?"

"It is magic of the earth, old magic, strong magic, intelligent magic. It has seen, it has purposed, it is so. It has come to pass. All will come to pass."

"Is this magic...Faerie magic?"

"Yes and no. It is older than the Faeries, but it is the essence of the Faeries."

"And you've waited here for me to show up for six thousand cycles?"

"Yes. It was a privilege, my Queen. I did not despair."

"How is it you that say you saw me on the Gnomes' throne and the wolves throne and saw me destroy the *Kataruk*?"

"I am a prophet. Mine is the gift of prophecy, of seeing. I have seen you and watched you since you crossed what you name Dwarf's Pass, east of the Mage River. I saw you coming. I saw you fulfill the prophecies."

This was strange enough for sure, but what did it all mean?

"Lend, give me *The Book of Secrets of the Queen*."

"Gladly, my Queen." He rose and went to a corner of the small room where he opened a compartment hidden in the floor, from which he retrieved a small, wood and gold bound volume. He closed the compartment and brought the book to Andreanna. "This fulfills my destiny."

"...Don't go taking any Final Journey just yet there, Lend."

"I shall not, my Queen."

Examining the book, she saw it was sealed in a way that made it impossible to tell how it was to be opened or where to loosen the lock, which she could not even find, for the gold-plated binding appeared to hold all borders of the book equally.

"Do you know how to get this opened, Lend?"

"It is not mine to know, my Queen."

"Great!" she grumbled.

"I believe it is sealed with magic, my Queen."

That gave her an idea. She took the Elfstones from around her neck and held them in her hand. Concentrating on the book, she squeezed the stones. Nothing happened. She concentrated on the stones. Nothing happened. She took the pin, given to her by the Gnome chief, and touched it to the book. The golden hardware glowed, and a hole appeared in the cover's center. She pushed the pin in with a click and the book opened in her hands. Yes, the key given to her by the Gnomes...but how...?

"I see, my Queen, that you have found the way."

"I guess I have." Opening the book, she read the single sentence contained on the first page, "*Upon the coming of the Queen to Pernham, she will release the **Bonawock** from their penance by...*" She gasped!

No, she would not!

Andreanna nearly got up and walked out, but instead, with restraint, she turned the page and read, "*Daektoch, who became unloved, unloving, unlovable, left and went to the outside world to live among the Humans who dwell there. He discovered the Black magic, or rather, it found him. Through its power, he passed himself off as one of the outsiders, and through it, lived many millennia. His name, before he was known as Daektoch, was Pezzikta. She who knows this has power.*" She turned to the next page and read, "*Though you do not yet believe, O Mighty Queen, it will be so. Be of a strong heart, O Long Awaited for Queen.*" She closed the book, not wanting to read more, and stuffed it into her pack. She returned her Elfstones and the pin to her neck.

"Tell me about the *Bonawock*, Lend."

"Ah, yes, the *Bonawock*," he sighed deeply. "The *Bonawock*... well, they were the people of Pernham. The name is from the Faerie language: *Bonawock*, meaning *The Collective of the Damned*. They were a simple people in many ways, but of great intelligence. As you have seen, they were great lovers of buildings, beauty, of gardens and paved ways. They were lovers of life and Humanity; yet they were innocent and without understanding concerning evil. They were too easily beguiled.

"This was of the original race of Humans, a purer race than those who inhabit the outside world. Their intelligence was great, using most of their minds' powers in contrast to the present race that uses but a fragment. When they saw, they understood. If you presented a child of Pernham with wheat kernels, he would understand bread as the end. If you gave wheels to another, he would mount them to a box and have a cart. If one looked at a hill of stone, the process of a stone building was obvious to him. Yet, they remained as children in their minds. They were governed by an elected council but had no laws. They lived at peace and in harmony with each other. The land was virtually free of disease, and we, for I was one of these fair people, lived hundreds of cycles until we were called to the Final Journey.

"When the *Kataruk* came, he beguiled them thoroughly. They did not understand evil. They were not evil but misled children. *Pity them, my Queen. Pity them*!

"The one who is now known as the Black Mage, Daektoch, was a boy when the *Kataruk* came. He fled when the sacrifices began; but not before he was corrupted with the lust for the power of magic as he saw in the Kataruk."

Their conversation went on into the night, Andreanna asking, Lend answering. As the first rays of the sun came through the great doors in the building's east wall, they finished their discourse.

"Will that be all, my Queen?" asked Lend.

"I think so, Lend."

"Do you give me leave?"

"I guess so."

"Thank you, my Queen. It has given me much pleasure having spoken with you and having served you all these cycles." And with that, he let out a long sigh and fell over onto his side...dead.

"Lend!" cried Andreanna, reaching out to him, his body turning to dust as she touched it. She fell back, aghast.

"What is matter, 'dreanna? Me sleep. Not tired anymore. Hungry now," said Fonta suddenly appearing in the doorway.

Something about this child was not quite right.

"Let's go outside; we'll eat there," she said, desiring to get away from the prayer room.

So, they went out of the building and found some stone benches around a table in a garden that did not contain a bloodstained altar.

"...an' then butterflies were flying everywhere, an' Ma say not pull their wings. Their wings are dusty colors. Ma say not to eat butterflies, but I eat yellow one when Ma not looking. Taste yucky! Worms taste better...an' then we make pies with mud, an' we leave them in sun, an' they get all hard, an' my sister taste one an' say it was yucky, an' so we...."

Having finished their break fast, they left the city. When they arrived to the city's edge, the *Bonawock* was there waiting.

"She comes.... Quiet.... How is it so quiet? No voices of children..." the *Bonawock* whispered.

Andreanna stopped abruptly, remembering what she had read, also remembering what Lend had said, *"Pity them, my Queen. Pity them".* Tears filled her eyes, causing her nose to get stuffed up. She sniffed at her tears.

"What would you have of me, people of Pernham?"

"She asks.... Tell her...no, she mocks, she will punish," the voices argued within the *Bonawock*.

"Ask!" she commanded, gathering her wits.

"We would be free of our guilt and shame. Send us away."

"The only thing I can do for you is to destroy you in the same way I destroyed the *Kataruk*. If I do that, you will not make the Final Journey."

"It is enough. To sleep in the darkness of forgetting would be a great and sweet gift indeed, O Queen...she is angry, do not speak such...," the voices warned.

"You would have me destroy you?"

"Do not answer.... Silence! ...Yes, Elven Faerie."

"Though you have no body, will that not be like murder?"

"No, we murdered ourselves! We would sleep and not know memory, not know pain, not know guilt."

"I don't think I can do this...."

"She is angry...stay yourselves...you will cause her to punish more...."

"I will join my companions at the cave and give you your answer at the rising."

As she slept, Andreanna dreamed. A beautiful Faerie maiden came to her.

"Behold, I am **balat,"** *she told Andreanna, "Essence of Destruction."*

*"But how can you be **Destruction** and be so beautiful?"*

*"The destruction I bring is that of justice, wisdom and, in this case, pity. There is nothing left for the **Bonawock,** but **balat**. Their sin and their guilt will not permit the Final Journey. There is no power or magic that can change this. What is left for them is for them to go into the silence and peace of nonexistence. It is a mercy you will do for them if you pity them. Too long they have paid for their transgression. There were none to free them. None but you. Even among the Faeries, there are none who can, by essence and law...who can free them. You are the only one. You are the first to possess **balat,** to be **balat**. The choice is yours."*

*"**balat,** is that not the name of the stone I wear?"*

*"We are one and the same, more so, because the curse of Daektoch blended with Elven Faerie magic and White and Black and Gray magic, when you were set free of the curse, **balat** is **one** with you. We* are ***balat**."*

Andreanna sat up in the cave in a cold sweat. The fire outside burned low. Baby lifted her head.

"Is all well, Alpha-female?" asked Baby.

"...Yes.... All is well, as well as can be, I guess. Just dreaming."

"Of rabbits?"

"No, other things."

"Deer?"

"No."

"What else is there?"

"Other things...." She lay down and went back to sleep.

The group left the cave at sunrising; the *Bonawock* waited in an eerie silence that seemed to permeate the mountain. The Mystics were still, as if the mountain held its breath, awaiting Andreanna's decision.

"Do you hold to your request," asked Andreanna as she approached the *Bonawock*.

"*We do.*"

"All I can do is the same I did with the *Kataruk*."

"*We shared in his evil; we will share in his fate. Besides, sleep and forgetting will be a welcome sweetness.*"

Andreanna reached for the chain that held the stone, *balat*.

"*No, please,*" said the *Bonawock*. They came forward; an arm and hand of mist extended from the form as if to restrain her. "*Please! Allow us to remember, as we go, our lost Humanity. The power is in you as it is in the stone. Please, we beg. Do this as Human to Human, for we perceive the humanity that is within you, also.*"

Andreanna was puzzled, not understanding what they asked for, but she stepped forward, reaching out. Her hand touched the mist's hand. With force, the sense of the *Bonawock*'s heart intruded into her mind. It was overwhelming! She was overcome with visions of life in the streets and homes of Pernham. She saw children playing, craftsmen at their work, lovers on the grass. It seemed that within a few heartbeats she witnessed the entire course of Pernham's history. They had lived, sang, ate, loved. They were Men, misguided Humans. She wept with and for them.

"*Let it be so,*" they said.

Without thought on Andreanna's part, the power of *balat* rose from her, wrapping itself around the mist, bringing *destruction* to them, sending them into nonexistence, into the sleep and rest that they longed for. It took but a heartbeat of time; the *Bonawock* were gone. Then, she piled stones where the *Bonawock* had stood, and finding a large stone with a smooth flat surface, she placed it on top. With the tip of her longknife's blade, she scratched into the stone "*balanna fe balat"* (forgetting in destruction). She did not know how she knew the words of the Faerie language, but somehow she did. Wrapping her arms about the large stone, she wept and mourned the passing of the people of Pernham, City of the Mountain.

The first prophecy of *The Book of Secrets of the Queen* had come to pass, *"Upon the coming of the Queen to Pernham, she will release the Bonawock from their penance by a great and powerful destruction, by the hand of her power. She will send them into darkness and forgetting; their name will be remembered no more."*

Silently, she wept.

"*Bonawock* sleep. Feel better," said Fonta. "Ma spank Fonta, then, she go to sleep an' feel better. Fonta had bunny. Dogs eat bunny. Bunny sleep an' feel better. Doggie sleep an' feel better too. But then Ma say that we go out an' play an' we...."

Sitting on the ground, Andreanna looked at the Gnome child. "Fonta,...you're a strange child."

Fonta's shoulders went up in a shrug, and her hands covered her mouth as she giggled. "Ma say that too." She giggled again. "Fonta want ride Baby!"

"Baby, is it alright if the child rides on you?"

"...why not? She's not much bigger than a tic."

It was the third course of the sun since the destruction, the *balat*, of the *Bonawock*. The two Gnomes were leading the group north. Boy and Baby followed behind Andreanna. Fonta still rode Baby, who seemed to have grown attached to the Gnome child as if she were a pup in her pack, and Boy tolerated her, remaining strangely quiet and withdrawn. Andreanna also was quiet. Her experience with the *Bonawock* had left her thoroughly depressed.

Among the Faeries, things were slowly but progressively worsening. Lethargy and unrest moved throughout the population. Many changed from their humanoid forms into that of stone manifestations, which were more stable, in order to attempt to stay the "sickness" that was among them. They did not know the cause of the sickness. It had never been so among them.

They waited....

*

Another three risings went by. On the course of the fourth rising, Andreanna seemed to come to herself. Looking about, she realized she had not paid attention to where she had been going for the past courses.

"Banta, Where are we?"

The Gnome went down on one knee and sketched in the dirt. "Mage River is here. River Rain here. Blue Mountains. Mystic Mountains. We are here," he said drawing a circle that encompassed several leagues.

"Any clue to where we can find the Faeries?"

Both Gnomes shrugged.

"One doest not find the Faeries. They find thee," came a voice from behind her.

In a flash, Andreanna had turned and had her sword halfway out of its sheath. "Fire and demons, Morlah! Blasted Druid, you scared me to death."

Baby and Boy snarled. Baby lunged at the Druid but sailed through the apparition.

"Easy, Baby. It's alright. He's pack."

Baby stopped her attack but stayed on her guard. Boy had peed from fear; the Gnomes rushed and took up positions in front of Andreanna, weapons ready. Finally, having reassured everyone, Andreanna got them to relax.

"Morlah, how'd you know where to find me?"

"I hadst been watching Mildra through the orb on mine staff for sometime, when it didst dawn on me that I hadst not seen thee for a while. So, I didst go in search of thee and found thee here. What doest thou, little one? Thou art far from home."

"Good question, Druid. Nan, the Faerie, appeared to me in my dreams and obsessed me with the thought of finding the Faeries. Don't ask me why."

"I see thou hast picked up a troop in thine travels."

"You've seen Mildra? ...How's Jerhad and Kendra? And the Elves?"

"Everyone is alive and well. Well, almost everyone. The Trolls have attacked Mildra, and now, they doest amass to the east, and the armies in Mildra have gone out to meet them. More battle is imminent."

"Oh dear. I should be there, but damned Nan wouldn't let me rest until I do this. You visited the Faeries...twice. How did you do it?"

"That, I do not know, little one. They will find thee in due time."

"Can you get a message to Jerhad, Morlah, please? I left without telling him what I was about because I knew he'd forbid it. He doesn't know where I am or what I'm doing; could you tell him not to worry? Tell him I'm alright.

"Oh, and look, Morlah!" She extended her hand, causing the power of *balat* to form a dark cloud of magic in her palm. The magic crackled with might.

The Druid raised an eyebrow. "That is quite impressive, little one. How is it thou hast come about this?"

"The stone you gave to Jerhad," she said. "She said she was formed by the blending of magics, and well, a blending with me."

"That is most interesting. I trust then thou art...who is that behind the rocks?"

Andreanna looked about. Fonta was missing. "Fonta, come out, it's alright. He's a friend."

Fonta stepped out from behind some large rocks she had been hiding behind, looking shy, head down and hands behind her back. Her foot toed at the ground, and she squirmed as if she needed to pee.

Morlah's eyes grew narrow, and he frowned severely. "I see thee, Fonta. I do not know what thou art about but...I willst defer," he said in a stern and serious voice.

"Take it easy, Morlah; she's just a baby. Strange...but still just a baby."

"Yes, thou art correct, I willst leave off. I trust thou willst soon find the Faeries. Trust me in this. They art closer than thou doest think. Ja speed." And he vanished.

"Druids...!"

After traveling most of the remainder of the course, Andreanna called a halt to the march. "If the Faeries want me, they can come find me! We're camping here until they do or until we get tired of waiting for them and go home. I've had it with this!" So, they set up camp, Boy and Baby leaving to go hunt.

"Will you not hunt with us, Alpha-female?" asked Baby.

"No, our meat is not quite the same, but if you have some extra bring it back, and I'll cook mine."

"Arrr!" exclaimed Boy. "She would ruin good flesh with fire!"

"You should try it. You'd never eat raw again," taunted Andreanna with a hint of mischief revealed in her eye. Boy turned and ran off, Baby following behind. Later that night they returned, their bellies full, and took up their positions as watch.

For the next three courses, they remained in camp, Andreanna using the free time to practice weapons and hone her skills. Fonta was strangely silent and withdrawn. Andreanna wondered at it but decided not to attempt to change it, welcoming the silence. The Gnomes kept to themselves, taking turns at doing perimeter checks around the campsite. Baby and Boy lay around and slept off whatever they had eaten, their bellies still taught with the meal.

The sun's golden orb crested over the edge of the horizon on the fourth rising, as Andreanna woke. She sat up in her bedroll looking around. The stone and bare rock where their campsite had been was now thick with lush green grass. Flowers and fruit trees flourished. The air about her was warm and vibrant. Before her was a long table set with woven baskets filled with fruit, vegetables, herbs, and greens. Earthen pitchers of sweet nectar for drinking and bowls of honey filled the spaces between the fruit dishes. Sitting along the table were...Faeries.

It is difficult to describe the Faeries' appearance. In recorded history, when seen by more than one person at a time, each one came away with a different memory of the Faeries. When seen by Dwarves, the Faeries appeared to be two-spans tall with coarse features, large noses, and often, the males wore beards. The Keeper and Nourisher, the Giant, during the rule of the Emperor Slonitakol III, claimed that the Faeries that visited him at the Gift were as large as Trolls and wore armor. But most were agreed that the Faeries had golden-blonde or platinum-colored hair. Frequently their movements and voices were accompanied by the sounds of chimes and tinklings as from tiny bells.

Andreanna saw small, Human-appearing people of platinum-colored and golden-blonde hair. Their eyes were elongated and slanted almond shapes of radiant blue as if the very heavens were hidden within them, their ears were Elven like and they were no taller that Fonta. All were of a slender physique and were clothed in gossamer gowns that were not transparent, yet flowed as if made of woven cobwebs. Every which way she looked, there were Faeries. Some speaking to one another. Others dancing. Others involved in chases. The Faerie King and Queen stood from the table and came to her.

"Welcome Andreanna, Queen of the Elves. Welcome! We thank you for coming in answer to our summons. Rise with your companions, come feast with us," spoke the King, with a deep bow at the waist. Fonta came and stood next to Andreanna.

The King looked at her, "*isini*, I see you have kept your charge well and brought Andreanna here safely."

Fonta stomped her foot and frowned at him. "You weren't supposed to tell."

"*isini*? You're a...Faerie?" blurted Andreanna.

"Oh, well! Now you know. Yes, I'm a Faerie," Fonta replied with a fair amount of exasperation in her voice.

"You're a damned, son-of-a-Troll, blasted Faerie?" spat Andreanna.

"Yes!" said *isini*, annoyed at her ruse being uncovered.

"You miserable little Gnome. All that chatter and talk... and the *Bonawock*...and the *Kataruk*, and Lend...you knew all along.... I should throttle you!"

"Hey, it was part of my quest, so relax!" hissed Fonta.

Andreanna turned to the King. "That is one strange kid... Gnome...or Faerie or whatever."

"Yes, we've thought so too; but we don't get to choose in these matters."

"Let's eat!" shouted Fonta, and she rushed off to the tables where she began to gorge herself, chattering to the other Faeries at an even greater speed than she had with Andreanna. She was everywhere, talking to everyone. More than once, Andreanna saw a Faerie roll its eyes at her prattle.

"Come, you will sit with us. You will eat and be refreshed, and then we will speak," said the King.

So, they sat and ate and drank. The food was wholesome, tasty and invigorating. Andreanna felt as if she had never been so awake or alive before. Her skin tingled and her senses heightened. What she did not know was that the food she ate was Faerie food and the Elven magic within her was being further awakened and heightened by it. The Gnomes were rather wide-eyed at it themselves; it seemed that they could eat vast amounts without feeling stuffed or overfilled; the more they ate the more they wanted.

Finally, the feast ended. Fonta stood on the table before them. "We have to wash her."

"Yes," said the King. "I believe that is what we should do next."

Chapter 12

"Wash me? Is it that bad?"

"Yes," replied the King. "It is. The taint of Daektoch's magic remains in you though you are well healed in many ways. But still, it needs to be removed."

"Daektoch?"

"The spell that he poisoned you with when he captured you still has its taint upon you. Come, we will wash it away." So, the Fairies all rose from the table and walked to a deep pool of transparent silver-white liquid that was nestled in a copse of tall rhubarb.

"Come with me, my darling Andreanna," said the Faerie Queen. They stepped behind a screen of Morning Glory vines, and Andreanna emerged dressed in a long, flowing, white gown of a material like that of what the Faeries wore, light as butterfly wings, yet strong as mail; it seemed to whisper as she moved. The Queen led Andreanna to the pool and directed her to slip in. The substance was wet, liquid, but without discernable temperature; she could not say if it were warm or cool. It felt invigorating and set her skin to tingling as if thoroughly scouring her clean. She gladly walked into the depths over to where the King and Fonta stood at the pool's edge.

The Faeries looked on.

"This is wonderful! What is it?"

"It is what you would know as argentus," said the King, "only in its liquid form."

Suddenly, Fonta reached out, took Andreanna by the hair, plunged her head below the surface, and held her there. Andreanna thrashed about, not having had time to get a lungful of air. The King frowned at Fonta.

"There are better ways to prepare one for such," he said, but did not intervene.

Andreanna was amazed at Fonta's strength. Fight as she could, the Human could not break free of *isini's* grip, rise out of the liquid or pull Fonta in. Andreanna's frantic struggles caused her to quickly run out of breath! She thrashed beneath the surface, in *igini's* grip. It appeared that Fonta was going to drown her.

The Faeries stood, watching.

"She does not understand, *isini*. Your ways do not please me," murmured the King. Andreanna noticed that she heard him speak as if she were standing besides him, unsubmerged.

isini was going to *destroy* her!

Was that why she had been brought here, to be drowned by the Faeries, in the mountains? She did not know where Tanodo and Banta were. Baby and Boy were out hunting.

Finally, Andreanna was at her end. She had to breathe. Her lungs heaved painfully. She would drown. Air burst from her mouth, her lungs pulling hard at the liquid in a spontaneous attempt to get air. She breathed in deeply, sucking the liquid in forcefully, but nothing happened. Or at least nothing bad happened.

She simply inhaled and exhaled as if it were air. Oh, the pleasure of it! It was as if she had never breathed in her life. It seemed that she inhaled into her arms and hands, into her legs and feet and toes. **Alive, alive, she was alive and free!** The element of magic, argentus, infused into her, cleaning her, making her live, reviving that which had never been alive! She felt as if she soared in the clouds, as if she flew on the wind. Sensing her relax, Fonta released her.

"You never would have convinced her to inhale while her head was in the liquid," Fonta said to the King. "My way saved us a lot of endless arguing and futile convincing that would not have got us anywhere. It would have just made things that much harder."

"I still do not approve," responded the King. "But it is done. I believe it does suffice. You may come out now, Andreanna." The Human rose from the argentus bath, glowing silver-white inside and out.

"Look!" hissed Fonta, pointing at a putrid, inky-black substance that floated on the surface of the bath. The Faeries approached and gawked. A few were heard gasping; murmured discussions rose from the group.

"What is it?" asked Andreanna.

"Daektoch's filth," spat Fonta.

"Daektoch's Black magic that still polluted you," echoed the Faerie King. His voice sounded like miniature bells ringing out in alarm. Fonta reached out and touched the inky slime, burning it with a touch of magic as it floated on the argentus.

"*Lanta pino annin* or...mission accomplished," she said.

Any other time, Andreanna would have had words or even fists for the stunt Fonta had pulled, but she felt *far too good* to harbor any ill thoughts. "Now what?" she asked, ready to climb to some lofty mountainous peak.

"Now you must help us," answered the Faerie Queen, radiating a beauty Andreanna could not describe.

"Help you what?"

"We do not exactly know. Fonta said we needed you and convinced us to let her bring you here," said the King.

Andreanna could now see that he glowed with an inner intensity of magic.

"Need me for what?" she asked eyeing the Faeries as if they might disappear.

"Come sit. We will speak," responded the Queen, guiding Andreanna. The Queen drifted a finger's breadth above the ground rather than walk.

So, they went out into a sunny field of red, yellow, white and orange daisies and sat on the thick mossy carpet that grew in its midst.

"Where did all this come from?" asked Andreanna. "It was a barren rock just yestercourse."

"The Faerie lands are not exactly in the same place or plane you were in then. Though, they are in the same location in the mountain. It would be difficult to explain beyond that," said the King. "But to the point at hand. For a few cycles of the moon, we have been becoming, for lack of a better word...sick. Many have taken on their stone manifestations in an attempt to stay this sickness. We are becoming, ever so slowly, lethargic and almost, one might say...weakened. Though our magic is great, it is not what it was. We seem to be losing ourselves. I cannot define it, for it is new to us."

"What am I supposed to do?"

"I don't know. Fonta insisted that you were needed, so here you are. *isini*, what of it?" asked the King.

Fonta shrugged. "I don't know what she can do. We need her, I got her. There she is. What will be will be. You can't be expecting me to do everything. I just know we need her. You figure it out. Why do you look to me to solve all this? I don't know...."

"*isini*."

"Yes, King?"

"Shut up."

"Yes, King," she pouted.

"So there you have it, Elf Queen."

"Elf Queen?"

"Don't you know? Did you not learn from your visit to Lend? Have you not heard? Was it not you who called Jerhad the Prince of the Elves, Prince and Sire? And if you are wed to him, would you not be Queen if he is to be King?"

"Well, that was just for fun. I didn't...I mean.. I don't.... Oh!"

"Well, let it suffice for now. We will ask you to stay with us for seven courses of the sun, and after that, we will allow you to return to your family. We hope that *isini's* request was not idle chatter," said the Queen, her words sparkling like diamonds as they came from her mouth.

"Idle chatter! I'll have you know...."

"*isini*!" commanded the King.

"What?"

"Shut up, please."

"Yes, King," she pouted again.

The Elves and Dwarves had been entrenched at Land's Break for two courses of the sun. Scouts had reported back saying that the Trolls should arrive by midcourse of the following rising. The precipice of Land's Break, varying from twenty-nine to twelve paces in height, ran from the Coastal Range to the sea cliffs overlooking the warm, green waters of the Korkaran Sea, which bordered the south coast of Frontmire. There were a few places where the cliffs had collapsed, leaving access from the eastern to the higher western portion of the plain. Sether Road, which followed the south coast, used one such breaking in the cliffs to connect East to West, near the cliffs that overlooked the sea.

It was at these more accessible points that the Elf and Dwarf Armies would concentrate their forces; it was doubtful that the Trolls would try to scale the cliffs in multitudes. Twelve smaller detachments were left free to move about and concentrate where the fighting was heaviest. Since Land's Break was six leagues long, it was impossible for even the largest of armies to defend it with any strength along its entire length; they would do the best they could.

Jerhad sat on top of a rise covered with lush green pasture, overlooking the area that would become the battlefield. Stanton arrived riding a gray mare, not the immense warhorse he had used in the Breezon Army, nor the lighter but more endurable cavalry charger. He would make due with what was available.

"Everything is in place. I'm not really happy with this position. We're spread out too thin. If the Trolls have ladders or can climb the cliffs, they'll swarm up here in no time," said Stanton.

"No helping that," answered Jerhad somewhat distracted by his own thoughts. "I've been thinking; we have a major part of our force here where the road comes up from the eastern flats. If we sent them to the other positions and I kept this one, it could strengthen the remainder of our line without compromising this point."

Stanton raised an eyebrow, "You sure you can do that? You sure you want to?"

"I can. You remember what I did to the Trolls that attacked Mildra seven cycles past don't you?"

Jerhad, with the use of the black Elfstone, *balan* (purification) and *licri*, had killed more than three thousand Trolls in a few spans of heartbeats. *balan* had cleansed the battlefield where the Dwarves had held the Trolls cornered in a canyon two leagues north of Mildra. When the Elves had joined the battle, peppering the Trolls with arrows from their positions on the cliffs above, the Trolls had bolted and forced the Dwarves back to a hill where the Dwarves rallied and held. Jerhad and his companions, coming south from the battle in Breezon, had arrived at that point and Jerhad, taking the battle upon himself, had used his magic to finish it.

"I know I can. I don't want to. Does anyone here want to be here? Does anyone here want to battle the Trolls?"

"I see your meaning," said Stanton with a grimace, scratching at the back of his head. "I'll make the necessary changes. Only, I'll leave you a squad of soldiers to protect you with shield and sword in case it should prove necessary."

"I'll think about it. They may just prove to be a distraction, and I might end up having to protect them. I'll let you know. A dozen at most might be adequate if we do."

"You look preoccupied."

"It's...Andreanna. I'm worried about her. Why would she leave like that, and where would she go?"

"You remember how Morlah used his orb to see and find things. Maybe you could do something like that to find her."

"Good idea. I'll have to try and see if...."

They were interrupted by what sounded like a solid knock on a heavy wooden door. From where they stood in the middle of the fields on the upper flats, the sound was quite out of place. They both looked about but saw nothing. Then suddenly, immediately before them stood Morlah, the Druid. He was translucent in appearance, pale as if he were a ghost, and his flowing robes and mantle were animated as if he stood in a stiff wind.

"Fire and demons, old man, I wish you wouldn't do that," exclaimed Jerhad.

"But I didst knock first, as King GladdenStone hadst formerly suggested," said the Druid.

"Is that what that was?" said Stanton.

"Yes. GladdenStone, the late Dwarf King, didst mention it once. Actually, the last time I didst visit him. He didst suggest that I shouldst knock, or something, before making an apparition."

"Well, I guess next time we'll know...not a bad idea...better than scaring the life out of one's body," agreed Stanton.

"Yes, I doest suppose, since thou didst not know the meaning of the forewarning, that the apparition wouldst be as startling.... Jerhad, I doest have a message for thee from the Lady Andreanna."

"Andreanna! Where is she? Is she alright?"

"Thou doest fret too much for her, Jerhad; she is quite capable. But, yes, she is of a good health and humor. She wast, when I last didst see her in the Mystic Mountains. It doest appear that *acrch*, or Nan, has summoned her to meet with the Faeries in the mountains. She is accompanied by two Gnome guards, two wolves and a Faerie who hast chosen to manifest herself as a Gnome child."

"Nan? Nan sent her!" Jerhad repeated incredulously. "If I get my hands...."

"Thou may as well begin at thine own throat if thou willst throttle anyone. For the magic that is Nan is also the magic that is in thee, young Elf-Friend. Be not overly distraught; she is with the Faeries; she couldst not be safer."

Jerhad kicked at the ground, turning a divot of grass, and pouted a bit. "Yeah...well...she better be or I'll...I'll.... What do the Faeries want with her anyway?"

"She didst not have a good grasp of that knowledge when I spoke with her. But she wast in good health and spirits and didst want me to let thee know where she wast."

"What were you doing in the Mystic Mountains?" asked Stanton.

"Looking for Andreanna. I hadst noticed that she had been missing from Mildra for a few courses, so I searched for her with mine orb and found her in the Mystics. I didst appear to her there and spoke with her. But enough of that.

"Let us speak of the matters at hand. The Trolls willst be here at the sunrising, midcourse at the latest. They art camped on the lower flats. Come, look." He passed his hand over the orb that was mounted on his black-polished-oak staff, bringing it to life. The staff was named *tenensil* by the Faeries, meaning The Watcher's Eye. The silver-white metal of Faerie magic glowed brightly for a few heartbeats, and then, the fist-sized orb became clearer than spring water. Jerhad and Stanton drew near, never having seen this magic. Within the orb, they witnessed a view of the Trolls' camp, which spread out across the flats.

"Must be sixty thousand of them," said Stanton.

"Fifty-five thousand eight hundred and forty-nine," replied Morlah. "Their numbers doest grow course by course." Stanton returned the Druid a sour look for the correction. Morlah appeared not to notice.

"I doest think we shouldst consider visiting them in the night," Morlah continued. "A little surprise may make them more wary of their folly."

"What do you have in mind, Druid?" asked Stanton.

"Raven and I willst be with thee in person shortly. At this time, we art sailing two leagues south of thee, off the coast, on the *MayBest*. We willst join thee in this exploit. Tell me what thou doest think, Commander, for I doest defer to thee in military strategy. I didst think that with the use of the archers, we couldst raise havoc in their camp and remain hidden. With the use of a bit of magic, a Gray spell, I couldst cloak the archers from sound and sight under the cover of darkness. We couldst come within easy bowshot of the camp, perform our mischief and return here before dawn. Thou wouldst leave all infantry behind to defend the passages in case of a subsequent assault, though I doest think that the Trolls know not of thine presence here as of yet, for they have moved without the use of scouts. I willst accompany thee and carry out mine own damage from the air, from The Raven's back."

"Sounds good to me," said Stanton, approving the Druid's plan. "Jerhad should stay back and help secure the infantry's positions."

"Not on your life, Commander! I'll be right there with the two of you!"

Both Stanton and Morlah nodded, deferring to his decision, which surprised Jerhad. In the past, he had more than once argued with each of them over a course of action. Now, it was with ease that he turned them, Stanton being most agreeable and Morlah unusually silent. So, they went into Jerhad's tent to iron out the details of the proposed attack.

Jerhad was in the upper branches of a Great Live Oak. Though the night was almost pitch-dark, *licri* gave him vision that made it as if he were under the midcourse's sun. Fifty-five thousand eight hundred and forty-nine Trolls covered an unbelievable amount of land! Jerhad could see the magically cloaked Elf archers moving into position on the north side of the Trolls' camp in spite of Morlah's magic. Hidden under the Druid's spell, they need not worry about being seen nor heard by the Trolls. Jerhad's position to the west was to protect the archers with magic when they retreated. Overhead, he saw Morlah sweeping in fast on The Raven. That would be the archers' signal, when Morlah attacked the south side of camp; the archers would let loose their showers of poisoned arrows. If not for *licri*, Jerhad's heart would have been racing with fear and excitement. Now, instead, he was calm, focused and felt full of the strength and the vitality of the Elven magic.

The first explosion startled Jerhad as Morlah went into action, throwing fireballs down into the camp from the heavens. Raven, true to his nature, could not contain himself with the battle at hand; he had to involve himself. He flew down to the mass of Trolls, and using his steel shod hooves, he danced across the Troll horde, leaving behind a wake of broken and collapsed skulls. For all appearances, The Bornodald looked as if he were prancing in a parade, as Morlah continued raining fire and death into the host. From the north came the cries of pain as the archers loosed their fury of death. Confusion among the Trolls quickly escalated to a frenzy.

balan rose in Jerhad's chest. He intended to cleanse the field of the evil that was there. Drawing on Ember to assist him in his focus, he intended to use the magic as a scythe on the west edge of the encampment and slay Trolls by the hundreds.

"It should not be so!" hissed Nan's voice from behind him. Normally, he would have been startled to the point of perhaps falling from the tree, but *licri* held him firm.

"What do you mean?" the Elven Prince asked, turning to the Faerie.

"You mean to fight the Elves' battles for them and slay by the hundreds and thousands. Stay your hand, Elven Prince."

"I will not! These beasts mean to destroy our homes and people, and you would have me idle? You'll have to do better than that if you want me to stop."

"The Trolls have Life and Health within them; they are not your true enemy; Daektoch is. I cannot abide such destruction, Elven Prince. It violates the essence of my being, and, in that you possess the magic of *acrch*, it becomes a violation of your own being."

"What do you suggest?"

Oddly, Nan was silent. She hung her head and vanished.

"Thanks a lot!" He spat into the night before turning his attention back to the Trolls. He would not stand by idly!

The diffuse light shining through the tent's blue canvas roof rudely woke Jerhad to a hammering, incapacitating headache.

"Awake at last, Jerhad."

Through squinting eyes, the Elf turned to see Morlah sitting by him.

"I didst fear that I wouldst need get thee to Parintia, to the Druid Healers. How art thou?"

Jerhad shielded his eyes from the light with a cupped hand. In a faint whisper, the Elf said, "The light hurts my eyes and my head hurts like I drank too much Dwarf's ale. What happened? How'd I get here? We were...."

"Yes indeed, what didst happen? We didst find thee unconscious at the base of the tree where thou hadst taken thine stand. Thou wast carried back and didst remain unconscious until now, it being two spans of the sun into the second course since our offensive. I wast hopeful that *thou* wouldst tell me what didst happen to thee."

Jerhad was silent for a span of heartbeats. "I began slaying Trolls with the magic of *balan*...and Nan appeared to me telling me to stop. That's the last thing I remember. She'd appeared to me before also, before I began killing the Trolls, and told me not to. I didn't listen to her, and then, I was here."

"Nan. Dost thou mean *acrch*?"

"Yes, one and the same.... I'm starting to not like her!"

"Speak not thus, mine Prince. The wisdom of the Faerie creatures is significant and shouldst always be considered."

"I don't know if I believe all that. Elves die from battle wounds, and she doesn't want me to heal them. Trolls threaten our people, and I shouldn't kill them. What's the point of having magic if you sit by and don't use it?"

"I doest see thine meaning, Jerhad...but...I doest beg of thee that thou wouldst give heed to the Faerie's wisdom. There art laws within the realms of magic, which thou hast not been taught. They art not laws as those that wouldst be made by men or Elves to govern themselves. But they art more as the laws that govern nature. Things fall from the sky, not up to it. Water goes to the sea and returns to the land by the clouds. These laws doest posses a universal wisdom," Morlah spoke, his hands motioning as if pleading for Jerhad's understanding.

"So it is with magic, Jerhad. These are laws that one using magic shouldst heed. If not, there canst be grave consequences. Thou art familiar with the phenomenon of blending for example. If a Black mage attempts to use White magic or vice versa, the effect is to neutralize the magical ability of the mage. Thou must observe these laws. Take heed; if Nan wast stirred enough to come to warn thee, the meaning wast of significance. Didst she say anything else?"

"She said something about her essence being violated or something.... I don't know what she means."

"Ah, that is it then!"

"What is what then?"

"Nan is of the magic of Life and Health. It is difficult for her to abide killing, even necessary killing. It doest create a difficult conflict to have the presence of a few manifestations of Elven magics within thee, Jerhad. There is a delicate balance thou willst need to achieve if thou art to survive its use. Until thou doest possess this wisdom for thineself, it wouldst be advisable to take heed of the Faerie's counsel."

"But what happened to me? Why did I pass out? Why does my head hurt like this?"

"Let it suffice to say that what thou didst do with the magic is equivalent to thee attempting to run through a stone wall."

"That's what it feels like," groaned the Elf, allowing his head to fall back onto his cot. "How will I learn these laws?"

"It may be profitable for us to sit and discuss some basic principles when we doest have time. Until then, doest give heed to Nan when she addresses thee."

"What of the battle?"

"All is well. We scored a mighty blow and suffered no loss."

Deep in the Mystic Mountains, in the land of the Faeries, Andreanna underwent lessons of her own. The Faeries attempted to teach her how to use the magic that she possessed, but the progress they made was slow. They were also quite interested in the black Elfstone, *balak*. There had been no new Elfstones formed in a few millennia, and besides that, this one was different. It was not the normally seen manifestation of the Earthen magic but a blending of the magics, argentus, Black and White. Also, there had been no outward personification of a Faerie creature associated with it, but rather it was intimately linked to Andreanna, her innate magic and something of her personality or essence. The phenomenon caused quite a stir with many of the Faeries who spent much time examining Andreanna and her magic.

The determined courses of the sun were passing, Andreanna still unsure of what she was doing there. She had been summoned to help the Faeries with their problem.

*How can I help such creatures, the embodiment of magic? They are the greatest power on the planet. I didn't even understand the half of what they spoke to me of when they instructed me in the use of magic. The only thing I have that they don't is the black stone, **balak**.* That was a thought. Maybe it was in this that she might help them. She would have to ask the Faerie King about it.

Meanwhile, Fonta continued to keep to her Gnome-child form. She also continued to talk incessantly, to the point that it was noticeable that the other Faeries often avoided her. The King commented that it had been several millennia since Fonta had assumed her true manifestation. At one point, she had taken on the form of the Gnome and remained as such since that time. She had no explanation to offer and often insisted she be called Fonta and not *isini*, though the Faeries still called her by her Faerie name.

So, Andreanna was fed, tended to and doted upon, and she even allowed Fonta to persuade her to take another "dip" in the argentus bath though it took a lot of effort to let herself breath it in on a voluntary basis. Fonta also seemed a bit possessive of Andreanna and often put up a racket of chatter that drove the others away, only to quiet after they had gone.

"Fonta, what do you think of this," asked Andreanna reading to her the prophecy of *The Book of the Secrets of the Queen* — "*Daektoch, who became unloved, unloving and unlovable, left and went to the outside world among the Humans who dwell there. His name before he was known as Daektoch was Pezzikta. She who possesses this knowledge has power.*"

"It is as it speaks. To know the true name of a wizard is to have power over him. To speak the wizard's true name in his presence is to take his power from him and render him without magic. To speak Daektoch's name in his presence will cause him to become a mere mortal again. Since he is some millennia of cycles old, he would likely turn to dust, for it is only his magic that sustains what resembles a living Human now."

"Why haven't the Faeries dealt with him?"

"I don't know. Why should we? He is of no direct concern to us. We have caused the magic to return to the Elves. We have given the Elfstones and the Earthen element of magic to the forging of *Gildar*. We have provided Morlah with the orb and the knife to enhance his magic. We are indirectly the cause of the added blessing of the magic you possess. We have caused the magic to awaken in Jerhad, the descendant of the Elven King Windemere, and set him on a course to be raised to become King of the Elves. That should be sufficient to deal with Daektoch. The planet needs a balance of power, not necessarily the elimination of one or the other."

Daektoch looked into the pool of enchanted liquid in its alabaster basin, which sat on a pedestal. The foul brew ceased from its troubled boiling as the incantation came to an end. The liquid's key element was that of fresh Human blood. Prisoners from Heros' jails were easily acquired by Daektoch's servants. Daektoch had had the basin retrieved from his study in Heros by the hand of his servants and brought to Mount Bahal. From his cliff-side perch, he looked within to see how his spell against the Faeries progressed. He watched with glee, witnessing the subtle change progressing, little by little. Had he attempted it in an instant, the Faeries would have understood what was happening and easily stopped it. But as it was, the slow, insidious separation from their power progressed, undetected. They would most likely not discover his work until he delivered the final and fatal blow.

Then Daektoch saw her! The "Elf's toy", as he referred to Andreanna. *This was noteworthy*, but he did not know in what manner. *What is she doing in the Mystics? Why is the Elf not with her? Can it be there is something afoot to thwart my plans?* He did not dare go after her, for the Faeries were still far too powerful for him, especially collectively, probably even individually. Fortunately, he was patient, for it would take but a few more cycles of the moon to complete the Faeries' destruction. He hated them so; it was a shame he could not finish it now. With a sigh of resignation, he turned his focus back to the Troll horde at Land's Break.

Stanton entered the tent where Morlah and Jerhad were. "Interesting reports returning from our scouts. The Trolls have fallen back three leagues since our attack. A lot of fighting going on within their ranks. Seems like the taste of magic and poison arrows was a bit much for them. It looked like, to the scouts, as if some want to retreat while others want to move forward. Regardless, they're in obvious disarray. I think we should be planning something before they reorganize. If you could pull off something like you did the other night, Jerhad, I think we'd have them on the run."

"He canst not," interrupted Morlah. "It couldst be his death to try such again."

"He left hundreds of them dead.... *Why* can't he?"

"That is what didst cause his unconsciousness. To kill doest violate the essence of some of the magic within him; he *must not* repeat such unless there is no recourse."

"But this could be the last blow!" insisted Stanton.

"I can't," bemoaned Jerhad. "Morlah's right. I almost split my head open, or at least it feels like that, with what I did. Let's leave it as a fortunate turn and come up with something else. So, do you have a plan for our next move?"

Stanton looked from Morlah and back to Jerhad for a span of heartbeats. "Oh, well. I probably should get my head examined by a Healer. Getting involved in the use of magic like that.... I wasn't like that in the past you'll remember."

"No, you weren't, were you?" replied Jerhad. "That's quite a change now that you mention it. Using magic must be contagious."

Stanton shook his head and frowned in self-reproach. His hand slowly swept across his chin and mouth. "Yes, I do have a plan. Here take a look at these maps. This is where the Trolls have withdrawn to...."

Chapter 13

The Elf and Dwarf infantries lay low, shielded from sight by the heavily leafed, wild Elderberry bushes that grew along the forest's edge. Out in the fields beyond was the Troll army, which continued in their arguing and fighting about their next move.

They were in complete disarray, not having set watch nor camp. Their backs were turned to the forest and their attention focused within to the leaders, arguing and fighting. It would soon be dark, not the best time for a confrontation, but the Elves and Dwarves were here, and this advantage would not last forever. The roar of Troll voices rose to a din.

The Dwarf and Elf ranks moved out at a trot, closing the distance to the Trolls, pikes pointing to the darkening sky overhead. The sound of their tramping feet was muffled by Morlah's incantation. When the infantry was within one hundred paces of the Trolls, Morlah came in on Raven from the opposite direction drawing his enemies' attention to himself with fireballs and bolts of magic raining down onto the southern edge of the swarm. Pikes leveled as the infantry closed the final gap to their adversaries, and then, the first ranks struck! Archers behind the infantry aimed high and released their tainted shafts far into the mass of invaders. The unarmed backs of the Trolls were peppered with arrows. Hundreds of them fell while others screamed out in pain and anger as the second wave of infantry struck and the first ranks fell back. Razor-sharp spear tips deeply penetrated into massive bodies. Arrow poisoned Trolls fell, their mouths and nostrils filled with blood-tinged foam as they struggled against paralysis, seizures and suffocation.

Morlah continued his onslaught from the sky, but then he noticed some Trolls off to the side cringe at something not quite in his direction. "Roll off to the side. Now!" commanded Morlah. The Raven instantly obeyed without question. With a loud whoosh, a huge bat-like creature bearing one of Daektoch's dark servants streaked by where they just had been. Daektoch had sent his fiends in to deter Morlah from his attack. These monsters were former Black mages that Daektoch had enchanted and changed into something between mage and demon. Their claws were poisonous; they were oblivious to steel and shaft and were able to disappear into a mist of vapor in their comings and goings. The only thing able to hurt them was White magic, argentus and Faerie magic.

A few of them had been changed into the winged creatures as a deterrence to the Druid's interferences. It was unlike Daektoch to use them against the Druid's and Elf's magic, for he had lost many of them in this way in the past. Their ranks had considerably dwindled. Daektoch had been reserving them for uses where success was guaranteed. Either this was a decoy, or eliminating Morlah's meddling was extremely important to the Black Mage now.

Meanwhile, the Trolls had rallied to answer the surprise assault, as the fourth and fifth ranks of infantry viciously clashed with them. The Trolls surged forward with a snarl, and the army began falling back under tremendous pressure. Elves were decapitated by and skewered on broadswords. Dwarves were brained by stone maces and trampled to death. The Trolls' size was a distinct advantage that was not easily overcome in face-to-face battle. The Trolls began to ravage the forward ranks. As Jerhad watched in dismay, scores of his troops fell with each passing span of heartbeats. Large Troll hands twisted heads from bodies, and blood spurted freely upon the field. Jerhad pulled his knife and began to draw on *balan*. Stanton put his hand on Jerhad's arm.

"No, you don't. Morlah said you mustn't...promised to skin me if I let you."

"We can't let them die like that!"

"They have to fend for themselves. They have their orders."

"I can't.... No, wait.... It'll be alright. I can do this a different way," he said as he walked forward, reaching down into his magic, drawing on the white, yellow, blue and green magic in various proportions. Behind him, Stanton watched, doubtful, undecided. Up between the Trolls and the infantry rose a solid, transparent barrier. The front line of the horde was pressed into the obstacle with those at the wall being crushed by the pressure from behind. Many died impaled on their own weapons, armaments that were turned back against them by the barrier and forced by the press of host behind them.

The Elven and Dwarf detachment retreated in double-time, falling back into the forest where they quickly filed onto a narrow trail that they had swathed on the way here. Under the cloak of night, it was doubtful the Trolls would find it until the army was well away. Jerhad dropped the barrier and followed Stanton into the forest, making their escape as the Trolls surged forward again.

Back in the air, Morlah had his hands full as he was engaged now by three of the bat creatures and their dark riders. Deadly bolts of Black magic flew at him from all directions. He was forced to put his strength into his defenses as Raven maneuvered a convoluted track in an attempt to avoid being hit by the bats and bolts.

"The army is escaped. I believe we shouldst do the same," mindspoke Morlah to The Raven. The smell of heat scorched air and hair wafted in the smoke of the battle.

"And leave the battle!" came back The Raven incredulously. "We can take these furry beasts. Just keep those bolts off of us, and I'll do the rest."

"No, friend. I know that battle lust doest fill thee, but methinks the odds art against us. Let us retreat that we mayest fight another course."

Raven hesitated for a heartbeat. "Alright, Druid, but only after this." He rolled up and then back the way they had been going, swooping down on top of one of the winged beasts. Raven's rear hooves struck the rider, sending him catapulting toward the ground, while his fore hooves split the bat-creature's head open, propelling it in a downward spiral, following its unseated rider.

"How is it that thou didst harm it? It doest require magic to kill one of these."

"Druid, are you still a child in your understanding? The Bornodald were born of magic. We are of the same origin as what you call Faeries but not wielding power as they do. We are created by it and, in some sense, contain it."

"I doest stand instructed. Now, let us depart." With which Morlah gathered a large fireball and sent it floating between them and the other two mages. The spherical inferno exploded, causing the winged beasts to flee in the opposite direction to avoid being swept away by it. Morlah drew up a cloak of invisibility, and he and The Raven disappeared into the night. Below, hundreds of Dwarves, Elves and Trolls lay dead or dying. The Trolls, in their usual bestial manner, consumed the carcasses of friend and foe.

"I'm going out on a scouting mission to take a first hand look at the lay of the terrain beyond Land's Break," announced Stanton the next rising. A constant stream of rain fell from the gray, gloomy sky. It left a cold dampness in the air about the field where the Elf and Dwarf detachments were entrenched. "I'm taking one squad of Elves and one of Dwarves with me."

"When are we leaving?" inquired Jerhad.

"You're coming too?" said Stanton, disapproval dripping from his words.

"I thought I might tag along."

"It's not good tactics to send your leaders into battle or out on errands."

"I wish you'd tell that to Morlah. Every time I see him, he sends me off on some errand; but by that advice, Commander, you shouldn't be going out either."

"Alright. Pack your bags and let's get going."

"Will you join us, Morlah?" asked Jerhad.

"No, for I have seen what doest look like trouble to the north in mine orb, and I must investigate the matter. The Raven and I willst be leaving imminently."

The patrol, accompanied by Stanton and Jerhad, spent the remainder of the course moving along the fields at the edge of the Coastal Range's forests. Finally, at sunsetting, they came to a small village that had been razed by the Trolls. They did a bit of scavenging for food and weapons and came up with little. They found no bodies and assumed the villagers had escaped before the arrival of the invaders. Camp was established, sentries posted, and soon, they settled down for the night.

The skies had cleared to a heavenly blue when Stanton awoke the next rising. The man made his way to a small stream away from the camp and washed his face. He was suddenly surprised to hear the sound of a soft sobbing. At first, he could not determine where the crying came from, but then, he identified it as emerging from a well that was still a little further from the camp. He went over to the well, not sure if it was some kind of trap.

"Hello?" he cautiously said.

"Help me," came a soft feminine voice that rose from within.

Carefully, Stanton looked over the edge into the darkness where he could barely make out the form of someone just about one pace down within the shallow, dry well. "Who are you?" he asked.

"My name is Ahliene. I had come back to the village for something, but then, the Trolls came and I hid in here. I hurt my wrist and can't climb back out."

Stanton extended his hand down to her, "Here, let me help you up." She took hold of his hand with her good arm, and, with one heave and a grunt, he had her up and standing on the ground next to him by the well. When their eyes met, he looked into her deep, wide, green eyes and gasped.

Before him stood an Elf girl (well, actually a woman, or female as they were referred to in the non-Human races) probably in her twentieth cycle. She had long, straight, golden hair, and though it was wet, dirty and clung to her face now, he thought it might be the most beautiful hair that he had ever laid eyes upon. Stanton gawked as her fair-skinned hand came up and pushed a strand of hair back behind her long slender Elven ear (perhaps a bit longer than most Elves' ears). Her marine-green eyes moved as if she were a bit shy to be standing so close to him. The female looked up into his eyes and back toward the ground. She had sharply cut, high cheekbones and a clean vibrant complexion. Her light-colored eyelashes made her almond-shaped eyes look all the more wide.

Stanton fell into her eyes' deep, light-green pools, drowning in them.

His heart had never pounded so hard in his chest, not in battle, not in flight, not in the most arduous training he could remember. He stood transfixed by the Elven beauty that stood before him.

"Thank you," she said as she composed herself, the trace of a smile breaking on her lips. Moist, full lips.

The Commander's hands trembled, and he began to perspire nervously.

"Are you alright?" she asked reaching up and touching his hand. Nervous energy shot through him like a bolt of lightening at her touch. He gaped at her.

"Y...Y...Yess. I'm fine. I have to go now. There's something 1 have to be doing. I just don't remember what it is right now."

Ahliene suppressed a giggle. "What's your name?"

"Name? Yess. What's my name? Good question. Oh, right...Stanton. That's it. My name's Stanton."

"Well, thank you for pulling me out of there, Stanton," she said looking at him with her head slightly tilted to one side, the profile accenting her beauty. "Will I see you again?"

"Yeah, right. I'm around all the time." With that, he turned and almost ran off toward a group of Dwarves gathered about the morning cook fire. Making his way to the Dwarves, Stanton spotted one known as StoneSon. Motioning with his head, Stanton called him away from the group. "Hey, StoneSon, come over here."

"Yes, Commander. How can I help you?"

"Yeah. Do you have any of those corndrippings on you?"

"No sir, Commander. I swore off the corn-mash drippings. No more for me. That stuff will rot your innards. Pickle your gizzard, it will."

"Don't give me that Troll-dung. I know you're still drinking the stuff. Cough it up or I'll let IronLeggs know you're still drinking."

"...Alright. You caught me.... I do not know how...."

"Shut up and give me the bottle."

StoneSon reached into his belt pouch and handed the bottle of clear spirits to Stanton, who quickly pulled the cork, raising a imploring protest from StoneSon.

"No, sir. ...Do not pour it out...please!"

Stanton ignored him, and raising the bottle to his lips, he poured a few fingers' worth of the substance down his throat and then re-corked the bottle. He wheezed a cough as his face reddened, and he handed the bottle back to the Dwarf. The Dwarf gawked at the Commander.

"...(cough) thanks...(cough, cough) StoneSon. You're, (cough) a good man. (cough)," he said, tears swelling in his eyes. As he walked away, he loudly said, looking back so the other Dwarves would hear him, "You're a good man. I'll see you get (cough) a commendation (cough)."

"Commendation for what?" asked Jerhad, pulling up short to avoid having Stanton walk into him.

"Nothing, he's just a good example of a soldier...."

Jerhad sniffed the air. "Have you been drinking?"

"...(cough)...What if I have?"

"You just got up. It's morning. And besides, you don't drink."

"Needed it to calm my (cough) nerves."

"Nerves? You just got up. I've seen you in battle. Your nerves don't get frazzled.... They're like steel. What's up?"

"Nothing. Are you through?" Stanton blurted, his temper flaring a bit.

It was then that Jerhad noticed Ahliene standing in the background by the well. "Ye gods, will you look at that. She's beautiful."

Stanton turned to look, attempting to portray innocence. Ahliene smiled and gave him a little wave, causing Stanton to quickly turn away and blush.

Jerhad smiled. "You know her!"

"No!" he abruptly insisted.

Jerhad laughed. "You dog, you know her."

"Just pulled her out of a dry well where she hid from the Trolls. Can't a guy help someone without everyone getting bent out of shape?"

"You dog! You've been bit."

"Bit? What? I just helped her up out of the well," he said, his face turning a brilliant red.

Now, Jerhad was laughing. The Elf fell forward into Stanton, laughing, tears in his eyes and his arms around Stanton's neck, holding himself up. He choked for breath around his tears and snorted.

"You've been bit," he managed between his gasps for air. "Wait till Andreanna hears about this. Squad Leader Stanton has been bit."

Stanton pulled away, pushing Jerhad back at the same time. "Get away from me. What's wrong with you?"

Jerhad waved back at Ahliene, still laughing. He slapped Stanton on the back. "You should see yourself. The whole war has been worth it for this one heartbeat in time. You should see your face!" Jerhad continued, laughing.

"I don't have time for this. I have work to do! I have to go...work the men in weapons training." And work them he did. He gathered a group of Elves and Dwarves for practice, setting them in groups of three or five, up against himself, and gave them all a sound thrashing.

A while later, Jerhad came by. "*Ahem*, Commander.... Don't you think you should save a few to battle the Trolls?"

Stanton stiffly stepped back. "...Yeah...well.... Everybody dismissed!" He stomped off toward the other end of camp.

Jerhad, laughing, called to him, "Bitten, Commander. You've been bitten."

A quarter span later as they were about to break camp, Jerhad came rushing past Stanton and thrust something into his hands. "Quick, take this and don't look behind you." Jerhad then proceeded to run to where the Dwarves and Elves were gathering, ready to continue their scouting. Stanton looked down into his hands and saw that he was holding a bunch of wildflowers. He looked up at Jerhad who was now looking back with a broad grin on his face in addition to having all the Elves and Dwarves turned watching in the Commander's direction. Stanton began to turn to see what he had been instructed not to look at, behind him.

"Oh, there you are, Stanton. I just wanted to say good-bye before...oh, they're lovely. Are those flowers for me?" asked Ahliene, who was coming up behind him.

Stanton was stunned. His hand involuntarily reached out, giving her the flowers. From behind, he could hear the roar of laughter from the Dwarves and Elves. It was also easy to make out Jerhad's laughter in the midst of it; it was the loudest.

"I just wanted to thank you again for helping me out of the well," she said taking the flowers from him. "My wrist is much better now. Prince Jerhad did something to it, and it's good as new. He's also arranged for a group of Elves to escort me back to Mildra; so I wanted to come say good-bye before we went." She stepped in close to him, stood on tiptoes and kissed him on the cheek, leaving Stanton a brilliant red and with knees and hands visibly trembling. He opened his mouth and managed to squawk.

Ahliene suppressed a giggle and left, thanking him for the beautiful flowers. Elves and Dwarves rolled on the ground with laughter as he turned back to them, displaying his blushing countenance.

"Prince or not, I'll get him for this."

It was the fifth course of the sun of Andreanna's visit to the Faeries. Fonta had had her bathe in the argentus daily even though Daektoch's taint had been banished and destroyed with the first. This course of the sun, she came out of the pool and looked about at the Faerie land around her.

"It's mildewed or something. Fonta, you're mildewed!"

"What do you mean?"

Andreanna came over, touched Fonta's skin, and examined it. She spit on her fingers and attempted to rub Fonta's 'stains' off. "It's like mildewed cloth. It's deep within and doesn't come off." She scratched at leaves with the same result. "Everything looks mildewed," she repeated looking about as she turned in a continuous circle.

"We must go to the King and tell him. This is what we've been looking for. I can tell. I can feel it in my essence."

A few spans of heartbeats later, Andreanna sat with the King and Queen, surrounded by a multitude of Faeries, many having come out of their stone manifestations, reappearing in their Faerie forms to listen to the discussion.

"...And you say it all appears mildewed?" the King was asking for the fourth time.

"Yes..." she replied in an exasperated tone, "I can't explain it beyond that...little grayish-green stains or spots on everything except the bath of argentus."

"That, O King, is significant. I don't know how, but it is the root of the problem. I told you she would do it," exclaimed Fonta. "But nooo.... You said it was all in vain. At every turn, you doubted me. After all, I'm a Faerie too; but nooo...."

"*isini*, ...shut up."

"Yes, King."

"You were right, *isini*. I commend you for your wisdom, action and persistence," said the Faerie King with a bit of a bow. "I shall be slower to doubt you henceforth. But now we have some evidence, we still are no closer to a solution, unless you, Elf Queen, have a suggestion, for none of the Faeries are able to detect in any manner that which you speak of."

"Not me. I don't have a clue. If it were as simple as mildew, I'd put you all out in the sun for a while, but you are already in the sun...and it doesn't help, so I guess it's not mildew. Faeries probably aren't prone to mildew anyway...are they?"

"Tomorrow is the sixth course of the sun that you agreed to remain with us. The following sunrising you will leave. We will have *isini* accompany you back to Mildra. I would ask you to look closely at what you have seen. Use the magic you have to assist if you can," instructed the King.

"But what of us, she-alpha," Baby was asking Andreanna at a later time. "We cannot go and live among the Elves. They are not pack with us, and they would kill us with their flying sticks as soon as they see us."

"That is a problem," she spoke to Baby. "I hadn't really planned on being your pack leader, but my male and pup live there, so I must be there also. I do not know what to do with you."

"I told you she wasn't true pack," grumbled Boy. "A true alpha doesn't abandon pack."

"Do you ask me to abandon my male and pup, Boy?"

His lip lifted as if he would snarl, but then turned and trotted off toward the forest.

"What if we find you another pack," asked Andreanna.

"They would not have us unless you became their alpha."

"That's all I need, to be Queen of the Wolves."

"What is queen?"

"...well...it's the alpha of all the packs and the alpha of all the alphas."

Baby gave the concept some thought and then said, "Is that not what you are? Is there an alpha that could stand up to you, that you could not defeat?"

"I guess not, but I don't care to go around killing wolves for no more reason than to show off my power, or for any other reason, actually."

Pralande Stewart, Commander of the Breezon Army, walked the top of the city's wall, as he did at the sunrising of each course. He surveyed the plains, which rolled on as far as the eye could see, the plains where many battles against the Trolls had been fought. Each course of the sun he would rise and walk the wall and then meet with the scouts for their reports, after they rode in from their tour along the Blue Mountains where they spied out the Trolls' activities. Since the last war, the Trolls had remained well within the boundaries of the mountains and had not caused trouble.

Stewart was diligent in his duties, and though he loved battle, he did appreciate peacetime, since it was more of a guarantee of being around and alive a little longer.

Like many of Breezon's officers, Stewart had been in the army since the age of eighteen cycles. The army had a mandatory four cycles of service for all its citizens, male and female; most quickly left its ranks after their obligation was over, but a few stayed on, making a career of military life. Stewart had been one of those who had remained, having no family left after his parents had died in a Troll raid on the southern border of the plains. He had quickly risen in rank, and after the last Troll war when a strategic catapult shot from the Trolls had killed most of the army's brass as they sat in morning review, Stewart was the highest-ranking officer left. The city officials had promoted him to Commander of the Army.

This course, as he approached the southern gate where the scout patrols were barracked, he found the scouts had already arrived and were waiting for him on the wall. It could only mean trouble, for normally he watched them riding in from a great distance.

"Commander, Sergeant Marcus ready with scouting reports, sir!" saluted a soldier, an old friend of Stanton's.

"At your ease, soldier. Deliver your report."

"Troops from Heros in full battle gear, marching straight for Breezon, sir! Two spans out."

"From Heros? You must be mistaken. They're just patrolling the Blue Mountains."

"I estimate fifty thousand troops, sir. More than just a patrol. Headed straight across the plains. Nowhere near the mountains."

Stewart paused. It did not make sense! True, there was no love lost between the two cities. And although each time

Breezon had asked the capitol city for assistance in the Troll wars that had been fought and had been refused, there had never been any open hostility between the cities. Stewart also had always thought it odd that Trolls had never attacked Heros, but he did not know what to make of it. But now, to have Heros marching against them? It had to be a mistake. There had to be another purpose for the troops to be out. Nevertheless, he would not be caught with his sword belt around his ankles.

"Soldier, sound the general alarm," he hollered to the watchman on the tower next to them.

The soldier blew his call on the brass bugle that had hung on his belt, and soldiers poured from the barracks and onto the walls while others closed and barred the city's gates. The wall soon swarmed with men.

"Sergeant, send two men out to meet them and see what they're about. Mitchell, better rouse the city council and get them together. I'll report to them as soon as our messengers return. Marcus, have the catapults drawn but not loaded yet. Archers at the ready and cavalry at the ready within the gates." He turned and gazed out across the plains from where Heros' army would come.

Humans fighting Humans? It couldn't be!

HeartStone, son of GladdenStone, son of StoneBreaker, King of the Dwarves in *Dolan* in the western Mystic Mountains, sat in the King's Chamber that he used to conduct his administrative duties. His right index finger fidgeted at the corner of a parchment that he had stared at but had not seen for the last half span, preoccupied with the Trolls besieging *Dolan*.

All Dwarf families had been withdrawn from the valley where their homes were and into the mountain fortress. It was probably just a matter of time before the Trolls found the valley and a way down into it. The Trolls on the western face of the mountain numbered some forty thousand. HeartStone was loath to bring his army into direct confrontation with them. Their size, weight and reach were strictly in the Trolls' favor. To amass any formidable size sortie would take too long; their foe would decimate them as they left the tunnels. The King had had ten thousand troops waiting in reserve to the north, removed from the mountain; the deployment had taken place at a trickle, the soldiers exiting through the long tunnels. But that did not give them the edge they needed to take on Trolls, even if the Dwarf Army outnumbered the Trolls two-to-one, or even if he recalled the troops that he had sent to Mildra. He was not quite ready to consider doing that.

HeartStone was restless and was becoming impatient. The Dwarves were well prepared to endure a long siege, but if the Trolls did not go away, they would still be forced to take action. He wished that his father were here, that the old King were still alive. GladdenStone would have known how to deal with this. He lifted his eyes to the ceiling and cried, "Father, tell me what to do!"

There was a knock. Before the King could decided whether to allow entrance or not, Morlah stood before him.

"Druid!" spat the Dwarf King. "Bah! By my father's beard, you will be the death of me, doing that!"

"But I didst knock just as thine father suggested, as thou well doest know."

"I still do not get used to it," spat the Dwarf King, his mood rancid.

"Art thou aware that there are Trolls at thine door?"

HeartStone huffed into his beard. "What is this? An attempt at humor?"

"Mayhapst, a feeble attempt."

"To answer your question, yes. And I do not know what to do with them. I have sat for spans of the sun with my counselors and commanders, but they are more filled with indecision than I am. I wish my father were here. He would know what to do."

"Unlikely, Dwarf King. There were times that he didst fret and falter as thou art doing now. Decisions such as these art not simple. There art many factors to ponder, thine people, thine soldiers, losses, enduring a lengthy siege, children whose fathers wouldst die...."

"Bah, Morlah, do not remind me. What am I to do? I have sent messengers to Breezon to ask that they send their army down to flank the Trolls. Perhaps between the two forces we could move them. But the messengers were sent out sixteen courses back and have not returned."

"There willst be no succor from Breezon, for they art beset with ills of their own. Six courses past, Daektoch didst cause Heros to move its army against them, and now they lay besieged. There hast been no battle as of yet. Breezon is loath to fight against Humans, and so they sit and wait."

"Heros? What, by my father's beard, are they doing that for?"

"Thou doest know that the council is in the sway of Daektoch's power, though they are unaware of his existence. They art complaining about some alleged land dispute, saying that the Breezon Plains were formerly theirs and shouldst be returned. There is no truth to the matter, but Daektoch controls them.

"The battle against the Elves hast not been engaged, except for two skirmishes. So far, the Elves and Dwarves on the flats fare well, as far as things in the war art counted.

"Here, however, thou hast not tasted battle. I wouldst suggest that thou doest so. It mayest dislodge indecision and remove imagined barriers. Confrontation is inevitable. Let it begin soon if only for a taste. The Dwarves are zealous in combat; doest not underestimate them.

"Only doest not go out thineself. Send thine commanders, as there is no heir to the throne old enough to rise to it yet. The office and person of the King must be preserved! Send messages to your detachment to the north to come from the west and attack. Then, doest send out another ten thousand from *Dolan*, coming from the east after the battle has been engaged and drawn away from the mountain. After the battle doest turn in the Trolls favor, withdraw the twenty thousand to the Land of the Gift of the Elves. I willst tell the Giants there to expect them. From behind the wall, they canst defend themselves and thou willst have nearly one fourth of thine army in a more usable position."

"Alas, Morlah, I fear your counsel is best, even though I hate to think of the lost lives this will result in."

"Minimize thine losses. The tactic used in the Battle of Breezon with the use of long shields was effective against the Trolls. Use them again. I am presently appearing to thee as I return to the Elves, in flight on The Raven along the east coast. I depart now, for an apparition costs much strength and energy when over great distances. Ja speed. Be of good courage."

Then the Druid's eyes rolled back, and he went into a trance and prophesied, "*At thine darkest hour, when all hope doest fail and thine army falls, look for help to come from the mountaintop, from* ***Dolan's*** *summit. There, I doest see a dark and fearsome power arising. A power to aid thee.*" He disappeared, leaving a puzzled and worried King.

Back in Breezon, the siege continued without bloodshed, but daily emissaries from Heros were sent to the walls ordering Breezon to surrender. Breezon had no intention of doing so. It appeared, for now, that Daektoch was content to paralyze the Breezon Army to prevent them from assisting the Dwarves and Elves. Extending his power over two armies in battle was perhaps a bit too much for him. He could take care of Breezon at a later time. They *would* need to be made to pay for their meddling of the past, for it was at Breezon that his Troll army had been defeated in the last war.

The sunrising for Andreanna's departure arrived. The Faeries assembled to bid her farewell. The King moved forward through their midst.

"Give me your Elfstone *balak*," he said to Andreanna. He took the stone and spoke to it in the ancient Faerie tongue, precursor to the ancient Elven tongue. He then handed it to the Queen who did the same, she passing it to the next and the next until each Faerie had spoken over the stone. The Elfstone glowed more and more strongly in turn.

The King then returned it to Andreanna, saying, "We thank you for coming. Forget us not. Our future is still bound to your destiny. This my essence speaks of to me. Your stone is bound to the earth, it will draw power from the earth, from the element of magic you know as argentus. Your power will be great, perhaps greater than all of the Kings who had the magic, greater than any of the Elven Kings who have been. With it, trample your enemies and rule your people. *acrch* to both you and your children and your children's children. Now go. Your fate and destiny await you."

Andreanna thanked the Faeries for their kindness. She turned to leave. As she took her first step south, suddenly, the Faeries' domain was gone and all that there was left to survey was the cold and bleak mountainous region that she had camped upon when she had arrived. With the wolves, Gnomes and Fonta in tow, she departed, heading in a generally southwestern direction. She hoped they could get to the River Rain's source and from there raft down to Dwarf's Pass. If so, she could be home in a dozen courses.

Four sunsettings later Andreanna camped in the cave where the *Bonawock* had met them. She was in a sullen mood again. Being back there reminded her of what she had done. Not that she thought she had done wrong, but still, it felt wrong to have ended the *Bonawock's* existence. True, they were a tormented, languishing soul, yet they had been Human with the whole of Human values, emotions, joys and pains.

The Gnomes stored their supplies and bedrolls in the cave, and then joined Andreanna, sitting under the deep-blue darkening sky, staring into the fire in silence as the stars, one by one, appeared overhead. The night's chill descended upon them.

"Fonta?" Andreanna suddenly said, as if awakening out of a sleep. "Did I get this right? By speaking Daektoch's true name in his presence, he can be rendered powerless?"

"Something like that."

"Then that's it. I can put an end to this Troll problem and Daektoch. I have what I need to do it."

"Maybe it's not really as simple as I made it sound," began Fonta. But Andreanna was not listening anymore.

Her thoughts meandered off into the possibility of finally and forever ending Daektoch's hateful memory and blightful presence in Frontmire and allowing the races to live in peace, allowing her family, her husband and her child to live without the threat of violence. Fonta continued in her explanation unaware that Andreanna was no longer listening to her nor even aware of her.

"...there's a lengthy preparation involving incantations and spells leading to the use of the name. The name is a fragment of the whole of the process, the crucial ingredient. If you have the spell, then the name is the key to making it work," instructed *isini*.

"...then it's settled," said Andreanna speaking aloud to herself, still oblivious to Fonta's supposed chatter. "We're going after Daektoch. I have what's needed."

"You do?" puzzled Fonta.

"Yes, yes. Do be quiet, and let me think about this."

The stars pushed their light into the darkening sky, as the group sat around the fire, everyone assuming the fragmented conversation was a whole. Andreanna was now lost in thought about what she intended to do. Fonta turned her attention to Baby and amused herself, playing like a pup with the she-wolf. The Gnomes sat attentive to the night sounds about them, devoted to the protection of their Queen.

They returned to the cave when the fire was burnt down to softly glowing embers. Baby and Boy took up positions at the cave's entrance as the still night air in the mountains became keenly cold.

The sunrise and its light brought new resolve to Andreanna. She was going to find Daektoch and put an end to the miserable beast, a rabid dog only fit to be destroyed. Break fast being finished, packs secured, the travelers took to their new route, a northeast bearing.

Buried deep within her, Andreanna bore a grudge of festering hatred for Daektoch, for his abuse of her when he had captured her several cycles past. He had almost brought her to an end, having left her in shackles and starvation in his castle in Heros. She was looking forward to giving him a taste of his own brew.

They left the land of the Pernhamites and descended into the deep valleys between the ridges of tall snowcapped peaks, hoping that the ground between the ridges would be more conducive to travel. The Gnomes took the lead, having *some* better idea of how to get north, being *somewhat* familiar with much of the Mystics. They planned to head in an easterly direction and, then, follow the coast to Heros. The Gnomes were nervous about the Black Mage, however; they were superstitious to begin with and extremely fearful when it came to magic. It was doubtful they would have the nerve to get as far as Heros, not only because of the mage but also because Heros was a Human city. The thought of hundreds of thousands of Humans was extremely unnerving.

By midcourse, they were laboriously progressing along the valley they had chosen, following game trails through the brush and rock slides. Travel became slow and arduous but continued on at a steady pace; however, by the end of the course, they found themselves turned straight northwest by a chain of mountainous peaks, which at this point were an absolute impasse to the east. They now faced the choice of going back a course's march or going on in hope of finding passage eastward, for Andreanna thought Daektoch to be in Heros.

Four courses later, the group, now weary, having chosen to continue on northward but having been unable to turn eastward, were forced to climb to exit the gorge they had been following. The climb was steep and dangerous, and several times, they came close to losing one or another member of the party. By sunsetting, they descended to and stood on the foothills that overlooked the Inland Sea.

Tanodo hissed in fear, "Danger...the water is bitter like the great sea. Legends say evil beasts live in *Obet. Obet* is the Gnome name for the waters. We should not be here."

"So, how do we continue and go east?" asked Andreanna. The Gnome looked to the ground in determined silence and resistance, having no answer for his Queen.

Banta spoke up. "We must go back. We cannot go this way."

Andreanna looked out over the still waters of the large, landlocked sea. The sun was setting, casting its brilliant-red colors across the placid water. Sparse, thin clouds of purple, violet and steel-gray streaked the sky from east to west. Flocks of geese flew low on the horizon but avoided the calm waters.

"Fonta, what do you think?"

"It's like the Gnomes say. These are ancient waters. The creatures that live down in the water and about the surrounding low lands, they are best avoided. Even the Trolls in the Blue Mountains, on the north shore, stay clear of the area. It's dangerous, but it has been traveled by Humans and Elves before. There's not *too much* danger for me, so it's up to you to weigh if you're up to the risk."

"Well, we're not going anywhere tonight, so let's make camp and we'll decide come sunrising."

The Gnomes set up camp and made supper. They were obviously disturbed and a little belligerent in their attitude as demonstrated in their work, which they now performed roughly and moodily. Once evening meat was over, Andreanna called Baby over.

"Baby, what do you know about the water down there?"

"None. Wolves just stay clear of the big water. There are no packs about it, and as cubs, all we knew was that it was a place for packs to stay away from."

"No more than that? You never asked why?"

"Cubs are rarely told why. Just to do or not to do. We're going hunting back in the forest the way we came. Will you come?"

"No, you go ahead, I'd just slow you down anyway."

The wolves trotted off, back toward the south, leaving the small group watching the fire. One of the Gnomes climbed some nearby boulders to take up position of sentry while the wolves were away. Andreanna cut a thick pole from a sapling and passed the remainder of the evening whittling at it. As she worried the wood with her longknife, she pondered how to get around the Inland Sea. She could hardly believe she would have to backtrack five courses of the sun to get around the mountain and avoid the sea. *She could hardly believe she was going after Daektoch*. The diversion would keep her away from her home longer, yet it was a diversion that was worth the effort if she could finally eliminate the mage. Though she deeply missed Jerhad and Kendra, a life without the wizard would be a blessing. The entire population of Frontmire had suffered far too long at his hand. War after war had been directly caused by him and his lust to control all magic, to possess it for his own or destroy it so no other could have what he could not.

With the sunrising in the clear sky tinged with colors of yellow, green and turquoise, Andreanna arose with the problem resolved in her mind.

"I'm going on alone," she announced to the Gnomes. "You can return to your people and let them know where I've gone. Baby and Boy, I realize we're pack, but I'll ask you to return south, and I'll meet with you later at the Gnomes' village. Fonta, I guess you'll do what you want to, regardless of what I ask." All but Fonta and Boy blurted out a barrage of protests.

The hot yellow sun had been up in the cloudless sky for nearly two-quarter spans. A hot, heavy, damp mist clung to them as they trudged through the brambles. Gnarled, sparsely scattered willows and alders grew about the tannic-tainted water that stagnated in the marsh at the eastern end of the Inland Sea. The odor of plant decomposition hung strong on the breezeless morning. Mosquitoes were thick in the air and leeches abundant in the deeper waters. Mostly, the water was ankle to knee deep, but at times they waded in water that was up to the Gnomes' necks. The wolves were very unhappy about the situation while the Gnomes trembled in terror at being there. Fonta had taken to walking on the water, chattering incessantly once again as Andreanna led the troop through the marsh.

Andreanna *had* meant to go on alone. She had not wanted to bring her companions' into this self-imposed misery; but when "the axe came to the tree", everyone had followed. The Gnomes, true to their leader and Queen, could not be made to leave in spite of her best efforts to dissuade them. "But we are pack," Baby had protested. That had settled the matter for the she-wolf. Boy would not be separated from Baby, so he begrudgingly followed, but not without having bared his teeth at Andreanna in an expression of what he truly felt for her.

Fonta did as she pleased.

"...and then in the Great War of the Magics, in the three thousand fiftieth cycle of the Faerie inhabitation of the land, the dark spirits, magic consuming beasts and all manner of foul creatures were driven back into the region of the Inland

Sea, where they are contained by magic to this time. Most of them devoured and killed one another, so only the foulest and strongest are left. Most lay dormant beneath the water now and a few wander about...." *isini* was chattering on, as was her manner.

"Say what! Why didn't you say something about this before?"

"You didn't ask. Most of these beasts prefer to consume magical beings and have no use for flesh. Though a couple might. There was the Ranter, a phantom sort of creature who at times appeared in some embodied deception and ate flesh; but most look for the taste of magic...Faeries, for example."

"And what about Elfstones?" asked Andreanna in anguish.

"Well, yes, Elfstones would be of that nature of things that would make a nice treat. But they probably would not be attracted to them unless you used their power."

After that, except for Fonta, the group had gone on in a despairing silence. Above the water, flies filled their eyes and ears and were sucked down into their throats and into their noses with almost every breath. Beneath the water, leeches and water chiggers attached themselves to exposed and available skin. The insects drew blood from the companions' skin as they dragged themselves on through the marsh, putting one foot in front of the other as fatigue began to claim them.

Fortunately, their travel passed with no more than fly and leech bites to show for injuries. By dusk, they climbed out of the marsh on the northeast side of the still, dark waters of the Inland Sea. Andreanna went through the squeamish process of pulling leeches from her ankles and lower legs. They climbed away from the water where the flies were thickest and went into the foothills overlooking the otherwise peaceful scene. Before long however, dark, threatening clouds rolled in from the west, the promise of a thoroughly drenched and miserable night, as well as an omen of evil to come.

They took shelter beneath the heavy bows of a cluster of towering pines and set a fire a short distance from the trees, though, within a short while they ended up dosing the flames with dirt, for the winds picked up and blew fiercely. The storm swept in towards them, the air dropping several degrees in temperature over the period of a few spans of heartbeats.

Then, in the last of the faint pre-storm light, with thunder rumbling menacingly about the sea, Morlah stood before them. "What doest thou here?" he hissed. "This is an evil place to be found in, and especially at night. Thou, Fonta, as thou doest call thineself, how is it thou hast allowed this? Thou doest know!" Fonta actually looked abashed and hung her head before the Druid. "Flee into the mountains, for all manner of evil lies in this place. Wait not for the sunrising, for thou willst not live to see its light if thou doest tarry." And with that, the apparition was gone.

Andreanna almost became physically sick and nearly vomited as fear was now added to her fatigue and sudden dismay. She only wanted to be in her home and in bed at this point, safe with her mate's warm body lying pressed against her. *What had she been thinking of anyway? Taking on Daektoch, the Black Mage*! She sat on the ground overwhelmed by the emotional fatigue of her whole journey, the killing, the death, the separation from her family, the war...and now, Morlah's warning.

Self-doubt and despair filled Andreanna and, given enough time, she just might have let herself drown in it. There were leagues of walking to return home, and nothing said she could make it safely. She was sick of her role as alpha she-wolf, Gnome Queen, and Faerie Savior. Maybe if she just lay down and slept she would never wake again.

Ah! Sweet sleep.... Like the Bonawock.

It was then that the storm struck in its fury. Large pines groaned as they bowed in the wind. Cold rain lashed at the group, huddled together for shelter. Within heartbeats, they were soaked through, and windswept debris choked them as the flies had earlier. The pine trees they had taken refuge under provided little shelter as the group clung together. All were disheartened, except for Fonta who seemed intrigued, if not delighted, by the storm.

"What is the Elf's toy doing out here?" came Daektoch's voice from behind them. Baby, on instinct, lunged at the wizard but was picked up and hurled through the air as by an unseen hand. Boy peed himself and, with tail tucked between his legs, disappeared into the darkness. Tanodo and Banta gathered their spears and stepped forward as Fonta muttered she had just remembered something and vanished into thin air.

The Gnomes attacked!

With a hissing searing, they were burned to dust and ashes, except for part of Tanodo's skull, which lay on the smoldering ashes still showing an eyeball and a few teeth.

Hatred...!

Deep, dark, evil and unforgiving hatred – bitter, angry hatred welled up within Andreanna's bosom as she turned to meet the mage. Her mouth opened. From it surged the full force of *balat!* It caught the mage completely by surprise, pounding him into the hillside, leaving a furrow of turned soil as if a plow had broken the ground.

Fire erupted from the mage's hands, attempting to consume her. Andreanna again spoke the words of *balat*. Dark, powerful, destructive and consuming words wrapped about the mage's fire and extinguished it. Andreanna, as one possessed, again and again spoke the words of her ebony Elfstone, rooting up massive pines, heaping them up on top of the mage who burnt the trees as they came down on him, seeking to blaze a path toward his nemesis. Andreanna's eyes appeared as black holes. A shroud of darkness rose up about her. She threw house-sized boulders at the mage. She opened pits at his feet. Destruction was her goal. *Destruction* was her power! Between the two, the mountainside was soon torn and ravaged. Boulders cracked and trees snapped. The ground about them was ripped opened. Daektoch was always kept on the defensive, not having time to attack in turn.

Werme was a sixty-pace-long water serpent, of a smooth, not slimy, green skin. Ever since he could remember, he had inhabited these waters, even before the *great feeding* when the Faeries had driven so many beasts into and about his home. There were vague memories of others like him, but that was some millennia in the past. He was partially amphibious but much preferred the turbid depths of the sea where, when awake, he reveled in the sensation of his long slender body's undulating movements through the dark waters. Otherwise, he slept. Tonight, however, the scent of magic was on the water, arousing his appetite. Tonight, he would feed again. He slipped silently along the weed-choked bottom, hardly disturbing even the lightest of silt, following the sweet perfume of magic.

Daektoch had been surveying the country in his alabaster pool, which was how he had spotted Andreanna.

The temptation was too great; to possess the Elf's toy was far too delightful a thought and opportunity. He had quickly called one of his bat-like, magically-mutated servants and flown off to catch his prize, unaware that within the half-Elf an ominous power had awakened.

As a prisoner in his Heros tower, her latent magic had been so deep that he had missed its presence, not that it would have deterred the wizard, for until Jerhad's awakening to magic, Daektoch had been the wielder of one of the most powerful known magics on the continent, other than the Faeries and a few dangerous creatures that lurked about the Inland Sea.

Andreanna grew in stature by the heartbeat! Her Human form and identity was being taken over by *balat*. **She was Queen!** Queen of the Wolves. Queen of the Elves. Queen of the Gnomes. This was a side of *balat* Andreanna had not seen, that she had not known. This was not the *balat* who had sent the *Bonawock* into peace and rest but *balat*, **Queen of Destruction!**

Andreanna continued spewing out the words of *balat,* tearing at the mage, who now in desperation threw every last resource of his power at her, as he stood knee deep in the brackish water of the sea. Andreanna drove him back with each word that she spoke, the mage caught up in the wave of her assault. Almost spent, Daektoch lashed out with a flurry of lightnings, hurling Andreanna back into a boulder, which she hit with a loud crack of her head. She lay unconscious.

The mage was panting, bent over with exhaustion. He sucked air deep into his ancient lungs. That was as close to being killed as he had ever come. That was as powerful a force or adversary as he had ever encountered. The Elf's toy had almost done him in, *but he had won*!

Then, giddy with exertion and his victory, he laughed. First, it was a single giggle. That was followed by a loud chuckle, and then finally, a full, hearty, belly-hurting laughter. He could not remember when he had last laughed so. It was possible that it was more than one thousand cycles. He laughed until he was bent over and on his knees in the water. But she was *far* too powerful to keep captive! He would have to kill her. He composed himself, chuckled a few more times and pointed his finger at her. Behind him, the water opened up as a cavernous maw, swiftly, silently raced toward the shore. The power from Daektoch's fingers was aimed at Andreanna's heart. It erupted from the mage toward its mark, but instead, the magic flared and lashed through the forest as Werme swallowed the Black Mage whole. It slithered backwards, returning to the sea's depths.

It was midcourse following the next sunrising, soft rain still falling and slowly soaking into the earth, following the end of the storm. Baby lay at Andreanna's feet, crying a continual soft whine of sadness and of the pain of her broken ribs. Her worried eyes scanned about as she lay with her head supported on Andreanna's legs. Boy was nowhere in sight. Fonta was gone, and Tanodo and Banta were a wet pile of foul-smelling ash. The forest about the raindrop-speckled sea was still.

Andreanna dreamed. *Faeries danced in gardens and sang amidst the sounds of tinkling and chimes. Fonta was there but shied away when Andreanna tried to approach her. Then, Nan was before her. Nan,* **acrch**, *Life and Health.*

"I see I must help you again, Elf Queen. Though distance separates us and I am bound to the stone in Jerhad's knife, I may come to you because of ties we have from the past. Foolish child, what are you doing in such a place?"

"You mean in these Faerie gardens?"

"No, but by what you name the Inland Sea. No good could come of it, but let us tend to your need. Take my hand, rise and walk with me."

So, in her dream, Andreanna stood and walked with Nan, who spoke to her of magic, control, and wisdom in its use.

"But I was going to finish him, destroy him. Then we could live in peace."

"Child, speaking the mage's name without the proper preparation and spells is as speaking in the wind."

"But Fonta said...."

"Fonta! Are you aware that that is the Gnome word for mischief? And her Faerie name means more of the same. And where is she now, now that she has done her foolish work? She fled at the first sign of trouble. You were more equipped to deal with the mage with your magic than what you thought you were armed with. Only, the unleashing of your magic was fearsome and terrible. I am surprised you took no injury from it."

"So, what's wrong with where I am; what's happened?"

"You are still at the seaside. The she-wolf is the last of your group left with you. The he-wolf has fled, the Gnomes are dead and you lie with a concussion from which you will **not** *awaken without my help. I have come to give of myself that you might be healed before some beast comes along and finds you and has you for meat, though you will retain a headache and weakness for a while as a consequence of your ways, that you may remember and perhaps learn wisdom. I will also heal the she-wolf of the cracks in her ribs.*

It was dark, cold and foul smelling as Daektoch slid along the slippery slope and stopped at the bottom in a pool of blackish-green putrid liquid. Anger and hatred made him spit and stammer. He slammed his fists against the walls of his dungeon prison. Fate *surely* was watching out for her. Where had she got that magic? Powerful magic! Formidable magic!

It had not taken Daektoch very long to realize where he was. *Fire and demons it made him mad.* He raged, cursed and spat for a while. Finally, he came around to his senses, enough to take the time to neutralize the acid bath he sat in, inside Werme's belly. *Now what?* He was probably at the bottom of the sea by now, the leviathan settling in for a long digestion. *How was he to get out of a creature that feasted on beings of magic? Could he cut his way out?* He was thankful (as thankful as Daektoch ever got) that the fiend did not chew its food. He hoped that he was not powerless against Werme, but there also was a matter of conceiving a plan that worked before he ran out of air.

Andreanna and Baby traveled for several courses of the sun, both exhausted, not fully recovered from their injuries. Course after course, league after league, they wandered aimlessly, not knowing where they went, simply putting one foot in front of the other until Andreanna was all but stopped, inching her way forward. Her mind was fogged with fatigue. She barely knew who she was. Her mind was a thoughtless void. Fortunately for her, *licri* had a mind of her own, for when Andreanna was just about to collapse, Boy came hurtling from the brush behind them and jumped, lunging for her neck. With one blinding motion, she reached out, took him by the neck and snapped it. His momentum carried them both tumbling down a steep, rocky embankment.

Down they tumbled, over and over, until they were a tangle of arms and legs lying at the bottom. Baby lay at the hilltop and whined.

In her unconsciousness, Andreanna dreamed again. *She was a large, pitch-black she-wolf racing through the forests, hot on the trail of one of the local packs. She ran on for courses without tiring, without eating, drinking or stopping to rest. The pack she hunted wearied, and suddenly, they turned and attacked! But she was too strong for them. As fangs lashed in the turmoil that followed, one by one she would pin them down. Each time she took one by the throat, the others froze in the position they were in, some in the air, some on their noses or tails. All stopped in the heartbeat of time they had been in. Then, holding the one she had in her jaws, she clamped down until it submitted or she killed it.*

Then, as quickly as the flurry had stopped, they were in the air again, the whole pack in motion, fighting against the large she-wolf in a fury of growls, snapping teeth and screams of pain. Not once did her quarries' teeth meet her flesh. Finally, the pack was all subdued or dead. She rose and pursued another pack. The dream lasted for what seemed to take a score of cycles of the sun, until all the wolves of Frontmire were subject to her or dead.

The longhaired, glossy-coated alpha of the alphas of the wolves stood on a snowcapped peak overlooking the entire land. She was Queen of the Wolves, Queen of the Gnomes, Queen of the Elves; she would be Queen of Frontmire. She would become the Dark Queen ***balat***.

More and more *balat* seemed to become Andreanna's identity. Her Human side was slowly becoming lost to her.

Emotions and memories faded. Faces of loved ones were lost. Compassion and mercy forgotten.

All would bow to her, the Dark Queen, or be destroyed. She stood alone above the earth now. She saw far away lands, the Homeland of the Giants, the Rock Trolls, the Karobs and the Parintians with their Druids. They would all bow to her or perish!

"Cease! You extend yourself beyond your authority, ***balat,****" came Nan's voice.*

And, yes, she would rule the Faerie magic and the Faeries....

"Cease, ***balat****. You forget yourself. She is not yours to take over."*

"Submit to me or you will die too, ***acrch****."*

Nan laughed. "You are not of a sound mind, ***balat****. You have no power over me."*

"Come then, let me see you, and we will see who rules who."

Then ***acrch*** *appeared in all her glory, radiating Life and Health in a blinding brilliance, causing the great she-wolf to step back, snarling defensively.*

"I warn you, ***acrch****, step any closer and I will deal with you as I have dealt with all others."*

"Come then, let us dance the Dance of Life."

"You mean...the Dance of Destruction." And with that, ***balat*** *rushed Nan, who opening her arms wide received the she-wolf, and as* ***balat's*** *jaws sought to latch onto her throat, wrapped her arms about her with a hold that was beyond the strength of steel, much like the strength of Life itself.* ***balat*** *yelped as if with pain at* ***acrch's*** *touch and now struggled furiously to escape. Her yelps quickly escalated to a guttural, bloodcurdling scream as she thrashed about, frantically seeking freedom.*

*"Now live, **balat**, but not as lord over the girl, for there is no health in you apart from her, only **destruction** onto **destruction** and **balat** onto death of her and thyself. Dance with me, **balat**, I am **acrch**. I am Life. I am Health. You are untamed, unlearned. The Black mage's magic has made you corruptible. Be healed or you'll die. The entire Faerie kingdom awaits your decision. You will be healed or they will come as one and put an end to you. Receive me. Submit. I am able to make you whole, to give you reason, to give you the stability and balance you lack. Receive me."*

*But **balat** fought all the more as if in terrible agony of pain or fear of being subjugated, perhaps both. On **balat** battled through the night and into the next and the next, not able to break free from Nan's searing touch. Finally, with all her might, she turned on Nan in an attempt to destroy her adversary. She rose up in her power, larger and larger. The she-wolf grew until her skin began to split, tear and peel, as if she were rapidly outgrowing a worn garment.*

*At last, **balat** was revealed, the Dark Queen in a Human form, wrapped in her black shroud, long strands of black hair moving of their own volition, as if blown by a gale. She wrapped long powerful arms about Nan and whispered, "Come, I will tell you a story of death and **destruction**, you miserable, meddlesome witch." She pulled her mouth close to **acrch's** ear and began to speak words of **destruction**. Her eyes were dark pools of hatred. Her words contained destruction for an entire planet and all who inhabited it.*

*Andreanna drifted in the darkness. There was nothing to see, feel or hear. That is, nothing except fear. Not terror, but fear. She did not know of what. She felt as if she were no longer in her body. Maybe no longer in the world. **Maybe she was dead,** came the suggestion. **Maybe! Being dead would possibly***

feel like this. Her fear eased a bit. This would not be too bad; there was no pain, hunger, thirst or fatigue. But what of her family? She could not tell. Did she miss them? **Not really. It was too dark. You really could not miss someone when it was this dark. What of your revenge on Daektoch?** A pity, but she would have to do without. **But you hated him so much! Yes.** And that was a pity too, for it had been a gnawing cancer within her, she saw now, eating at her when she did not even know it was there. It was this that had given **balat** foothold to take over and become the anarchist Dark Queen, Ruler of All, including Andreanna.

"It was?" Andreanna asked.

"Yes, it was," came a familiar voice.

"But **balat** doesn't rule me."

"Then where are you now?"

"I guess I'm just dead."

"Not dead, child, but you've lost your identity to **balat,** and she has pushed you back within her own in an attempt to dominate, to be an entity separate from you."

"But are we not the same person?"

"Somewhat. Like the opposite sides of the same coin."

"Then I'm not dead?"

"Not yet, but soon. **balat** is fighting for supremacy. If you do not regain control, she will succeed. Then, the Faeries will have to destroy her, for she is far too ambitious and destructive now. Without you, she has lost her balance and is no longer the beauty you once met but a specter who names herself the Dark Queen."

"Am I dreaming again?"

"Yes and no."

"Are you Nan?"

"Yes, little one. It is I who speaks to you, but that is unimportant. You must take control soon or be lost."

"Faeries! " Andreanna sighed. "What do I do?"

"You must regain control of your Human vessel. ***licri*** *is innate to you. Her strength will be yours. What do you see?"*

"Darkness."

"Close your eyes. What do you see?"

"Darkness."

"Open your eyes. What do you see?"

"Darkness."

"Close your eyes. What do you see?"

"Darkness."

"Open your eyes. What do you see?"

"Darkness.... No, wait. I see...a...star?"

"It is the self that you seek, your identity. Reclaim it."

acrch *and* ***balat*** *were locked in combat. But* ***acrch*** *just hung on and spoke into* ***balat's*** *ear.* ***balat*** *did the same but with a frantic thrashing back-and-forth, locked in dance. Finally,* ***balat*** *collapsed, and* ***acrch*** *stepped back.*

"It is time," ***acrch*** *spoke.*

igini *suddenly appeared, the magic of* ***harmony****, the purple stone on Jerhad's knife. She lunged and wrapped her arms about* ***balat****, standing her up, and when it looked like the "dance" was just about to begin again, she kissed* ***balat*** *on the mouth.*

"You can't do that," said Andreanna. "We're both girls."

igini *smiled, kissed her again and disappeared.*

A stone pressed hard into Andreanna's back as she opened her eyes, looking up into the late, clouded, gray sky that threatened rain. Attempting to move off of the stone, she noticed that she was holding something in one hand. She turned her head to look. It was Boy's dead body, neck broken, and throat torn open and dried tongue hanging out of his mouth. Her hand reflexively pulled away. She got up on one elbow, testing herself to see if anything was broken.

Then she saw; scattered around her were some forty or more dead wolves. Almost all males, their throats ripped open. Baby sat off in the distance on a hilltop, looking anxious. Andreanna stood, her legs wobbly, and gazed about. It was then she noticed it, off in the distance at the foot of the mountain - the river village of Rain's Bottom.

Chapter 14

Andreanna entered Rain's Bottom at about midcourse after the following rising. It was a quaint little village, but she was a bit uneasy about it, remembering Jerhad's experiences here. Some drunken trappers had attempted to rob Jerhad and Stanton in the night while they slept in the *Blushing Maiden Inn*. Stanton had ended up killing three of them. The fourth had fled. But for now, it was sunlight, and there were men and women milling about the streets, busy at their course's activities, as well as children playing about. So far, it looked peaceful enough.

The village streets were muddy and marred with wagon wheel ruts, forcing her to carefully choose her way. There were shops and mills dotting the village's main street, and many dilapidated homes crowded together on streets going up the hills and away from the river. Andreanna was making her way past The Mill's Inn, when there came the sounds of a violent ruckus from within. There were loud thuds and crashes mingled in a melee of shouts. Suddenly, the door burst open and a figure came hurtling though the air towards her and plopped into the mud at her feet. She looked down at it, and the figure looked up at her. It was a Dwarf!

"Pleased to meet you, Missy," said the larger than average, powerfully-built Dwarf. He appeared to be middle-aged, with the expected long beard of a color not too different than the mud he was in. He was a bit...plump (if one is polite about those things) around the waist and had intense brown eyes.

A man wearing a white but richly-soiled apron came to the door and shook his fist at the Dwarf. "You ain't welcome here no more, SixFists. And I don't care if you *do* pay with gold! You ain't welcome here no more! Take your business elsewhere."

Andreanna looked back to the Dwarf. "Is that really your name?" she asked.

"Not my real name, but it's the one everybody knows me by."

"What kind of name is that?"

"Well, let me explain it to you," he said picking himself up from the mud and attempting to wipe the thickest of it off. "You see, a long time ago, I was in a tavern much like this one, looking for a good fight. Well, I spotted my man, a big burly brute he was. So, I start to making some comments about his sister. I didn't know his sister. Didn't even know if he had one. Well, he goes and gets all riled up and comes after me. We fought like Moor Cats. Later as they carried him out, he mumbles something like, 'It was like fighting someone with six fists'. So the name stuck."

"You mean you went in looking for a fight?"

"I did. What of it?"

"Why?"

"Because I like it. Always have. Ever since I was tall as the end of my father's beard...loved a good brawl. It got me kicked out of *Dolan* though," he said with his face scrunched up in regret. "So, I just lives up in the hills behind Rain's Bottom now. Come down to town for them. There's always a trapper or soldier, or someone who doesn't know me going through who can be enticed into a good brawling. This time, though," he said with some disgust, "the man had twelve friends show up as soon as we got to working it. They joined in when they saw I was going to get the best of it. There's six of them laid out on the floor though." He laughed.

"Well, Missy, I don't recall you. You're not from around here are you?"

"No...I've been...traveling and was just passing through on my way home."

"And where would your home be?"

"Mildra."

"Mildra? That's Elf country. What's a pretty little Human pony like you doing in Elf country?"

"My mate is an Elf."

"Well, I guess that would explain that then. I'm about to go have something to eat over to *The Blushing Maiden*. You could come along and join me if you've a mind to. Promise I won't pick a fight with you," he smiled, his eyes full of mischief. "I like to do my fighting in places I don't care to eat in; but the *Blushing Maiden*...," he said smacking his lips. "Miss Molly is the best cook in all of Frontmire. She's got strawberry and rhubarb pies cooking, and a shepherd's pie that will melt you, it's so good. I hear she uses nothing but the freshest shepherds."

Andreanna laughed. "Alright, SixFists, I'll join you. I was looking for a place to eat. *The Blushing Maiden*. My husband spent the night there once."

"Did he now? What was an Elf doing up here? We don't see them often."

"Well, that's a long story. Jerhad didn't really get to enjoy his stay."

"Jerhad? Of Mildra? Jerhad, Prince of the Elves Jerhad?" he asked, stepping around before her and putting up his palm to stop her from moving forward.

"Well, yes, I suppose you could call him that...."

SixFists bowed deep at the waist, "I am moved with honor at meeting the mate of the Prince of the Elves. Now, I must *insist* that you join me and let me treat you to a meal. It would be a rare privilege, Queen of the Elves!"

Andreanna blushed. "Don't call me that. Andreanna is my name."

So SixFists, a full head-and-a-half shorter than the Human female, escorted Andreanna to *The Blushing Maiden*, strutting proud as a peacock, and led her into the inn.

"Master Kline," he bellowed as they entered. "Come quickly, for you have a dignitary coming to dine."

Master Kline slowly walked towards them, wiping his hands on his apron, "I like you, SixFists, but I 'ardly thin' you meri' the title of dignitary."

"No, no, not me. Her!" he said thrusting his thick thumb out towards Andreanna. "This is the mate of the Elf Prince who caused all that ruckus several cycles back. Jerhad, Prince of the Elves."

Master Kline stopped, his brow wrinkling up, and stared intently at her, "Is this true?"

Andreanna nodded her head, almost fearfully.

Master Kline rushed forward, taking her hand into his and squeezing it warmly. "My dear, i' is an 'onor. We've 'eard so much abou' your 'usband and 'is doings. And you, married to an Elf!"

"Well, I'm part Elf myself," she said, more so, for not knowing what to say.

"Well, don' jus' stand there. Come in, come in," said Master Kline, and he led them to a table just off from the kitchen and then rushed off through the open kitchen door.

"EEEK!" came the often-heard shriek from the kitchen, and then Miss Molly, Master Kline's wife, came rushing out toward Andreanna. "You're tha' cute li'le Elf's wife? Wha' a darling boy 'e was. I'm so sorry about' all the trouble though. And look a' you. Wha' a beautiful woman you are, though you could use a li'le cleaning up if you don' go mindin' me sayin'. I'll be' tha' poor Elf never knew wha' 'appened to 'im after 'e laid eyes on you.

"And you, Master SixFists, 'ave you been rollin' in the mud agin?" She grabbed Andreanna and hugged her, suffocating her, drawing her face into her more than ample bosom. Releasing her, Miss Molly asked, "Wha' can I ge' you to ea'? And 'ow on earth did you ge' into this 'ooligan's company. No' tha' 'e's a bad sor', bu' all 'e does when 'e comes to town is ea' and figh'. Otherwise, 'e's a 'armless fellow. Oh, I've go' to get me pies ou' of the oven. Master Kline and the girls 'ill look after you ou' 'ere." Then she went back off into the kitchen on the same whirlwind that had brought her out.

So, they ate their lunch, talking all the while. Afterward, SixFists sat back to a large mug of cold ale, the only cold ale in all of Frontmire, and the largest bowl of tobac Andreanna had ever seen, except for that of the Giants', of course.

"So how were you planning on getting home, Missy," the Dwarf was asking just before drawing another heavy draught of smoke from his pipe and blowing smoke rings toward the ceiling.

"I thought of hiking up along the north side of the Rain and crossing at the falls and down through Dwarf's Pass."

"Don't think that's a good idea, Missy. The area around the falls is said to be swarming with Trolls, and there's been a few strays along the north side of the river."

"I can take care of myself. I have to get there somehow. And I've been told that there are Trolls massing to the east, so I can't go that way. I can't go straight south either. So what do you suggest, Master Dwarf?"

"I suggest that I escort you home," he said as he stared into his pipe's bowl, at the coal of burning tobac.

"Escort me?"

"Your Jerhad is said to possess one of the King's tokens. It's my sworn duty to render him assistance. I do believe I would be considered derelict if I was not to help you at this time."

"You don't need to do that. I can take care of myself better than you can imagine, really," she said a bit irritably.

"No, *I'll* be coming along when you leave. Besides, I may just like to try my hand at fighting with a Troll. I'd be more than glad to instruct one or two of them on what it means to encounter SixFists, the six-fisted Dwarf." He looked up from whatever mesmerized him about the burning tobac and grinned at her.

"SixFists, how is it you talk differently from other Dwarves. A regular Dwarf would say 'cannot' or 'will not'. You say 'can't' or 'won't'."

"I don't! I wouldn't!" He gasped. "...I do! Well, I had never thought about it, but I guess I do. Funny, all these cycles with Humans is looking like it's rubbing off on me. Oh, my father's beard! I do hope that's the only thing rubbing off on me from them." Then looking at Andreanna, and with a trace of a blush, he said, "Begging your pardon, Missy."

Much later, evening meat also being finished, Miss Molly came from the kitchens to talk with Andreanna. "You'll be spendin' the nigh' with us of course. I won' take no for an answer. It's a small way of payin' your 'usband back. Why 'e and tha' soldier jus' li' out of 'ere in the middle of the nigh'. Didn' ge' the mornin' meal or a full night's use of the room, already been paid for in full an' all.... Well le' me tell you, tha' soldier boy pu' them trappers in their place. Now, you come with me, an' I'll fix you a 'ot bath an' ge' the girls to wash your clothes.

"You'll jus' love me homemade soap. Pu' lavender in i' jus' to irrita' the men folk. Makes them smell like girls." With that, she slapped her knee and bent over laughing. "I' was a joke me mother an' I 'ad used on me brothers once. I' worked so well tha' I use i' to this very course. Always ge' a commen' abou' the men smellin' like girls." She laughed again, tears filling her eyes, and then she breathed in deeply to regain her composure.

Andreanna sank into the depths of the hot, steamy, lavender-scented, soapy waters of her bath. The sweet herbal scent relieved her tension and fatigue as the water that washed away her grime. Oh! She could not remember the last time she had bathed. *Ye Gods! Could it be that long ago*? She soaked in the heat of the bath and in the fragrance of the soap and let every muscle relax and every fold soften and moisten. Ah, life just could not get better than a heartbeat like this, when you got what you had not in a long time, something you loved that was meant as much so to spoil oneself as to serve an actual function. When the water began to cool, she set herself about to the task of scrubbing herself down with all vigor.

Lounging about her room, Andreanna felt somewhat more like her old self again. But, she could not make heads or tails of the events she had experienced. She was apprehensive of the changes that had taken place in her. And now that she was in the very room that Jerhad and Stanton had been in during their brief sojourn at the *Blushing Maiden, s*he missed her mate and Kendra acutely.

As she reflected on recent events, she suddenly became aware of a noise outside her window. *What was it*? It sounded like, growling dogs or maybe someone being strangled. With shortsword in hand, she slowly opened the window. It was much louder, but she could see nothing. Returning with an oil lamp, she peered out the window, and finally identified the source of the racket. SixFists was sleeping under her window obviously for the purpose of exercising his snore.

"Hey! Hey, SixFists. What are you doing?"

The Dwarf roused and looked up at her. "Not to bed yet, Missy?"

"What are you doing?"

"Getting some sleep. Why, Missy?"

"Do you always sleep on the ground *outside* an inn?"

"Oh, that. Just making sure the Prince's Missus is safe. I'll be alright." He turned and repositioned himself to continue his vigil, even though he meant to sleep through it.

"There's an extra pallet with a straw mattress in here. You can sleep on this side of the shutters."

"Oh, no. I couldn't do that. I'm alright. Honest. Don't you go worrying about me."

"I insist."

He sighed. "Does this mean I won't get any sleep until I do as you say?"

"Yup."

He stood up and said, "Watch yourself, I'm coming through." He pushed his blanket in, and then, he hurtled the windowsill like a deer, landing inside with a two-footed thud of boots. Wrapping himself in his blanket, he winked at her. "Thanks, Missy. See you in the morning. Some say I snore. Just throw a boot or something...."

Early the next rising, Andreanna left Rain's Bottom with SixFists in tow. She had not put up much resistance, for it was evident that the Dwarf had made up his mind and was going to tag along regardless of what she said. The Dwarf carried a small pack, with food and a blanket, and a short-handled war-axe in his belt. He was in a jovial mood and hummed softly as they walked along. The air along the river was rich with the scent of cedars, ferns and grasses. By midcourse, they had come to the end of the trail they followed leading west out of the village.

"We'll have to move away from the river and into the denser wooded forest to make the travel easier. Less underbrush," remarked SixFists. "I don't know if you've noticed, Missy, but we're being followed. We picked up a customer about two spans ago, following behind not too far back. You got any enemies?"

"A few that I can think of and would rather avoid, but they wouldn't follow behind. They'd just come in and have it over with. How about you? You must have a few enemies?"

"That I have, Missy, but most of them are too lazy too walk this far to have at me," he laughed and stepped off the path's end through the shrubs and came up face-to-face with a wolf. "Step back, Missy. I'll take care of this if you don't mind," he said, drawing his axe from his belt.

"Oh, but I do mind," said Andreanna putting her hand on SixFists', to hold back his arm, preventing him from finishing the move that would have freed his axe handle.

"What say you?"

"She's with me. SixFists, this is Baby. She's been traveling with me. Baby, the Dwarf invited himself along. We might as well consider him pack. He would fight to the death to defend me, I expect."

Baby did not seem too happy, and she turned and ran off ahead in the direction they were traveling without responding.

"You mean to tell me you talk to that wolf, and she understands you?"

"It's Elf magic that I picked up along the way. It allows me to speak with and understand everyone including animals, at least, wolves. I haven't tried it on anything else. But I was able to talk with the Mountain Gnomes with it."

"Mountain Gnomes!" exclaimed SixFists. "They are a mean bunch. You have been with them?"

"I have. It's a long story. I'll tell it to you on the way." She pulled out the brown Elfstone and showed it to him. "Here, this is an Elfstone. It allows me to communicate with Gnomes and wolves."

"Can I examine it?"

"Sure," she said, taking it off and handing it to him.

"Well I'll be a son-of-a-*bedak**," he exclaimed after examining it for a heartbeat. "Missy, you know what you've got here?"

She shook her head, wondering what he was talking about.

"This is *monit*, the Elfstone of shape-shifting."

"What?"

"Look here at the mounting. That's Dwarf work if I ever did see any." He worked at the mounting a couple of heartbeats and then removed the stone. He looked within the base of the gold mounting and nodded. "Yup, just as I thought. Look at this, Missy."

She looked within the mounting and saw an inscription, but she could not read it. "What's it say?"

"Oh, here. Hold the stone and try again."

She did as instructed and looked again. This time she read, "*To bind the Elves and Dwarves – **monit***".

"That's it! That's the Elfstone given to the King in *Dolan*." He then reassembled the stone and fixture. "Now, how was it? Ah, yes.... It was some two or three millennia back when

---

* *bedak* – Dwarf word for female Troll.

the Elves still lived in what's now called the Breezon Plains. It was given to the Dwarf King by the Elf King as a gift. *monit,* the shape-shifter. It's said that with it, one can change his shape into that of rock, tree or animal… even to look like another person.

"That explains how you can talk to the wolf. Its power allows the change of sound and speech also. It disappeared from *Dolan* about eight hundred cycles past. No one knew what had happened to it. Where did you get this?"

"The chief of the Mountain Gnomes gave it to me. He said something about me being their Queen."

"Well, I'll be a son-of-a-*bedak*!" he said handing it back to her, at the same time letting out a long low whistle.

About one span before sunsetting, SixFists called a halt for the night. They had come to a stream, which flowed into the Rain, and they followed it along its gavel shore to the river.

"Good," said the Dwarf. "GraniteTop's canoe is here. Friend of mine. Depending on where he is, his canoe is either up at the portage at Barrett's Fall or down in these parts. He let's me use it, and he walks if it's not here. He's good like that. Not that I wouldn't take it anyway," he grinned. "Tomorrow, we go by river." They pulled back into the forest a ways to what appeared to be a well-used campsite and settled down for the night. Darkness enveloped them and their campfire under the moonless, overcast sky.

"Well, Missy. First watch or second."

"None."

"Say what?"

"The wolf will watch for us. She's a lot better at it."

"Are you sure about this, Missy?"

"Let me check." She called out to Baby, who apparently was just on the opposite side of the bushes about their campsite. "Oh, you surprised me, I didn't think you were that close. Will you watch for us during the night?"

"Is he staying?"

"Yes, I think he'll be with us for some time. Is it a problem?"

"The Dwarves have not been wolf-friends. They have hunted us and killed our kind for many cycles."

"And you have hunted and killed their sheep for as long."

"So? We both eat sheep. *We* do not kill Dwarves."

"Probably because they don't taste good," teased Andreanna.

Baby just looked at her, obviously annoyed.

"SixFists, Baby bears a grudge against the Dwarves because they kill wolves."

"I have never killed a wolf in my entire life, I swear. If the wolf is a friend of yours, then she's a friend of mine and no harm will come to her of my hand."

Andreanna repeated SixFists' words to Baby.

"I'll watch. I'll be off in the brush a ways so the stream doesn't interfere with my senses."

As they got into the canoe the next course of the sun, Andreanna turned to Baby and asked, "Are you getting in with us?"

"I think I'll just follow along from the shore. It doesn't look too steady."

"You'll have to walk, when you could get a free ride."

"I'd rather run." And with that, she turned and ran off going upstream towards Barrett's Fall.

It was a span after midcourse, the travel being easy with the spring floodwaters being past, when Baby showed up on a sandbar and barked a high-pitched warning.

"What is it?" asked SixFists.

"Trolls," replied Andreanna.

Baby ran back, disappearing into the forest. Shortly thereafter, a dozen or so Trolls appeared on the muddy beach and waded into the water towards the canoeists.

"Let's move out towards the other shore," cautioned SixFists.

The Trolls dug into the river bottom with their hands when they were a bit more than knee deep and pulled out some large stones, which they proceeded to hurl at the canoe.

"Watch those stones, Missy. One of those will kill you dead."

They doubled their effort and soon were out of the Trolls' throwing range. The Trolls then proceeded to follow them upstream, wading along the shore. Suddenly, the Troll who brought up the rear let out a howl. Baby had got hold of him by the calf and was hanging on, with deeply embedded teeth. As the others came to aid their comrade, she tore at the Troll's leg, let go and quickly vanished into the forest. The wounded Troll limped badly as the others resumed trailing the canoe.

"I think she's hamstrung him. He's not moving well. Sure has lots of courage, she has," observed the Dwarf.

Not long later, Baby struck again, tearing at the last Troll. The previously injured one had fallen behind and was apparently abandoned by the group. Again, she injured the Troll, leaving him crippled and growling in rage before disappearing back the way she had come. The remainder of the group bolted after her, throwing stones and spears.

"I see her game," laughed SixFists. "She's going to lead them on a goose chase. That's one smart she-wolf you got there, Missy."

"I think she's got me more than I got her," mused Andreanna. "Which side of the river do we camp on? I really hate to abandon her to camp on the south shore. This pack thing means a lot to her. It took a lot of convincing for her to leave me while I was in Rain's Bottom."

"If it's important, we'll take care of it. We camp on the north shore. Besides, she'll give us plenty of warning if there's trouble."

Later that night, just as they were thinking of bedding down, Baby came into camp carrying a partially eaten rabbit and offered it to Andreanna. The carcass' entrails hung from its torn body.

"No thanks, Baby, I just finished eating a little while ago. I couldn't eat another bite."

"More for me then," responded Baby.

"Baby, the Dwarf insisted we camp on this side of the river in spite of the Trolls being around, for your sake."

"The Trolls are no longer around. They're off chasing me down towards the Humans' dens." Then she stopped and looked at SixFists. Slowly, she went over to him and sniffed him. "He could be pack." She picked up her rabbit and went into the brush to finish eating it.

Chapter 15

The next four courses of the sun went by without event, Andreanna and SixFists in the canoe, and Baby following along on the shore. Birds chirped as the sound of paddles churned the placid water between stretches of turbulent rapids. At Andreanna's request, Baby also provided them with some whole rabbits to help restock their provisions. SixFists cooked them up nice and tender, which was no small task over an open fire. The smell of roasting meat was a welcome comfort. The Dwarf turned the remaining meat to a quick-dried jerk by laying thin strips on the hot rocks that he placed by the coals of their fire. Baby watched the meat cook, as if it were being wasted. Andreanna tossed her a piece of the rabbit jerk.

"Try it, it's not cooked, just dried."

Baby sniffed at the meat and then picked it up and chewed at it a couple times before swallowing it. "It was tender when I brought it to you," she said, reproaching Andreanna.

"It's supposed to be tough. It will keep for many courses of the sun like that. Besides, if you take the time to chew it thoroughly, you get to enjoy it longer. It's more fun."

"Hunting is fun, not chewing hard flesh."

"Think of it as a bone," suggested Andreanna.

Baby stopped and sniffed the wind. "The big two-legs come."

"How far?" asked Andreanna.

"As far as a deer will run before he can run no more."

"SixFists, more Trolls are coming. Maybe some half a span off."

"Alright then, let's pack up, get the fire out and make tracks. We'll have to travel in the dark"

Soon, the three were jogging along at a slow pace, moving upstream. Now that they were near Barrett's Fall, they would leave the canoe behind and go on foot. Not far from the passage that led under and behind the fall and across the river, Baby, who was in the lead, stopped.

"More big two-legs up in the hills above and some across the water," said the she-wolf.

"What is it?" asked SixFists.

"Trolls. There and there," Andreanna indicated.

"They're everywhere. I know I'll catch a tongue lashing for this, but you *are* the Prince's spouse. Follow me."

The Dwarf took to running at a pace that Andreanna found hard to keep up with. Just when she thought she would have to ask him to slow down, she found *licri's* magic as if by chance, and drew from its strength. Her eyesight became as sharp as when under the midcourse sun. Soon, she was running with ease and could have easily doubled the Dwarf's fast pace.

"*Now,* you run like a wolf," Baby seemed to laugh.

Arriving at the base of the thundering waterfall, SixFists stopped and looked at Andreanna. "Never did see a Human that could keep pace with a Dwarf like that. You're made of some pretty stern material there, Missy." He turned to a stone at the cliff's base and, after fumbling behind it for a heartbeat, rolled it to the side revealing a small tunnel entrance. He motioned Andreanna to follow.

Baby hesitated. "Dwarf den – no place for a wolf."

"It's alright. Come on."

"No. I'm not going into the Dwarf's den. Maybe this one is friendly, but there is the scent of many. I know you must find safety, and the big two-feet don't care about me, so I'll roam out here and find you later." She turned and ran into the thicket.

Once they were inside the cave, SixFists returned the stone to its position and locked its mechanism. Suddenly, magic orbs giving off a soft-bluish light came alive about them, lighting the way down the tunnel. No sooner had they passed one than it would go out, and the next few ahead would light up. They moved down the tunnel at a swift pace.

The tunnel was a smooth bore through the solid granite and was of a height that a Troll could have walked in with only a bit of a bowing of its head. It was as wide as it was tall.

A couple of spans later, they came to a widening of the passageway where several wooden bunks with straw mattresses lined the walls.

"We stop here for the night," said the Dwarf. They each chose a bunk and laid their blankets on them. "That cave over there," pointed out SixFists, "has fresh running water on one end. The seat over where the stream goes back into the rock is for... well...you know." He pulled his blanket over his head. "You can throw something over the light-orbs if the light keeps you awake." He soon was asleep and snoring heartily. The sound of the water trickling through the rock mingled with the Dwarf's snores as if in some odd harmony.

Andreanna stood in the garden behind her home. Turning, she saw Jerhad coming up behind her.

"You look lovely tonight," he said, as he placed his hand on her arm. But something was wrong. His hand felt stubby and hard. The skin was like leather.

Suddenly, Andreanna woke and sat up to find herself nose to nose with SixFists, his hand on her arm.

"Sorry, didn't mean to startle you, Missy," he whispered. "Listen."

For a heartbeat, all she could hear was her own heart beating loudly in her chest, but after a bit of adjusting, she heard the distinct sound of feet echoing through the passage from a distance.

"What is it?"

"Trolls."

"How do you know it's not Dwarves?"

"Dwarves wear boots. Them's bare feet. The Trolls have found a way into *Dolan.* They have to be stopped. Wish I could send you for help, but you'd get lost on your own in these tunnels, and I'm not up to leaving you here alone, so I guess you're coming along. I have to stop them and find how they got in before the whole Troll army gets in here."

"How are you going to stop them?" she whispered.

He lifted his fist up so that it sat between his and her nose. He stared into her eyes from over the knuckled weapon. His eyes narrowed menacingly. "Ain't met a creature yet who could stand up to it. Did I tell you about the bear I knocked out once? ...Well, maybe another time. For now, we've got work to do. Let's get going."

They gathered their packs and took off in the direction of the plodding feet.

They had been traveling for less than a quarter span when SixFists pulled up short. "They're not far now. Doesn't sound like there's too many of them," he said pulling her by the arm to get her ear closer to him so that he could whisper into it. "You stay here and I'll go see what I can do. If I don't come back, or I shout a warning, you take off, back the way we came, and take your chances in the tunnels."

"I'm coming with you."

"Now listen, Missy. You're the Queen of the Elves, and I have a responsibility to you and your mate, not to mention the Dwarves. You do as I say." Without waiting to see if she would listen, he took off in the direction of the Trolls, leaving Andreanna standing in indecision that grew into a state of paralyzed inaction, which seemed to hold her back as if she were held in hardening mud. Strange the effect SixFists had on her like that. Usually when someone tried to tell her what to do, it only led to her determination to do the opposite. Now, she stood frozen in the eerie light of the blue orbs and gazed at the darkness in the tunnel where the Dwarf had disappeared.

She did not have to wait long for him to find his quarry, for within a of couple dozen spans of heartbeats there came the sound of an awful melee from the darkness before her. There was grunting and bellowing of Trolls intermingled with dull thuds, which she assumed was the sound of the "six-fists". It sounded sickening to hear the mashing of fist on flesh. Then, from the tunnel came SixFists' voice.

"There's too many of them, Missy. Run for it."

And run she did. Dropping her pack and setting a firm grip on her staff, she took off in the direction of the fighting.

Arriving to where the Trolls were, she saw several sprawled about unconscious or unable to get up, though they were going through the moves of attempting to do so. In the center of the cave was a mass of bodies locked in a desperate struggle.

Then, she caught sight of the Dwarf - truly a sight to behold! With a mighty jump, he would catch a Troll at the throat, drag it down and let go a flurry of fists, resembling a blur of windmill blades under stiff winds, and the Dwarf was gone to another before the first hit the ground. He moved so fast that none of the other Trolls were able to lay a hand on him, but it was obvious the effort was beginning to cost him, for his breathing was heavy and sweat poured freely down his face.

SixFists climbed up one Troll, struck it unconscious, pushed off with his feet onto another, knocked that one out, slid down before it began to fall, ran between its legs and laid hold of another. An artist working in his own medium.

Andreanna stepped up behind a Troll, who was intent on the fracas, and struck him hard with the butt of her staff at the base of its massive skull. With a loud crack, the bone fractured, and the Troll folded in on itself, crumpling to the ground. She disabled three more in this manner before the others became aware of her presence. A small group broke away from the whirlwind of a Dwarf and came after her with shortswords and maces.

Now, she wished she had spent more time with Stanton learning what the Giants had taught him on fighting larger opponents, but then *licri* awoke in her again, slowing the scene before her. Stepping forward, she drove the staff into the closest Troll's belly, driving the wind from him and leaving him breathless on his knees. Pivoting on one foot, she came around, and her staff met the next just below its brow, blood gushing from its nose as it fell back full length. She cracked the first one's skull with a jab, thrusting behind her, not even bothering to look back at her mark as she stepped past. The next one's knee inverted and fell into the line of its fellow's swinging mace. The Troll's head broke open. A shortsword got turned into another Troll's side, eviscerating it. She disarmed another before bring the staff around as hard as she could up between its legs, a blow that would have caused most males to cringe at the sight thereof.

Step by step, she made her way through the swarming Trolls, leaving a trail of dead and maimed bodies behind her. Within herself, she grew, her magic filling her, becoming more and more a part of her until it seemed to ripen and blossom into fullness. *balat* merged with *licri,* and she became an instrument dealing out death to all who stood in her way. Another Troll dropped, and she stepped aside to let it hit the ground where she had just stood, bringing her staff around as she spun ready for the next. She stopped. There stood SixFists panting hard. There were no Trolls left. The magic within her went still. She swooned and collapsed.

When she woke again, she almost vomited. The cave was filled with the sickly sweet smell of blood, as if they were in a slaughterhouse.

"What happened? Why so much blood," she asked looking around.

"Well, I'm glad you weren't awake to witness it, Missy," he grimaced. "I couldn't be letting these Trolls go waking up to have another throw, so I slit their throats."

At that, she turned away and did vomit.

"Sorry, Missy. There wasn't any choice on the matter," he said almost embarrassed.

"No, it's alright. I know it had to be done. But it still doesn't sit well with me to see all this death and killing."

Looking somewhat affronted, SixFists replied, "But yours were almost all dead when I got to them."

"That doesn't make me like it any better. Besides, a lot of that was the Elven magic's work."

"So it is true. The Elves do have the magic. I was a bit busy at the time, but I did get a chance to see some of the fighting you drew. That's the first time I seen anything move faster than my fists. And that's a fact! What a fight it was too!" he chuckled. "Those Trolls, their skulls are so thick I had to hit them four or five times to knock them down. What a fight! I may just have to retire after this. Don't expect there'll be anything to compare to this ever again.

"Come. There's a bunk hole a little ways off. Let's get away from this mess and catch our breath. Then we can see if we can find how these boys got in here and collapse the tunnel in that area."

It was a few spans later that Andreanna woke. Looking around she saw that the Dwarf was missing. She got up and put her pack back together and then went and washed up. Then, she drank at the small feed of the underground spring that flowed through the bunk hole. She felt unusually refreshed and in a state of excitement. *Must be the fight, or the magic. Ye gods! Hope SixFists isn't rubbing off on me! But all that killing! Even if they were only Trolls.*

She probably would not have thought much of it in the past, but now after her experience with Fonta and her changed perspective of the Gnomes, she wondered if these Trolls recognized families. Parents? Children? Did they love? Did they play and laugh? It made her queasy again to think about it. What if someone would kill her family in the same way? She drifted into a sullen mood, her excitement turning to anxiety.

Deep within the mountain, a distant rumble brought her out of her reflection that was turning to guilt and depression. A tunnel had collapsed. SixFists must have found where the Trolls got in and caved in the passageway. She hoped he was alright. A cloud of dust blew through the tunnel.

A couple of spans later the Dwarf showed up, mumbling to himself. He entered the bunk hole and then stopped to look at her.

"Ah, Missy. I see you've slept your fill. We should be on our way as soon as I've taken a few mouthfuls of food and refilled my water skin." He went to the spring, washed his face in the cold water, and slurped a few two-handed draughts.

"Did you find how the Trolls got in?" Andreanna asked him as he filled his water bottle.

"I did," he grumbled.

"Was that you collapsing the tunnel that I heard?"

"It was at that, Missy," he grumbled.

"What's wrong?"

"Wrong?" he said, turning to face her.

She nodded but did not say anything.

"Trolls came in the same way we did. That's what's wrong! Don't know how they found it. I was sure we hadn't been followed or seen. But find it they did and came into *Dolan*! It's never happened in the thousands of cycles the Dwarves have inhabited it. And now, it looks like I let them in. HeartStone will have my hide when he hears of it! Damn it, I'll have my own hide if *he* doesn't. Do you realize the disaster that could have happened if we hadn't stopped them? Trolls in *Dolan*!" Then he stopped and beamed, "But that was one wonderful fight we had there, wasn't it, Missy?"

They traveled the rest of the sun's course in the light of the pale-blue orbs, through the tunnels without speaking. SixFists was in the lead; the pace he set was fast. He appeared to know his way about. Andreanna was exhausted when they stopped, not having used her magic to help herself. She had been lost in thought, thoughts of killing living beings. Trolls or not. Yet equally disturbing, she felt at home with the fact of it. It was the magic of *balat* (destruction, in the ancient Elven tongue). *balat* was a part of her now, and she found that killing was becoming easier. It wasn't that it was random senseless murder but nevertheless, the snuffing out of life that could not be restored....

Andreanna had become increasingly depressed as they had traveled. Not for the first or last time, she longed to be back home with her family and not know any of this. *Damned Faeries and their magic! Why could they not take care of their own affairs? If they were so powerful, why did they not deal with Daektoch and bring all this to an end*? As usual, answers did not come, only more questions, frustration and depression.

Soon, scenes of BlueHill in its destruction, razed to the ground seven cycles past at the hands of the Trolls, came to her. She remembered finding the charred bodies of her parents and sisters in the ashes of their burnt home, the entire community a heap of burnt rubble and scattered, dismembered corpses. She had been spared only because she had been away and had sailed into Parnham Bay and BlueHill the course following the devastation. There, she had found the destruction and witnessed the atrocity committed by the Trolls, wishing she had died with the others. It was there she had met Stanton and Jerhad and had almost immediately fallen in love with Jerhad who had been able to convince her to go with them, sailing to Breezon.

But now, the loss of her family, the pain of the loss and all the other difficulties that had led her to this place and time seemed to be threatening to swallow her and drown her in sorrow. She felt as if the very mountain's weight pressed down upon her, making her breathing difficult. All the hardships they had suffered came back to one point, Daektoch! To make matters worse, she had thought she could just walk up to him and neutralize him with one word, his name. That had been that miserable Faerie's fault. *Fonta! Where had she gone off to anyway*? She was better off without the Faerie, regardless of where she had gone.

"Missy?"

Andreanna looked up to see the Dwarf staring at her.

"Missy, you look like someone died."

"They did," she choked out.

"Who did?"

"My parents, my sisters, the Trolls, the Elves, the Dwarves, the Druids.... Everyone but the one who's responsible for all this." She started to cry.

"Oh, Missy, now don't go doing that. I don't do good with crying females. I mean...well, I just don't know.... That's probably why I never hooked up with one for my own. I just don't know what to do. Especially when they go and start crying and stuff," he fidgeted.

"I'm sorry, but I feel so awful, so helpless and alone." She sniffled loudly.

"Ahh. Helpless you're not. I saw you take down those last six Trolls. Helpless you're not."

"Not helpless like that," she sniffled. "There's so much death and suffering. So much wrong. It seems that trouble just comes looking for good folk who are just minding their own business, just living out simple harmless lives. Yet, trouble seeks them out and grinds them down. I'm just so tired of it. It hurts so much."

They sat in silence for a while, except for Andreanna snuffling back tears once in a while. Then SixFists got some wood stored in the bunk hole and made a fire near an updraft shaft made to clear smoke and act as a chimney though wisps of the pine wood smoke could still be smelled in the chamber. The fire and its scent gave the hollow a cozier feel. He got his stuff out of his pack and started cooking. After a while, without looking up but still staring into his work and into the fire, he spoke in a low voice.

"I can handle a bear with my fists, a man and even a Troll. But I can't help what's ailing you, Missy. Everything you say is true. It's as if the wicked don't suffer half as much as the good, and yes, folk die, get sick, get hurt. It's as if the gods are set against everything good *and* evil, as if some force out there is bent on the destruction of everything and everyone that was ever created. Yet, for all that, we still have good things we can enjoy and love. Sometimes you can forget the bad and just take the good." He went silent again.

Andreanna looked at him with a new regard. "I didn't know there was that much depth to you, SixFists. You surprise me," she said, brightening a little. "You're right of course; it's all we can do, that is, take the good. There's enough evil to swallow us all up. When I'm with Jerhad and our family, life couldn't be better. I just wanted it to stay like that. No sorrow, sickness, pain...or death to interrupt us. It's not asking all that much.

"What's more, nobody asked me. I mean nobody asked me if I wanted to live in a world that has all the bad possibilities. If they had, I would have cast my vote against it. Even at the best now, I've lost my parents and sisters, and then eventually, we'll lose Jerhad's parents, and then Jerhad.... I don't want it to be this way anymore. So many times when we traveled from Heros to Canon, we could have died. It made me so aware that the time will come that Jerhad will die, too. I can't even begin to deal with that. I couldn't stand being without him."

SixFists nodded and dished out the savory, beef hash he had made; they ate in silence and then turned in for the night.

Early the next rising, they rose, a bit of sunlight shining in through the airshaft.

"We should come out on top of the mountain late in the sun's course. Maybe at sunsetting if we're too slow. This tunnel is separate from the others, a safety precaution. We'll need to come out before we can go down into the tunnels the army uses and then to where the Dwarves live." They ate a cold breakfast and set out for the mountaintop.

Just as they started, Andreanna put her hand on SixFists' shoulder.

"Thanks," she whispered.

"For what?"

"For listening. For not discounting me as some hysterical female. For not making fun of me or telling me I wasn't making sense. For being a friend. If you ever get yourself a female, SixFists, you'll do just fine."

He blushed, turned and took off, going up the tunnel toward the mountaintop.

The Dwarf Army had been harrying the Trolls for six courses of the sun, using speed, since the Dwarves were surprisingly fast considering the length of their legs. Archers would pepper the Trolls' rear ranks as they sat in the siege of the Dwarves' mountain stronghold and then disappear into the forest. After dark, small sorties would rush out of the night, chopping neck and limb from sleeping Trolls. The Trolls became antsy, not to mention wired from the sleeplessness they endured. Even when they did lie down, sleep eluded them, every sound causing them to bolt upright from their near slumber.

But the tactic turned against the Dwarves on the night of the fifth course. The Trolls set ranks four deep on their outer perimeter. As the Dwarves emerged from the tunnels, they were swept away by the charge. Dwarves were strewn about, brained, decapitated and dismembered. The hitherto secret tunnels were left open, and the Trolls swarmed into them.

Levers were tripped, causing massive cave-ins. Hundreds died. But others followed and cleared the rubble, large hands hardened from cycles of mountain existence heaving heavy stone until the tunnels were cleared. Again, Trolls swarmed into the tunnels only to result in further cave-ins.

Sheer cliffs encircled the Dwarves' valley to the east with no access to the bottom. But under the guidance of a few Rock Trolls being used as commanders, they soon had dozens of tripods with pulleys lowering large platforms full of Trolls to the valley's floor. By next sunrising, those in the valley numbered in the thousands, equipped with battering rams, hoping to break the barriers that kept them out of the stronghold.

Within, extensive lengths of tunnels leading to the basin were collapsed, barring access from the valley. Leaving a token defensive force within the mountain, the Dwarf Army left their defensive position and exited through the tunnels on the mountain's top in order to engage the Trolls on the west face. With the Dwarves now in battle ranks, they moved down the steep slopes to engage in combat. Messengers had been sent around to the western flank and given the Dwarf detachment there the battle plan and the orders to attack on signal. As the east ranks closed with the Trolls, rams' horns blared, filling the morning air with their solemn reverberation.

For the first span of the sun's course, the foe was in disarray and took heavy losses, but then, the Trolls rallied, turning the tide against the Dwarves. Hundreds upon hundreds fell on both sides, littering the mountain terrain with bodies and blood coursing down the stone slopes, giving the Dwarves a gruesome advantage of having the slope below made slippery with the life of its defenders. Nevertheless, the Dwarf ranks were being decimated. The battle raged on throughout the sun's course.

Near *Dolan's* summit, in despair, his guard fanned out before him, King HeartStone stood watching the slaughter, when a hand came down on his shoulder and a female voice said, "Peace, King HeartStone."

Startled, the King threw himself and rolled a few paces away, coming up with his battle-axe in hand to find himself facing Andreanna and SixFists.

"Sorry, didn't mean to startle you," grinned Andreanna.

"Who are you, Human female?"

"I'm Andreanna, mate of Jerhad, Prince of the Elves."

"What are you doing here? Should you not be home? The last I heard, you have more trouble than needed back there," he retorted, relaxing his hand. Behind him, the violent clash of battle, the cries of pain and the stench of death continued to escalate.

"It's a long story, Sire, but since I'm here, maybe I can help."

The King raised an eyebrow, and his beard appeared to twitch.

Andreanna smiled. "I know I don't look like much, but from the look of things, every heart beat counts for hundreds of lives. Trust me and call a retreat."

"Retreat?"

"Quickly, please, I can help. I am part Elf and possess magic that will make a difference."

"...Magic..." spat HeartStone, snorting a huff into his beard, chewing on his lower lip, hesitating, desperate.

Behind Andreanna, SixFists nodded to the King.

Suddenly, Morlah's prophecy returned to HeartStone's mind, "*In thine darkest hour look for help to come from the mountaintop.*"

"Alright." He called to the squires with the horns to call a retreat.

They looked at each other in disbelief.

"Do it!" commanded the King with a growl. Turning to Andreanna he said, "If you don't come through, girl, I'm personally going to skin you alive!"

"Nothing like putting a bit of pressure on a girl, eh, Sire?"

"I have the entire Dwarf nation in peril of annihilation here. I do not have time for games or foolishness," he snarled.

"Follow me," commanded Andreanna.

With his guard in tow, the King followed, making his way down through the retreating Dwarf ranks who made their way toward the peak. The Trolls were now before them, a mass of fighting, ravenous beasts lost in the frenzy of battle, all the resemblance of ranks and order long forgotten.

Andreanna held her hand up to stop her entourage. "Wait here, Sire. I'll take care of this," she said, her voice deepening and taking on an eerie hollow and resonating quality, as if spoken from the land of the dead. She walked forward, her stride becoming strikingly graceful, her pace slowing but lengthening, her stature growing and her body transforming into a black shrouded female figure, tall (twice her usual height) and slender.

Her robes moved about her as if by enchantment. Long elegant hands with somewhat skeletal fingers showed through her sleeves, and her long black hair lazily flowed as if by the wind in the still, early evening air. The aura of *Power* and *Destruction* grew, pulsing about her.

The Dwarves fell back in fear, giving her a wide berth. She stopped and surveyed the mount. Her eyes turned dark and ominous, promising menaces of death. Slowly, her eyes scanned down to the distant Parnham Bay, to the Korkaran Sea, and to BlueHill where Andreanna had lived with her parents. The half-Elf realized now that she had never resolved her grief for them, had never had time to mourn her murdered family. She had been swept away into one adventure after another, then wedded and finally had her first child. Then, the excitement of living with the Elves, a people with a passion for life, had consumed her. Andreanna had never resolved her anger against the Trolls and Daektoch. She had never so keenly felt the pain of her losses as she did now. Surveying the Dwarves, now in full retreat at the blaring of rams' horns, she turned back and saw SixFists. Andreanna smiled at him, sending him scurrying back toward the tunnel; she observed the King standing, planted to the mountain, fiercely gazing at her in awe.

Turning back, she faced the Trolls, her power now felt by them even from the hundred paces that separated them. They stopped, their eyes fixed on the obsidian Mistress of Destruction, the Dark Queen, now in *harmony* within herself. Now come into her destiny.

"Return to your homes in the Blue Mountains or be destroyed." Her voice resonated with power and with an otherworldliness.

The Trolls, confused and fearful, knowing they were indeed threatened, looked each to his fellow, not sure what to do. Through the mass came a Rock Troll, a battle mace in each hand. He eyed Andreanna, then the King and the Dwarves, and then bellowed, "Charge! You will feast on Dwarf flesh tonight, my brothers. Charge!" With which, the whole of the Trolls as one surged forward and up the slope.

Andreanna's, the Dark Queen's, eyes rolled back in her head, leaving only their whites showing as the words of *balat* erupted from her mouth. The Rock Troll leader was picked up, his head ripped from his body and then both hurled back into the rear ranks of the Trolls. The enemy before her were torn and shredded in mid step, as if each had been a volcanic mountaintop bursting forth, erupting with millions of stones' worth of pressure pent up and finally broken through. Limb and viscera were hurled, strewn about. Eyes burst from sockets. Tongues were torn from mouths. The Dwarves, including the King's guard, fled in terror. HeartStone stood, stern, determined and undaunted. Truly, he was ***King of Dolan.***

Andreanna continued sweeping her *Destruction* along the ranks of the Trolls for nearly one half span of the sun's course. The mountainside turned into a torrent of blood and body parts coursing toward the sea. Thousands upon thousands of Trolls were caught in the path of *balat*, in the path of *destruction*. With mere dozens remaining, they turned and ran for their very lives, blind horror twisting their minds into irreparable insanity.

"Missy?" came a voice from behind her. The Dark Queen turned and viewed the two Dwarf worms that stood behind her. "Missy? Are you alright?" asked SixFists.

Then, she came to herself. *Ye gods! What was she becoming?* Andreanna stopped, transformed into her Human form, swayed and fell back into the arms of the King, who in one leap was at her side, seeing she was spent far beyond what she could withstand.

The mountainside was silent. The Dwarves stood in a terrified awe. No victory cry went up. No praise. No hail of victory. For nearly one-quarter span, the army stood motionless, surveying the holocaust-like *destruction* and devastation. The King himself carried Andreanna back into *Dolan*. At long last, the army coming to itself, reorganized defenses. Patrols were sent out to seek their wounded and gather their dead. Groans of agony rose, mingled with the stench of gore.

It was midcourse six risings later when Andreanna awoke. The King was at her side holding her hand. "You have come to at last, Queen of the Elves."

"Who are you…? Where am I?"

"You do not remember?"

"No.… Oh, my head. I feel like I have been trampled and dragged through a knot hole backwards…twice."

"It is you who have done the trampling, my Queen. I am HeartStone, King of the Dwarves. You are in the Dwarf stronghold, within *Dolan*. It has been six courses since, in the midst of a fearsome battle, you came down from the mountaintop and annihilated the Troll forces besieging us. You saved the Dwarf nation from extermination.

"My Queen, the Dwar...no...*I* am at your service as long as I shall live. My sons and my son's sons will also be, or by my father's beard, I will return and haunt them to an early grave. I swear it on my father's name and by my father's beard. I am your servant, as will be the Dwarf nation."

"Easy, King. Don't get excited; it makes my head swim."

"Enough talk for now, the Healers will want to see you for more care now that you are awake." With that, he stood from the bed's edge, went down on one knee, bowed deeply, and then, he stood and left.

Daektoch sat inside Werme's belly at the bottom of the Inland Sea. Twice he had been caught up in fits of rage again, his anger and ill-temper getting the best of him. They would pay! They all would dearly pay for this. He would make them suffer as much as possible. He would not let them die if he could prevent it, for death would end the misery that he intended to visit them with. Long would they suffer before he allowed them the escape of death. The Elf, his toy and especially Morlah. Daektoch hoped to make them suffer long and sweetly. But each had magic and it would prove difficult to capture and hold them for torture. Or maybe...yes...he remembered a spell, one for painful eye-burrowing parasites. He smiled.

But for now, he needed to get out of Werme's belly. How? How much magic could the Werme absorb and digest was the question. What could it not digest? Since Werme's diet was that of magic and magical creatures, it was possible that Daektoch could not outright injure it, for its digestive tract would be suited to deal with such. Cunning was what was required.

Daektoch attempted to mindspeak with his bat-like servants but found that the Werme's gut did not permit it. He knew a good vomiting spell, but he was not sure he wanted to be vomited out while at the sea's bottom. His anger began to rise, but he controlled himself. The dark prison stank of vomit, and its slimy secretions began to eat at the Mage's skin. If only he could lure the beast to the surface and then have it vomit or keep its mouth opened long enough for him to get out. From there, his winged servants could fly by and pull him from the water. He had a plan!

Daektoch sent out a thin strand that contained a powerful fragrance of magic up through Werme's throat. Odd! His magic seemed to falter; it did not respond well to his will. He increased his concentration and sent out the tendril of the scent through his captor's mouth and back into its nostrils, using the magic to tickle its sense of smell and appetite in attempt to lure the creature to the surface. Daektoch experienced relief as he sensed the long, serpentine body begin to undulate through the water and rise towards the surface.

Daektoch attempted to squeeze himself up Werme's esophagus, endeavoring to get ready for his escape. Werme's throat swallowed against him and slid the mage back into its belly. The relieving pressure in the mage's ears indicated that he was getting closer to the surface. If only he knew which way the shore lay, he might get the creature closer to land. Werme had leveled in his swim, following Daektoch's bait. The Mage cast the vomiting spell and sat near to his escape route. Somehow, the mage found himself becoming quite nauseated. He tried raising wards to protect himself from the backlash of the spell but found his magic responding feebly. He mashed his fist against the slippery stomach walls. Damned Elf's toy! How had she managed this?

There was one last chance for Daektoch. But he would have to hurry, for he sensed that his ability to use his powers was going awry. The leviathan was digesting his magic. With much difficulty, the mage transformed himself into a mist. He was able to flow up to Werme's gills and pass through into the seawater. But the mist was not made to enter into water and in a last effort of despair, Daektoch had to materialize back into a solid form to avoid being dissipated into the sea and being left unable to reform.

The Black mage thrashed about on the surface of the Inland Sea, unable to swim, frantically calling to his winged servants. Werme circled back, seeking the scent that it had followed but was now lost. One of Daektoch's servants swept in just above the sea's surface. With immense clawed feet, it plucked the mage from the water and began its climb toward the heavens.

Werme struck. It latched on to the wizard's leg and allowed its massive weight to fall back into the sea, dragging mage and servant down with it. Daektoch's winged servant screeched as it frantically fought to escape and to rescue its master. Werme's weight slowly dragged them down toward the briny, dark waters. Daektoch's leg, pierced through with sharp, needle-like teeth, was close to being ripped off. In that the great serpent wanted both for its feast, it took efforts not to tear the leg off and be left with but a fragment of a meal. It would seek to drown its prey and then eat.

Slowly, the serpent's prey was drawn closer and closer to the water. Daektoch screamed in rage and pain. Just then, a second of the wizard's bats flew in to help. The mage latched onto it with a strand of magic, struck it unconscious and rammed it into the side of Werme's head. The great sea creature, in reflex, released Daektoch and, with cavernous jaws, took the bait. Daektoch was lifted away from the water as the leviathan swallowed the immense creature in two hideous, gulping swallows. Werme sank back into the sea. Daektoch escaped. As they flew away, the Black mage cursed and spat at his servant, commanding it to get more altitude lest they be picked out of the sky by some other beast.

Chapter 16

The Troll forces that had destroyed Canon were now camped in the southern plain, just out of bowshot from Land's Break. It was not much of a camp; they did not build fires or pitch tents. They simply stopped their advance and milled around, some lying in the grass to sleep, or they gathered in groups and spoke of the cattle they hoped to feed on. Their losses had numbered nearly four thousand in the combined assaults they had sustained. The Trolls, loving to eat and fight, were now ready to move on to fulfill these lusts, having been brought back under Daektoch's control through the agency of his wraith servants. Their fears of assault from Morlah were pacified now that they had cover given to them by the flying creatures. The near proximity of the transformed mages also allowed Daektoch a much stronger hold on their simple minds, allowing him to persuade them to pursue the destruction of the Elves.

The Dwarf and Elf armies on the upper flats waited in an anxious dread to see what the next course of the sun would bring. They would be there to meet the Trolls, for they had homes and families to defend. There were no thoughts of flight. There was no recourse for them.

Blood-red tendrils of light pierced through the clouded sky as the sun's golden orb crested on the far eastern end of the Coastal Range when the attack came. Most of the Dwarves and Elves were still sleeping when the sentries' rams' horns sounded the alarm, breaking the otherwise peaceful silence of the cool, still morning.

"Battle formations! Battle formations!" cried Stanton from the back of his horse, whose eyes rolled wild with nervous excitement. Dwarf and Elf scurried about in disarray, the Elves bordering on panic, but it was not long before they stood in ranks ready to meet their foe. Everyone stood in silence as the stampeding mass of Trolls made its way toward the road leading to the upper flats, while other Trolls scurried up the cliffs at random.

Morlah stood with Jerhad at his tent door attempting to hold back the Elven Prince from taking part. "Remember Nan's admonition. And remember what happened last time. Vow to me thou willst remain here."

"I vow nothing, Druid! I will hold; but I *will not* allow a slaughter."

"Let it suffice then. I willst go with The Raven and help as I can." He leapt onto Raven's back, and the great Bornodald rose into the sky with powerful strokes of his huge wings, nostrils flaring and ears pinned back for the battle rage that took him over when he prepared to fight.

The Trolls, now carrying shields for the first time, penetrated the archers' assault and soon clashed with the pikes, which met them in a straight frontal charge. The steep road slowed the them and gave the Elven squads momentum that carried the first lines back to the bottom of the hill. There, the fighting grew fierce and the battle turned against the Elves' ranks. Many fell under the heavy blows of Troll maces. Elf and Dwarf heads were crushed and bodies broken. Trolls collapsed with spears skewering their necks and chests. The battle escalated. The assailants broke the defenders' frontline. Clashing metal rang with awful ferocity. Trolls twisted heads from bodies and threw the carcases at their enemy.

Jerhad watched in horror. Just as he was about to go down to the battle, Morlah and Raven came hurtling through the sky from the rear of the Troll army. Morlah hurled fireballs into the rear flanks. The distraction broke the advancement, and the Elves began the laborious retreat, fighting each step of the way back to the top of the hill. The Trolls hammered them at every step.

Trolls began to swarm the flats to the north and south of the camp, causing the Dwarf posts along the cliffs to be hard pressed to prevent them from gaining a foothold on the upper plain. But the Dwarves rallied and swept along the cliffs and, by sheer weight of numbers, drove many to their deaths over the edge and onto the boulders and rocks strewn along the lower flats. Yet, no sooner had the Dwarves cleared a section and moved on than it was again swarming with their foe. Jerhad watched in dismay at the carnage of Troll, Dwarf and Elf taking place before him.

"Nan, where are you?" he spoke into the empty air before him.

"I am with you and within you," came the answer, but not into his ears.

"Let me see you."

"No. Speak, Elven Prince. What is it you require?"

"Don't you see what's happening? What am I supposed to do?"

"I do not know. It is yours to use the wisdom of the magic. I am not a warrior. I cannot say. Only, do not slay as you did before."

"Great!.... Why don't you just leave if you're no more help than that."

A second wave of Trolls moved up the road just as the Elves rallied and charged again. The Dwarves continued sweeping the cliffs clean of Trolls; in the distance, Morlah was seen engaged with the flying black creatures. Although the Dwarves were doing fairly well, the Elves were taking tragic losses. They fell by the score. Cries of pain filled the air. The grunts of laboring combatants mingled among the groans of dying soldiers. The smell of dust mingled with the scent of death.

Through gritted teeth, Jerhad cried out in frustration, his heart torn at witnessing his people being ravaged. Rank upon rank were falling to the Trolls, whose superior weight and strength made them too great an adversary for the Elves in a face-to-face engagement.

Archers on the cliffs poured arrows into the horde's flanks. The Trolls hit by the poisoned shafts thrashed in convulsions, with spit and blood frothing from their mouths and noses.

And then it came to him! Elfstones glowing, Jerhad unsheathed *Gildar*.

"Desist!" hissed Nan in some distant thought or voice. He could not tell which.

With magic blazing and power radiating, Jerhad ascended into the sky, rising on a straight upward course until he was almost to the height of the low, overcast clouds that blocked the sunshine from the battlefield. With the might and power of the Elfstones focused through his Elven blade, he began carving a fissure from the far Coastal Range and in a southerly direction toward the coast. The ground opened with a loud grumbling and shudder. Earth heaved and boulders belched from the ground as the flats split open some twenty paces wide and sixty paces deep. The earth opened under the Trolls who were now in full retreat, frantically seeking to get clear of the great maw opening at their feet. Troll, Elf and Dwarf fell to the ground at the violent quaking that was separating the Elves and Dwarves from the larger mass of their enemy.

When the trench was completed to the cliffs overlooking the Korkaran Sea, Jerhad stopped. He stood as it were, in his celestial position, like the apparition of a god. The Trolls on the far side fell back and, finally, turned and ran as Jerhad looked down on them in a display of a fiery aura of magic that raged about him, revealing a fearsome power and awesome might. The winged creatures turned and fled. The Trolls remaining on the westward side of the chasm were quickly slaughtered or jumped to their deaths in an attempt to escape the presence of the Elven Warrior.

Raven hovered before Jerhad, his mighty wings catching the wind.

"An impressive and resourceful demonstration, Sire," said Morlah. "Thine magic truly is an awesome force. Greater, I believe, then any Elven King since the reign of Broanaldire, the first King. Again thou hast delivered thine people for the time being."

Below, a great cheer went up from the Dwarves and Elves. Then, as one, the Elven Army went down on one knee, lifted their weapons to the sky, and with a loud exclamation cried, "Hail, Jerhad, King of the Elves!" The Dwarves responded accordingly repeating the praise, "Hail, Jerhad, King of the Elves."

Jerhad flushed with embarrassment. His magic faltered due to the distraction. Morlah, ever vigilant, reached out and grabbed the Prince by the collar as he began to fall; the Bornodald folded his wings and dropped with them as if in an orchestrated movement, allowing Morlah to pull Jerhad onto the Bornodald's back and into a seated position.

"Fire and demons, what happened? Good thing you were here. I don't know what I would have done," said the Elven Prince as Raven unfolded his wings and glided toward the ground.

"Magic does require constant concentration, Elven Prince. Something I think thou willst remember in the future. Now, let us go assess our losses," said Morlah. He felt Jerhad's head slump down against his back.

"I can't, Morlah. I can't look on all those who fallen. O ye gods, there must be over a thousand of them. Get me to my tent. I need to rest...and hide."

But no sooner had he stepped to the ground than Jerhad spotted a dying Dwarf where the wounded were being gathered. He went over to the soldier, pulling back the crude bandage from his chest, where he saw a gaping hole, through which he could see straight into the Dwarf's viscera. Jerhad groaned in horror and with compassion, his hands instinctively going to the wound. A silver-white light radiated from Jerhad, cleansing, healing, closing the wound, and leaving the soldier still weakened but with the promise of Life and Health.

The Dwarf looked up into Jerhad's tear-filled eyes and, in a weak, faint voice, whispered, "Hail, King of the Elves." Jerhad moved on from there, down the ranks of the wounded, cleansing and closing wounds; but not using enough magic as to make them completely whole, for there just was not enough time to take for each if he were to save as many as possible.

Jerhad heard Nan speaking within him. "It should not be so, but I will not protest, for the Life and Health of each of these is dear to me also."

Late that night, as the last light faded from the still overcast sky, now threatening rain, Jerhad stumbled into his tent in exhaustion. He had attended to the more severely injured and wounded while the Healers frantically tried to match his pace tending to the lesser injuries. Too many times,

Jerhad had been too late to help and had simply stopped to close the dead's eyes; too many had died waiting. Some, he had passed by, knowing it would take too much time and energy to save. Morlah followed at his side without speaking a word. Throughout the ordeal, the Druid's hand was on the Prince's back, lending him strength from the argentus in his orb. Unfortunately, the Druid's magic did not lend itself to healing, but he could assist the Elf in this way. Before Jerhad had returned to his tent, Morlah had spoken to him.

"Thou hast shown much wisdom in these matters, Elven Prince. I doest salute thee. Now go to thine bed and sleep, for such an extreme use of magic canst draw greatly from one's strength. When thou doest awake again, eat and drink much. Thou willst need to replenish thine resources. Magic as yours is inherently tied to your own body's strength; therefore, be wise in its use and your own body's maintenance." After that, he mounted Raven and flew off to see what the Troll horde was up to.

The rain fell lightly, pitter-pattering on the army's tent tops under the dark gray morning sky, reflecting the mood of the defense force's camp. A detachment had been sent carrying the worst of the wounded, not yet fully recovered, and the dead back to Mildra. Jerhad slept late and, after eating a large meal, went back to sleep until the third quarter of the sun's course at which time Morlah visited by apparition.

"The Trolls have withdrawn about one league east. It doest appear that Daektoch's servants have managed to take control of them again. I didst allow Raven to rest overnight, but now we are headed north to see if we can see any evidence of Daektoch's goings and comings and to see how things in Breezon fare. Stanton appears to have the army here under control. Continue to rest for another course. I shouldst return within one dozen courses. Ja speed." And, in his customary fashion, Morlah was gone.

For the next six courses, the army held its position. Scouts, now going and coming from around the north end of the fissure Jerhad had created, reported no movement of the Troll host. Reinforcements of both Elves and Dwarves arrived on the seventh course, bringing news of the devastation of the Troll horde that had besieged *Dolan*. Messengers told of a dark specter that had destroyed both Troll and Dwarf armies leaving *Dolan* strewn with bodies and a torrent of blood. Later messengers reported that the specter had only destroyed the Trolls; for the time being, any threat from the north was gone.

Stanton, who had been in the thick of the battle, went about attempting to shore up the army's morale. But he himself was filled with self-doubt, blaming himself for the high number of casualties the army had taken. He became sullen and withdrawn and was seen talking with StoneSon on several occasions, leaving with fits of coughing after meetings with the Dwarf and his distilled concoction.

It was on one of these visits to StoneSon that Jerhad caught up to Stanton.

"You're at the corndrippings again. What's going on?" But, Jerhad did not press him, knowing it was more serious than just "a girl", having heard reports of Stanton's mood from IronLeggs.

"I don't think I'm your man. You should find someone else to lead the Elf Army; maybe IronLeggs would be willing to take over."

"And why should I find someone else? You're the one who has made an army out of this group of farmers and fishers, almost overnight. You're the one who's trained them and allowed them to survive this long. You can't go taking responsibility for what the Trolls are doing. This is what made you leave the Breezon Army seven cycles ago; you can't handle seeing your troops being killed.

"But I'm telling you that there's no one better qualified, not in all the land of Frontmire, to do this job. I can't handle standing by watching the Elves and Dwarves butchered and not use my magic; but one thing I have learned, what Kassandra taught me: that I can't take responsibility for what others do. And you can't either. You're doing a great job with little to no resources. No one could do better under the circumstances."

"How do you know about why I quit the Breezon Army?"

"I didn't travel half the continent with you and not get to know you. After what we went through, you were pretty easy to figure out. Now, Commander, pick yourself up. Harden yourself like you did when you took command of Breezon. We have a job to do!"

But Stanton could not receive the Prince's admonition.

And so it was, four courses later, that Stanton stood on the cliffs overlooking the Korkaran Sea and wondered if he would be better simply jumping off the precipice or running off to hide deep in the Mystics or maybe moving to Rain's Bottom, a place fit for a derelict such as himself. There he could drink Master Kline's ale until his coin ran out. By then, he would be some seventy cycles old, and he could just lie down and die. No more giving orders sending hundreds and thousands to their deaths. No more thoughts of wives and children having to be told of fathers and mates dead in battle.

He could almost hear the report used with the families of the dead, as used by the Breezon Army, "*...under Commander*

Stanton Ferrell's orders, marched to battle and died in defense of his home and people...."

Ye gods, how could he face any of them, being the one who sent them out against such odds; over and over he sent them out, knowing many would die, knowing they were out-matched. Stanton could handle battle as well as or better than the next. He could slay in self-defense or war and not be bothered. He could face his own mortality and battles that brought the promises of death, but he could not handle sending others to their deaths. If the Human Commander had a weakness, it lay there.

"Stanton," came a soft and familiar voice from behind him.

He turned to find himself looking into those wide, green, Elven eyes once again. "Ahliene," he gasped. "What are you doing here?"

"The Healers were looking for helpers, so I volunteered to come out with the relief group that came with the reinforcements a couple courses ago. I had been busy until now with bandage changes. Some of the males told me you had come this way, so I came to see if I could find you to say hello."

Stanton's eyes dropped, and he began turning away, lost within his turmoil.

"What? Are you unhappy to see me...?" Ahliene asked, her countenance falling.

"No, it's not that. Well.... It's just that...I have something on my mind," he said turning back to face her. "Something that's sort of eating at me.... I don't know.... I don't know what to do."

"Well, that sure is a surprise, after everything I've heard about you. I didn't think there was anything you came up against that you couldn't handle..." she said suppressing a giggle, "except maybe a 'girl.'" Again, she suppressed a giggle and a smirk.

Stanton looked up at her and again was caught in the pools of her green eyes, making his heart pound within his chest. He took a deep breath, trying to get hold of himself, but then had to laugh in spite of his mood. "You're right.... There's very little that scares me or is too much of a challenge, except 'a girl'...especially one like you," he said, his face flushing brightly.

"Why, thank you.... I think that was a compliment, Commander."

Stanton flushed even redder.

"Can we walk?" she asked, taking his arm, turning him and propelling him by his elbow along the cliff-side path. "Am I allowed to ask what troubles you? All the males are talking about it, and worry is written all over your face, and I can keep a secret if needed – honest." Below them at the cliff's base, the surf pounded the rocky precipice with the same ferocity that the Trolls had pounded Stanton's troops.

Stanton did not resist but allowed himself to be herded along, his whole body electrified by the sensation of Ahliene's hand on his arm, his whole focus on that one sensation. Without realizing what he was doing, he poured his heart out to her, telling her of his concerns, unloading his problem, though little by little he began to realize what he was doing. But then it was too late; he had spilled his guts, revealing his weakness, and worse of all, to *a girl*.

"Oh, that is so sweet. I would have never guessed that a male like yourself, a soldier like you, would ever even think of such a thing, let alone be bothered by it. I would have thought you to be like a stone."

"Sweet?" stammered Stanton.

"Yes. The fact that you care about those under your command, the fact that you care if they live or die, and that they're not just tools that you throw into battle to obtain your goals shows that you have compassion within you. It shows kindness and concern...character.... That you're not just some hardened killer."

"It does...? "

She stopped him and forcefully turned him to face her. "Commander! If you didn't feel the way you do about your males and their deaths, that would be a cause to worry. The Elves and Dwarves will fight with or without you. Our lives and homes are at stake. *We have no choice*. We have no options. Our land is being invaded; *we have no choices*. Our army will stand to the last male if need be.

"We all appreciate your help and expertise. The soldiers respect you. With you, there might be a few more of us alive when this is all over. Do you hear me, Commander! With your help, there might be a few more of us alive when this is all over! As for me, I thank you for how you've helped us so far." She stood on tiptoes and kissed him on the mouth, holding her kiss for a span of heartbeats before she turned and left, leaving the warrior trembling nervously.

The second watch of the night had just come on, campfires still burned as many Dwarves were still up telling stories, which was their habit. Watch fires burned along Land's Break's edge. One heartbeat, all had been peaceful in night, and the next, the air was filled with the blaring of rams' horns, their bone-chilling call filling the darkness. Messengers arrived at a run to Jerhad's tent, Stanton showing up on their heels, still pulling his pants up and barefoot, just on time to hear the Elven scout's report.

"Trolls moving fast, coming down through the mountains. They ambushed several scouting parties.... I think it was those black things. That's why we didn't get word sooner. They'll be here within one or two spans."

"Fire and demons," cursed Jerhad. "What now, Commander?"

"We fall back," directed the soldier. "We can't face them here, or else it will be finished here at our expense. We fall back and try to make the best of it. Maybe find another place to make a stand." He sent messengers throughout the camp to let them know they were to be packed and moving within the quarter span. Stanton was shouting orders as he returned to his tent to finish dressing. Jerhad stopped and considered his Commander for a few heartbeats; he seemed like his old self again.

A solitary horn sounded the start of the retreat. The Dwarves would march in ranks to the south of the Elf infantry. If the Trolls attacked, the Dwarves could flank them in an assault. The Healers, cooks and others were sent ahead in ox-drawn carts, while the formation of the Elf Army formed a rearguard. They moved swiftly but in an orderly fashion. The archers were set out to the north keeping pace with the infantry. In case of an attack, they would stop and let the Trolls go by until they could flank them with showers of poisoned arrows. With all players in their places, they set out for Mildra. Jerhad gave up his horse and sent a rider bearing messages back to the town.

The sun was at midcourse, the heat of it intense, as the armies came to a halt for their first rest under the cloudless summer sky. They were at the abandoned village of Lindhal, so they used the village's wells to restore water supplies before setting out again. It was not long before scouts caught up to them, bringing more information.

"Trolls will overtake you by nightfall at this pace," said the Dwarf.

"Commander?" inquired Jerhad.

"We need to do something to slow them down. Unfortunately, that would mean a couple dozen squads sent on a suicide mission. There's nothing else. It's up to you, Elf Boy."

"I'm not ready for that just yet. Can't we just double our pace?"

"In this heat! They'll be on us, and we'll be unfit to fight if we do that. Can't do it!"

"Well that leaves one choice then. I'll stay behind and stall them."

"You think that's a good idea?"

"No. You've got a better one?"

Stanton grimaced and shook his head. "I'll stay behind with you. I probably can't do much, but who knows, you might need a hand with something."

"I'm staying alone. You go on with the army. We can't afford to lose you."

"Me?" Stanton laughed. "*You're* going to be king of this outfit and *you* can't afford to lose *me*?"

"King...whatever...I want you with the army."

"IronLeggs can take over for a while, Princey. I'm going with you and that's final." The Human punctuated his statement with a poke of his iron-like finger to the Elf's chest. Jerhad winced.

Anger crossed Jerhad's face for a heartbeat, but then, he burst out laughing, "That's more like the old Stanton

I used to know, Commander," he said, slapping Stanton on the shoulder. "Come on then, let's go see what we can do. And get those squirrels in your head working overtime because I don't have a plan."

The mass of Trolls had grown since the last confrontation. They swathed the path nearly one league wide across the flats as they came on at a pace that reminded Jerhad of a wolf pack on a hunt. From within a lone stone farmhouse, Stanton and Jerhad watched the oncoming horde. The two had gone back almost half a league to where they saw the dust of the Troll movement rising in the distance. Having found the farmhouse, they decided it was as good a place to make a stand as any. A drainage trench stood between the fields and the house.

"Too bad we didn't bring the archers," Stanton remarked. "That trench would have been a good site for an ambush."

"Until they were overrun with Trolls," finished Jerhad.

"Just a thought...."

"That's it! That's just the thought we needed. Now, let's see if I can do this."

"Do what?"

"Watch. Watch the trench."

Stanton looked out the window where suddenly one Dwarf and one Elf each carrying a pike, rose and rushed off in a full charge toward the Trolls. When they had gone a dozen paces, they vanished. "What was that?" asked Stanton, obviously startled.

"An illusion of an ambush, Commander."

"Two soldiers doesn't quite make an ambush, Elf Boy."

"But what if I put the illusion of some sixty or eighty thousand battle-crazed Dwarves and Elves out there? Might it slow the Trolls if only for a heartbeat?"

"I doubt you'll buy much time with it, if any. If they only clash with air, what's the use?"

"Let's give it a try. There are other things I can do if necessary."

"No you don't! Morlah has already chosen the outhouse that he'll nail my hide to if I participate or let you do that stuff again...hey, wait a heartbeat. Remember that wall you made the Trolls smack into back on the lower plains in our second engagement with them? What if you made it uneven like a weak frontline, so that the Trolls don't really immediately understand that they aren't in battle? Say we put a lot of shields in our front line. Have some of your imaginary troops fall, and then, have the army retreat...or even better, routed to the north into the mountains. Now, that could buy us one course or more depending on how long you can hold your army together and on how long the Trolls persist in searching for the missing troops."

"Excellent, Commander. That's what I pay you all that gold coin for."

"Elf boy.... You haven't paid me anything."

"Haven't I? Well here, have a couple of these. Nice likeness of me on them, too." Jerhad fumbled in his belt pouch and flipped Stanton a couple of golds that had been minted in Mildra.

Stanton bit one. "At least it's real. I'm impressed."

Jerhad rolled his eyes and shook his head. He turned his attention back to the Trolls' advance.

"That's probably close enough for a charge from our side," said Stanton.

"Here goes nothing," said Jerhad, pulling his knife to get more power and focus into what he was about to do. The Elfstones on *Gildar's* handle shone brilliantly, except for *balan* and *acrch*. Then, with an ear-piercing battle cry and the resounding of rams' horns, line upon line of infantry rolled out of the ditch in formations to match the width of the Trolls' advance. Their faces were distorted with rage and hatred as they rushed off to their deaths. When they had closed half the distance to the Trolls, they all began letting out bloodcurdling howls, bringing the Trolls to a halt.

"Nice touch, but don't scare them off just yet," frowned Stanton, a might wary of Jerhad's magic.

The Trolls stood and looked at each other and back to the minions charging them. Overhead, a winged creature flew in with its rider, attempting to send the Trolls forward again. The black creature was aware of the illusion but was unable to communicate it to the Trolls. It circled above the plain; its presence and the winged beast's screeches instilled apprehension throughout the horde. Without Daektoch's control, they would have bolted. The army rushing toward them appeared completely mad. The Trolls dug their heels in and prepared for the clash.

The magic worked perfectly. The first two lines of Trolls let out an oomph of a groan as the wall hit them, but then, Elves and Dwarves fell everywhere. The Trolls quickly pressed the advantage as several more ranks of attackers suddenly fell. The Elves and Dwarves began dropping their weapons, turned tail and ran. The Trolls stood, somewhat puzzled, but several of their leaders shouted orders, and the mass pitched forward in pursuit of the army that fled toward the mountains.

"So far so good," said Stanton.

"I don't know how long I can keep this up," panted Jerhad looking a bit pale. "This is taking a lot more effort than I expected."

"Let more of them fall or just vanish if it will make things easier for you. The Trolls probably won't figure it out for a while. Just get them to the mountains. Can you maintain the illusion that far?"

"I think so. It's getting dark; if I can just last until sunsetting, then it won't matter." Time wore on. Jerhad visibly tired before Stanton's eyes with each passing span of heartbeats.

"Just a little longer, Jerhad."

Jerhad looked at his Commander. "What happened to 'Elf Boy'?

"Oh...nothing. Just trying to help...."

Jerhad smiled. "Actually it does a bit."

"Close enough to the mountain in this light. Let it go."

Jerhad released the illusion and fell back against the wall. "I need to sleep."

"Those Trolls could spend courses searching the mountains unless those black things get them back on our trail again." He looked down at Jerhad to find he was talking to himself, for Jerhad was already asleep. "Well, Elf Boy, you pulled it off again." He smiled. But then suddenly, he went cold, and his breathing became heavy.

Stanton's sword, *ursha*, Defender of Life, sang as it slipped from its sheath, as Stanton whirled about to find himself face-to-face with one of Daektoch's dark servants. The creature breathed a hissing sound as it stood in the doorway, slightly crouched, sword drawn. Stanton would have liked to get it outside, away from Jerhad, but he did not have the option.

The creature stepped forward, and Stanton went to meet him, hoping that whatever Nan had done to his sword at Moreau's Ford still worked. For without the power that *acrch* had instilled into it, he was perfectly helpless against this foe. The creature was a medium height and thin. Its garments were pitch black as if they defied light to fall upon them, its face lost in the darkness of its hood, and its very presence projected a strong sense of consternation.

With the first clashing of steel, Stanton knew Nan's magic still worked, for fire erupted from the blades as they met. The battle was on! Stanton was at a distinct disadvantage with Jerhad in a deep sleep behind him. He could not maneuver as he would have, for he needed to protect his Prince. Again and again, the blades collided with force, first the one attacking and the other defending, and then the other attacking and the first defending. Swords reverberated with violence. This shade fought with great skill, unlike the others that the soldier had fought in the past. It feinted, lunged and defended with the flowing grace of a Weapons Master. It beat Stanton back again and again. The Human was hard pressed to hold his ground and keep the beast away from Jerhad.

The conflict raged for nearly a half span, and just when it looked like Stanton had taken the upper hand, in the heat of the battle, he forgot that his foe was not merely flesh and blood. He allowed their blades to slide hilt to hilt, coming nose to nose with the creature.

Deep within its cowl, it smiled, and then, Stanton felt it rake its lethally poisonous claws across his side. His chain mail, containing a trace of argentus, as it was made by the Dwarves, saved him from being torn open, but the tip of one claw found purchase and dragged across his skin. He stepped back and spun around, *ursha* decapitating the creature whose body thrashed and writhed about for some one half span. Stanton dropped to his knees as he felt the poison of the foul beast's claw rapidly course through him as if he had been bitten by hundreds of vipers.

"Jerhad, you must wake up," said Nan.

"But I'm too tired; besides I didn't violate your stuff.... Let me sleep."

"No, you must wake up. You did but let the magic's wisdom guide you. You did well. But Stanton needs you. Wake up."

"Where...what does Stanton need?"

"He is dying. Daektoch's servant has wounded him, poisoned him. You need to wake up and help him. He is necessary."

"You mean I'm not awake?"

"You sleep. The battle has been fought at your very feet without rousing you. Wake. Stanton is in need of you."

"I don't know how to wake up if I'm not awake now. This seems like being awake to me."

Nan sighed deeply and stomped her foot. "Mortals! You still hold Ember in your hand. Concentrate on me to revive you from your exhaustion. Concentrate!"

Jerhad felt **acrch** *glowing within his hand and then within his bosom.*

"Concentrate!"

Jerhad saw Nan, or rather Nan's essence, and drew on it deeply as if drinking from a spring.

Suddenly, Jerhad opened his eyes and found himself sitting at the wall where he had slept. Stanton lay a few paces from him with the headless creature a bit further off. The head was lying a few steps away, a ghoulish, skeletal face revealed. Jerhad went to Stanton who was in his last breaths. Stanton gasped, stopped breathing for a couple spans of heartbeats and gasped again. The soldier's face was swollen beyond recognition, and his fingers resembled thick, pork sausages. His skin was mottled to a bluish purple overlying a sickly gray color. His throat gurgled each time he exhaled, and foam bubbled through his nostrils.

Jerhad slid Ember under Stanton's chain mail and slit it opened like parchment. Then, he tore the Human's shirt opened to find the grossly inflamed scratch Stanton had taken. It streaked a hideous bluish mottling out from the wound. Jerhad lay his hand on the wound and poured *health* into it. Although the venom within nauseated him, he pressed on, infusing Life and Health into Stanton.

"No," cried Nan. "Not like that. You're killing yourself."

"Get lost, Faerie."

"No, you'll kill yourself. Use the knife. Don't touch the wound!"

"Now you tell...." He fell over unconscious.

That was how the Dwarf detachment found them the next rising. IronLeggs had sent a small patrol back to see what had become of Jerhad, Stanton and the Trolls. They had not seen the Trolls, who were still searching the mountains for the army, but they found Jerhad and Stanton unconscious, feverish and in an appalling condition. Litters were lashed together with use of poles and blankets, and the Dwarves took off at a run, carrying the Commander and Prince back to Mildra.

The Dwarves ran nonstop all the way, taking turns every span of the sun's course at the four corners of the stretchers, carrying the two fallen leaders back to Mildra in two courses time, passing and leaving the main body of the army far behind, though IronLeggs joined them. They arrived as the sun rose on the third course. They carried the two to Jerhad's home.

Catrina met them at the door and had both of them placed in Jerhad's room, sending for the Healers at the same time. Of course, these were not Druid Healers, and the Elves' ways with herbs and poultices fell far below the need.

"O ye gods, they're burning up! Get those blankets off of them," said Catrina, surprisingly composed. She had some elder females help her take their clothes off while some males got a cool water bath ready to attempt to break their fever. Then, she cornered IronLeggs.

"What's happened to them? There are no wounds, except for that partially healed scratch on Stanton, though it looks hot."

"We do not know for sure. We found them like this with one of Daektoch's creatures slain by them. Judging from Stanton's mail, we think they fought, and Stanton took a scratch from its claws. The scratch already looked like it was partially healed, but we cannot tell what happened to the Prince. He has been the same as Stanton, feverish and at times delirious and breathing a bit ragged. I am on my way out to rejoin with the army. If there is anything you need from us, get hold of SteelHand. But I doubt our Healers have any advantage over yours. What we need here are Druid Healers."

"Or magic," Catrina muttered to herself as IronLeggs left.

Chapter 17

Meanwhile Andreanna was having trouble with *balat* again. Though *igini* (Harmony) and *acrch* had both attempted to balance her, *balat* still was of a strong will, as was Andreanna, for she was *of* Andreanna.

"You will be subject to me," said ***balat****, the Dark Queen, to Andreanna.*

"What in the gods' names is it with you? How can you become the dominant identity if we are one?"

"I can, and I will."

"We'll see about that." Then, Andreanna took hold of ***licri*** *and* ***monit*** *and held them to herself, depriving* ***balat*** *of access to both. Using* ***monit****, she transformed herself into a great serpent covered with coarse, dark-green scales, which glistened with a multicolored hue at each movement.* ***balat****, deprived of access to* ***monit****, was unable to assume her transfiguration of the specter of the Dark Queen. But instead, she appeared as a female child the color of oiled coal. Eyes, ears, tangled hair, hands, and feet were all like the color of the pitch that bubbled from the earth in the northern Mystic's tar pits.*

The serpent laughed, "So that's the problem. You're nothing but an undisciplined child. That's easily remedied." The serpent lunged, catching ***balat*** *and wrapping herself about the tiny body.* ***balat*** *screamed and kicked, for without access to* ***licri*** *she was significantly weakened, and she could not just destroy her opponent. After all, they were one, even though she refused to* *admit it. The serpent's coils wrapped her securely until only head and hands could be seen; and then, the constriction began.*

"I can live without you, ***balat****, but you can't without me. Yield to me, or I will finish what the Faeries didn't."*

"Never, you witch. I'd rather die than be subject to you. I ***am*** *the* ***Dark Queen****."*

"You can be so, but only if you are subject to my will."

"Never! We will both die." ***balat*** *began speaking her words of destruction as the serpent tightened its hold, crushing the child* ***balat****, impairing her strength and power and holding her in control. The struggle lasted for spans into the night; neither relenting in the contest, but slowly* ***balat*** *began wearing out, for she had not the strength of* ***licri.***

Finally, as the sun rose over the peaks of the Dwarves' home valley, ***balat*** *gasped, "I yield."*

Suddenly, Nan and ***igini*** *were there, each in turn placing their hands on the side of* ***balat's*** *face.*

Nan kissed her and said, "The kiss of Health."

Then ***igini*** *took hold of her and kissed her saying, "The kiss of* ***Harmony****. Be whole,* ***balat****. Be whole and harmonious."*

The serpent spoke to the two, "Do you think this will do it or will I have to take this brat over my knee repeatedly?"

"I think all will be well," said Nan, "for this time we kissed her when she was in submission. I think she will be well, only keep her away from ***monit*** *and* ***licri*** *except under your control until she shows that she can be trusted. If she rises up again, then destroy her, for we have done what we can. If we need to come against her, we will have to destroy you as well; we cannot distinguish, but you have the power within you to bring about her demise and end without taking harm to yourself.*

Andreanna woke up drenched with sweat, a Dwarf Healer sitting at her bedside. "Ahh, the Queen of the Elves awakes at last."

"How long have I been asleep?"

"Four settings of the sun have passed since you spoke with King HeartStone. You have been delirious but without fever for much of that time. Here let me give you some herbal medicament while I send for the King and SixFists. They have been worried about you, as we have."

It was the second course since Jerhad and Stanton had been carried to Mildra. Catrina sat at their bedsides speaking words of well-being to them, remembering how she had affected the dying flowers, but not comprehending what she attempted; nevertheless, she did, with magic, stay much of the venom's effects. Outside, the efforts at raising the wall redoubled, knowing it was a matter of time before the Trolls' arrival. All four Giants were about again, Mordock and Kassandra back to their usual strength and health. Mining of the gold came to a halt, and the laborers were pulled to work exclusively on the wall. The *MayBest* was sailing on the afternoon tide to deliver another load of gold bullion to *seilstri*. They promised to immediately return with their best Healers.

Ahliene rushed into the room to Stanton's side, just having returned from the plain.

"How are they?" she asked Catrina with worry in her eyes.

"Not well," Catrina said shaking her head. "The fever returns sooner and is harder to break each time it does return. Neither has awakened. If they don't wake to take some water soon, they will die.

"Who are you? What are you doing here?"

Ahliene blushed. "Well, I heard of what happened, and I was concerned...."

"Then the rumor is true. You have a thing for Stanton! Word is that you turned the Commander's head.... Why don't you stay and help me care for them?"

"I had heard tell that when the Prince's mate was sick at *seilstri* the Healers used a sea-reed's stem, Red Kelp I believe, to get food and water into her. Could we think of trying that?"

"Ye gods, I do believe I remember Morlah telling of it. Oh, but I do wish he were here. Let me speak to the Healers. They have all left for now, seeing there wasn't anything to be done here. Perhaps we could try."

Two settings of the sun later, the wall was three paces in height at its lowest mark and some of it was four or five paces at the northeast corner. The Dwarves and Giants worked by sunlight and by night with the Trolls' arrival imminent. The Giants had not slept in four courses, while Dwarves and Elves worked one-half course shifts. The pace of the labor was frantic as they anticipated the impending attack.

Jerhad and Stanton were now being given water and herbal mixtures. The Healers had begrudgingly agreed to attempt it, fearing they might end up drowning them. After much heated discussion, Ahliene had come up with the idea of blowing in the reed to determine if it bubbled in the stomach or in the lung, listening with an ear to the body. The Healers had submitted to this reasoning and had begun treatment for fever and dehydration.

Two courses later, the Healers from Parintia disembarked from the *MayBest*, rams' horns simultaneously announcing the Trolls' arrival. On that note, the Giants, Dwarves and Elves ceased their labors. The Giants went to their tents to get some sleep, leaving instruction to wake them at first sign of attack. One-quarter of the troops were sent to sleep, one-quarter left on standby and the other half in formation within the walls. The Trolls stopped on the field about one-eighth league from the now *city* of Mildra. It appeared that the Trolls would rest before their assault began; therefore, another half of the troops were sent to sleep.

In Jerhad's home, the Druid Healers put everyone out of the sick room, raising vehement protests, and went to work. One span later, they emerged. Kristi, one of the Druids' chief Healers approached Catrina and Lewin.

"It is good that thou hast given them water. I doest doubt that Stanton wouldst have lived much longer. Jerhad is not as bad, but we hadst to put them both into the Druid Sleep to prevent them from getting worse. They art both infected with poison, which is of Black magic in its origin. The only ones with the ability to deal with this further are Master Filinhoff who because of his age wouldst not be willing to make the journey, and Morlah. Doest thou know where he canst be found?"

"He's gone north to spy out Daektoch's movements, but we don't know when he'll be back," responded Lewin.

"We canst either wait," said Kristi, "or move them to *seilstri*. They shouldst not deteriorate more while in the Druid Sleep. Thou doest need to continue giving them water, and I willst give thee a recipe to nourish them in the same manner.

"Fear not, for it was a case exactly like this one, which wast the source of the discovery of the Druid Sleep; they willst recover. We doest need to gather some freshly cut herbs to treat them with."

Later that night, Ahliene, sitting at Stanton's bedside, sleeping with her head on the bed and the Healers slumbering in the next room, was awakened by the sound of someone calling her name. She raised her head, looking about, wondering if she had been dreaming.

"Ahliene," spoke the voice again. Tinkling sounds permeated the night air along with the fragrance of Health.

"Who is it? she whispered, straining her eyes in the dim light of the oil lamp, trimmed low.

"It is Nan. Do you know me?"

"Nan? I don't think...."

"Not the name. Listen to my voice."

Ahliene smiled. "No.... It can't be. It's not true...."

"It is. I will show myself. Be not afraid." Nan appeared before Ahliene in the same form of the little old lady that had appeared to Stanton in Moreau's Ford.

Ahliene was somewhat startled. "That's not you...."

"It is in a manner. Let it suffice for now lest we be interrupted. Hear my voice."

Ahliene relaxed and smiled again. "I was to the point in my life where I thought that I had made it all up. That you were a child's fantasy. Oh, but I still can't believe it.... All those times you visited me when I was a child...but why?"

"I have a great love for you, Ahliene. Among the Elves, you exclusively bear the magic of *acrch* in such purity. It is not with the strength that the Prince possesses, but it is purer. I have come to you, for it is time that your magic be awakened. The Druids have done what they can, but it will not be enough soon enough. Both Stanton and Jerhad will be needed and very soon, and besides, Stanton's descendants are tied by Destiny to the future of this land. Come and embrace me."

Ahliene stood and went to the little old lady and bent down to hug the stooped form.

"Oh, I do love you so, Nan," Ahliene said as she kissed Nan on the cheek. Releasing Nan, she stood and gasped, for there stood *acrch* in her true form, her long silver hair streaming, sky-blue eyes radiating with the essence of Life and Health, which shone in brilliance about her, along with its sweet fragrance.

Then the Faerie vanished. "Hear me, dear heart. Open yourself, your heart, and the magic will lead you," Nan's voice spoke within her. Then, the *acrch* Elfstone on Jerhad's knife, hanging from Jerhad's belt in its sheath at the head of his bed, began to glow. Ahliene went to it, slowly reaching out with one finger and touching the stone.

"Oh!" her soft voice exclaimed. "I see you clearly now. Oh, Nan, you *are* beautiful!" Then looking down, she saw that her hands and arms glowed softly with the silver-white glow of *acrch*. Her breathing deepened as if in excitement, and she found herself in love with Life and Health. Not that she previously had not, for ever since she had been a child, she had often dreamed of being a Healer but had always been somewhat repulsed by the use of herbs as a means of healing, which had left her with no alternative. Hence, she had abandoned the dream. Her childhood visitations by Nan came back to her clearly. It had not been her imagination. She had never spoken of it to anyone, not parents or siblings. And now, she understood why she had never been sick at any time in her life, for Nan's influence on her and the magic of *acrch* (even though dormant) within her had had its effect.

But something else was awake within her. An intense love for Stanton, as if their destinies had become tied to each other's, and she had some responsibility for getting him to the fulfillment of his. She turned away from *Gildar* and started towards Stanton's bed but stopped short. *No, her duty lay first to her people.* She went instead to Jerhad, pulling a chair up next to him, sitting near him and then studying his face. He was a handsome male, and though she had not known him until several courses past, she now felt she knew him intimately. Magic answered to magic. She took his face in her still glowing hands and softly kissed him on the lips.

"Be strong, be healthy, live long, my Prince. *acrch evandol, poncourse cantalti enaduat*," she spoke in the ancient Elven tongue, even though it was foreign to her, unaware that she had. Slivers of the whispers of power hung suspended in the air between their lips as Ahliene broke the kiss. The glow of her magic spread across Jerhad's skin. He took a deep breath and let out a sigh, as if comforted. Her touch revealed that his fever no longer burned. He shifted a bit in his sleep, the first movement he had shown since his return.

This was her calling! Her destiny! This was her purpose for being. To be a Healer using the Elven Faerie magic. Satisfaction and fulfillment flowed through her, raising a new sense of excitement. She quickly stood and returned to *Gildar*, drawing it from its sheath, feeling as though she were one with the Elven blade. Ember's might pulsed within her. The argentus in the steel made her skin tingle, and the Elfstone *acrch* glowed even more brightly. She gasped, filled with joy, tears flowing down her cheeks. *Oh, would that all the Elves would come into the magic of their destiny. What a wonderful world this would become!* She stood holding Ember, basking in the magic, communing with it, drinking it in, being strengthened by it and finding wisdom through it.

Finally, after some span of time lost to her, she returned Ember to its sheath and turned to Stanton, the soft glow of dawn lighting the far eastern sky. She went to his bed and took his face into her hands, kissing him on the lips. "*acrch evandol, poncourse cantalti enaduat*, my darling," she spoke, watching the glow of *acrch* spread across his skin, repeating the effect it had had on Jerhad. "Sleep now, my love."

She rose and went out of the house into the early morning only to be sickened by the thought of the impending invasion. Inside, Stanton stirred restlessly in his bed.

Meanwhile, elsewhere in Mildra, in varying degrees, several of the Healers were displaying the power of *acrch* as they tended to their work. Others, (was it a coincidence?) among the scouts began having an uncanny ability to detect the Trolls and their movements. Some found that they could improve morale and unite their people to the Elven cause with their mere presence and others that they could clean spoiling food, wounds or infections. Evidences of magic began to spread throughout the population, each member having some portion of its manifestations. A few had two or three abilities. Kendra was able to perform several different magics with the ability to combine them, looking like she would soon surpass her father's abilities.

This soon changed the whole demeanor of the Elven population, who in its entirety was now in Mildra. Their outlook became more positive and more serene. Though sober and aware of danger, they went about their daily duties and activities with less worry and despair. They found themselves with time for more laughter, song and fellowship with both Elves and Dwarves.

Since Ahliene's coming into the magic of *acrch*, Jerhad Prince of the Elves continued to improve but was, as Stanton, still asleep. The Druid Healers had marveled at the quick change toward recovery, speaking to each other in whispers as they re-examined the two that course. Ahliene feigned sleep as she sat in the rocking chair in the corner. The Healers were reluctant to bring the two out of the Druid Sleep so soon, not having understood the changes.

The Dwarves and Elves had constructed a relatively defendable wall. The entire population had put its effort to help the army in its completion. It was far from being an impregnable wall for the Trolls, but it would prove a difficult barrier. On the outside, the entire wall was surrounded by a dry moat, as Stanton had recommended. This trench was finished with a lining of stone on both sides and paved within, made with a two pace drop at its outermost edge and ten paces in width. The dugout was a difficult obstacle in itself; it also added two paces of height to the battlement, now giving them a rampart of five paces in height. All the dirt from the dry moat had been piled on the inside of the wall in ramps leading to its top in hopes of allowing the use of the infantry to charge assaults coming over the wall. They now worked on completing a one-and-a-half pace parapet on the battlement's top.

Andreanna was not recovering as she should have from her exertions in magic. Each course of the sun she would rise, eating large amounts of food, often concentrating on meats. By the end of the sun's course, she would feel better and have energy again, only to waken the next rising soaked in perspiration and with extreme fatigue, thirst and hunger. This went on course-by-course, causing deep concern among the Dwarf Healers.

The Dwarf King found her looking out of one of the royal castle windows, high in the cliffs overlooking the Dwarves' valley.

"There you are, Elf Queen. I have come to see how you fare."

"Same as yestercourse, same as the course before. I awake weak, exhausted and famished. If this doesn't stop, I'll eat you out of provisions."

"The Healers are concerned for you. They wish we could get you to the Healers in Parintia, for as you know, they are skilled above all others. But there are still a few Trolls about to the south and no ships in Parnham Bay. I would urge you to remain here and rest. I would fear for your safety should you go wandering south." Then he grinned. "Perhaps I should fear for the safety of the Trolls you might meet instead...."

During the past two courses, Andreanna's memory of her assault as the Dark Queen on the Trolls had returned to her. She was in horror...not at what she had done but at the fact that she was not appalled by what she had done. Thousands upon thousands of dead Trolls for Daektoch's sake. Why would he not he leave the poor beasts alone in their mountains? She lay in her bed and wept.

There was a knock at the door. The door opened and a Dwarfish head popped in. "Can I come in?" asked SixFists.

"SixFists! Yes, come in, please. Oh, I'm so glad to see you."

"I have someone with me. Come in, Grams."

Behind SixFists, entered an elderly female Dwarf whose face was crevassed with age, her features thickened with the cycles, her intense dark eyes almost lost in folds of sagging brows and behind her shoulders her long white hair flowed to the ground. But her posture was Dwarf-tall and upright, and she moved with the grace of one familiar with nobility. She was clothed in a long maroon dress made of very rich and fine, velvety material.

"This is Gram, Missy. Gram is my great-grandmother. The King's great-grandmother too and GladdenStone's grandmother."

"The King's?"

"We are cousins."

Gram approached Andreanna, who got up and bowed. "There is no need for that," she said, her voice strong and firm. "I have wanted to meet with the Queen of the Elves." She hesitated "...and maybe out of curiosity...the Dark Queen." She seemed almost apologetic.

"Well...come in and see," Andreanna smiled, trying to disarm the awkwardness.

"I'll be leaving you two ladies alone," winked SixFists. And before Andreanna could object, he stepped out the door and closed it behind him.

Andreanna spoke to the elder Queen. "Here, please sit. I'm honored to meet you...."

"Gram. Everyone calls me Gram. I am the oldest living Dwarf in *Dolan*. I have survived two hundred eighty-six cycles, and if I have my way I will another two hundred eighty-six. Previously, the oldest Dwarf ever known was two hundred twenty-one cycles. It seems like yestercourse I was but one hundred cycles....and you should have seen me then. I was still quite a catch," she laughed. "My mate, RavenStone, guarded me jealously though I do doubt that any Dwarf would have ever given a first thought to touching the Queen.

"But as for you, dear, I am told you are part Elf and possess an awesome power. I do not know if you are aware that you set the whole of our army into a panic. Not a small task, for Dwarves are not easily intimidated. Would you like...to tell me about it...your magic that is?"

So, Andreanna sat on the floor before Gram, feeling somewhat in awe of the old Queen; she told Gram the story of her troubles, of the coming into magic, of its effects on her and of her travels with SixFists.

"SixFists," repeated Gram, shaking her head. "He has always been something of the black sheep because of his fighting. The Dwarves tolerated him long for my sake. He has always been very dear to me. Looks just like his great-grandfather RavenStone, spitting image of the old King.

"But now to the matter I really came for. Among the Dwarves, every few hundred cycles, rises a seer, one who foretells the future, one who sees and unravels mysteries and secrets and such things. I am such an one who was visited with the gift.

"Ever since you have wakened from your ordeal, at night when I have laid down to rest, I have sensed a presence in the form of a curious or peculiar magic within *Dolan*. And suddenly, the presence is gone only to return at dawn. Since you are the only one visiting *Dolan*, I assume that it is you whom I sense. Therefore, I have come to spend the night with you. Perhaps I can help you and your healing, if I can unlock your secret. But I will ask your permission to do so, Queen of the Elves."

"Why not? Anything that helps me feel better is fine by me. And please, Andreanna, not Queen of the Elves."

"Very well." Gram pulled a tiny gold bell from her sleeve and rang it. The door to Andreanna's chamber opened, and servants came in with trays of food and bottles of wine. One maid carried Gram's nightgown and laid it out on the bed, while others assembled a large cot with a feather mattress on it.

"You don't need that. You can sleep with me," said Andreanna. "The bed is big enough for six of us."

"I know...the cot is for you. You would not deprive an old female of the little pleasures in life would you?"

Andreanna blushed at her presumption.

Gram laughed. "My dear, I have been spoiled beyond measure by the Dwarves for cycle upon cycle; humor me and allow me my little treats."

So, they settled in for the night, eating dainties, drinking wine and talking about stuff more on the level of girl talk. Late in the night, they went to bed, Gram in the large bed and Andreanna on the cot set up next to the bed. They had just settled in when Gram sensed the same presence that she had on previous nights.

"Andreanna?" spoke the Dwarfess.

There was no response. The old Queen rolled over and turned up the wick of the oil lamp at her bedside, pushing back the night. Slipping out of the bed, she walked around to the cot where Andreanna slept soundly. Gram pulled up a stool and sat next to her, placing a hand on Andreanna's arm.

Visions flashed rapidly through the Dwarfess' mind. She observed as an immense, howling, pitch-black she-wolf on a mountaintop, called the packs of Frontmire together for the hunt. Mounted upon the canines were Mountain Gnomes, brandishing spears and bows. She witnessed pack after pack sweep down from the mountains in response to the call and pour onto the western flats. Gram watched through the she-wolf's eyes, the she-wolf surveying all of Frontmire. Then suddenly, Andreanna was gone, bodily.

"Elf Queen, Elf Queen, Elf Queen," she whispered, shaking her head. "No wonder you are so tired...running and hunting throughout the night." Gram placed her hand on the cot and, with her consciousness, was able to follow Andreanna into the plain, a large dark she-wolf, alpha of alphas, leading thousands of wolves and Gnomes on the hunt, converging on the Trolls' flanks.

The Trolls were waiting, the wolf and Gnome attack having become a nightly event. But the wolves were too fast for them and scattered through the horde, inflicting their damage. More often than not, Trolls would miss their mark with their stone maces, injuring the others about them. Chaos spread through the host, the wolves quickly hamstringing many as others distracted the two-feet, Gnomes peppering the immense beasts with spear and arrow. The alpha she-wolf, flanked by a smaller female, took down hundreds, catching them at the throat and breaking their necks. The attack continued through the night and onto the dawn, until suddenly, Andreanna was in her cot again. Her hair was soaked with sweat, and she panted hard, tongue hanging from her mouth.

Gram rose, got some water and towels and cooled the Human down, washing her and changing her garments. Then, she climbed into bed and went to sleep. At about midcourse, Andreanna awoke to sounds in the room. Servants came and went, Gram now dressed in a long, green, silk dress. A banquet of food was laid out.

"Andreanna dear, so good of you to join us. Come sit with me and we will have break fast as soon as you refresh yourself. Do you take honey in your java?"

They sat and ate and continued their chitchat for a while. Finally, Gram reached out and touched Andreanna's hand.

"Andreanna, dear, you have a problem that we must put a stop to."

"I do?"

"Yes," smiled Gram. "Do you know the black she-wolf?

Andreanna blushed, embarrassed.

"How much control do you have over her?"

"I don't know. I've only known her in dreams. I didn't know she was real or that she was *me* until she killed some wolves who wouldn't submit to her...to me...her."

"While you slept last night, you went hunting Trolls. Not in a dream. You vanished from this room and went out onto the plain to the east of Mildra with all the wolves and Mountain Gnomes of Frontmire, hunting and killing Trolls."

Andreanna turned pale. "Oh no. It's *balat* again. Gram, you've got to help me. I don't know what to do. The magic is acting on its own."

"Do not get yourself upset. Obviously, you are only trying to help the Elves. It is all very natural, dear, that you are trying to help your people. But it has to stop. You are wearing yourself down, as well as exhausting the wolves and Gnomes. They have no time to hunt for food; they will not eat Troll flesh except under great duress. They have all been without adequate food or rest for several courses. You need to rest too.

"Now eat and regain your strength. Later, we will walk in the valley. One tunnel has been reopened and the Trolls there dealt with. We will stroll the gardens to the west. Fortunately, the Trolls did not destroy much, having been intent on gaining access to the tunnels. We did lose a lot of livestock though. And," she chuckled, "I think I have a solution to your problem."

That night as they sat in Andreanna's chamber, they ate and drank again. They spoke of Andreanna's adventures but later ended on the topic of Andreanna's family.

"You miss them desperately, do you not, child?" asked Gram.

"Well I hadn't...life was so busy. I mean, it hurt and I missed them and cried sometimes, but lately it seems to be getting worse. I feel now like I thought I should have felt then. But it's too much, now."

"That is the problem with Humans," said Gram shaking her head. "You do not participate in your people's making of the Final Journey. You remain alienated from it and do not find the release that such brings to the living as well as to the dead who make the Journey. This is what I perceive your problem is: You have too much that is unresolved. Your speech is filled with longing for your family and hatred of your enemies. This is why the magic within you is not at rest and is having difficulty finding its 'harmony'. Here, have another glass of wine. Tell me about your family, your parents and sisters...."

Andreanna went on and spoke of them to Gram. The longer she spoke, the sadder she became.

"Tell me of BlueHill and how it was to live there," said Gram. "Here, let me fill your glass."

Andreanna continued talking, becoming sadder and sadder, Gram repeatedly refilling her glass with wine. It was past half moon's course when Andreanna began to sob. Gram stood and went to her, wrapping her arms about the weeping girl.

"There, there, dear. Go ahead and have yourself a good cry."

And cry she did. Andreanna wept long and hard, Gram providing her with towels to blow her nose on while she sobbed out her story and sorrows in drunkenness. Finally, not long before dawn, Gram poured Andreanna a glass of wine from a different bottle.

"Here, drink this."

Andreanna drank again. "Oh, this is good. What is it?"

"It is wine mixed with Mountain Wood Betany, Myrrh and Fortis Root. It will help you sleep and avoid the headache in the morning. You have had *a lot* to drink," Gram laughed.

"Thanks, Gram. I never did know my grandparents. I'd like you to be my Gram too."

"I am everyone's Gram. Another grandchild should be bearable. Here, lay down in the bed."

"What about the cot?"

"It is alright. We will sleep together."

They climbed into bed, and Gram had Andreanna lay her head on her sturdy shoulder.

"Gram?"

"What is it, child?"

"I like you."

"I like you too, Andreanna. Now sleep."

Andreanna was soon asleep. Gram remained awake, stroking Andreanna's long auburn hair, singing Dwarf lullabies as if she held a baby. She sang to the breaking of the dawn and then rose and went to her own chambers to sleep, leaving Andreanna in her drunken somnolence in her own room. Andreanna had not hunted this night.

A couple of courses later, Andreanna almost felt her old self again. She was cheerful and rested. But she had not seen Gram again, either; neither had she hunted. When she inquired about Gram, she was told that the elder Queen spent much of her courses giving audience to petitioners and assisting such in resolving their problems. The King was too busy for such work, and Gram had, since her time of being wed to RavenStone, taken the job upon herself.

Then, as Andreanna walked through the valley gardens one course, two of the King's guard approached her, rather cautiously, and requested that she follow them. She was led back into *Dolan* and through a series of passageways until they came to two great oak-timber doors that were guarded by fierce-looking Dwarf soldiers, who opened the doors to allow the three to pass. Magical orbs, revealing a grand hall finished in oak planks, brightly lighted the room. The ceiling above was so tall that it was out of reach of the lamps' light. The room was big enough to be a ballroom, but instead it was filled with seating, forming an arena around a long table where there sat twelve Dwarves and the King. Andreanna was made to sit opposite the King. All eyes rested on her.

The King cleared his throat, looking a bit antsy. Andreanna noticed SixFists sitting off to the side.

"Elven Queen, we are deeply grateful to you for saving our people," began HeartStone. "Without your intervention, it is sure we would have perished. We are in your debt. However...."

The "however" brought anxiety to Andreanna's heart, not sounding promising.

"However, it has been brought to our attention that you have within your possession something that belongs to the Dwarves. An Elfstone. An Elfstone given as a gift to King HammerStone, ancient King of the Dwarves, by King Amberset, King of the Elves in that age. It disappeared from *Dolan* some eight hundred cycles past and was never seen or heard of again, and now, it seems that it has been recovered and is in your possession."

Andreanna looked to SixFists, who hung his head and averted his eyes.

"We would request that you restore the stone to us," concluded the King.

"Restore? It's mine. I mean the Gnomes...gave it to me."

"It was not theirs to give," said the King, casting his eyes down, blushing, and looking plainly embarrassed. "How it came into their possession is unknown. We would like to have it back."

"Aw, come on, cousin, let the girl keep it..." said SixFists.

The King glared at SixFists, causing him to sink low into his chair.

Andreanna was aghast. *How can they do this*? *monit* was a part of her, as were *balak* and *licri*. They could not take it! It would destroy her very being to lose the stone now. "Is there no other way?" she pleaded.

"No," said the King, clearly uncomfortable with the situation. "The council has expressed their desire to have it back."

"**Pay her!**" boomed Gram's voice from the doors of the hall.

"What?" said the King.

"**I said pay her!**" rumbled the strong and determined voice, echoing throughout the mostly empty arena.

"Gram, please, you should not be here," replied the King with patience. The Dwarves around the table writhed in their seats, agitated by her presence. Gram marched herself to the table and took up a position next to Andreanna, like a she-bear over her cub.

"**I said pay her!**"

"For what?" asked a bald-headed, long-nosed Dwarf named Bandolt.

"For what? Are you fools?" Gram seemed to rise in stature, her presence full of authority, though in reality, she had none. Her deportment demanded respect and obedience. "Who is it that saved your beards from the Trolls? Who is it that saved your mates, your children, your homes? Are you fools? Is this how you were raised, HeartStone? A pat on the back and 'job well done' and you are off the hook? Would your father have settled his debt that way? I dare say, not!"

The council appeared intimidated. HeartStone bit his lip to avoid grinning and suppressed a chuckle.

"No! GladdenStone would have lavished her with gold and jewels and dozens upon dozens of his copper tokens of favor. He would have laid his beard on the ground as a carpet for the Elf Queen to walk upon. And here you are, miserable wretches that you are, trying to get a stone back, lost since who knows when. You do not even know how or if you can use it. What is worse is that you do not even need it!"

Now some of the council hung their heads in shame for having been involved in the farce. A couple of members appeared angry but lacked the courage to confront Gram.

"I changed your diapers, HeartStone. And you too Glimmer and you too," she exclaimed, pointing her finger in another Dwarf's face. "Every single one of you sat on my lap at one time or another. Every single one of you sneaked into my room at one time or another for help or for advice. Well, I come to get paid for all that. This course of the sun, I collect my dues. If you persist in this travesty, I will denounce you all before the nation.

"What shame you have brought upon us, seeking a trinket from the one who saved your beards, may they fall from your faces!" spat the Dwarfess.

The council gasped!

SixFists laughed, but Gram turned him an eye that made him wither and shut up.

"Who started this anyway?"

No one moved. Finally, HeartStone stood.

"*Oooh, dooo* sit down! I know you better than that. I will not let you take the heat for whatever fool started this." She glared from face-to-face, finally resting on Glimmer. "You. I am going to tell your mother!" she threatened with a wagging finger. "Wait until your mother hears of this!"

Glimmer's countenance fell, and his head dropped as if he had been skewered with a spear.

"She beat your greedy bottom often enough. I thought she would have beaten that out of you a long time ago. Look at you, your beard to your knees and you are no wiser than one who has no whiskers at all. I am shamed before our guest for being part of this nation, who repay her in this manner.

"Andreanna," Gram bellowed, "what is your fee for having saved our lives. Do not hold back now. We are worth something, though one could not tell by the demonstration this rabble has put on. What is that, you say?"

Andreanna's jaw hung opened.

"You say the Elfstone would be all you ask for? **No!**" she gasped. "**You cannot be serious!** Is that all we are worth? Was saving our lives at your own peril *sooo* trivial that all you want is an old Elfstone that was lost to us? You do not want thousands of golds and thousands of silvers? You do not want us to be your servants forever? You are not asking we give our children to you as slaves? Why do we mean *sooo* little to you, that all you want is an old stone?"

By now, all heads about the table hung down in shame. But Gram was only getting started. She went on, calling on her ancestors to witness the Dwarves' rudeness and impudence. She called on the gods to wipe out such a lowly people and save the Trolls instead. She called to the former Kings and threatened their very beards for having given seed to these who now ruled. On and on she went. Ancestors of the council were cursed and damned, the nation called to mourn in sackcloth and ashes and the heavens commanded to bear witness against their crime. Then she stopped, her voice still ringing in the council's ears, in the silence of the hall. The

King and council breathed as if she had beaten them with her war-mace.

"Come, child," she said to Andreanna in a tender, motherly tone. "Come with me; we must take you to the Healers to see that no harm has come to you." She pulled Andreanna to her feet, turned her back to the council and propelled the half-Elf toward the doors. At the Council Chambers' doors, the guards stood, wide-eyed, and looked for help from the King as Gram approached. He nodded, and they quickly opened both doors wide to allow Gram and her charge to pass.

The two females passed through the doors, turned left down a corridor, Andreanna being forcefully ushered quickly away with her elbow in Gram's iron grip. As they went, Andreanna thought she heard Gram begin to cry. She was just about to say something to her when she realized she was wrong. Gram was laughing!

Gram suddenly opened a door, stuffed Andreanna into a small storage closet, and squeezed herself in, closing the door behind herself, as she broke into gut-splitting laughter. Magic orbs lit up the small space.

"Did you see their faces?" she gasped, tears rolling down her creviced face. "Dear King-mate, forgive me for taking charge of the council like that; but oh, it was grand." She continued laughing. She laughed and snorted, giggled, chortled and cried. She wiped her nose on her sleeves. Andreanna stood in shock! It took a while, but finally, Gram composed herself enough to speak.

"Ah," she said wiping her tears away. "In all my cycles, I never once meddled in the council's affairs." She sniffled a bit and sucked in some air. "Oh, my, my. Oh, my." She cleared her throat. "That was fun, was it not?"

Andreanna stared, her jaw still hanging slack.

"Glimmer's mate came to me this rising, telling me what he had been grumbling about – the stone. She told me he intended to call the council over it. He must have been able to sway enough of them to get the vote on it. Stuff like that always gets put to a vote. Glimmer always prides himself on being unreadable. He must still be in shock that I singled him out." She laughed again. "I have been working myself up all course for that dissertation. I even wrote some notes on my hand," she added, showing Andreanna some ink markings within her palm. "Just a few key thoughts. Ah, but I was on a roll and did not need them." She fell against Andreanna and laughed again. Now Andreanna started to laugh, the shock of the whole experience lost with the revelation of Gram's antics.

"Now, you must forgive HeartStone. For in these matters, that is, matters that have been put to vote in council, he sticks to what is decided whether for or against it. I know well enough that he does not approve of some of Glimmer's ways. Glimmer was greedy as a child, and it appears that he has not outgrown his failing.

"Alright...let us get ourselves together here. We need to look stern. The whole of *Dolan* will be talking about this shortly, and we need to look the part." She opened the door to the closet a crack and peaked out. Then, she stuck her head out and looked the other way. "All clear; let us go. Walk and look angry. We will go hide and laugh some more in my chambers." She suppressed a laugh with a cough, and they headed down the hallway once again.

Morlah again sat on the quarterdeck of the Druid Queen, which lay at anchor north of Mount Bahal, out in the Maring

Sea. He had been there for six courses of the sun as time in the land of the living was counted. He was tired in ways that even the Druid Sleep would not easily take care of. He was emotionally drained from the centuries of struggle against Daektoch. *Or was it just the fact of having been alive over six hundred cycles?* He could not tell, but he did feel a weariness deep within his being. *Perhaps if he could have, like Master Filinhoff, just stayed at the keep, pursuing his studies.*

Morlah had seen too much in his time. Too much pain, too much sorrow, too much hardship, too many people he had loved who had died, all leaving him with an emptiness that could not be filled. Yet, he was the appointed champion of Frontmire; the Faeries had chosen him as the one responsible to bring a balance of power between the forces of good and evil back to the land. They had given to him the element, which was the very source of Faerie magic, argentus, to the forging of *tenensil* and *tenenden*. They had taught him in the magic's use and control. They had told him of the future, like that of the Phoenix rising from its own ashes, of the King of the Elves, one who was descended of Windemere. They had given him the Elfstones that were in Jerhad's knife.

For centuries, the Druid had sought the heir to the throne; though the task in itself had been fairly simple. Finding the King's lineage in the Books of the Genealogies, Morlah had sought out the eldest of each generation, sending them on an errand to deliver a package to Canon, and then, he himself going there and awaiting the arrival of the parcel. The innkeeper of the appointed inn would pay for the receipt of the purse and return it to Morlah, who waited in the next room.

The problem was, though, that if the package made it to Canon without the awakening of the magic of the Elfstones in the handle of Ember, then it was the sign that this was not the appointed heir. Generation to generation, the Elves had passed the blade, *Gildar*, to the eldest son, at times, Ember all but forgotten in some pile of junk. Each time Morlah sent the eldest on this mission, he would speak a spell, given to him by the Faeries, opening the knife's power to the ability to awaken. If it reached Canon, it would return to its dormancy.

It had not been long before he had known that he had found the heir in Jerhad, for the lad had been on the trail for but a few spans when Morlah became aware of the magic's release. Morlah had watched Jerhad flee from the Gnomes, using his magical argentus orb, *tenensil* or The Watcher's Eye. He had witnessed the Elf's flight north and up to the Rain and to Rain's Bottom; it had all been witnessed through the use of the Druid's argentus orb, acting as a window into the distance that separated them.

Morlah had been severely tried, restraining himself from interfering. The Elves had to come into the magic with minimal interference; *that*, the Faeries had made clear. Fate was to govern subsequent events. The heir would prevail!

But now, Daektoch was about again, a substantial force of magic and not for the good. He would destroy Jerhad and the Elves if given half a chance. *Was Daektoch something that was better left to the Elves? Was it too much meddling and intervention on Morlah's part to seek to deal with the mage himself?* Morlah did not know. What he did know was that in spite of having found the heir to the Kingdom and the joy it and Jerhad had brought him, he was still left with a bone-weary, dog-tired fatigue.

Morlah gazed south across the water toward Mount Bahal, not seeing the mount for his thoughts. The *Druid Queen*, ship of the ancient, murdered Druids, a ghost ship, rocked gently at her anchors, with groans and creaks of the ancient vessel's masts and tackling. She had been a beautiful ship, owned by the Druids, but in those times, she had been christened the *Ryer's Maiden* after the name of Ryer's Clan who later were renamed "Druids".

The clan had been a benevolent, kind and studious people. Later, when Daektoch tried to annihilate them, they became reclusive and withdrawn, closing themselves within *seilstri*. It was then that the local people had labeled them Druids, a title which they later adopted for themselves.

The Druid crew, seeking out their enemy in Heros, had all been slain except for one. The *Ryer's Maiden* was towed out to sea by some unknown party and burned. She had become a ghost ship then, with the souls of her murdered crew aboard awaiting the time of vengeance against their killer, longing for respite, seeking the release that would allow them to make the Final Journey.

Morlah had summoned them out of the void that exists between the lands of the living and of the dead some seven cycles past, using the *Druid Queen* as a means of quick transportation. For she existed in a timeless plain, allowing her to travel great distances in an instant or in a cycle. It made no difference to her, since time was not a factor. The crew of the *Druid Queen* had been instrumental in the victory in the Battle of Breezon against the Trolls, for their presence cast terror into the hearts of mortals up to half a league away. With the knowledge of this, they had discomfited the Trolls and eventually caused the rout of the entire hoard, leading to the death of tens of thousands of Trolls. Now, they waited and watched for Daektoch, pining after their revenge.

"Well thou canst stare at her until she doest crumble, but thou willst not be any closer to a solution," spoke the Druid Queen's captain to Morlah, referring to Bahal. It was with great effort of magic that Morlah protected himself from the terror of the dead when among them, but he had finally come upon a spell that made their presence tolerable and even comforting at times.

"This is true, Captain, and I am not any closer to a solution of what, if any, measures I shouldst take against the mage."

"We doest have the matter in hand. Why doest thou not attend to some more needy matter?"

"There are none at this time that art needier than that of the mage."

"Seeing that dealing with the mage is not possible, methinks that thou shouldst look back to the land, to the south, for I have heard the souls of many wailing as they left their bodies. Multitudes have died, of the Trolls, Elves and Dwarves! There art stirrings of powerful magics to the south."

Morlah sat up straight. "When?"

"Over the past three courses."

"Why didst thou not speak sooner?"

"Because it didst appeared that thou didst need time for the sorting out of some thoughts, and now, it doest appear that thou hast done so to the furthest that thou art able to at this time. Now doest go see to the land."

"As always, Captain, I am in debt to thee and thine wisdom." He mindspoke to The Raven who was out grazing the fields along the Breezon River. Within a span, the two were flying south toward Mildra.

Morlah had been alive, over six hundred cycles, since the Druids were still known as the Clan. He had been an energetic young man of multiple interests and achievements including the study of weapons, alchemy, White and Gray magic, as well as being a scribe. The Druid was of a determined and focused mind, not easily discouraged or deterred. Cycle upon cycle he had watched, waited and worked at his mission as given to him by the Faeries. In all these cycles, he had been single-minded in his purpose. Frontmire's champion had foregone most pleasures offered by life, had foregone the love of a mate and, to an extent even, had refrained from finer foods, clothes and any other thing that might distract from his purpose.

Morlah was known by many, especially the leaders of the races, except for that of the Trolls. The Druid was known for his kindness, generosity and fairness among the common people and for his wisdom and judgment among the leaders. He made it his practice not to interfere with the doings of the races, but he did frequently offer his counsel. Of the Dwarves, he had often asked for and given assistance, and so, he was held in great favor by them even though he had never obtained the copper-coin token of the King's favor. Perhaps it was because he was too powerful an individual. *Wast it for fear or that the Dwarves had never thought he wouldst have need of such? No matter, it did not worry him. That wast the way it hadst been and wouldst be.* The Dwarves had never withheld anything he had requested of them anyway.

It was the Dwarves, in fact, that had assisted in the forging of the blade of magic. Deep in the mountain where the molten lava stream flowed, the Dwarves had their forges, the magma used to smelt ores. Morlah and the Dwarf King, AlhadStone, under the hand of Derrin son of Kalborn, had formed *Gildar* with the best of Dwarf steel, with the addition of a sprinkling of the magic element argentus. With the steel cooled, Morlah had mounted the Elfstones into the handle of wrought and twisted steel. The Dwarves had fashioned the mountings to lock permanently as each stone was snapped into place, all, except for the stone *acrch*, which became the contents of the purse that the eldest male Elf of the King's line carried to Canon each generation.

It was to these, the Dwarves, which Morlah now flew. Morlah and Raven soared to a small village covering one-half the distance to *Dolan*. After having put down behind an orchard to conceal the Bornodald, Morlah walked into the village of Arbor for a night of rest. This had been one of the villages destroyed by the Trolls in the last invasion, the same attack that had devastated BlueHill, Andreanna's hometown.

Arbor had been rebuilt since, but not to its former state. The few who had escaped came back to erect shacks and small buildings, as if their very spirits had been broken along with the devastation. Because there was a fair amount of coming and going between the Dwarves and Breezon, a Breezon merchant had built an inn here. It was one of the few villages along the way that had been rebuilt.

Morlah came to the inn, Mandy's Pride, and seated himself in the dining room, showing himself as an old man. The few who sat about the dining hall seemed intent on one topic, the battle at *Dolan*. Morlah quickly pieced together events from what he heard as he ate the fish chowder being served with fresh bread. The biggest question was where the Trolls had come from, for in the last invasion, Arbor had been straight in the path of the Trolls. This time, it was speculated they must have traveled through the mountains, for they had not been seen along the road here. Then, to add to the excitement of it all, a band of Trolls had gone north not two courses past in what appeared as a blind terror, as if chased by demons, not even bothering to stop to harm a blade of grass in Arbor.

Morlah decided that matters in *Dolan* were settled for better or worse and that he would return to Mildra instead.

Chapter 18

The army was ready. There were Trolls as far as the eye could see, waiting for some command that would cause them to swarm the city. Daektoch's plan was to sweep the plain from east to west and amass all the Elves in Mildra, and then, he would push them into the sea never to be seen again. He had kept the Dwarves occupied at *Dolan* so that they would not meddle. Breezon was in up to her dregs with her own troubles. There was no one to help the Elves. No one, except for the Elf with his magic and Morlah. They were the only threats to his plan.

Everyone waited. Many of the Elves perspired with nervousness. The Dwarves stood, solemn and determined. This would end it all. This is where the war would be decided. Even though the wall was up at a reasonably defendable height, it was not a substantial enough defense for the size and number of invaders they opposed. The thought was, in many minds, that they were all about to die.

Back at Jerhad's home, IronLeggs had tried persuading the Druid Healers to wake Jerhad and Stanton, but they resisted. They both had been too sick, and even though it looked like they were recovered, the Healers were reluctant to wake them lest they only be afflicted again and worsen. The two patients were both, for all appearances, healed, but how could that be? How could they have eliminated the poison so quickly? For that matter, it was a wonder that Ahliene had been able to heal them and not take harm as Jerhad had.

Perhaps it was because the wounds were old when she had worked the magic of *acrch* upon them, or that Jerhad had taken the brunt of the harm and the evil.

IronLeggs cursed. He wanted Stanton in charge of the army. Not that he himself was unable to lead them, but he knew that the Elves would respond better to the one who had trained them. He also wished he had had time to get the field better prepared, but all labor had gone into the battlements, and no one could have been spared for other tasks. Had they enough time, he would have dug pits, planted rows of stakes, built traps and set snares, constructed catapults and large crossbows for the launching of sharpened beams that would have skewered eight to twelve Trolls at a time. Instead, they had one catapult capable of launching ten to twenty rocks at a time and a bit of boiling oil; but with such a low wall, the oil would not be as effective as it should.

IronLeggs sighed. He wished GladdenStone were here. The former King had had a way of shoring up the Dwarves' hearts for battle. He had moved them in ways that had seemed to double their effort and effectiveness in the past. IronLeggs was a seasoned warrior and experienced commander. He knew that he was up to the task, nevertheless, doubt gnawed at him. Maybe it was simply that he was keenly aware of how greatly the odds were stacked against them. Even if the entire Dwarf Army had been here, it was doubtful they could withstand this enemy. Sparing a few heartbeats of thought for his mate and offspring, he resigned himself to his fate.

IronLeggs did have one surprise for the Trolls however, but it was going to be gruesome. He hoped, by his father's beard, that the wind would be blowing easterly when it happened. The dry moat had been lined three spans deep with straw that had been soaked in barrels of heavy fish oil that was laced with lamp oil. It was a one-time effort that would scorch thousands and leave their burnt carcasses strewn before the wall. The stench had the potential to become paralyzing if the wind brought the smoke and stench back into the defenders' faces.

The archers were equipped with poisoned arrows. Barrel upon barrel of the paralytic toxin had been made; only they would run out of arrows long before the poisonous concoction did. The entire population was ready. Every male, female and child old enough to hold a weapon was armed. The plan was to fight until there was no one remaining alive. The army would fight first, and then once they were gone, the females and children would take their places. Perhaps a few would survive.

Then the Trolls came!

IronLeggs had the archers up at the parapet and the infantry at the base of the slope leading to the top of the wall. Dwarves and Elves holding torches waited, watching IronLeggs, throats constricting with nausea as they readied themselves to perform their own atrocity. A rumble of Trolls' grunting rose over the din caused by tens of thousands of charging feet.

When the Trolls arrived at the dry moat, they slowed, dropped into the ditch and then crossed to the wall, not taking heed of the straw at their feet. They massed along the wall and began their attempt to scale it.

IronLeggs nodded to the squire holding a ram's horn. The horn blared, and the torches were dropped into the moat. It was a matter of a span of heartbeats before the entire moat roared with flame and cries of pain. The horrible stench of burning oil, flesh and hair rose from the trench. Again, IronLeggs nodded, and the horn sounded.

The archers began releasing volley upon volley into the mass of Trolls who stood on the opposite side of the trench. Dark smoke rose, thick, blocking the view between the two armies while archers continued pouring arrows through the black billows.

Suddenly, an Elf, Hash, Jerhad's friend, ran up from the infantry lines, his hands engulfed with fire. Those about him gasped and set out to assist him, but he hissed at them! They backed away. Hash jumped up onto the parapet, fire flowing from his hands and into the flames below with a loud noise of crackling. The heat grew intense, much more than was justified by the straw and oil. Then further down the ranks a way, another Elf was at the parapet doing the same, and a few heartbeats later, yet another, until the heat was so severe that the archers had to back away.

Magic! It was the magic awakening!

Come sunsetting the fire burned itself out. When the smoke cleared, the Trolls could be seen in the distance, having withdrawn to the place of their initial stand. Beneath in the moat, were charred stone and fragments of bones. The fire had been so extreme that much of the stone lining the moat was chipped and cracked. Heaps of bodies lay piled along the opposite side of the trench, poisoned shafts riddling their corpses. The quick-acting toxin left the dead bloated with blood oozing from ears, noses, eyes and mouths.

IronLeggs had the north gate opened (for they had not placed a gate on the east wall) and sent out four squads to scavenge arrows from the fallen Trolls. The defenders had survived the first wave.

Then as darkness fell, cries of pain and turmoil came from the Trolls' northeastern flank. It took quite a while before someone climbed onto a rooftop for a better view and claimed that he thought he saw wolves attacking the Trolls. Daektoch's wraiths were nowhere in sight.

Sunrising brought the sound of rams' horns announcing an attack; everyone was ready, waiting in their positions. The Trolls stampeded to the moat, running the obstacle course of bloated bodies. They seemed to hesitate a bit as they crossed the moat, looking each to his fellow as they came on. Once at the wall, a horn sounded, and the archers released their arrows across the moat to break the momentum of the charge. This continued until the Trolls were about to come over the wall, the Trolls not using ladders but forming living pyramids. The following Trolls climbed up on them and were able to catch hold of the wall's top; they performed this with surprising speed and agility, for their strength was tremendous.

The archers fell back. IronLeggs remained by the parapet. He nodded. A ram's horn blared, sending ranks of infantry charging up the slope onto the wall with the heavy treading of booted feet, toppling the invaders from the fortifications with the use of pikes, lances and a clash of force. Skewered trolls fell back from the battlement, most with torn necks or gouged eyes. The first rank of defenders fell back and the next line struck, the fifth, the sixth, the seventh, again and again. Each time, the Trolls fell from the wall. Each time, the infantry remained unscathed. Then, a two-fold call sounded from the squires' horn and hot oil gushed out through spouts in the wall, the spouts that Stanton had recommended.

Torches were dropped, and this time, dozens of Elves ran forward, hands flaming, turning the moat to the intensity of molten lava and incinerating the Trolls within. After the last of the foe were pushed from the wall, the archers came forward and hailed death on those who stood on the opposite side of the trench and watched the raging fire that cut them off from the Elves and Dwarves.

At sunsetting, with the extinguishing of the fire and subsiding of the smoke, it was seen that the enemy had once again withdrawn. A great cheer went up from the Elves and Dwarves; but as the sortie went out to scavenge arrows, the Trolls sprang a trap, for many had lain in wait among the fallen. As the scavengers gathered arrows, Trolls suddenly surrounded them. The archers rallied to the wall, but shooting now had to be at careful aim in order not to hit their friends. Only eighteen of the two hundred that had gone out returned. The four Giants, who had charge of keeping the gate, prevented their adversary from entering into the city, and finally, the gates were closed. The greater Troll mass watched on. They were too far out to join the melee, but they roared in approval, for they had finally struck a blow, though it had cost every Troll involved in the trap its life. IronLeggs sent out a second sortie to scavenge arrows as the wolves and Gnomes struck the Trolls' camp for the second night. The city was now out of oil.

The third rising brought the Trolls back in a swarm. In unison, they hurled themselves towards the battlements. This time the archers struck at them as soon as they came within range of their longbows. With a vociferous whoosh, the catapult launched volley upon volley of lethal missiles. The Trolls rushed the wall, and the infantry took over as the archers continued shooting above the infantrymen's heads. Now, in several places along the parapet, it was observed that both male and female Elves struck at the Trolls with magic, hitting them with unseen forces, fire and bolts of magic. Their foe was bowled back from the parapet into the swarm below and many killed. The fire-wielders soon stood on the parapet, burning their enemy and clearing them from the wall, from the positions that the Elves held. Hurled maces took out several fire-wielders, and a barrage of stones and spears came hurtling over the wall. Other Elves took positions behind the fire-wielders and surrounded them with the glow of the white Elven magic of *urcha* (shield or defender in the ancient tongue). *urcha* deflected stone and spear.

But the momentum of the infantry had been broken in a few places by the hurling of various missiles, and the Trolls came pouring over the walls in these positions. Lehland, leading a dozen or more Elves, appeared with longknives and rushed these them. The band of Elves glowed with the magic of *licri* (strength or mighty) and Lehland also with *esord* (foe-finder). They moved about the Trolls as if the beasts stood still. To the observer, these Elves moved with blinding speed, slitting throats, stabbing beneath breastplates, hamstringing others and severing hands that grabbed at the top of the fortifications. Trolls were eviscerated as they gained the battlement's top; their eyes were pierced with longknives as heads rose over the parapet. Soon, the small group of defenders led by Lehland reclaimed the wall and fell back to allow the infantry to return to its work as the group moved further down to clear the attackers from another foothold they had gained. It was not long before there were several other groups similar to Lehland's.

To the north, the Giants dropped down into the mass of Trolls who had come up against the gate with a battering ram. With longswords, they swathed a clearing before the gate and held it. DiamondHeart tore the battering ram away from the Trolls, using it as a scythe, clearing a circle of six paces about him. There, the enemy was mashed by the Giant's weapon and fell by the score.

But the defenders began to tire as the scourge rolled on and on and on. The sun witnessed the butchery as it ebbed across the heavens. Trolls were now climbing the heap of their dead and clambering over the wall without assistance. It seemed that for every beast that was felled, a dozen took its place. At the gate, the Giants sweat profusely and breathed heavily; they went back over the wall, bringing the battering ram with them.

The situation began looking desperate. More and more, the Trolls made it over the parapet. Elves and Dwarves were cut down. Lehland and his group, and the others like them, were pressed hard to keep the wall cleared. The assault on the defenders flowed like water, and their efforts seemed to become like an attempt at stopping the Mage River's spring floodwaters from overflowing her banks.

Then suddenly, without explanation, the Trolls ceased and retreated; it was sunsetting. Defenders fell to their knees, exhausted. The blood-red sky darkened as the sun dropped below the horizon, promising beautiful weather and bloodshed for the following rising. Troll bodies were heaped up to the parapet and defenders' bodies were strewn about the top of the wall by the hundreds.

The wolves and their Gnome riders swept down from the mountains. The Mountain Gnomes shrieked their battle cries.

IronLeggs burst into Jerhad's house. "It is over, Druids. Time to wake the boys up!" Again, the protests came. IronLeggs reached up and took Kristi by her vest, drew her down nose-to-nose and gave her a solid shaking for good measure and emphasis.

"Listen to me! One more course or so of this and we will all be *dead*. So, what difference does it make to you if they die from you waking them up too soon or from a Troll walking in here and crushing their skulls in with a mace? **Tell me! I want to know what the difference is!"** he growled as if fueled by the volcano Bahal.

Kristi grew pale. It looked as if she would faint. But then, she composed herself and said, "Thou art correct. I didst not realize the situation was so desperate. Give me one span."

IronLeggs turned and left, huffing into his beard and muttering into his whiskers.

Jerhad opened his eyes, looking up to the ceiling. It was familiar. *Yes, it was his room.* Confusion swept over him. *He wasn't supposed to be in Mildra. How could he be in his room?*

"Ye gods, well it's about time you woke up," said Catrina. "Trolls are everywhere, and there you lie, sleeping like a baby. I thought you'd just die in your sleep. Ye gods in the heavens, Jerhad. You should have seen it. I shot three Trolls in the heart with my bow and...."

Yup. He was home. He did not know how, but he definitely was home. He propped himself up on one elbow and looked at Catrina and the small gathering in the room. He noticed the Druids and then Stanton, who was just awakening on a cot next to him.

"Why does you and me sleeping attract such a crowd? You up, Commander? I think we slept in." They got up and ate, for they were both ravenous, and IronLeggs, who had been called in, gave his report.

"...and with the heap of dead Trolls out there lying against the wall, tomorrow's charge will simply run into the city. Sure am glad to see you two about again. If we are all going to die, I would just as soon it was under someone else's command."

Jerhad and Stanton stopped, forks halfway to their mouths, and stared at him.

"Flatlanders!" spat IronLeggs. "That was a joke. Long story behind it. Guess you had to be there. I will tell it to you sometime."

Jerhad shook his head. "Real funny there, IronLeggs. Give us a couple heartbeats here, and we'll join you at the wall."

IronLeggs stood on the parapet of the battlement's northeast corner when Jerhad and Stanton arrived.

"Gnomes eat my heart!" exclaimed Jerhad.

"Mother-of-a-Troll! Will you looked at that mess!" whistled Stanton. "I thought you were exaggerating when you said they'd run right in over the wall." He stepped off the fortification onto the mountain of dead Trolls, surveying the situation. "You did great, IronLeggs! Looks like you had your hands full."

"That we did, Commander. But I do not think our best effort would have played out if Lehland and his boys had not come up with...magic. They were able to take care of what would have been our undoing. Then, Hash and the other fire-wielders...well, I will just say...I am glad they were on our side."

"Elf Boy," said Stanton, stepping back onto the wall. "Why don't you clean this mess up for us? They're already dead, so I don't expect I'd get in trouble with Morlah.... Speaking of which, has anyone seen the Druid lately, IronLeggs?"

"Not a whisker of his beard, Commander."

"What do you mean 'clean up this mess'?" asked Jerhad.

"Like you did last time and the time before. You incinerated the bodies of the dead Trolls with your magic."

Jerhad's lips twisted, and his eyebrows contorted. Finally, he said, "I guess I could. I guess there's no reason not to. It would sure help out in tomorrow's battle." He looked around.

"Only, would you have the sentries move everyone away. I really don't want anyone to see me do this."

From their tents and about campfires, the Elves, Dwarves and Giants watched the intense glow of light moving along the wall.

"Looks like the Prince is at work," said Kassandra. "It gives me great joy to know that he and Stanton are well and that the Prince is back to his former self. Let us allow him to finish his work, and we will go greet him."

In the darkness of the night, the whole city watched the brilliance of Jerhad's magic burning the Troll carcasses. Jerhad finally finished the exhausting task of reducing to ashes the mountain of dead Trolls. Stanton had suggested those along the opposite side of the trench could be left for now; they would slow the Trolls' momentum in the next charge. A howl was heard in the distance, the howl of the great she-wolf. Jerhad turned and looked out into the night wondering at the sound, feeling as if, somehow, he knew her.

Later, the Giants found him as he returned home.

"Elf Prince," called Kassandra. "It does my Giant heart good to see you about again. Mordock and I wish to thank you for saving our lives, though, to make the Great and Final Journey is not a fearful happening for us. To be reunited with BondBreaker and others who have made the Journey would be a great joy. But for now, we rejoice in being here with the Elves and Dwarves."

Jerhad went to meet her and, when she had bowed herself close to the ground, he hugged her, though his arms barely made it around her neck. "Kassandra. Mordock. It gives my tiny Elven heart great joy to see you about again. May we all be united in the end, in the Final Journey. But for now, let's see if we can stay alive a little longer."

Mordock bellowed a laugh and slapped his knee. "I believe our Giant ways are rubbing off on the Prince. Yes, I believe we will be united then as we are now. But I do see your meaning. We should perhaps look to delay that journey a while longer."

Sunrising found Elf, Dwarf, Giant and Troll ready to battle again. Jerhad approached Lehland and what had now become his twenty organized squads of 'hunters'. As Jerhad came up to them, Lehland stepped forward and embraced him.

"Whoa!" blurted out Jerhad, falling back a step. "Easy with that stuff. You're cocked like a bow at full draw."

"What stuff?"

"You don't see it? The magic! *licri*! It's pent up like a dam waiting to burst from within you. Unbelievable!" said Jerhad touching Lehland again. "Are all these males like this?"

"I'm not sure what you see or what you're asking, but I think we're all close to being the same. Some more, some less, but basically all the same. When it takes us, it's like everything just stops. We walk around. Everything about us seems immobile. Spears and maces creep by. You'd have to run into them on purpose to be hurt by them. Each course the numbers grows. There are nearly two hundred of us now. And then, there's the fire throwers. There's some four hundred of them this rising.

"Hash got it.... I mean...he got brained with a mace while he was throwing fire on them. He fell into the mass of them. Ye gods, I hope they didn't eat him. Either way, it was fit that you burned them all. He'd have liked to know it was you who sent him off to the Final Journey with a fire like his." There were tears in Lehland's eyes, but before either could say anything more, the horns raised the alarm.

Stanton, Jerhad and IronLeggs gathered together up on the wall at the northeastern corner. The Commander watched the horde swarm toward them, as he leaned with one hand on the pommel of his drawn sword, whose point rested on the battlement.

Stanton turned to the Dwarf and said, "IronLeggs, take over. You already have a feel for this and its momentum. Take over. I just want to watch for a while to see how things go."

"Yes, sir. I don't mind as long as someone else is calling the shots," he winked.

"More of that joke?" inquired Jerhad.

The Dwarf nodded and grinned, turned his back to them and ordered the squire to call for the archers to release their first volley. Ram's horns blared.

The battle raged as before, but with the fire throwers now protected by those who wielded *urcha*; access to the wall became more difficult for the Trolls. Lehland and the 'hunters' stood back and waited for a breech of their defenses. Suddenly, the air was filled with a flurry of stones thrown by the Trolls. Instinctively, Jerhad's hand shot up, and the stones were all hurled back into the mass by his magic.

Stanton watched as the host surged forward. Down toward the center of the east wall where the fighting was most fierce, the Trolls poured over the wall, but in a blur they all lay dead at the feet of a squad of 'hunters'. The Giants were outside the gates again, clearing away another group that had brought up a battering ram, but this time there were Rock Trolls among them. There, the battle rose to a new level of ferocity!

"Here," said Stanton to an archer. "Lend me your bow." Sheathing his sword, *ursha*, Defender of Life, he took a deep breath and brought the arrow down on its mark, held for a heartbeat and released the poisoned shaft. The arrow struck one of the Rock Trolls in the ear. It collapsed.

The other Rock Trolls paused a heartbeat, not knowing why their comrade had fallen, not having perceived the fateful wound. This heartbeat of hesitation cost them their lives as the Giants took the advantage. DiamondHeart crushed one Rock Troll with the battering ram. Its skull broke open and its ribs splayed out through its chain mail, in shards. Another was decapitated by Mordock's sword. Kassandra, in fury, lay hold of the other and twisted its head from its body with her powerful bare hands. The four Giants jumped the wall and were within the gates again, having secured the second battering ram. Mordock raised a salute to Stanton and bellowed, and then his face broke into a wide grin. Stanton waved back, but then suddenly, he turned and ran toward the town.

"If I did not know him better, I would say that he was deserting," said IronLeggs.

"Maybe he is," grinned Jerhad. "He really doesn't like doing this...."

"And I do?" asked IronLeggs.

"More than you will admit to, but your point is taken. However, the Commander has a soft spot for the males he sends into battle, and he'd rather not deal with it."

"Do you think it is different with others?"

"I suppose not. I really hadn't considered it before...."

"Where do you think he went?" asked IronLeggs.

"Hang around a bit. We should find out soon enough."

They turned to watch the infantry push a wave back from the wall in another charge. The battle was hot and fierce. Metal clashed upon shield and armor, helm and mail. The Trolls growled, grunted and gnashed their teeth as they fought to gain the parapet. The hunters were now busy in several places, for the dead were piling up. Daektoch threw them in by the thousands as a means of paving a way for the others. The catapult launched with a loud whoosh, but then Jerhad noticed that it threw a large, brown, flowing mass into the air. He looked toward the catapult where he saw Stanton, Lehland and some hunters. He looked back and saw the brown mass opening up. It was a trawling net with stones lashed about its edges. It fell onto the Trolls, turning about a hundred of them into a laboring press of bodies. The whole of the charge behind them piled up, coming to a stop for a few heartbeats before the others climbed over the heap and trampled the those who were trapped on their journey to the wall. With another whoosh, a second net was in the air. Again and again, the nets went up.

Damn it, he'll immobilize the fishing fleet if he launches all their nets, thought Jerhad.

The battle toiled on with the invaders unable to gain the wall but for a span of heartbeats at a time. The infantry tired and began to show signs of slowing. Jerhad slipped Ember from its sheath and struck its point between two stone blocks of the wall, pouring *licri* down into its length. Abruptly, the infantry, as one, shouted as if they had been stung, and they surged forward in *might* and bowled back the Trolls over the parapet once again.

"You show wisdom, Prince of the Elves," spoke Nan within him.

"Faeries!" he hissed; he had not become any fonder of her. Then as suddenly as it had started, the Trolls retreated for the night, just as a wolf's howl was heard, turning Jerhad's head toward the mountains for a span of heartbeats. He wondered at her howl. Then, he went out to burn the dead Trolls from the trench.

"There are no more arrows," said IronLeggs to Stanton. "And we are low on pikes and lances. Fighting is going to become hand-to-hand soon. Not good!"

Having been unwilling to take a chance at another ambush, they had been unable to replenish their supply, and now, there was not a shaft left in the city. The other weapons suffered a terrible attrition. There was no relief in view.

The overwhelming odds should have been daunting as well as discouraging, but as magic blossomed within the Elven population in its various manifestations, their courage and determination grew. *igini's* influence was also great, for she had never ceased her activity even as Jerhad had lain unconscious. Her sway even spilled over to the Dwarves, who on this last course came to themselves and took up singing battle songs as they fought.

Stanton stood alone on the wall late that night, alone except for the sentries. Suddenly, behind himself, he sensed a presence. Just as he grasped *ursha's* handle, he smelled the sweet fragrance of Jasmine. He immediately knew who it was. Without turning, he said, "Hello, Ahliene."

She gasped. "Oh, you startled me. I didn't think you knew that I was here."

He turned to meet her.

"Well-met, Commander," she said.

"I take it that this isn't a coincidence." He suddenly felt strangely at ease with her as she stepped closer. He felt her presence or was it her magic? Then, he recognized within her perfume the added fragrance of the magic of *acrch*, for he had known Nan back in Moreau's Ford when he had participated with her in saving Jerhad. The fragrance was clearly that of Nan, yet it emitted from Ahliene. "It's magic..." he said.

"What's magic?"

"I smell it. It's the magic of...Life and Health. The scent is coming from you."

"Commander! Are you part Elf that you should smell magic?"

"Not that I know of. Is it?"

She nodded. "Yes, yes," she said somewhat excitedly as she drew in closer and placed her hand on his arm, sending nervous energy from her touch through him. "Nan came to me. I am able to heal. In fact, nobody knows this, but it was through me that Nan healed both you and the Prince."

So, that was it. He could feel it now, as if he were still connected to her, as if through her he had Life and Health. It was what had allowed him to sense her presence. But there was more. There was another bond, as if the destiny he had sought to fulfill in assisting Jerhad seven cycles past had taken a turn and that Ahliene was tied to himself and the fate of many. Not only that, but he suddenly found himself wanting this fair Elven maiden, to take her into his arms, his life and his future. His heart pounded wildly.

"Well, I'm sure you have a lot on your mind with the Trolls and all.... I'd better be going. I just wanted to see you. Besides, I need to tend to the injured again." Without waiting for him to reply, she turned and left, leaving him standing there thinking of her and not of Trolls.

Sunrising found the defenders readying to meet the Trolls again.

"Commander," said IronLeggs. "I would like to move all the Dwarves to the north wall where the fighting has been the lightest and give the east wall to the Elves."

Stanton raised an eyebrow. "Go on."

"Something is happening with the Elves and what we have seen of the magic at work. It seems that the more of them there are together, the more powerful it becomes. Something is working amongst them, and I think that mingling the Dwarf squads with them will slow it down. Just a few observations, sir. I would like to see what happens if my thinking is correct."

"Hmmm." Stanton thought for a bit as Jerhad came up to them. "Go ahead, let's try it and see what happens."

"What's going on?" asked Jerhad.

"IronLeggs' got a theory. I'll explain it to you once we're all set up." Just then, the archers took their positions on the wall.

"Thought we were out of arrows," said Jerhad.

"So did I," answered Stanton.

Calling a nearby Elf archer over, Jerhad asked, "Where did you get the arrows? We were out, yestercourse."

The Elf, Daniwcil, pulled a shaft from one of the three large quivers he carried on his hips. Together, they contained some two hundred arrows. He handed the arrow to Jerhad. "Take a look at this! Unbelievable! I hadn't believed it if I hadn't seen it with my own eyes."

Jerhad took the shaft. It was a perfectly-formed, well-polished arrow, brownish-tan in color, with a hardened, wooden piercing head lashed to the tip. Then, he noticed something different on closer inspection. It was brown from the bark that covered it. "How...? Look at this Stanton."

"It's the children, Sire...or rather the magic," said Daniweil. "When they heard we were out of arrows, a few score of them got together around the oak in the market circle. Well, before you could say mother-of-a-Troll, they had these shafts growing out of the roots, perfect shafts. I've never seen a straighter arrow. The roots of the tree keep growing them out, and the children cut them to rough lengths. We've been at it all night putting the tips on and feathering them. Thousands of arrows, sir. Thousands."

Stanton let out a low whistle. "IronLeggs might be onto something after all...." The rams' horns sounded, alerting them to onset of the renewed assault. "We'll find out soon enough."

The battle was on again with thousands pouring across the dry moat and up against the wall, while hundreds fell from the thick flurry of arrows pouring down on them. As the Trolls scaled the wall, the archers drew back and the infantrymen rushed forward. Many of the Elves were without weapons.

"What the blazes are they doing?" cried Jerhad.

"I don't know...."

As the Elves met the Trolls, scores of fire-wielders were revealed. Invisible forces pushed other Trolls back over the wall. Some Trolls turned to dust.

Jerhad gasped. "Ye gods...the whole line, it's, it's... They're all alive with magic. I can feel the pulse of it...the strength of it."

"That was what IronLeggs was talking about. He thought it would work better without the Dwarves' presence." A score of Trolls, having gained the wall, were flung away to the rear of their ranks. Suddenly, a huge wave of water came rushing down the trench along the wall sweeping all the way down the east side and out toward the sea. Stanton stepped back.

"What was that?" he gulped.

"Water drawn from the Mage River up north of the town and brought here by magic," Jerhad said, perceiving the source and activity of the magic. The entire trench had been washed clean of living and dead Trolls. Those on the outer edge hesitated a heartbeat, but then the momentum of the charge behind them carried them toward the wall. Again, the archers came forward and rained arrows into the mass, but now the arrows changed and could be seen penetrating two to three Trolls deep. Apparently the poison had become increasingly lethal, for the Trolls dropped in their tracks the heartbeat they were touched by the shafts, whether in vital areas or in their limbs.

Another large wave rushed down the trench and washed it clean once more. The Trolls turned and ran. They headed toward the mountains, but just as it looked like they would leave for good, the winged beasts with their riders appeared and circled about. The Trolls cowered as if in tremendous pain or agony. They soon were under control again, but it looked like the attack was over for this course of the sun.

Course after course the battle raged, the tide turning one way and then back the other. The defenders now survived the mental pressure and the physical drain through the effects of the magic alone. The Dwarves endured because they were Dwarves. At sunsetting at the end of the fighting a few courses later, Jerhad noticed that the wolves had not attacked the Trolls for a while. Neither had the she-wolf howled in the night. Strange. He felt as if he missed her.

At three quarter moon's course, the horns announced a new offensive. Elves rushed to the east wall and the Dwarves and Giants to the north wall. Jerhad, using Ember, lit up the scene with the pillar of light only to see wave after wave of Trolls, worked up into a frenzy, coming for them.

Something seemed different. Their enemy seemed more determined, maybe a bit madder. Overhead, the winged creatures circled high above the battlefield. As the Trolls made the wall, there was a loud 'oomph' as if someone had got the wind knocked out of him. The Elves were bowled back, many falling to the ground and others tumbling down the ramps. But they came back, clashing with their foe, only to be thrown back again.

"What's happening?" asked Stanton.

"Black magic," hissed Jerhad. "But I can't see where or what it's doing or how. But the effect is obvious." Each Troll seemed to be ten times as powerful as he previously had been. A huge wave of water rushed down the trench, but when it had passed, the Trolls were still there. They had locked themselves arm in arm as a mass tied to those on the wall and those on the opposite bank. The majority survived the wave. They surged forward again, more and more of them gaining the wall. Again, the Elves rallied with fire and power, pushing their enemy back to the parapet before they could turn the momentum to their favor.

"Easy, Elf Boy," said Stanton. "Don't jump in just yet. They're holding their own for now." The battle raged on as the sun rose. At times, the defenders had the upper hand. At times, the archers were able to come forward and slow the charge, only to be pushed back each time the Trolls gained the wall. The attrition was horrific. Elves, Dwarves and Troll bodies piled up, making the front increasingly difficult to manage.

At midcourse, a solitary horn sounded behind them on the northwest side of town, signaling that the Trolls were somehow coming around the end of the northwest wall. Just then, they heard a shout up from above and saw Morlah sweeping down, riding on The Raven, the Bornodald snorting wildly in excitement. Jerhad saw him as if for the first time.

"Greetings, Bornodald," he mindspoke to Raven.

"Greetings, Prince. Your magic has become quite lively, and you are now capable of mindspeech. This is a welcome surprise. The Druid is a bit...monotone at times."

"I heard that," interjected Morlah. "Jerhad, the Trolls are coming down by the thousands on rafts. I wouldst go intervene, but the heartbeat I doest, the winged beasts willst be upon us."

"We don't have the forces to send there. We're barely holding on here," mindspoke Jerhad to the Druid. "The Dwarves and Giants have their hands full on the north wall." Morlah and Raven landed. "Well, I guess that leaves me," said Jerhad.

"No! Thou canst not..." said Morlah as he slipped from Raven's back. Raven set himself up to kick Trolls off the wall as their heads came over the parapet; their heads seemed to explode from the blows from Raven's rear hooves.

"Give me another plan then, or I go."

"I have nothing to give thee, I doest fear. Thou hast reason. Thou canst not allow the Trolls to ravage the town and come in behind thee. I willst accompany thee. Come, we willst go on the Bornodald."

"No. I'll meet you there." In a blur, Jerhad was gone. He took up the position on the hill above the docks where the Trolls were amassing.

Morlah and the Raven came down behind him. "What willst thou do, Elven Prince?" asked the Druid.

"Same as before."

"But the *acrch*...."

"*acrch* or no *acrch*. I'll die here if I have to, but while I still breathe, Druid, I will not allow our people to die needlessly. This course's battle has taken some kind of turn, a turn for the worse, and I fear that without some kind of miracle that this is our last stand. Though magic has risen powerfully among the Elves, Daektoch has come up with something more potent. I think we may all die here."

He turned to the Druid. "Morlah, I've said nasty things about you at times, but I know you've only tried to do what's been for our good. Thanks!"

Jerhad turned and went forward to meet the Trolls who now came up the hill from the river. A rainbow of colors and power began swirling around the Elven Warrior as he gathered his might.

"Let us die with him, Druid. Let us go. They wait for us," said Raven as he and Morlah watched Jerhad go.

Morlah looked up into the sky and located the winged beasts. "Yes. If the Elves doest die this course of the sun, then I guess we may as well follow them, for then all our travail willst have been futile." He mounted the Bornodald and looked about. He sighed, long and deeply. "Friend, I wish we could have known each other in better times."

"What times are better than these: when friend defends friend and we fight for our lives, homes and everything that is dear? Battle makes heroes, draws deep on warriors and proves their mettle. Hearts feel the whole spectrum of emotions. And then, we make the Final Journey as one if we fail.

"No, Druid. These are the best times for the likes of you and me to have known each other. We did our best, and for a season we prevailed. I salute thee! Let us go to the battle." The great Bornodald rose into the air and closed the distance to the closest of Daektoch's beasts.

Then suddenly, it was as if the world had been turned upside-down. Time stood still for a few heartbeats, but for those involved it seemed to last forever. Elf, Dwarf, Human, Giant, Bornodald, Troll and dark wraith felt as if there was no air left to breathe, felt as if they could not move and as if their bodies and spirits were disassociated. The whole of the scene about them seemed to slur and bend to the south; feet stayed planted to the ground, but bodies appeared elongated and leaned southward as if stretched by cyclonic winds. Within each mind was the thought that the end had come, that death was at hand. The ground shook. Sound ceased. Numbness stole sensation. To some, it felt like they had drunk a full bottle of corndrippings in one gulp. Each being became isolated from all others. They saw those before them, but the other's presence was meaningless.

In *Dolan*, Nan stood before Andreanna. "The Faeries have gathered in council. It is requested that you attend."

"What? You're crazy! I'm not going on another trek through the mountains, Faeries or no Faeries and that's final. If you think...."

"Andreanna," Nan interrupted. "It is not necessary. With the magic of *monit,* you can shape-shift time and distance. In an instant, you can appear in essence, not in body, as yourself or in body if you use a combination of magics and go as the Dark Queen."

"I can?"

"Allow me to touch you."

Then, Andreanna's mind was opened and her understanding enlightened, and she was able to appreciate what Nan was saying. "Alright then, I'm on the way.... Wait. Is this like Morlah when he travels in apparition and his body lies helpless as he's running around like a ghost?"

"Only if you go as yourself. If you come as the Dark Queen, you will be there completely without need to worry about such things. The only restriction is that you must return to where you departed from before you can transform again into your Human form."

"Will you be there?"

acrch nodded.

"See you there. Wait! How do I get there from here?"

"Just visualize where you want to be, just as if you were to go on foot. Visualize and go. It will happen."

Andreanna stood at the foot of the long table lined with Faeries. She was shrouded in power, her skin dark as oiled coal, her eyes threating *destruction*. The King and Queen rose to greet her.

"Dark Queen, you have come," said the King.

"I have," she said, her voice sounding eerily strange in her ears.

"Let me look at you. May I?" he asked. She was not sure what he meant, but she gave her consent; the King reached out and touched her.

"Oh, my, but this is interesting. Your magic has blossomed impressively. White, Black, Gray magic blended with Faerie magic, your innate Elven magic and your Human self. This has never been. Most interesting. But also somewhat fearful."

"What do you mean?"

"The magic of *balat* has never been manifested in Elfstone nor in any other form. The form of the Dark Queen, as you well know, has its potential problems. I do hope you, Andreanna, keep *balat* in check. She is a bit, how should I say...compulsive and self-willed."

"But I am *balat*."

"Well, no, not exactly. It is more like saying that your finger is part of the total of you. It is not *you*. But for now, it appears that *acrch*'s and *igini*'s interventions are effectual and that *balat* is subdued and keeps in harmony with your other magic. But that is not why you are here. Come, the Faeries sit in council. You may choose to participate or simply observe. You will sit between the Queen and me." So sitting at the end of the table, the Dark Queen met with the Faeries.

"What's going on?" asked the Dark Queen.

The Faerie Queen indicated that she should be silent.

Then, two Faeries came from an alcove with Fonta between them. They escorted her to the opposite end of the table where she sat, and the two Faeries remained standing behind her.

"*isini*," spoke the King, "you have been charged with gross and harmful behavior and *mischief*. And though it is as your name means, in your nature to do mischief, it is felt that your behavior has been excessive and has endangered the course of destiny, fate and that of Andreanna, the Queen of the Elves."

"Wait. No.... I mean...," blurted Andreanna.

"Please be silent, Andreanna," said the King. "Observe and be patient. The charges are brought by myself, *isini,* not Andreanna. We have long purposed and planned to restore the balance of magic in the land. You, Fonta, with your mischief, have endangered our purposes. For many cycles, we have endured you because you simply are as your namesake. This we do not begrudge you, but you have increasingly become out of control and now have endangered our purposes for the good of the land and of the magic. Do you have anything to say?"

Fonta hung her head and shook it. "I'm sorry, King."

"We will put it to a vote as to whether we take action and have you stand in judgment. All hold hands."

The Faeries about the table united, including Andreanna and Fonta. Andreanna was startled as she made contact with the King and Queen's hands, for through them she knew the mind of each as they gave their consent to have *isini* judged.

"Andreanna, you do not speak your mind," mindspoke the King, arousing her from her thoughts.

"I don't know. She's just a child...."

"Not so. She is a Faerie creature of a dozen millennium of age. She should be accountable for her actions."

"I don't know...."

"Let it suffice then. It is unanimous other than your abstaining, Dark Queen. For now, watch and see." Thoughts flashed around the table of Faeries as they mindspoke with each other. Andreanna was unable to follow the discussion because of its speed and the multitude of speakers.

Finally, the King stood. "It is settled then. *isini*, you are hereby sentenced to be limited to your manifestation of magic as an Elfstone. You will no longer be permitted a humanoid form. You will now revert to your Elfstone manifestation."

Andreanna gasped. "You can't...she's just a...no you can't."

"It is done. It will be so."

Fonta stood, not appearing at all disturbed by her sentence, and suddenly, she was gone. One of the Faeries standing behind her chair stooped to pick something up from the ground and walked around the table, giving it to the King, who in turn extended his hand before Andreanna. She looked within his palm to see a beautiful, radiant opal. Andreanna, who had stood to see what the King held, got a bit light-headed and weak in the knees and sat back down with a thump.

"You misunderstand, Elf Queen," instructed the Faerie Queen. "Many Faeries live, by choice, the entire course of their manifestations as such. They are quite content. It is not the punishment you imagined it to be. She will be well and content but confined in her mischief also. It is now to be determined though, to see if she will remain with us or as the council has judged...to go with you. What do you say?"

"With me? Why? How?"

The King spoke. "The council feels that, since her transgression was against you, she should be yours to have as an Elfstone, as the two you already possess. Only, because of her mischief, she would need to be kept subdued, as *balat* is. Elf Queen, *isini*, or Fonta as you know her, expressed that she would have it to be so, also."

"She did?" sobbed the Dark Queen. "I don't know. I mean, poor Fonta in a stone."

"She expressed that she is very fond of you and that she would be with you," said the Faerie Queen.

"She did? I kinda like her too, even if she was a pain in the butt. She really did mess things up there at the end, didn't she?"

"Yes, and she abandoned you when the mage attacked you. She should have defended you to her own destruction. Together you would have fared better against Daektoch. Besides, if you have her with you, you can speak with her when you choose to, *but* she cannot blab incessantly if you do not permit it."

"Alright. I'll take her then."

"May I have your two Elfstones and key?" asked the King. She removed *monit,* the key to the lock of the *Book of the Secrets of the Queen* and *balat* from around her neck, handing them to the King. He spoke to them as he held them cupped in his hands and passed them to the next Faerie who did the same.

Eventually, the stones were in the Faerie Queen's hands who in turn delivered them to Andreanna saying, "Here, dear. Take these and wear them always." Andreanna looked down to see the Elfstones and key all mounted on a heavy golden chain, *balat, monit*, *licri, isini* and the key.

"We have added an expression of *licri* in Elfstone form to concentrate and focus her power, which is in you. These will serve you as the stones in Jerhad's knife do him. Wear them wisely and proudly," said the Faerie Queen.

Andreanna slipped the chain over her head. She felt a sudden rush of magic course through her. She recognized Fonta among them and smiled. Then suddenly, she gasped. "I see him!"

"Him?" asked the King. The Faeries about the table stirred.

"Daektoch!" she hissed. "The mildew or mold I said was on everything? It's Daektoch! He's cast a spell that is slowly cutting you off from the argentus. The spell appears to be tied into the very fiber of the world: powerful! That's why you felt weakened.

"Why that bastard! *I'll* take care of him!"

She gathered herself up in the fullness of the Dark Queen and her magics. The Faeries gaped at her! The King and Queen stepped back, horror on their faces. The Dark Queen knelt down on one knee and with one hand gouged through the soil, to where she found a vein of argentus below Daektoch's influence. The air about her grew dark, lightening flashed and thunder rumbled. She enveloped herself in the darkness of her power. Her might churned about in wrath and viciousness. Putting her hand to argentus, she drew on its strength in its purity. Magic coursed through her in pronounced intensity, causing her to throw back her head and howl, whether in pain or ecstasy she could not tell. Her eyes burned with the fire of magic as she placed her other hand on the Black-magic-tainted earth.

With every ounce of her potency, the Dark Queen lashed out at Daektoch's magic! She unleashed a torrent of her power back along his spell's trail toward him. She followed its tainted path back to Mount Bahal, down through the crater into caverns and the labyrinth. There he was, feeling quite satisfied with himself and his evil. He looked up as the consciousness of the Dark Queen entered his chamber, just before her magic lashed out at him, tearing at him, thrashing him within heartbeats of his destruction and breaking his spell against the Faeries, also breaking his hold on the Trolls and the spells that he had set for the last battle in Mildra. She lost contact as the mage's spells broke, unable to finish him off as she sought to do.

A harmony of music...or was it fragrance...or maybe the sky was bluer. Sweetness, pleasant sensations and other indefinable feelings of ecstasy rose up about her. She raised her head to see large flowers breaking from the ground, fruit visibly growing on trees. The air cleared and the mold and mildew shrank and disappeared. Chimes and tinkling rose about her as Faeries danced about in festivity.

"Oh, my!" said the Faerie Queen. "I feel my old self again. Andreanna you did it! Just as *isini* said you would. It was you who was needed to do this. But what did you do?"

"I knocked the mage on the head and broke his spell which was insidiously separating you from the argentus." Within herself, Andreanna felt the stirrings of *isini*. She turned within and spoke to her. "You knew it all along, didn't you?"

"I did, Dark Queen. It was necessary that my magic become part of you for you to fulfill the saving of the Faeries. Only, I didn't know the how's and why's of it, and therefore, I couldn't explain it to the King and the others; the King wouldn't have combined the magics to produce the needed effect on my word alone."

"You sacrificed yourself for this."

"Not sacrificed. It is as the Faerie Queen said. I am content. More so, I am very happy to spend my time with you and within you."

In Mildra, the Trolls were gone. They had simply dropped their weapons and fled into the mountains of the Coastal Range, heading back to the Blue Mountains. Daektoch's servants, overhead, had shrieked in dismay, turned and flown north toward Mount Bahal. It could not be! It could not be over! It must be some kind of trick. They were all gone. Dwarves and Elves stood staring out to the empty field. The silence was unnerving.

In a rush, Jerhad and Morlah returned to the eastern battlements, back from the river. Then Stanton was shouting orders that the wounded needed to be tended to and the dead gathered. The Giants embraced each other and spoke to each other in their native tongue. The Dwarves took up a victory song in the Dwarf tongue. Taking them by the elbow, Stanton turned Jerhad and Morlah, moving them toward town.

"Jerhad, my boy. Morlah, my man. I don't know what happened, but I really think that it's over. Something has happened to take Daektoch's control away from the Trolls. I know that it's only midcourse of the sun, but I'm going to buy you two a few pitchers of ale."

They had not taken two steps when a solitary ram's horn sounded an alarm. In shock, the three turned and looked out in the field where in the distance, some thousand paces away, stood a tall (three times the height of a Giant) dark, shrouded, feminine figure of solid black. Her long hair flowed about in the breezeless air. An ominous stillness cloaked her.

Morlah gasped and said, "I doest not know who she is, but I sense that she is powerful beyond belief. I shall take to the air upon The Raven and attack at once."

"No, Morlah," said Jerhad with a gleam in his eye, holding the Druid back with a hand on Morlah's arm. "*This one is mine*! Step back everyone."

The Elves and Dwarves gave him a wide berth. Drawing on his magic, Jerhad grew in stature. Taller than Trolls, taller than Giants, the Prince grew until he matched the dark specter's size. He stepped over the wall and took off at a run toward the figure who remained motionless. Each step he took shook the ground as he gained momentum in his rush on the obsidian figure. As he reached her, he crouched and lunged, wrapping one arm about her neck and the other about her waist, throwing her off balance and pushing her back until she was bent over backwards with one foot on the ground and the other in the air.

He looked deep into her eyes and said, "Did you do something with your hair, my love?"

She laughed. "I didn't know if you'd recognize me. I really needed to see you and this was the only way I could come without delaying a few more courses.... You like my hair?"

"I love it more than life itself. But even so, apart from the change in hair, you look...*different*."

"I'll make you look different if you don't shut up and kiss me!" She wrapped her arms about him and kissed him hard. Back at the wall, the armies gasped. The Prince was obviously locked in some kind of mortal combat with the creature.

Morlah mounted onto The Raven. "I must assist him."

"Wait," cried Catrina running up to them. "It's Andreanna. She's come back."

"Andreanna?" asked several voices in disbelief.

"Yes, I was in the house with Kendra, and suddenly she looked up, pointed this way and said, 'Mommy'. Ahliene is bringing her now. I went to pick her up, and when I touched her, I saw through her eyes what she could see from within the house. So I ran out to warn you not to hurt her."

"She doesn't look like she'd be easy to hurt. Are you sure it's her," asked Stanton again. Just then, Ahliene ran up, carrying Kendra.

"Mommy, Mommy," Kendra cried with delight. Suddenly, a dazzle of sprinkling lights appeared before her, and she leapt from Ahliene's arms and onto the sparkling magic that immediately turned into a large dove that flew off toward the couple still locked in an embrace out on the field, carrying Kendra to them.

The Mountain Gnomes returned to their homes, The Dark Queen's magic lingering with them, giving them a sense of her presence. The wolves would no longer prey upon them, thereby fulfilling the prophesy. She was the Queen of the Gnomes and Queen of the Wolves. Baby remained with one of the wolf packs that had attacked the Trolls, eventually rising to become an alpha-she-wolf.

Several courses later, ten thousand Dwarves arrived in Mildra, coming down from *Dolan*. Andreanna was with them as was King Hearthstone. As Jerhad approached them accompanied by Stanton, Morlah, IronLeggs and others of the Elf and Dwarf leaders, the King fell to his knees and put his face to the ground. Ten Dwarves stepped forward and each laid a large canvass sack on the ground before the Dwarf King. With a slash of longknives, the sacks' contents were spilled, revealing gold, silver and gems.

"I am in your debt and service as is the Dwarf nation forever. We are your servants. You may do with us as you please," said HeartStone.

Jerhad raised an eyebrow.

Andreanna came forward and hugged Jerhad. "It's a long story. Humor him," she whispered into his ear.

"Alright then, HeartStone. You can start by getting up. You're already short enough when you're on your two feet," Jerhad said, winking at Andreanna who rolled her eyes.

"Ah! Males! That's not quite what I meant. He's serious," she whispered as the King rose as commanded.

"So what's this all about?" asked Jerhad.

"Andreanna, the Queen of the Elves, saved the Dwarf nation from destruction at the hands of the Trolls."

Jerhad's head drew back in surprise. "That was you!"

She nodded.

"We served her poorly in return," continued King HeartStone. "I have come to apologize on behalf of myself and those involved. She gave us our lives; we return them to her and to you."

"You'll explain all this later won't you?" asked Jerhad to Andreanna in a whisper.

She nodded.

"No problem, King HeartStone. Our people are one! Without the Dwarves, we would have not survived the battles we have fought here. If you so desire, I will accept your offer. You will be our servants and are commanded, from this course of the sun forward, to guard our borders to the north all the way to *Dolan*."

The King said, "You jest with me, my brother. Alas, you put me to shame. For you deal more kindly with me than I deserve. The Dwarves have hitherto been known as a noble race. We will with all our might keep your command even though you do pull at this old Dwarf's beard. It is difficult for me to bear my shame. May I live to bring honor to my name and that of the Dwarves once again."

"How about a couple of ales, HeartStone. That usually lightens the mood. Did you bring any tobac?"

HeartStone came forward and embraced Jerhad. "You truly are a Prince, my lord. And your mate is truly a Queen." He pulled a large pouch of tobac from within his tunic. "I had brought this as my last resource in obtaining your forgiveness," he grinned.

"Great! Somebody start a feast or something; whatever you do to get a feast started," cried Jerhad. "DiamondHeart, how about a fire fit for telling stories."

"It will be done, my Prince," the Giant laughed, and he and Tahmat headed off toward the forest to get a tree.

Andreanna clung to Jerhad, arms around his neck, her face buried in his shoulder and one leg wrapped about his. They looked like two turtledoves in courtship.

"Stanton, my man!" Jerhad extended his hand to his Commander. "Thanks. We couldn't have done it without you. The kingdom is yours, whatever your heart desires."

"How about a small farm with a house, big enough for a wife and couple of kids."

"You dog!" cried Jerhad.

"What's this?" Andreanna asked, her head popping up.

"Stanton, my dear, is in love, and now, it looks like he's about to be wed."

"Ah, wait...I haven't asked her yet."

"Stanton? I didn't know you had it in you, Squad Leader. Anyone I know?" inquired Andreanna.

"I don't think so, but she's at your home taking care of your daughter and bread ovens in the market. I think you'll like her, though she's not *at all* like you," he laughed.

"Great, let's go ask her!" said Andreanna, taking off at a run toward the town.

"Hey no, wait.... Don't...!" Stanton protested with dismay.

"Forget it, Stanton. You'll never catch up with her. May just as well wait here to see what the answer is."

Morlah shook his head. "Thou doest all have far too much energy for me. Thou doest make me feel like an old man."

"Yeah, yeah! Tell us about it, Druid." They laughed at him.

"I willst stay for the feast and a few courses more. But I have seriously spent myself and willst soon be in need of the Druid Sleep. Stanton, if thou doest hurry, I wouldst be honored to attend thine wedding."

"Stop pushing! I don't even know if she likes me."

"Come on! The way she flutters those green eyes when you're around...." Jerhad, raising the pitch of his voice and batting his eyes, said, "Thanks for the flowers, Stanton."

"That's it! That's the last straw!" Stanton rushed forward, putting the Elven Prince into a headlock. The Commander rubbed his knuckle hard on the Prince's skull as the two fell to the ground in a tangle. Jerhad was laughing too hard to commit himself to the battle.

Two courses later, Stanton and Ahliene were wed. Stanton stood proud as a peacock. Andreanna and Catrina cried through the whole affair, and Morlah had a tear in his eye. Jerhad put on a display of magical flashing lights in the darkening evening sky with sparkling glitter raining down on everyone, as if raining peace and comfort on Mildra's inhabitants.

Earlier that same course, the Giant schooner, *The Hammerstar,* had pulled into port, and a celebration fit for Giants was on. A couple of courses later, Morlah and Raven left on the *MayBest* and returned to *seilstri*, for Morlah was far spent and in need of restoration that only the Druid Sleep could mend. Messengers also arrived from Breezon, saying that the confrontation with Heros was over and that, for the first time in hundreds of cycles, there were plans for cooperation between the two cities.

Andreanna and Jerhad sat back beneath an ancient Silver Willow, watching the ongoing festivities, Kendra playing with Kassandra off to the side. Andreanna clung to her mate like Moor Ivy to a Cypress. She whispered into his ear causing the Prince's eyebrows to rise and his face to blush fiercely.

"What do you mean, '*Do it* with the Dark Queen'?!" he gasped.

She giggled and snuggled in closer.

Made in the USA